The Journey Home

NEVER give up on your dreams! Keep pursuing them until they become a reality!

The Journey Home

Bethany Rodgers

THE JOURNEY HOME

For more information contact:

Bethany Rodgers

www.bethanyrodgers.com

bethany@jrodgers.net

Cover Photo by Priscilla Du Preez

Book and Cover Design by Bethany Rodgers

ISBN: 978-1-7372218-0-7

First Edition: August 2021

Acknowledgements

The task of writing a book is no easy feat, and I know I couldn't have done it without some amazing people God placed in my path to help guide me through the process.

First and foremost, I have to give credit to God. He is the one who gifted me with the ability and passion for writing, and it is truly an honor to be able to further His kingdom with that gift. I hope this book touches the hearts of those who read it, and it brings them closer to Him.

To my wonderful husband, Jim. You have supported me through every crazy idea and adventure I have come up with. You have supported me on this journey for the last 6 years, and I know you are just as excited to see the finished product as I am. I cannot wait to celebrate the release of this book with you and all the books in the future. I love knowing you will be by my side for all of it, and I wouldn't want to do this crazy, joy-filled life with anyone else.

To my wonderful children, Jay and Janie. The memories of writing this book will always be weaved throughout the memories of the beginnings of your stories as well. I started this book right after Jay was born, and I would write during his naps, and I continued throughout the years into Janie's naps as well. I will always cherish the unconditional love y'all have shown me and how much y'all have taught me about God, life and myself.

To my amazing Life Group: Michael, Beth, Rob, Karen, Matt, Tara, Jesse, Kari Ann, Britt, Daniel, Jessica, Jake, Paige, Patrick, Bethany, Eric, Joy, Ashley, Matt, Blake and Dana, you have all taught me so much about God and life and how we can thrive in this life with God. We have shared many stories, laughs, great conversations, meals and Bible studies through the years. I am so thankful God chose for our paths to cross. I know I wouldn't be who I am, and this book wouldn't be what is it without all of you and the influence you've had on my life.

Elizabeth, thank you for reading my book and offering critiques. I know how busy your life is, and it means so much to me you wanted to do that for me. I love watching our kids grow up together, and I hope we can continue to grow our friendship through God.

April, you have been the best support system during this journey. Thank you for reading and critiquing my book when I couldn't bring myself to read for edits one more time. Thank you for having an answer for every question I texted and always being a huge support system. You will never know how huge your support was for the success of this book, and I am thankful each and every day God brought us together in Sunday School, so we could be in each other's lives.

Thank you to Priscilla Du Preez for taking the beautiful cover photo and allowing me to use it! You can find more of her amazing photography on unsplash.com and follow her on Instagram @andyourstorycontinues

Finally, thank you to everyone in my family who offered love and support over the years to see me through this process. Sometimes it was watching a child or two while I powered through a chapter and sometimes it was just listening to me complain about a section that wasn't working out. You have all helped in more ways than you will ever know, and God worked through all of you in this process beautifully.

Table of Contents

Ch.1

Charlie Cochran returned to his office and collapsed into his chair. He knew his new job as the youth pastor of the church would be challenging and rewarding, but he had underestimated how emotionally difficult it could be. He had spent the last hour in the head pastor's office sitting next to the pastor and listening to a woman from the church, Marianne Ward. She told them both about her estranged daughter Annabelle who had run away from home three years earlier, and who everyone in the family seemed to have a strained relationship with. She explained her own guilt for not seeing the pain inside of her daughter and not being a source of comfort to her. She described the tug of war she had felt between her loyalty to her husband and her love for her daughter. They had both been constantly at war with one another over what she admitted was her husband's need to be in control especially in his daughter's life. She even confessed her fear that she had lost her daughter forever. Charlie listened as she begged him and Pastor Maxwell to please pray for her daughter and pray that God would give them a second chance at their relationship and a chance to repair the damage. As Charlie listened, he felt a weight seem to settle on his chest, and now as he sat in his office, it was still there. A weight and something else, the silent nudging deep within his soul that he recognized to be from God. He thought about them, and it seemed as if there was an internal ringing of a phone with God on the other end of the line, reaching out to him, ready to have a conversation. With the heaviness and the nudging in full force, he obeyed and bowed his head to pray.

"Gracious and heavenly Father, I come before you now to ask you to please heal all the souls out there today, Lord who are hurting and broken by this world. Please grant them peace and reveal your mighty love and grace to them now, Lord. I want to specifically lift up Marianne, Lord. I met her today for the first time, but I can already tell she knows your power, and she has a mighty spirit for you, God. She is hurting right now. She is hurting over the loss of a child who went out into the world and has seemingly been lost in it. I ask that you please restore this relationship and help them each heal from their wounds. God, I also pray that Marianne's marriage and bond with her husband will be mended. It is obviously strained at the moment, because of her guilt and belief that she had to choose between her husband and her daughter, but you and I both know that isn't the case. Please help her to see that she will never have to choose, because you will always guide her and help her along her journey. I also pray for Annabelle specifically. Though I have not met her, I know that when she left, she must have felt broken in some way. I hope she has found some peace in you, but if that's not the case, Lord, will you remind her, so she can dwell in your grace and forgiveness and blessings once more. I ask that you show her that she has so much here to return to. I know returning would be hard and probably scary for her, God, but she has so many people who care about her here. Please let her remember that. I also want to thank you for the forgiveness you freely give us each day when all we must do to accept it is just ask and accept you. Please guard our hearts and minds and turn them to you, bringing us closer to you so we can influence others. Please remind us that we are never too far from you to receive your grace and forgiveness. It's in your holy name I pray. Amen.

< < > >

Annabelle woke with a start. She looked around groggily trying to get her bearings about her before emerging from the warm bed. She glanced over at the clock and realized it was almost lunchtime. Then she remembered why she was still in bed so late in the day. Her shoot the night before had run long, and she had grabbed a late dinner. She had gone out to party with some friends, where she ran into Jake, who, of course, ended up trying to go home with her at the end of the night.

Why couldn't he just realize she wasn't ready for sex? He was always pushing her, and she was starting to feel bad about always saying no. Annabelle had told herself time and time again that he was being pushy, and she was mad at him for it, but deep down she knew it was more than that. She was worried if he wasn't having sex with her, he would be getting it from someone else, and she knew that was the wrong reason to have sex with him, but sometimes she entertained the idea. If she lost him, she would be completely and utterly alone, and that thought was scarier than anything she had ever faced. She had tried to work up the nerve to give into his desire several times, but every time she felt like she was getting close to progressing further, something always stopped her. She couldn't quite put her finger on it, but she had a feeling it was deeply rooted inside her and was planted there by all the preaching she had sat through as a child and teen growing up in church. Whenever that realization struck her, she turned her anger on her parents for forcing her to go to church and honestly on herself for continuing to buy into all that Christian stuff when she hadn't stepped foot in a church in three years. The thought of all of it made her crazy, and she grabbed a pillow, placed it over her face and screamed into it. She had learned in her three years of independence that sometimes; you just have to scream and get it all out.

Annabelle stopped screaming just in time to hear the phone buzzing on her bedside table. Without removing the pillow, she felt around blindly for it and when she found it, brought it to her ear under the pillow.

"Hello," she said hesitantly, because she had broken her rule of never answering the phone without first checking to see who it was.

"Anna? Is that you?"

"Hey! Yes, It's me. What's up?" Annabelle said. She was happy to hear her agent, Christy's voice on the other end of the phone instead of someone else. like her mother or her perfect, never-does-anything-wrong sister, Jill.

"You sound like you're in a tunnel or something. Are you okay? Maybe something is wrong with your phone."

"Nope! Everything is fine." Annabelle said, as she hurled the pillow off her face. "I'm fine. Everything is fine. How are you?"

"I'm good." Christy said sounding not completely convinced. "So, I have some exciting news. I just got a call from a magazine, and they want to feature you on the cover and in a few inside shots."

"Oh my gosh! Really? That is fantastic news. Christy, this is the big break I have been waiting for. Which magazine is it? What designer do I get to wear? Do you think they will let me keep the clothes?" Annabelle knew she was rushing through the words, but she couldn't contain her excitement. She had been waiting to hear those words for three very long years, and now they were finally here! This was going to be her big break. She just knew it."

"Whoa slow down! So no, you won't be keeping the clothes, because there won't be any clothes."

"Wait. What?"

"This shoot is for the magazine Lust. They were looking for someone with an innocent 'girl next door look', and when they saw your picture, they thought you would be perfect."

"Christy, Lust is the magazine where the models…" Annabelle trailed off, afraid to finish her thought for fear she would be right.

"Pose nude, yes, that's correct. But Anna, don't think about it like that. Think about it as a way to break into a whole new industry. You've tried for three years to break into the modeling world the old-fashioned way, and this is just another avenue to get where you want to end up. You can make a name for yourself this way too. Both roads lead to the same destination. You'll just be driving a different car to get there than the one you had planned on."

"Yeah, I guess that makes sense." Annabelle said, reluctantly.

"Trust me. This will be so great for your career! Just say yes, and I'll call them right away and let them know."

"Okay. Yes! If you think this is a good move, then I'll do it!" Annabelle said hearing confidence in her voice she knew she wasn't feeling on the inside.

"Great! I'm going to go and call them, and I'll text you the details of the shoot. It will be a few days from now, so until then, get good sleep, eat well and get in some exercise. Oh, and make an appointment for one of those spray tans. Spray tans always look good, so make sure you don't show up without one. Ciao!" Christy said in a flash, and then hung-up, leaving Annabelle's head spinning.

Annabelle hoped she was making the right decision. She felt a small inkling in her heart that this wasn't what she needed to do, but her brain told her if she wanted a career and to pursue a lifestyle as a model, she had to listen to Christy and take this step, so that's what she decided to do. She thought briefly about texting Jake to go out and celebrate, but Christy had given her some direct instructions on what to do to prepare, and she didn't think getting herself tangled up in a stressful situation would ever be on Christy's list. She dialed the number for the tanning salon and made an appointment later that evening for her spray tan. As she hung up, she imagined her life far into the future, when salons would make house calls for *her* tans instead of her going to them. "One step at a time." She thought to herself with a smile.

Jill lay back on the pillow of the hotel bed, sweaty and breathing heavy, her whole body electrified from her toes to the hairs on her head as Jason's ran his fingertips lightly along her arm.

"That was amazing." He said, looking over at her.

Jill drew the sheets up to cover her nakedness as she propped up on her elbow to gaze at him. She had been looking at and exploring his body for weeks now, and the sight of him still made her go weak in the knees. He was gorgeous, and yes, she had dated cute guys before, but they were just boys. Jason was a man. He was muscular and strong in all the right places, and unlike the others she had dated, he had the ability to grow facial hair. She loved the feel of his beard on her skin and the rugged way it made him look. Above all, Jason always made her feel like she mattered and like there was no one else in the world he would rather be spending his time with. Jill knew she would never get tired of the way he made her feel. She smiled at him as she rolled onto her back and groped around the side table for her phone. She finally felt it and held it in front of her to check the time. She was shocked it was so late, and she turned back to look at Jason with the saddest look she could muster.

"What? Is it already time?" He asked, shaking his head.

"Yes, I have to leave in a few minutes, and anyway I'm pretty sure we are inching close to check out."

"You're probably right. What am I saying? You're always right, my love." Jason said rolling over to give her a quick kiss.

"Am I? I'm pretty sure I've been wrong before." She said playfully.

"No, you're never wrong. You're perfect." Jason said, kissing her again but deepening the kiss this time.

"Jason, as much as I would love to repeat what we just did, although I'm sure we can't top that, I don't have time. I must get home by a certain time, or my mom will start to worry, and what I will end up walking into will be a weekend full of chaos. No one wants that. Trust me."

"I know. I'm just going to miss you and miss this while you're gone."

"You can come with me." Jill said teasingly as she raised up again to look at him.

"Honey, you know I would love nothing more than to come with you and meet your parents, but this weekend is bad for me. I have so much work to do, and if I go with you, I'll be entertaining your parents all weekend and won't get anything done. Next time I promise I will be there." He said pulling her in for one more kiss.

Jill grumbled playing off her hurt and focusing on the task at hand, getting dressed. She had been pushing Jason to meet her parents for a while now, but he always had reasons he couldn't come. The reasons, she had to admit, were always good and realistic, but she always felt like he was holding back and purposefully not wanting to come home with her and meet her parents. She didn't understand why. Their relationship had progressed rapidly, and she was happy with him and couldn't wait to take the next step and get engaged. She wanted to make sure he had already met her parents before that happened. She reached over the side of the bed and started collecting her clothes. Then she sat up, and as she was re-clasping her bra and putting it back in place, she felt the bed shift as Jason sat up behind her.

"So." Jason started. "Have you thought anymore about dropping the class before you get turned in for plagiarism?"

"Honestly, no. That hasn't been on my mind recently." Jill said, smiling at him until she saw the serious look on his face.

"Jill, you really need to think about it. Dropping the class won't affect you the way a plagiarism violation will. Just trust me and drop the class. It will be better in the long run."

Jill stood up to pull her jeans back on much more frustrated and a lot less satisfied than she was just moments before.

"Jason, I really don't want to talk about this right now, okay? I am about to go home and see my parents, and I don't want this lingering over my head the entire time I'm there. Please just drop this, and I will think about it later." Jill said, a note of frustration rising in her voice.

"Jill, I'm just saying you really need to make a decision before a decision gets made for you."

"Jason, can we *please* just drop it. I am so tired of having this conversation, and I will *not* have this conversation right now. What we just did was beautiful, and that's the last thing I want to remember from this moment, so I'm going to go. Call me later when you're ready to talk about something else, anything else except this." Jill said, yanking her jeans up, buttoning them and grabbing her bag. Her hand was on the knob when she heard Jason speak again.

"Jill, c'mon. We really need to talk about this."

Jill was through the door and halfway to the elevator before Jason had a chance to say anything else. As the elevator doors opened and she stepped in, she thought about what Jason had said. Then she thought about going home and facing her parents and all their questions and expectations. She couldn't tell them anything that would upset them. Annabelle had broken them when she ran away, and Jill had stayed to pick up the pieces and be the perfect daughter they needed. She couldn't be the one to break their hearts for a second time. She had already made up her mind not to say anything to them. She wished she could explain everything to Jason, but for some reason, she didn't think he would understand.

When she walked off the elevator and through the lobby, she felt lighter. She was walking away from one source of tension and into another, but for one brief moment, she would be in between both worlds and would get a chance to breathe. She hoisted her bag higher on her shoulder and made her way out the front doors and across the parking lot towards her car. She unlocked the car and crawled inside to set her bag on the passenger floorboard. Then she sat upright in the driver's seat and put on her seat belt. She cranked the car and looked in her rearview mirror giving her eyes a chance to glance upward toward the window to the room where the gorgeous man she was so in love with was still inside. She ached for him in the pit of her stomach, and her toes curled at the thought of him, but a sense of stress and negativity was starting to cloud her image of him. She took one final look out of her rearview mirror before she backed up and pulled out of the parking space toward the road. As she left the hotel parking lot, she found she didn't have the urge to look in her rearview mirror back towards Jason. Instead, she fixed her eyes straight ahead, and she took a deep breath as she proceeded forward.

Ch.2

Charlie leaned back in his chair and stretched his arms over his head. This has been a long day, and after the conversation with Marianne earlier that afternoon, he had been carrying around a nagging feeling in the pit of his stomach. He wanted to just ignore it and hope it would go away, but he knew it wouldn't. Besides, he wasn't the type of person to let something like this win and drag down his spirits. He heard a soft knock on the door and looked over to see Pastor Maxwell standing there. Charlie waved him in and then sat upright in his chair with his hands clasped on the desk in front of him.

"I just wanted to stop by and see how you were doing. I know that meeting today got a little intense, and this is your first time sitting through anything like that, so I just wanted to come by and see how you were feeling about it." Pastor Maxwell said with sincerity dripping from his voice.

Charlie took in a deep breath and gave a small nod of his head as he thought about what he wanted to say in response. He hadn't always been so particular about his word choice, but he had grown a desire to be very intentional with his words over the past few years. Words carry so much power, and he wanted to make sure that his words were always necessary and true.

"Honestly, that was a tough conversation for me. A lot of what she said cut to my core, and I have been torn up about a lot of it ever since." He said looking into Pastor Maxwell's face to show him he was being honest and wasn't holding back.

"Why do you think you're taking it so personal?" Pastor Maxwell asked him with genuine curiosity in his voice.

"Because those are probably the same types of things my mom said about me to our pastor and the same prayers, she asked for about me. It's hard to be in a situation where you're getting a glimpse at the people you hurt when the worst parts of yourself were in control. It's hard to have a front row seat to the pain you caused the ones you love. I know if her daughter had any clue as to the pain she is personally inflicting on her parents, she would feel the same way." Charlie said feeling the sorrow all the way into the depths of his soul."

"I can imagine that would be difficult. I had no idea this would bring out those kinds of feelings for you. I would say I'm sorry, but I believe God puts us in the position he wants us to be in to receive what we need when we need it. In that case, I'm glad you had this experience, because it might give you a better perspective and more insight later in your life." Pastor Maxwell said.

Charlie nodded his head and realized even after speaking his feelings aloud the feeling hadn't dissipated at all. He knew feelings that he felt so completely could really tear you up from the inside out if you weren't careful and didn't deal with them. He was acknowledging them which was good. Now what could he do to deal with them? He looked up at Pastor Maxwell and asked if he would mind if he said a quick prayer for Marianne again and his own mother and the feelings he was feeling. Pastor Maxwell nodded, and both bowed their hands as Charlie began to pray aloud.

God, I don't know why, but I know that you love me so completely despite my flaws and everything I do wrong. I do my best God, but I know I fail repeatedly, but you are always there to pick up my pieces and help me to stand on my own two feet again, and for that, I can never truly thank you enough. There aren't enough thank yous in the entire world to show my true gratitude for salvation and everything you have done for me. I come to you now with a heart of thanks and a broken soul that is still grieving. I am grieving for my past and the hurt I inflicted on everyone I love, especially my mother. She's the greatest blessing from you aside from my salvation. The world says I will never fully be able to make right all the pointless and terrible things I put her through, but I know that you say everyone can be made new in you. I have asked for forgiveness from my past discretions, and I know you have granted me the forgiveness I sought. I have seen you bless my mother for her obedience to you even in the hardest times, and for that I thank you.

I want to come again and ask for healing for Marianne in her situation, and I would like to ask that you open the eyes of her daughter, Annabelle. She is seeing as the world sees right now, but you can change her sight. You can show her how you see, and with her new sight, she can have some clarity to avoid a life of mistakes and regrets, and she can focus on a life that is rich and full of your love and blessings. Please God, I beg you to open her eyes and open them wide. Pour into her soul all the truths she is ignoring, and please grant her healing in her life and in her relationship with her family. There is so much brokenness, God, but we are all broken people who are made whole and new again in you. I ask all of that in your precious, holy name. Amen.

Charlie felt better as he looked up at Pastor Maxwell who nodded his head in approval. The weight felt as though it had gotten lighter, and he could live with that for now. He would continue praying and being healed from the inside out.

"That family has a lot of heartache to face and overcome, but I know they can do it. Stick with them, and you'll see it too." Pastor Maxwell said as he stood.

"A front row seat to God's power? Of course, I wouldn't miss that. I love watching God at work." Charlie said as he stood and came over to Pastor Maxwell. The two of them hugged and walked towards the door of the office.

"I'll see you tomorrow." Pastor Maxwell said as he turned to head towards the main doors.

"See you tomorrow." Charlie agreed then he turned and made his way back over to the desk to get his phone and call his mom.

When she found herself in her parent's driveway rolling up to the house, Jill realized she had lost the battle. She had spent the entire 3-hour drive to her parents' house trying to think of everything but Jason, but now that she was here, she realized he was the only thing on her mind. Their relationship was great, and it had been a whirlwind from the beginning, but there was something about it that was gnawing at her. Something she couldn't quite put her finger on. Her mind drifted back to the early days before she really knew him when they would talk about school and her classes and his classes, and she remembered how she was initially drawn to his intelligence and his confidence in his field. She remembered how they would take walks or share a meal, and she felt like she could listen to him talk forever. Now, she had to admit, their relationship had become a lot more physical which meant there was a lot less talking. She missed the early days when he would whisk her away to out of town art showings, restaurant openings, theater performances, you name it, they went no matter how far they had to go to get there. If they could be back to fulfill their obligations the following day, they went. She loved being part of his world. It was so completely different from the small-town life she had been raised in. She had never known how much she wanted a different life until Jason had pulled her into his. Now, she couldn't imagine anything different.

She remembered their first kiss. They were in a gallery for the opening of a new exhibit a few towns over. Jill remembered seeing a painting with various shades of red strewn about the canvas and golden flecks highlighted throughout. Something about the painting had awaken her on the inside. It was like she was being set free. Jason had come up behind her and slid his arm around her waist. Without thinking, she had turned and closed the distance between them in a matter of seconds. With her body pressed as closely to his as she could get it, she kissed him hard and full. The kiss had probably only lasted a few seconds, but to her, it felt like it had lasted so much longer. She had said so much with that kiss, and from that moment on, she couldn't stand being apart from him. She craved his closeness and his touch in a way that she felt like she ached for it when she was away from him.

Raindrops started to hit the roof and the windshield, and before she knew it, the sky had opened, and rain was falling heavily all around the outside of her car. She put the car in park and remembered the first time she had allowed their intimacy to progress, and they made love for the first time in an old, abandoned gardening shed on campus. It had been raining that day too, and she could still remember the sound the rain made on the tin roof as it played the soundtrack to their intimate expression of love. She remembered so much about that day: the sound of the rain, the smell of damp earth, the softness of the earth underneath her body, and the coolness of it against her bare skin. As she thought about it, a smile played at her lips. It was such a completely random place, but she treasured it and found so much beauty and connection there. It was one of her favorite memories.

The spontaneity they once had was gone from their relationship now. Now, when they wanted time alone, Jason would book them a room at the Hilltop Suites. Jill had to admit the rooms were nice, and it was nice being able to avoid her roommates and anyone who would ask questions, but the monotony of it was getting to her. She missed the newness and the thrill of their relationship. She hadn't told anyone about them trying to respect Jason's wishes to keep things private a little while longer, so sometimes, she wanted to sneak him back to her bedroom in her apartment. The thrill of potentially getting caught was just what she thought they needed, but she could never convince him. Instead, they met up at the Hilltop whenever they needed more than they could get from each other at a restaurant or an event, and Jill was always satisfied, but she also always left feeling like there was something off. She was hoping a weekend away might awaken her hunger for him a little deeper, and maybe that would be the spice she was looking for. If nothing else, maybe it would teach her to appreciate what she had right in front of her and stop wanting things to change.

She was so lost in thought her heart jumped into her throat when someone banged on the window of her car. She looked over to see her dad standing there in the pouring rain with an umbrella. She waved at him and turned off her car. Then she grabbed her bag, motioned for him to step back, opened her door and jumped under his waiting umbrella. He held the umbrella over them as they huddled together beneath it and hurried into the garage trying to avoid as much as the deluge as possible.

"Hey sweetie, welcome home." He said to her with a hug once he closed his umbrella.

"Hey dad" She replied hugging him tightly as well. Her father had always been complicated when it came to his relationship with her sister, Annabelle, but with her, things had always been great between them. Jill had learned a long time ago to just do whatever her parents wanted and be whatever they expected her to be, and her relationship with them would be great. It was suffocating at times, but it had been the driving force in her applying to Hineman University, which is where she met Jason, so everything seemed to work out in the end.

"So how was your drive?" He asked as they proceeded inside.

"It was uneventful." Jill stated.

"Well, that's good. How are things going with school?" He asked as they came into the kitchen where her mother was busily putting ingredients into a big pot on the stove.

"Yes, sweetie, how is school going?" Her mother asked cheerfully.

This is the part where she should come right out and tell them about Jason or about the plagiarism violation or her choice to drop a class. She could just slide the last on in nonchalantly and then they could have dinner and forget all about it. She could convince them it was no big deal. She had it poised on her tongue ready to say it, but when she opened her mouth to respond she found that none of those things came out. Instead, she lied and said, "School is fantastic. I am having so much fun there." After hearing it come out of her mouth, she really had to fight the urge to not literally smack herself on the forehead. School is fantastic? What was she thinking? School wasn't fantastic. She was in trouble, and she had to decide to drop a class or be charged with plagiarism. Either way, that class would result in an F. She knew her parents wouldn't see that as being fantastic. As for having a lot of fun at school, she guessed what she had been doing with Jason had been fun, so that really wasn't as big of a lie as the first one had been. Either way, she had blown her chance at telling them, and she didn't know if she would be able to muster the courage to tell them later. They were both smiling at her proudly, and she plastered a fake smile on her face and smiled right back at them.

After a few minutes, Jill excused herself to her room to put her bags up and freshen up before she had to be back down again for dinner. Now that she was home, her life seemed a lot messier and a lot more complicated than it had this morning. How was that even possible? Her life hadn't suddenly changed. For some reason, she was able to lie to herself more when she was with Jason. She hadn't even been gone that long and already she couldn't wait to get back to him. She never should've come home this weekend. She had the feeling things were going to end up in disaster. She texted Jason to let him know she made it, and she lay back on her childhood bed and decided to give her mind a rest until it was time for dinner.

< < > >

Annabelle listened intently as the tanning technician went over the procedure with her, or at least she tried to listen. There was so much she had been doing to get ready for the photo shoot. Her agent had made several appointments for her. She had already gone to the hair salon to make sure her length and color was where it needed to be then she had a nail appointment to make sure they didn't look terrible like she never got them done which was the truth. It cost way too much to keep her nails done all the time, so she only got them done whenever she had a big shoot coming up. Now, it was time for her spray tan. This was the first time she'd had a spray tan, so she was listening and trying to understand the procedure and what to do, but her mind was also drifting to other places like Jake and the upcoming shoot. She had thought she would have days to prepare, but Christy had called her back a little later after speaking to the magazine people, and it turns out, they didn't need such a lengthy timeline. They wanted to fast forward things. She had tried to call around and make her own appointments, but with time being an issue, she let Christy call and book her appointments after finding several places were all booked up on such short notice. Christy had some clout that Annabelle didn't have yet. She wished she had it, but she was hoping in the future after this shoot, she would have some. The tanning place Christy had booked was extremely nice. Annabelle really couldn't afford all this pampering, but after getting paid for the shoot, she was pretty sure she could cover it.

"Okay, so I'll be back in about 5 minutes." The tanning tech was saying. Then she turned and exited the room.

Annabelle was left completely alone in a small room with 5 minutes to undress and be ready. She quickly undressed and took the paper shower cap and covered her hair with it. She could not afford another hair appointment if her hair was to get accidentally sprayed. Then she stood there naked in a room knowing any moment someone would be walking back through the door. She tried to calm her racing heart as her anxiety picked up, but she was losing the battle. She tried to encourage herself with having confidence in her body and knowing she looked good, but she was still naked. How was she supposed to be naked in front of multiple people tomorrow if she couldn't be naked in front of this girl? She willed herself to get a grip as she heard the door creak open.

"Are you ready?" The petite young, blonde technician said as she came in the room.

Annabelle wasn't quite sure how to answer the question, because ready wasn't what she was. Able to endure? Sure! Ready? Would she ever really be ready? She listened as the girl instructed her how to stand and what do as she sprayed each part of her body with a cold watery mist. There were several times throughout the procedure that everything in Annabelle's head was pushing her to grab her clothes and bolt, but she stood her ground to prove she could do this and that she wasn't going to look like a crazy person. She willed herself to stay calm through it all, and at the end of it, she found herself standing naked in front of a fan while the tanning spray dried, and she realized she had done it. She had been completely naked in front of someone. She decided if she could do it in front of one person today, she could do it in front of multiple people tomorrow. She had no idea if that was true, but she told herself it was anyway.

After drying for 10 minutes, she was instructed to put on some loose dark clothes. She put on some back flowy pants and an off the shoulder black slouchy blouse. She had to admit walking around with no bra felt a little more freeing that she would've thought. Maybe that's how she could look at the shoot tomorrow like an experience to free herself from her past and all the negativity there and to create a whole new version of herself who was free and confident and could do tough things like do a naked photo shoot or for goodness sakes having sex with her pseudo boyfriend.

Jake and Annabelle had broken up several times at this point, always whenever he felt she was being too clingy or too involved in his life or just too much girlfriend. He would say they needed some time apart. She always hoped he was home and missing her, but she had heard several times he had been seen out with other girls and left with them. She had brought this up to him only once, because when she did, he got angry and reminded her they weren't together. When she reminded him, they were only taking a break, he had conveniently felt the need to let her know that he had needs in his life, and she wasn't fulfilling them. She had been cut to the core by his words, and she thought about being finished with him completely, but there was something about him that always kept her coming back for more. She was sure he knew that too. Every time he wanted to get back together; she was always right there ready to make it happen. The only thing that hadn't happened was the sex, but she still couldn't sleep with him which probably played a role in their latest separation.

Annabelle smiled on her way out as the girl at the front reminded her to go home, stay in the same clothes and not shower until morning to let the tanning spray set. This would give her an actual excuse if he came calling. He couldn't touch her or mess up her tan, or Christy would be furious. Jake was also in the modeling world, so he knew how it was. You had to do what you had to do to get the role. It was always as easy as that. Jake *would* understand that, right? Annabelle hoped so, but as she drove home to settle in for the night, she really wasn't very sure.

Ch. 3

Charlie woke that morning with a new feeling growing in the pit of his stomach. His phone call with his mom and prayer the night before had helped alleviate the nagging feeling he had been carrying around all day with him, and he recognized this new feeling as being something more. He couldn't quite place the feeling, but the word that came to mind the fastest was dread. He had a horrible, dreadful feeling that today was going to be very impactful. The only problem was, he couldn't place whose lives would be impacted by it. He made a note to call his mom on the way to the office and check in just in case it had to do with her, and he would check in with Pastor Maxwell when he arrived at the church to see if any families in the congregation had anything happen overnight. Aside from that, he couldn't think of much else he could do except pray and wait for God to show him the part he would play in whatever was coming.

Heavenly Father, You give us the gift of choice and decision to choose our own paths and chart our own course in life, and in obedience, we are to choose to align our path with the one you have chosen for us. I know that isn't always the case, but I pray for those struggling today with choices to be made and those whose paths have strayed far from the course you set for them, they would choose the right path today and start making their way back to you. You have the power to move mountains and create into existence our entire being. You knit us together in our mother's womb, and you have loved us longer and more completely than anyone else. Therefore, I know when we are following in the course you set for us, we will be thriving. I want that for everyone, Lord. My desire is for everyone to know the joy that comes from living a life purely and completely for you. I pray that for those struggling today with their path and those resisting you today that you give them a nudge in the right direction. You never forsake us though the enemy will tell us time and time again that you do. Never have we spent a single second without you by our sides. Some people need reminding of that today Lord, and I pray you speak to their souls and remind them who you are and how much you love them. I pray for protection over my friends and family, Lord. I pray you watch over them and watch over those I am just starting to get to know, Lord. I once again lift up Marianne and her family. They have been on my mind and heart lately. Please walk beside each of them today and every day and point their path back towards you and each other. It is in your precious and holy name I pray. Amen.

< < > >

Jill woke to the smell of cinnamon and sugar in the air. She got up and pulled on a robe before heading out of her bedroom and descending the stairs to the main level of the house towards the kitchen. She saw her dad behind the counter pulling a try of piping hot cinnamon rolls out of the oven. Knowing her dad hadn't made homemade cinnamon rolls, she glanced around for her mom. Her dad looked up and noticed her enter the kitchen.

"Your mom just left to run and pick up something, but she left us these if you're hungry." He said gesturing to the pan of cinnamon rolls on the stove.

"I'd love one!" Jill exclaimed! She got up to grab 2 plates as her dad put some icing on two of the cinnamon rolls. She grabbed 2 glasses as well and filled them with milk and set the plates on the counter beside her dad and the milk on the counter where they would be sitting.

"It was great having you home last night, kiddo." He said smiling. "It was nice to have the house back to feeling alive again. It gets a little lonely sometimes when it's just me and your mom, and we miss you when you're away for long stretches."

The dinner had been nice but also uncomfortable. No one mentioned Annabelle, and it was like she hadn't existed at all, ever. The discomfort also mingled with the news about school which Jill had chosen not to tell anyone yet. She wanted to say something last night and just get it out, but they were so happy, and she couldn't do it. She had decided to try the divide and conquer method. It would be more painful having to say it twice, but once she got a reaction from one parent, she could easily gauge what the reaction from the other parent would be. She did know that no matter what, she had to tell someone. This secret was eating her alive, and if she didn't let it out, she didn't know what she would do. She had broken the news to Jason last night that she hadn't told her parents. He had been pushing her to do it, and she had promised him today would be the day. She had to admit with her mom gone, this did seem like the perfect time. She sat down at the counter as her dad came over with the two plates of cinnamon rolls and set a plate at the counter for each of them. She took a few breaths to clear her head. The cinnamon roll wasn't as appetizing as it had seemed just minutes ago. A sick sour feeling coursed through her stomach and replaced the hunger pangs she had just been feeling. Jill looked over at her dad who was busily unwinding his cinnamon roll, and she decided it was now or never.

"Dad, there's something I need to tell you about school." Jill started hesitantly. Even she could hear the lack of confidence in her voice, so she tried to channel some confidence He looked over at her happily chewing on a piece of cinnamon roll with some sugar still on his bottom lip.

"We talked about your school last night, and you said everything was good. I don't need any specifics as long as everything is fine."

"That's the thing, everything isn't fine, exactly." Jill said quietly as her father put the piece of cinnamon roll, he had been holding back onto his plate and looked fully at her.

"You see. There was this paper, and I umm. Well, I, umm. The short version is that I'm under investigation for plagiarism, and if I don't turn myself in, I'm in danger of being expelled from school, and I don't know what to do." Jill said as her voice cracked on the final words. With her head in her hands, she started sobbing.

"What? Jill, what are you talking about? You're the most honest person I know. No matter what kind of trouble you would be in growing up, you always told the truth no matter what. I refuse to believe that now you would be stealing and refusing to confess and tell the truth. That isn't like you at all. So why don't you tell me what this is really about."

Jill both loved and hated that her father knew her so well. If he knew her less, she would be able to pull off this lie and get away with it, but he did know her very well, at least parts of her. He knew her well enough to know she wouldn't be cheating on a paper and get caught for plagiarism, but she suspected, the truth would come as quite a shock to him too.

"Okay. The truth is," she said wiping her tears and bracing herself for the impact of the bomb she was about to drop, "the plagiarism story is just a lie to distract from the bigger thing that is going on. My professor for my English class. I'm in a relationship with him, and he thinks someone might have found out and is going to turn us in which would get him fired. This whole thing has turned into such a mess."

"You are in a relationship with your professor? How old is this man?"

"He's older than me. He's close to thirty."

"So, you're telling me, a thirty-year-old man is seducing my daughter and then making you lie to me and everyone else, and you are okay with that? You are going to let someone ruin your life over what?"

"Daddy, it really isn't like that." Jill started to say until he cut her off.

"Well, it sure seems that way. I bet he even sent you here this weekend to lie to us to see if we would by it didn't, he?"

"Well, not exactly." Jill said shrinking under the weight of his anger.

"Jill, wake up. He's about to ruin your life, and I'm sure there's only one thing he is after, and he wants to make sure he gets it. Please tell me he doesn't have access to that yet." He said noticeably trying to stay calm.

"Well…" Jill said sheepishly, some pinks highlighting her cheeks.

"I tell ya. I really thought *you* were smarter than that. I thought *you* knew better than to get mixed up in some mess like this. I would *never* think *you* would be the one getting involved in this mess. This is more something Annabelle would do."

"I'm not perfect, and I'm sorry, but I love him, and when you meet him you will see why."

"I will never be meeting him because this relationship isn't going any further than this moment. Give me his number, so I can call him and give him a piece of my mind." He yelled already red in the face and sweating.

He grabbed for her phone next to her on the counter, but she was too fast, and she grabbed it before he could get to it. He started moving toward her like he was going to wrestle it from her hand, but as she backed away, she saw him clutch his chest and fall to the floor. He was down for only a few seconds before her panic set in. She knew something was wrong, but her brain couldn't compute what she should do. She just stood in panic and fear watching her father suffer. In a matter of seconds that felt like hours, the door had opened, and Marianne had walked in. She took one look at the scene in front of her and took out her cell phone and called 9-1-1. She started compressions, and she was able to keep them going until the ambulance arrived. The whole time. Jill could do nothing but stand back and admire the aftermath of the chaos she had created. If her dad died, she would *never* forgive herself for this. The paramedics had him on the stretcher and out the door in a flash, and Marianne went along to ride in the ambulance. Jill said she would follow in the car, but as soon as she got into the car and closed the door, the silence washed over her and all she could do was lean her head into the steering wheel and cry.

< < > >

Annabelle had woken early full of excitement and had even arrived at the shoot early. She was trying to keep her nerves at bay and just focus on what she had to do. She had been pleasantly surprised with how well her tan had turned out after the excess had washed off in the shower, and she had to admit it did make her feel sexy which is exactly what she felt she needed today. Once inside the room though, her confidence started to wain as she was faced with the task in front of her. She was starting to doubt whether she would be able to do this. The first task was easy, undressing. The next task would be more difficult. She was supposed to put on her wardrobe, which upon entering the room she had seen, consisted of a pair of Ugg boots and a blue, tan, and white plaid blanket scarf. Annabelle took a deep breath and picked up the boots and scarf. She started trying to put the boots on when she heard a knock at the dressing room door. Startled, she dropped one of the boots that she'd been clumsily trying to put on her foot with one hand while the other hand held the other boot and scarf. She looked up in time to see the door open a few inches and a face appear.

"Anna, two quick things: first, we really need you to hurry it up and get out here, so we can start shooting before we lose the light. Also, your phone has been going crazy out here, and we can't seem to shut it up, so if you could come and help us out with that, that'd be great. Thanks!"

Annabelle looked towards the girl with a stunned expression on her face. She was trying to process everything the girl had said. She knew they would be shooting outside, which frankly made her more nervous, but she hadn't thought about the fact that the light would be changing every half hour or so. She really was going to have to hurry. Also, the phone crisis puzzled her. She could've sworn she put the phone on vibrate and put it into her satchel. No one should be able to hear it. She quickly slid her feet into the boots and put the scarf around her neck on top of her bathrobe and looked up at the face that was still in the door.

"Awesome, just come out like that, and we will get everything in place, so you can take your robe off at the last minute. It might be a little chilly out there if a breeze or something were to blow, so everyone will understand. Follow me!"

Annabelle saw the head disappear from the doorway, and she stopped to take one last look at herself in the mirror. She was mentally prepping and telling herself that this was going to be her big break. After this, she would be more well known. During her inner monologue another thought crept in. She heard the words, "Remember your body is a temple with which to honor God", echo through her mind. She stopped to figure out where that came from. She hadn't been to church since she graduated from high school and moved away about 5 years ago. Her body was not a temple for God. Sure, she ate healthy for moments like today, but she'd defiled her body in more ways than she cared to remember over the years. She was certain God knew about that, and he didn't need her excuses. If he really cared, where had he been all these years while she struggled to keep it all together. No, God had turned his back on her just like her parents. She had proved she didn't need them, and she would prove to God that she didn't need him either. With one last glance in the mirror and smile at herself, she rounded the doorway, and her eyes went in search of the face from before.

She spotted her walking briskly towards the snack table. When she turned to make sure Annabelle was behind her, Annabelle noticed the girl for the first time. She was short with an athletic build and a cute pixie cut. She looked like she was in her early 20's. On her head, she sported a head set that was attached to a box clipped onto her hip by a wire running up her back. She carried a clipboard in her hand and Annabelle noticed she was wearing tennis shoes on her feet as well as comfortable pants and a comfortable top.

"Ah", Annabelle thought to herself, "She's a lacky." Annabelle had seen this kind of ensemble before. It was always worn by those who fetched coffee, ran errands, and basically, just did all the running around the important people didn't have time to do. Annabelle had been offered that job once, but she turned it down. Nothing about being paid to basically serve others thrilled her. She didn't want to serve others. She intended to have others serving her.

Annabelle followed the girl through a maze of people and equipment until they finally came to a doorway which opened onto a patio. The girl went ahead of Annabelle and retrieved something off a chair next to the doorway. When she turned back around, Annabelle could see it was her satchel, and she could hear a ringtone coming from inside.

"Wow, I'm so sorry about this," Annabelle said as she rummaged through the bag to locate her phone. "I really could have sworn I turned it off. I hope I didn't mess up anything."

"It's fine", the girl said, but we do need it turned off before we can continue with the shoot."

"Absolutely," Annabelle said as her hand closed around the phone and drew it from her bag. She glanced at the screen before switching the button on the side to silent. She was shocked to see her sister's picture appear on the screen along with her name and number. Annabelle had no idea why her sister would be calling her. She knew how important of a day this was to her. She had stressed repeatedly how this day was her big break. With hesitation, She glanced at the girl and saw that she had gone back towards the photographers to mingle amongst them for new assignments to carry out. Annabelle quickly turned away, swiped her finger across the phone to answer, and said hello.

"Annabelle, I'm sorry to have to call you like this. I know this is a big day to you and all," Jill said in a rushed voice. "I just wanted to tell you that Daddy just had a heart attack, and he's being taken by ambulance as we speak to the county hospital. Momma is riding with him in the ambulance, and I'm following in the car. This was so sudden, and we really don't have a clear guess on how he's doing. Do you think you can come? "

Annabelle had barely been able to process everything her sister had just told her. Did Jill say their father had a heart attack? She was asking if Annabelle could come home. That meant it was serious right? "Jill, I'm kind of in the middle of something. Do you need me to come right now?"

"Well, yeah. I mean, he's alive right now, if that's what you're asking, but it would be nice for you to be here. This is happening suddenly, and there are no guarantees with life, and I know he'd love to see you."

At the mention of her dad wanting to see her, Annabelle scoffed. She knew that was coming from her sister. Her dad had written her off years ago when she broke off her engagement, turned down her scholarship to a big university, and uprooted her life to pursue something that her father determined to be as he called it "flesh feeding flesh". In his world, everything had to feed the soul, and she had never fit into that mold or lifestyle the rest of her family had adopted. She'd been raised in church, but she'd learned long ago that you didn't make it through life on a hope and a prayer. You made it through life by working hard and going after the things you want.

"Look, I'm busy right now, and it sounds like dad isn't going anywhere for a while, so I'm going to stay here until this is finished, and I will let you know later when I might be able to come. I have to see if I can move some things around."

"Are you serious? Our father is in the hospital probably dying, and you can't come because of your "job" as you call it?"

"Yes, Jill. I am working, and I can't lose everything over someone who would be happy to see me fail. I'm not going to let him win like that. He does *not* get to control my life anymore. This is my life and my choices, and he will *not* affect them!"

"You're so selfish and ungrateful sometimes. I don't know where all this bitterness and hatred has come from, but you need to hope it doesn't take root inside of you, or you're going to end up a lonely, miserable person one day. Call me if you can make time to come and see our father while he's fighting for his life in the hospital. In the meantime, I'll pray that God will soften your shell of a heart long enough to let you see what's important."

"Jill, if God cares so much and doesn't want me to do this shoot, then, why doesn't he just stop it. Isn't he supposed to be oh so powerful? Someone so powerful should be able to pull off something small like that. I guess your big God doesn't care about individuals like me."

"Of course, he does! He loves and cares about you, but he's letting you follow your choices that will lead to consequences either good or bad. I'm certain God has been working on you for a while, but you've probably been unreceptive. If he wants you to pay attention, he will demand it from you. Don't you worry."

"Good. I'll be waiting for that. Bye Jill."

Of all the ridiculous things Annabelle had heard, this was by far the craziest. Jill thought God would come down and stop this shoot and demand her attention and care about one person out of millions. Yeah right. I'd like to see him try.

Annabelle had no more than placed the phone back into her satchel and turned around the face the shoot again when she heard it. Were her ears deceiving her? She looked around and within an instant she heard it again, the low rumble of thunder off in the distance. In another quick second, she saw the sky overhead darken and lightning flash across the sky. She watched as people all around her rushed to grab equipment and move it inside. It was a sea of chaos as the sky opened and released a downpour over everyone and everything still in its presence.

Annabelle grabbed her satchel and ran inside to save the beautiful boots on her feet. Once inside she heard the photographer and the director of the shoot arguing over whether to make it inside. The photographer kept insisting he had to have natural light, or the shoot wouldn't work. Finally, the director gave in, and said everyone would be called with the date and time for the next shoot. Annabelle didn't think much about it. During this time of the year, pop-up showers weren't uncommon. There was nothing abnormal about this day.

She headed back to the dressing room to change. She felt a pang of sadness in her heart when she removed the boots and had to leave them behind in the dressing room. Without the shoot being over, there was no hope of her being able to bring them back to her house to occupy space in her closet with all her other gorgeous shoes that she owned, but she couldn't afford to go anywhere nice enough to wear them. That was her life in a nutshell. Stacks of boxes of beautiful shoes and beautiful clothes she would never be able to wear until she hit her big break. She resolved to wait for the phone call and hope for better results next time.

When she got to her apartment building, she unlocked the front door and strolled inside. She went over to her mailbox on the mail wall, and she grudgingly placed the key in the lock and opened it up. In the sea of white envelopes, she noticed multiple red stamps with various phrases like "final notice". She knew she was behind on bills, but she kept hoping if she ignored them, she'd end up getting the money before things got worse. She was saving every penny she had to continue paying rent. She didn't want to have to end up moving. She liked her location, and she felt safe here. She pulled out the envelopes and found her bank statement mixed into the sea of red and white. When she opened it, she gasped at the low number she saw. She hoped the company would call soon with another date for the shoot. She didn't have enough money in her checking account to afford another month in her apartment. She'd been lucky to get the apartment on a month-to-month lease, but it was nearing the end of the month, and she was still short an extreme amount of money.

She grabbed the envelopes and placed them in her bag then she headed for the doorway to the stairwell. As she passed the elevator, she slowed a bit and thought about pushing the button and just riding up to her apartment on the 5th floor, but a little voice in her head reminded her that she couldn't pass up any chance to get in a quick workout. She took a deep breath and quickened her pace as she continued towards the stairs. After the first flight, she regretted her decision, but she kept imagining how great her legs would look in the pictures, and multiple companies were bound to call and offer her job after job once they saw how great of shape, she could keep her body in. She let her mind wander to all the things she could do with the money from all the jobs once she'd paid off her bills and become famous. She would live on the highest floor in the nicest building and take the elevator all the time, because at that point, she would be able to afford a personal trainer. No more agonizing stair climbing for her anymore!

When the sign for the 5th floor appeared, Annabelle was exhausted. Her legs ached and burned and were begging her to stop, so they could recuperate. She finally saw the door and sighed with relief after she wrenched it open and stepped over the threshold into the lighted hallway. It wasn't the nicest apartment complex in the city by any means, but to Annabelle, it was home. The walls were a light yellow with chipping paint here and there, and the floors were covered in a dark green style carpet. The yellow of the walls was supposed to help with illuminating the overhead fluorescent lights, but they didn't help much. The hallway was dim even in the daytime. The familiar musty smell of the hallway wafted into her nose and reminded her to hurry to her unit. When she made it big one day, she wouldn't be able to forget where she started, but she hoped she'd be able to forget the smell. Although, she had a suspicion that for the rest of her life, anytime she smelled that musty scent, she would be instantly transported back to this place in her mind.

Annabelle trudged forward down the entire hallway to the last door on the right. She rifled through her bag until she found a set of keys. She opened the door and breathed in the much more pleasant scent of vanilla. The scent was being expressed from one of the scented plug-ins she'd hidden behind her couch. "Oh, the simple joys in life." She thought to herself. After a day like today, she was ready to settle in for the night and relax.

She stepped over the threshold and closed the door behind her. She scanned the entirety of her one room apartment in less than a minute. She was thankful she had been able to find enough work to generate a small profit that combined with her savings allowed her to afford this place without having to have a roommate. Annabelle could barely fit into the space herself, and she had no idea how anyone could fit two people into this space. She was also thankful she'd made the bed and folded it back up into the hideaway in the wall this morning. With the bed folded up, the room almost doubled in size. The apartment had 4 different distinct sections at any given time: kitchen, bathroom, living area, and entertaining area. The entertaining area was nothing more than a threadbare sofa and colorful rug she'd salvaged from an apartment 4 rooms down when the tenants were evicted. She'd seen them around, and they always seemed clean, so when she saw the eviction notice on the door, she went inside to find anything salvageable. She noticed the sofa and rug and after giving it a thorough once over to make sure it wasn't hiding any undesirable creatures, she managed to maneuver it out of their apartment, push it down the hallway, and maneuver it into her apartment. She had even placed a partition around the area that was considered her bathroom to spruce it up. She'd found the partition at a flea market, and she fell in love with its quirky charm, bright purple color, and Asian lettering. On down days like today, she liked to believe the Asian symbols stood for something positive and empowering. She would look at them, take a deep breath, and convince herself that everything would be okay. She had 2 cabinets in her kitchen area that were home to her random assortment of mismatched dishes and silverware. After years of collecting one piece at a time, she'd finally accumulated enough to be able to have four people over to eat at one time. The cabinets and counters were an olive color, and the only thing she could find to make it better was a dishtowel she'd found at the store. She dishtowel had a brightly colored flower design, and it helped to add some happiness to the room. The glade plug in was, in her mind, a necessity that was worth every penny. It kept her from getting too depressed and claustrophobic in this tiny space.

She dropped her keys back into her bag and dropped it onto the old, rickety table she'd salvaged from the side of the road. The table had 3 good legs and one broken, short leg. Books had been placed under the bad leg, so the table could function and support a small amount of weight. Annabelle had been so proud of her find. She had big plans to sand it and put a new finish on it, and she had even thought about trying to fix the broken leg. She had spent an entire Saturday watching HGTV and convinced herself she could accomplish any task. She went to bed that night full of excitement for all the Sunday projects she'd planned, but when Sunday morning rolled around, she wasn't as enthusiastic, and her plans all seemed to be pushed to the back of her mind until they eventually dissipated. Her table still sat on its broken leg, the couch still had a big tear in the back of it, and the 90's wallpaper was faded and peeling off the walls all around her. She looked around at the hodgepodge of pieces making up her furniture collection. Despite the disheveled look of the place, everything here was hers. She had salvaged, saved, and accumulated everything here piece by piece. She wasn't proud of the condition of everything, but she was proud that it was all hers.

Annabelle walked over and slumped on the sofa. She grabbed a blanket to put over her legs while pushing back on the pillows behind her to fluff them in just the right places. She opened her phone to check the time and saw she had a text. It was from Jake, her pseudo boyfriend. In her mind they were always together, but if you asked him, they had a strained relationship. He would say they weren't together randomly, but he would change his mind a few days later. She stuck with him, because he was a fellow model in search of stardom. She felt like he really understood her, and he was extremely good looking.

Jake: I hope everything went well today. You're going to be a big star someday. Can I take you out tonight to celebrate?

Annabelle: Things got delayed today by the weather. I'd still love to go out, though. What time?

Jake: I'll pick you up at 5:30. I should be done with my shoot by then. Speaking of things getting delayed, I think tonight's the night. Wear something sexy and then make sure to wear something sexier under that for me find later.

Annabelle: Okay see you then.

With shaking hands, Annabelle dropped the phone on the couch. The whole time she'd been with Jake, she had been able to keep putting off the physical side of an intimate relationship. She'd told him time and time again she wasn't ready. Had she just agreed that tonight was the night it should happen? She wasn't sure how to feel about that. On one hand, she was relieved the pressure was off her to make that call, but deep down, she still felt like she wasn't ready. Maybe she should just go with it and see where it led. She could always fake food poisoning or something tonight after dinner if she needed a quick getaway. Yes, she decided. She wouldn't worry or stress out. She would be easy going and just see where the night lead and how she felt about it then.

She glanced at her phone again and realized it was nearing 4 p.m. She needed to hurry to be ready in time. She decided to add a little insurance to the night in the chance it went south. She typed out a quick message to Jake letting him know she had been feeling a little nauseated earlier, but she was hoping it would pass in time for dinner. Then she went over and drew back the curtain for her bathroom corner of the apartment. She turned on the water and filled the tub with a combination of perfectly warm water and bubble bath. She got in the tub and soaked for a few minutes before getting to work washing her hair. She got out of the bath and wrapped her hair in a towel while she wrapped herself up in her plush bathrobe.

She set about washing her face and applying crest white strips to her upper and lower set of teeth. She hadn't had the money to have them whitened by the dentist, so she'd settled for a box of white strips. So far, they'd helped whiten her teeth which had been stained by coffee, sweet tea, coke, and other forbidden pleasures. With the white strips applied, she went to her rolling rack in the corner and selected an outfit. It needed to be something perfect. She wanted something he would like, but she also knew it was important to keep him guessing and wanting more. She went over to a plastic 3 drawer container and opened the bottom drawer. The drawer was filled with magazines. Gorgeous women lounging, standing, lying seductively, smiling, blowing, kisses, and looking flirty stared back at her. She carefully slid the magazines to both sides to open the center. Underneath all the magazines in the very center were a few select lacy pieces of lingerie. She selected a black bra and panty set to accompany the slinky black dress she would be wearing tonight.

Annabelle put on the lingerie and eyed herself in the mirror as she turned this way and that way inspecting every inch of herself. She wanted to look good for tonight. Her morning hadn't gone as planned, and she just needed something to work out for her. Surely it wasn't too much for the universe to just let her be happy for once. After all the missteps and bad decision making, she'd endured over the past few years, she wanted to know that some part of her plan had been good and come to fruition.

After getting dressed and sliding on some black stiletto pumps, she sat on her couch and waited anxiously for her date. She picked up her phone and glanced at the time. The time said 5:28. Jake should be here any minute. She did everything she could think of to pass the time without staring at her clock nonstop. She surfed the internet, looked around to see if she could straighten anything up, and finally she gave up and texted Jake.

Annabelle: Hey, I picked out something I think you will like. I can't wait for you to see it.

Jake: Oh, I forgot to tell you. Some of the models from the shoot wanted to go out and grab a bite. I told them I'd tag along.

Annabelle: Oh, I guess it's good to get to know other people in the business. Anyone I know?

Jake: No, probably not.

Annabelle: Weren't you doing the shoot with a girl named Stacy?

Jake: Yes, I did shots with her today.

Annabelle: I thought she was the only other model there.

Jake: A couple other people are meeting us at dinner.

Annabelle: Thanks for the invite. I guess you didn't want me to mess up whatever it is you've got going with Stacy.

Annabelle had known Stacy for a few years, and what she knew about her wasn't good. Stacy didn't understand there were boundaries decent people wouldn't cross. None of that mattered to her. As far as she was concerned no one was off limits. Annabelle also knew what she lacked in experience in the sexual department, Stacy made up for in all her many years of experience combined.

Jake: I don't know what you want me to say. Me and you aren't together. We haven't been together for a while. We go on dates, which are fun, but we're allowed to see other people. I'm not saying I'm seeing her like that, but I'm keeping those options open.

Annabelle didn't know what to say. It was true that they had technically been in an open relationship for the past year. She always tried to pretend it wasn't that way, but Jake would always do something to make it glaringly obvious. She replied with a statement that although it was a lie, it was also her last-ditch effort to keep him from straying from her.

Annabelle: If you go out with Stacy tonight, don't call me when things go south. I won't sit here waiting around for you!

Jake: yeah okay!

She could just imagine the smug expression on his face. He knew what a lie her message was. She had always been there waiting for him when he came crawling back. He probably thought she always would be there. For some reason, she couldn't break the hold he had on her. He was the only stable thing she had going in her life, and even he wasn't that stable.

She felt like someone had punched her in the gut. She knew he was going to go off and sleep with Stacy, and she wouldn't hear from him for a few weeks until Stacy got tired of him and tossed him aside. Same story, different girl. She pushed herself off the couch and got out of her clothes and into some comfy sweatpants and a baggy t-shirt. She had just grabbed a blanket and snuggled back into the sofa when her phone started ringing. She picked it up and saw it was her agent. "Please be good news", she thought hopefully. She answered and placed the phone to her ear.

"Hello."

"Anna, hey, it's Christy. I hope you're doing well. Listen, I just heard back from the magazine about the shoot this morning."

"Did they reschedule the shoot? This morning was a nightmare with all the rain and chaos", Annabelle said interrupting, "But I was there, ready, and on the set willing to do whatever it took to get the shots."

"Yeah, they've decided to go in another direction. They thought they wanted the girl next door look that you bring, but they've decided to go with someone more well known in this industry. This is the business. Keep your chin up, and I'll call you next week if I can get you another gig. Ciao"

With that, she heard a click, and her agent was gone. She sat for a while just staring at the phone in disbelief. Jake didn't want her, and now, the magazine didn't want her either. This was a nightmare! She put the phone next to her on the arm of the sofa, dropped her head in her hands, and sobbed for a good 5 minutes straight. She was counting on that magazine job to have rent money and to cover living expenses for another month. What would she do now? She thought about her sister's urgent phone call from earlier. Could she really go home and face everyone? Could she go crawling back and admit defeat? No, she knew she couldn't and wouldn't go home and admit she'd failed. She couldn't tell everyone they'd been right. She thought about it a few seconds longer and a plan started to form in her mind. Yes, she *would* go home, but she'd do it under the guise of being there to help care for her ailing father. Yes, that could work, but it was very well known that she and her father had been at odds for years. Everyone back home knew that, and they also knew he'd been a huge part of why she'd left home in the first place. She'd have to come up with an answer to why she'd come back to help take care of a man who frankly didn't deserve an ounce of her help. Luckily, she had a 4-hour bus ride to figure it out. She had one thing left to do. She picked up her phone, took a deep breath, and called her sister. Jill picked up after only two rings.

"Jill, I thought about what you said, and you're right. This is a time for families to stick together. Tell everyone I'm on my way and to expect me tomorrow by 11 at the latest. "

"Wow! I'm pleasantly surprised! What changed your mind?"

Annabelle said the only thing she could think of in that moment. The thing she knew would cut right through into her sister's soul. "God did." She said it so confidently that she almost believed it herself, but God making her go back home, really? Yeah, right would she believe that. Today hadn't been her best day, and things hadn't worked out at all how she'd planned, but that wasn't going to make her start believing there was some all-powerful being pulling the puppet strings to make her do whatever he wanted. No Way!

Ch.4

Charlie couldn't believe the words he was hearing straight from Pastor Maxwell's mouth. Was he serious? Marianne the same woman he had just met the other day who had sat in Pastor Maxwell's office in front of them both and poured out her heart and asked for prayers for her daughter and reconciliation for their family had just called Pastor Maxwell to tell him her husband, David had just been rushed to the hospital by ambulance after suffering a heart attack at breakfast that morning. She had also mentioned the youngest daughter, Jill had been there when it happened, but Charlie mentally noted no one had mentioned the older daughter, Annabelle. There was no mention of her being around when the accident occurred, or if she would be coming to the hospital. Charlie didn't want to pry, but he wondered, considering David's obviously fragile condition, was Marianne afraid to mention their estranged daughter? He truly hoped this was God's way of bringing everyone together. This wasn't the way he would have planned it, but it really wasn't about him or what he wanted. This was about God, and he knew God always had a plan. The two pastors decided it would be best to pray for the family and the situation, and they each had a few things to tie up, and they would go separately up to the hospital for comfort or counseling or whatever the family needed at this time. Charlie and Pastor Maxwell leaned forward in their seats to rest their elbows on their knees, and with clasped hands, they bowed their heads onto their hands as Charlie started.

"Dear gracious heavenly father, you have brought this family to us and shone a bright light on them. We are listening and paying attention, and we are ready to help in any way we can. We know you are the great physician, and you can heal in more ways than just physically, so we come to you and ask you to mend their hearts and souls. Mend them to be on fire for you and to seek you in all things. Mend them to heal the ache their relationship strain has caused, and God, we ask you to use this as a time of healing to mend the hurt that led to the separation. Every member of this family needs to be strengthened and renewed during this time, and you are the mighty healer. We know you can do this. We humbly ask to be your servants during this time and to deliver whatever you would have us deliver from you to them. Please let us be your hands and feet and go out and touch as many lives for you as you would have us to. God, I also pray you watch over the daughters and help them heal. The youngest, Jill was a witness to the accident, and I'm sure she is scared and afraid. Please help her with healing from the pain, trauma, and uncertainty of this time. Help her to focus on you and know you are unwavering, and you have already gone before her and made a way for her. During this time, renew her spirit and her obedience to you. I also pray for the older daughter Annabelle; I pray she would use this accident as a time of reconciliation for herself and her family. Draw her back to you, Lord. Help her to see there is a clear path to you and how easy it is to navigate. Please use us in any way you see fit to progress your plan and your Kingdom. In your precious and holy name, we pray. Amen."

< < > >

Jill put down the phone and paused for a second letting her sister's words sink in fully. Was Annabelle serious when she gave credit to God? Jill hoped with every fiber of her being that Annabelle had been telling the truth but knowing how her sister had been the past few years, she doubted it. She'd watched her beautiful, full of life sister go from a God-fearing, church loving youth to a down and out young adult who was basically just existing. The few times she'd seen her sister, there hadn't seemed to be any life left in her. It had all been pushed aside by the bad decisions and too much pride to admit she needed help. Jill hoped this was finally a cry for help from her sister. She knew the only people who could be helped were those who wanted it.

Jill heard the familiar buzz of her phone against the hard surface of the table as she received a text. She glanced down to see it was her mother texting to find out where she was with the list of items, she'd asked her to retrieve from the house and bring to the hospital. Jill looked over at the bag on the table beside her full of things like toiletries, extra clothes, snacks, tablets, etc. She sent back a reply text telling her mom she was leaving the house now. When her mom had asked her to collect these things and bring them to the hospital, she knew that meant sitting up there just waiting for something to happen or some answers. Jill hadn't known how to tell her mother she didn't want to do that. She didn't want to sit there in a hospital room staring at her dad as he lay in a bed hooked up to all sorts of machines while doctors tried to diagnose what caused his heart attack. She knew exactly what had caused his heart attack, and she was not about to let her mother in on that secret. The last thing she wanted was to be in the hospital room when he woke up. She didn't want to watch as his eyes searched questioningly wondering why he was there and then focused on her, remembered the exchange they'd had to trigger the heart attack, and then settled their gaze on her with shame and disappointment.

She'd been trying to come up with a way out. She needed something to distract her mom, so she could slip away and not be stuck at the hospital until that inevitable moment came, or worse, her father would never wake up, and she would be left with the realization that she had killed him. She didn't know if she'd be able to live with herself and her secret. For that reason, she prayed multiple times today that God would heal him, and he would wake up, so she could have a chance to explain things to him. She knew God heard her prayers, because she always felt a sense of peace and calm after praying. She'd never heard God's voice aloud, but she could always sense his presence in her times of struggle and weakness. For that reason, nothing had ever really been as bad as it seemed. She knew she would forever have someone in her corner through every trial and adversity.

Although she felt God's calming presence, something felt different about this situation. It was more intense and real than anything she'd been through before. She felt like she was trying to stay afloat while doubt and uncertainty kept creeping in and trying to pull her under. This day-to-day struggle was very intense and draining, and sometimes, she wasn't sure how she was able to manage at all. She hadn't told anyone her secret except her dad. After his reaction, she was afraid to tell anyone else. Her mother had too much on her plate, and her sister would revel in her screw up too much. Annabelle hadn't always been the black sheep, but once she turned that corner and accepted her new role in the family, she'd been constantly screwing up right and left. Jill assumed Annabelle would like nothing more than to see her seemingly perfect sister knocked down off her pedestal by a mistake. Jill decided, she just couldn't give Annabelle that kind of satisfaction, but she *could* use Annabelle's visit to her advantage.

Annabelle and her dad butted heads about everything which was the main reason she hadn't been home to visit in years. Jill hoped that Annabelle's arrival would spark enough controversy it might keep her dad's attention focused on her sister and off her. She could only hope. Without thinking, she even said a quick prayer to that effect. Afterward, she instantly felt guilty for praying to God about something so selfish, so she bowed her head and asked God to forgive her and give her strength, courage, and peace for what was ahead. She even said a quick prayer for Annabelle's safe travels and peace within the family. When she was satisfied with that prayer, she opened her eyes, took a deep breath, and glanced down at her phone. Remembering her mother was waiting for her at the hospital, she tossed her phone in her purse, grabbed the "hospital stay" bag and hurried out the door to the car.

On her way to the hospital, she blared Casting Crowns and let their words carry her away from reality and into a peaceful place where she could be the good girl, she knew she was deep down inside, instead of the tarnished girl her father would now see when he looked at her. "We know we were made for so much more than ordinary life. It's time for us to more than just survive. We were made to thrive!" She belted the words out at the top of her lungs allowing the truth behind them to wash over her and get deep into every crevice of her being until she felt like she would explode with the desire to praise God. It was all she could do to keep from throwing her hands up towards the heavens and singing out to God while driving down the road. The only reason she didn't was the feeling there was more in this life she was meant to accomplish before she was meant to meet God face to face. She was going to make it her mission to stop surviving from day to day and begin thriving in her life. That would give her a nice goal to work towards while she worked out her troubles. She also vowed to read the bible more and grow closer to God, so she wasn't putting up any barriers between his unfailing love and her healing.

Suddenly, shuffle on her iPhone selected the next Casting Crowns song, "The Well". An entire song about leaving your past decisions, mistakes, and everything else behind at the foot of God and allowing him to be all the fulfillment you need. She couldn't help but smile as she listened to the words and felt like God was speaking them directly to her. He had truly gifted these talented people with the ability to pen and deliver his message of God's love to the masses. Anytime she was searching for answers, she would listen to them, and she would have all the answers she needed.

She blared her music and praised God all the way to the hospital. When she got there, she followed the signs to parking and pulled into the garage. After parking and grabbing her things, she hurried in the direction of the elevator. She found the elevator and was inside waiting for the doors to close when she heard someone shout, "Wait, hold the elevator!" She quickly stuck her purse in between the two doors and the doors began to open. She saw an older man hurrying towards the elevator. She noticed his familiar dark hair, tall frame, and glasses folded and hanging on the pocket of his suit jacket. She glanced down at the bible he was hugging to him like a football and immediately smiled.

"Hey Pastor Maxwell. How are you?"

"I'm great, Jill, but I'm afraid I should be asking you how you are, or how your family is?"

"We're doing the best we can with Dad's situation. We still don't know the cause or the prognosis, so we're still in the waiting game. That part gets old."

"I'm sure that part will be over soon. You know, the good Lord has a plan for everyone, and this is just part of his plan for y'all. We aren't meant to understand it, but in due time, he usually reveals to us how all the pieces fit together."

"That is so true!" Jill said it seriously, and she meant every word, but she wished at times like these she could say something more profound and meaningful. Deep down inside, she had an urge to spill her soul to the pastor and ask him to pray for her and tell her everything would be okay, and it wasn't her fault. She wanted to, but she didn't. Another part of her was afraid of seeing the same look in his eyes she'd seen in her fathers. She didn't think she could handle seeing disappointment etched across his face. She let the enormity of the situation wash over her, and she started to feel ashamed and embarrassed from deep within. She could feel the feelings rising and trying to take over as she assured herself it would all be okay. The stress must have shown on her face because she was snapped back to reality by Pastor Maxwell's words.

"Jill, are you okay?"

Jill let his question enter her ear and settle into her mind as comprehension began to allow the words to take shape. Was she okay? On a physical level, she was fine, but on an emotional level, she felt like she was drowning in her guilt and embarrassment. Finally, she knew what had to be done. She looked at Pastor Maxwell and asked of him the one thing she knew could rescue her from all her grief.

"Will you pray with me."

His eyes widened for a split second and then settled as a smile washed over his face. He nodded and motioned her closer. Once she had stepped closer to him, he laid his hand on her shoulder and began to pray aloud.

"Heavenly Father, I come now to lift up Jill and her family. We know that you are the great healer, and in this situation. We ask for healing of David's heart as well as healing of the hearts of his family members. No one knows your plans, but Jill has made a commitment to follow you wherever you would lead her. Bless her, Lord, in all areas of her life. Help her to find the peace she is undoubtedly seeking in this time of trouble and allow your peace to wash her clean of worry. We know your peace can pass understanding, and we pray for that right now. Please continue to watch over this family as David is overcoming this small obstacle. Please allow this to grow and strengthen this family. Help them to thrive, Father. It is in your precious, holy, and wonderful name we pray. Amen"

Jill opened her eyes and lifted her head to look at the pastor. The heavy weight of the burden she'd been carrying had been lifted. She felt like she would fly away if she decided to jump right then. No matter where her situation would take her, she was reaffirmed in her knowledge that God was in control, and he would lead them on the path he had already set for them. She would be okay.

"Thank you", she said to him as a smile brightened her face. "I really needed that."

"You're very welcome. Anytime you need someone to pray with you, just let me know. My door is always open."

The elevator door slid open, and they both stepped out onto the sleek, cold hospital floor. Jill had always hated hospitals, and she was instantly reminded of the reasons why. It always felt cold and miserable here like there was no life to this place. She looked around at her surroundings as the elevator door closed behind them. To the right she saw a corridor of doors. It was room after room of despair and devastation as far as she was concerned. This place seemed devoid of happiness. She looked left and saw a long hallway that ended with a door that had big letters on the front stating anyone who wanted to get past the doors would have to have a hospital badge with clearance. Jill also noticed a sign directing all passersby to turn right down another hallway to locate the bathrooms and cafeteria. Directly in front of her was a nurse's station where two nurses were busying themselves with their duties. One of the nurses, a short plump woman with short, spiky brown hair with blonde highlights and hot pink scrubs, was busy writing something down on a clipboard in her hand. The other nurse, a tall thin Asian woman wearing lime green scrubs and a hot pink zebra print headband to hold back the fly aways from her long ponytail was busy typing into the computer.

Pastor Maxwell turned to Jill and asked, "Do you know which room it is?"

"I don't", she conceded. "I was only up here briefly before, and we came in through the emergency room. I'm completely turned around right here."

"No worries. I'm sure we can ask those kind ladies."

Jill saw Pastor Maxwell take a step towards the ladies, so she decided it'd be good for her to follow. She hurried after him until they came to the big desk labeled "Nurse's Station" in the front of the room. She stepped up hesitantly next to Pastor Maxwell as the two nurses stopped what they were doing and looked up with smiles.

"Well, Hello, Pastor Maxwell, we haven't seen you up here in a few days."

"Hello, Faith! I always do enjoy coming up here and seeing you! I wish I could say all of my trips up here were to visit and fellowship with believers like yourself and Joy." At the mention of her name, the other woman smiled brightly at him as he looked towards her and nodded. "Unfortunately, I am up here visiting with a family who has suffered recently. This is Jill," He said motioning towards her. "We are here to visit her father, Mr. David Ward. He was brought in yesterday after suffering a heart attack. Can you point us in the direction of his room? The nurse typed something into the computer and then let them know they were looking for room number 735.

Jill wanted to take a minute and compose herself before confronting whatever she would find in that room, but Pastor Maxwell started walking that way. Without thinking, Jill grabbed the bags she'd set on the floor and walked off after him. She was not ready for this, but she didn't know any other way to delay it. She started noticing the numbers on the walls outside of the room. She thought to herself this was a lot like when you were looking for the correct number on a mailbox and you had to slow down to check every single one. They passed room 703 and Jill grew a little more anxious. She tried to calm herself by taking deep breaths, but the air was cold, and it had the faintest smell of the sawdust they used to clean up vomit at schools. Jill was starting to remember why she hated coming to hospitals.

"Hospitals are the worst kinds of places, so cold and impersonal. Who would want to end up here after a traumatic accident when you're just happy to be alive and ready to be surrounded by loved ones? I definitely wouldn't." Jill thought to herself.

She was also overcome with the thought that this cold and impersonal place would be the worst place to die. Some of the rooms they passed had open doors, and she could see people lying in the beds hooked up to tubes. Some of the rooms had televisions that were on and blaring, but no one seemed to be watching anything. She hoped all these people she was seeing were just sleeping and not dead. The thought made her shudder with a chill that ran rapidly from the top of her neck down her spine. She took in another breath and formed a silent prayer in her mind for her father. She asked God not to let him die in a place like this. She begged God not to take him now in this way, and she promised God she would try harder to be the person he wanted her to be, if he would just save her father.

When Jill was sure she couldn't bear another second of being in this place, Pastor Maxwell stopped and Jill noticed the room number by the door, 735.

"We made it!" She thought joyfully. There was a moment or two when she wasn't sure they would make it. She peeked inside hoping it wouldn't be like all the other rooms, dark and depressing with a loud blaring television.

She saw her mother sorting things on a table by her father's bed. He looked like he was sleeping, and Jill hoped he was. She was pretty sure one of the zillion machines he was connected to had to be monitoring his breathing, and it would surely start beeping to alert them of a problem if his breathing stopped. Jill knew her mom and knew she wouldn't be trying to find things to keep herself busy if there was a problem. Jill knocked softly on the door to announce their arrival. Her mother looked up quickly as if she'd been brought back to the present by the sound. Jill, not knowing what else to do, smiled at her mother and held the bags towards her.

"Thank you so much!" Her mother said. "Just put them over there by the windows. I'm trying to freshen this place up, so it isn't so dreary in here."

"Will he be here that long?" Jill asked with concern rising in her voice. If he had to stay extendedly, maybe things were worse than she thought.

"The doctor doesn't know yet." Her mom assured her. "They've been running some more tests this morning. I promise you will know something when I know something,"

"I think I can live with that." Jill said with a more natural ease back in her tone.

"Pastor Maxwell. It is so truly great to see you!" Jill's mother said as she hurried over to him.

Jill watched as Pastor Maxwell put his arm around her mother to give her a hug and assure her that everyone was praying for them. He opened his bible and pulled out a card for her that he announced was from the "Whole congregation". Jill doubted every person in the church knew about the card, but it was a sweet gesture. Jill made herself busy taking over what her mother had been doing. She started unloading the bags she'd brought from the house. As she was unloading the last bag, she overheard part of the conversation her mother and Pastor Maxwell were having. It seemed to be about her sister. Jill listened a little more intently and could hear her mother telling the Pastor all the concerns and regrets she had surrounding her sister. Jill's heart ached to hear her mother think even for one second that Annabelle had chosen this path, because of some parenting flaw she'd had. No, it wasn't her mother's fault. The blame all lay on Annabelle. She had allowed the devil to come in and push God out. She would hear the Pastor praying with her mother, and Jill felt odd continuing to unload the bags during this sacred time. She closed her eyes until the prayer was done and mouthed an "Amen".

"I have a new intern this year." Pastor Maxwell announced. "I've asked him to join me up here, so he can get to know families on a more personal level. He just graduated from seminary, and he will be with us at Grace until he is called by a church for Pastoral duties."

"I cannot wait to meet him" Jill heard her mother say.

Jill hoped her mother genuinely wanted to meet him, and it wasn't because she wanted to set up one of her daughters with him. Her mom was notorious for doing things like that.

Jill turned to say something to her mother when she heard a rustling. In a matter of seconds, the room fell silent, and everyone turned to look at the man in the hospital bed. His feet were moving under the covers and his eyes were fluttering behind his eye lids. Jill felt the anxiety catch in her throat. She had prepared herself for the moment she would see him again after their fight, but now, she didn't feel very ready. She kept reminding herself how lucky she was to have this moment. Her mom rushed over to his side, and immediately hit his call button to alert one of the nurses to a change in his status.

All at once, the room became alive. It was buzzing with nurses coming in to check on him and his vitals and look at the papers that were coming out of one of the machines. Jill was happily allowing herself to get lost amidst the crowd. She backed away to a sofa by the window and had a seat. She had a great view of her father, but she was hopeful his view of her wasn't so great. She could see his eyes were fully open now. A doctor had a small pen light he was shining in them to check their responses. Jill sat and waited.

Just as quickly as the rush had come, it had disappeared. Once again, it was just the four of them in this room. Jill could see her mother leaning down and whispering things in her father's ear. She had herself plastered to him hugging his head to her, and he had his arm loving on hers. Jill knew better than to interrupt this moment. Her mother suddenly remembering people were in the room, gestured towards Pastor Maxwell to announce his presence to her father. Pastor Maxwell came over to shake his hand and tell him how happy he was that God had spared him. There was more prayer and celebration for this amazing miracle.

Finally, the moment Jill had been dreading was upon her. She noticed her father's gaze begin to drift her way. She braced herself for the aftermath as their earlier confrontation would become clear in his mind. He looked at her with a vague expression. There was no anger behind his eyes, instead they just seemed cold and distant.

"This is worse." She thought. "I want him to show some kind of feeling and say something" she pleaded to God, but there was nothing on his face.

Jill felt the tears beginning to well up in her eyes. She needed a break from this. She couldn't sit here and take this.

"I'm going to go get some coffee" she announced.

"Honey, your father just woke up. We can get coffee later. Right now, it's important you stay here." Her mother said pleadingly.

"Someone should get coffee for dad. I'm sure he's tired." She spoke.

"I'll do it." Came a voice from the door.

They all turned to see Annabelle leaning against the door frame. Her shoulder length chestnut hair was more vibrant than the last time anyone had seen her, and it made her blue eyes pop She had on jean shorts that were cuffed at the bottom to make them shorter and a black tank top with a crocheted cream vest. On her feet she had her old, worn in cowboy boots. They were her trademark. She wore them everywhere. She was so tanned, toned, and "fixed up" the rest of them probably wouldn't have recognized her without her boots on.

"It's about time the old man decided to wake up." She said with a hint of laughter in her voice.

The room was silent as they all stared at her. Jill didn't know what to do. She hadn't told anyone Annabelle was coming because she hoped it would help her situation. It turned out, it had in fact helped her situation. She was pleased with herself. For once, her plan had worked without backfiring.

"Yes, why don't you go." Their father said. "You can come back when you have something worthwhile. A college education or steady plan for your future would be nice, but coffee will do for now." Her father said in a cold, hard voice.

"Nice to see you too, pops" Annabelle said before turning on her heels to head down the hallway.

The room was silent as the tension started falling around them. The thick air from earlier was thinning and becoming almost bearable. Jill could hear them commenting about Annabelle's hasty arrival and pondering how she's gotten here and how she knew where they were. Jill turned to stare out the window to avoid any more eye contact and questioning looks. She drew up her knees and rested her arms around them and hugged them to her. It felt nice and secure. Right now, nice and secure was all she would get, but it was also all she needed.

Ch. 5

Charlie had ridden in plenty of elevators in his life, and to be honest, this wasn't his first ride in a hospital elevator, although he wished it was. Being in this elevator brought back emotions and memories he didn't have time for right now. He was going to make himself available for a family during an uncertain and tragic time in *their* life. He needed to be alert and ready for anything that could come his way. Things from the past could wait in the past until he was ready for them. Ever since arriving at the hospital, he had an unmistakable urge to pray for Annabelle. He found it slightly odd, because he didn't know her at all, and he had no idea what specifically to pray for, but he felt God telling him again and again to pray for her, so he did. He closed his eyes as he felt the elevator moving, and he poured his heart out to God for her.

"God, Please protect Annabelle during this time. Please protect her heart and her soul because they are very vulnerable especially right now. Keep her heart from being swayed by feelings, and keep her soul fixed on you, so she will know how to determine the truth of any situation. Please give her the strength to return during this time and to start making amends and putting the pieces of her relationships back together, God. She needs a good dose of strength right now to walk in and face what she will have to face. Please guide her and keep her in your loving embrace. I also offer myself up as a willing servant. If I can bring her back to you, I humbly accept anything you would have me do to help further your kingdom. In your precious, loving and holy name I pray. Amen." Charlie whispered as he felt the elevator come to a stop and heard the doors slide open. He stepped out of the elevator refreshed and renewed for the task ahead.

< < > >

Annabelle was clutching the drink machine with a death grip while giving it the stink eye. She'd dealt with enough crap today, and she wasn't going to take any from this drink machine. She'd beat her Dr.

Pepper out of it if she had to. She picked up her foot and shot it backwards to build up enough momentum to kick the machine into submission when she felt her foot make contact with a stationary object. It only took a second before an audible grunt sounded too. She leaned forward and rested her head on the awkward, uncomfortable side of the machine taking a few slow breaths to steady her nerves and build enough courage to turn and face her victim. When the air was thick with tension, and she could feel the victim's eyes boring into the back of her head, she pulled her head up and whirled around to face the person.

She was face to face with a man who was tall about 5'11 with what she could tell was a muscular build under his suit jacket. It wasn't muscular like a weightlifter. Instead, he resembled the build of a runner or swimmer. It was a little hard to tell with his jacket on. She also noticed his deep green eyes that were looking at her innocently enough, but they seemed to be looking straight through her into the very crevices of her soul where her deepest darkest secrets were kept hidden away. She also noticed his dirty blonde hair which seemed to go perfectly with a tan that almost matched hers. She wondered briefly if his was fake too, but then realized it was most likely real which brought forth a pang of jealousy. Luckily, he was wearing a grin of sorts. It wasn't quite a full smile, but it did make him seem amused. She concluded that a man who was smiling after being kicked couldn't be all bad.

"Nice Leg". The man said.

"Excuse Me?" Annabelle said not quite sure she'd heard him right. Had he been checking her out before she kicked him? No, that couldn't be it. He said leg, not legs. What a strange comment.

"When someone has a good throw or good right hook, you say 'nice arm', but I don't know anything about your throwing ability or your right hook."

"yet" She inserted warningly. What kind of game was this creep playing?

"Point taken" he said backing away with his hands up in front of him in mock surrender. "I was only pointing out that I said, 'nice leg', because you have a mean right kick. Let me guess. Did you play soccer?"

"Why? Did you?" Annabelle said looking pointedly at him. She was not about to spill her whole life story to some strange, man in the middle of a crowded hospital when all she wanted was to get her Dr. Pepper and get the heck away from him. Better yet, she really wanted to be home on her beautiful, repurposed sofa enjoying her quaint, private apartment she might never see again.

"You seem very guarded. Has anyone ever told you that?"

"You're very nosy. Has anyone ever told you that?"

"Yes." He said with a smile.

"Well, you clearly didn't get it. Let me help by saying that this conversation has gone on long enough. I don't intend to spill out personal things about myself to a stranger in the hospital. I'm sorry for whatever has brought you here, but it's not worth going around looking for any type of emotional connection to try and mask the pain you're feeling. Okay?"

"Wow, that's some serious psychological talk right there. Where did that come from?"

"I didn't pay for that advice if that's what you're getting at. Annabelle said with her arms folded across her chest. "Anyway, I'm sorry I kicked you. It was a complete accident. My rage against the machine got a little out of control, and I accidently unleashed it on you. My apologies. Unfortunately, this," she made a gesture with her hands pointing back and forth between the two of them, "isn't going to go any further than this little incident. You were simply in the wrong place at the wrong time." She stepped aside and started to walk away from the man.

"What if I wasn't in the wrong place."

"Let's review the facts. You were standing in line to get a drink, and you got kicked hard in probably your shin by a girl wearing some heavy cowboy boots. I wouldn't really consider that a 'win' in my book, but you can go right ahead and call it what you will."

"How can this be the wrong place if this is where God wanted me to be?"

"God? Oh please! Now who is spouting off craziness. God is supposed to be loving and all powerful. Why would he have placed you in the way of danger? Wouldn't he have just kept you from getting kicked, or allowed you to magically find a cold can of unopened soda sitting somewhere far away from the dangerous girl in the cowboy boots?"

"God doesn't exactly work like that. Being a follower of God doesn't mean you don't have to weather the storm. It just means you're guaranteed to always have someone to watch your back and be there all the time for you, and someone you can always count on to show you the way."

"That's what we all need right? Someone to force us into a tiny box and make us do all the perfect and right things. I'm sorry, but I don't like being put into a box like that. I want to be free to be myself."

"God doesn't force us to do anything. We make all of our own choices, and he is there for us no matter what."

"Whatever you say, Church Boy. I must go join my family. Umm I'm sorry again about the whole kicking you thing."

Annabelle turned a corner and started walking down a long corridor. It wasn't long before she was aware of footsteps behind her. When she came to the elevator, she pressed the "up arrow" and waited for the elevator to arrive. She was suddenly aware the footsteps had faded but someone was standing behind her. She wanted to, no, she needed to turn and see who it was. She hated the feeling of knowing someone was there, but not knowing who they are or how close. She glanced behind her, and she immediately recognized him. She heard a ding announcing the arrival of the elevator, and she turned back and walked forward into the elevator. She turned to face him with an incredulous look on her face. He hesitated for a minute and walked forward with his hands up in mock surrender.

"I promise if I could take the stairs I would, but that'd take forever, and let's face it. You do kind of owe me. I mean you did just inflict bodily harm on me."

"First of all, that was an accident. You know that was an accident. Second, I don't think my accidently kicking you should warrant *my* getting stalked." She said pointedly.

"I promise, I'm not trying to stalk you. I just have a family to visit that is all. Once we are off the elevator and parting ways, you won't ever have to hear from me again. You might want to, because let's face it, I'm pretty hard to forget."

"Ha! "Annabelle laughed "Bad haircuts, awkward adolescent moments, and braces are all things that are hard to forget. You'll be a piece of cake to forget. I can guarantee you that."

Annabelle reached forward to press the button marked "7". She waited a second to see if he would also choose a number or at least tell her the number he wanted pressed. She glanced over at him, and he was grinning.

"Weird" she thought. "So, Church boy, I'm not sure when the last time you were on an elevator, but it does help to push the button with the floor you need to go to."

"My number has actually already been pressed."

"You cannot possibly be going to floor "7" too." She said disbelievingly.

"Believe it or not, I am going to floor "7". I'm going to room 735 on the 7th floor to be exact. I'm visiting a man who just had a heart attack, and presumably his family if they're there." He said matter-of-factly. He was hoping this would prove once in for all that he was not in fact following her, and he did have his own reasons for being there. He was hoping she would see that everything thus far had just been a coincidence, but when he glanced over at her, he could see that her expression had become more incredulous, and she seemed more guarded than before. He wanted to ask her what was wrong, but she started talking before he could say anything.

"Let me tell you what you will find in room 735. You will find a grouchy, know it all man lying in a hospital bed hooked up to machines and complaining, because he hates being stuck anywhere and every fiber of his being is telling him he needs to be constantly going and outside on the move. You will find a woman, his wife, strutting around trying to organize and fix everything she can possibly find or make up that has a problem, because she is beside herself with worry and most likely a milli step away from the edge of breaking down in tears. She's a fixer, and she doesn't feel useful if she doesn't have something to fix, clean, organize, cook, etc. The thought of feeling useless terrifies her to the depths of her soul. You will also, most likely find a girl who is doing whatever she is asked to do with the most polite and helpful façade painted on, because she wants everyone to think she is perfect. Her perfect little halo will be glowing and not a bit crooked. That's what you will find in room 735." She said these things to him in a voice that he could tell was dripping with sour undertones.

"That's very informative. Do you know them?" He asked thinking he already knew the answer.

"They are my family. My mom, my dad, and my sister, but no, I guess I really don't know them very well at all. To really know someone, you must pay attention and listen and stick around. I've never been much good at that." She said in the most honest tone he'd heard from her. "Wait. Why are you going to visit my family? Should I know you? Did we go to high school together or something?" She asked while she looked intently at him as if she was trying to place him somewhere in her memories.

"We actually haven't ever met, but I've heard so much about you from your mom. I'm Charlie Cochran." He said as he extended his hand to her. "You must be Annabelle."

"Actually, it's Anna." She said looking at his hand, but not extending hers. "What do you mean you've heard a lot about me from my mother?"

"Nothing bad. It's just that your mom came and talked to me about you once. I almost feel like I already know you."

The elevator stopped moving, and the doors opened to signal their ride was over. Annabelle stepped off the elevator and without waiting for him started briskly walking down the hallway to the right. She was halfway down the hallway when she stopped abruptly and turned around to face him. Her face was a wash of confusion and concern and he could see every wall she'd let down in the elevator had gone right back up again. Only now, the walls were higher and thicker than before. He braced himself for her as she started striding back towards him down the hallway.

“Listen, I don’t know what my mother told you about me, but she got it all wrong. I’m a mess. I make the wrong choices, I date the wrong guys, and I basically just make a mess out of everything I touch. I’m sure she talked me up and made me sound all great and wonderful, but trust me, I’m not. I come with lots of baggage. Do yourself a favor and forget everything you’ve heard about me. Actually, just forget about me.” She said and turned to start walking back down the hallway.

“You really sell yourself short. You know that.” Charlie said catching Annabelle off guard. She turned to face him, and he could see the walls were beginning to crumble but only for a second.

“Trust me. This is better than the disappointment you’ll get if you pursue me.”

In that instant, the walls were back in place and impenetrable. He watched her turn and continue down the hallway. He wondered what had happened in her life to make her such a hard person. He knew she needed the help only God could provide if she had any hope of letting her walls down. He would add her to his prayer list and pray for her daily and nightly and let The Lord work on her.

When Charlie arrived at the room, he saw the scene She had perfectly described. Her mother was busying herself fluffing her father’s pillows, straightening his blankets, asking him if he was comfortable about 10 times in the matter of a minute. He saw a girl who looked younger that Annabelle standing by her mother’s side and listening intently to instructions.

“That must be the sister” he thought. She resembled Annabelle, but for all the edges Annabelle had that were rough, her sister’s were smooth. She had the same piercing blue eyes and petite stature as her sister, but her hair was a strawberry blonde instead of brown. Annabelle had been right to say her sister wore a perfect façade. Charlie thought she wore it well, but he knew 9 times out of 10 there was trouble brewing under every perfect façade. He felt intrigued to find out what she was hiding under it.

He glanced towards the back of the room and saw Pastor Maxwell standing with a bible in hand. Charlie grinned. He had never seen Pastor Maxwell without a Bible in his hand. It was a comforting and peaceful reminder that God was in control amidst all the chaos of this hospital room. He glanced around for Annabelle knowing she should be here, but not quite able to find her. He stepped into the doorway and spotted her just inside the room on the right side leaning up against the door frame. She was just seeming to lean and watch. He wondered if it was all too much for her seeing them all like this. He determined her proximity to the door was mostly likely so she could make a quick escape if she needed to. He could sense how guarded she was in this moment and how thick the air around her felt with tension.

Marianne stopped scurrying around long enough to notice Charlie in the doorway. Annabelle felt incredibly awkward standing next to him in this moment and hoped her mother didn't try to make a joke about how cute they looked together or how perfect they were for each other. She couldn't even believe her mother was trying to set her up with someone while her dad was in the hospital. Didn't her mother have any shame?

"Oh, Pastor Cochran, it's so wonderful to see you! I was hoping you would come by. I know David is really looking forward to having someone to talk sports with."

Pastor Cochran? Annabelle allowed the words to enter her ears, but they seemed to be stuck in there. She was having the hardest time processing this new information. He's a pastor, and apparently her mom has invited him to talk about sports with her dad?

"Annabelle, have you met Pastor Cochran? He's the newest addition to Grace Baptist." Her mother said.

More pieces of the puzzle were taking shape in her mind now. He is new to their church which would explain why she had never seen or heard of him before, and he's a pastor. Did that mean Pastor Maxwell is retiring? She turned to look at Pastor Maxwell. He still looked young like he had a lot of years left to give. Why would he be retiring now? That didn't make any sense, and where did this new Pastor even come from? She hadn't detected any strong accents that easily tied him to any specific place.

"No, I'm not stepping down." Pastor Maxwell said as if he could read her mind. "Pastor Cochran here is fresh out of seminary, and I'm letting him get his feet wet with being a pastor while he searches for a church where he will be a head pastor." Pastor Maxwell finished and looked over at Charlie, his young protégé, with admiration.

"Pastor Cochran is a wonderful pastor" Marianne exclaimed.

Annabelle wasn't sure why her mom was trying to sell her on him. She glanced around the room nervously. Her eyes went from one person to the next until they settled on her sister who was in the corner sitting in a chair and looking out the window. How had her sister escaped all of this? She was getting to daydream and pretend she wasn't even here while Annabelle had all eyes on her like a little lost kitten trapped in a cage. She glanced at her father, but he wasn't looking at her. Of course, he wasn't. She was the last person he wanted to see. She looked at Charlie and plastered a fake smile on her face.

"Congratulations on being a wonderful pastor. I'm sure that will take you far." She said with just the slightest hint of sarcasm in her voice.

"Annabelle!" her mother exclaimed while Charlie gave a soft chuckle.

Apparently, her mother had picked up on the sarcasm. She was now glaring at her as if she should apologize, but Annabelle stood her ground. She wasn't going to apologize until someone told her what was going on. She felt trapped like this was a huge set up. No one was saying anything. She could feel the room getting hotter by the second. She suddenly felt very flustered and became very aware of her breathing. She closed her eyes for a second and drew in a long breath to steady herself before she spoke.

"Mom, I've already spoken to Pastor Cochran about everything, and I think in time he will understand." She ignored the confused look on her mother's face simply writing is off as an act as she continued. "Pastor Cochran, I am flattered that you would even indulge my mom's romantic ideas for even a second, and I'm also flattered that you would try to see me in that way, but like I said before, I'm not girlfriend material. I especially am not girlfriend or even wife material to someone who is going to be leading a church. I really don't know what else to say except to assure you that I am flattered."

Once she finished her soliloquy, Annabelle noticed everyone's expression had turned to confusion. Surely her mother had been clear about her intentions for setting Charlie up with her. Her mother had been trying to play matchmaker with her since she and Brian broke up in high school, and her mother had been trying to marry her off since she was 18. Why would now be any different. Charlie looked at her sincerely, or was it a look of pity? She wasn't sure. She glanced at her mother and saw it written all over her face. It was pity.

"Annabelle," Charlie began "I am also flattered you would consider me to be a potential person interested in you, but I actually have other intentions for being here and meeting you today. "

"Oh." Annabelle said nervously. "What would those intentions be?"

"I actually just found out the lady who was lined up to be my secretary has decided to stay home and help take care of her grandchildren. You might know her. Mrs. O'Malley?"

"Yes, I know her". Annabelle said wondering exactly where this was going. Mrs. O'Malley had 3 daughters, and she didn't even have to wonder which of them had procreated first. It had to be Bridget. She was always the boy crazy one when they were growing up. Annabelle looked back at Charlie expectantly. Her eyes were urging him to continue.

"Well, that means I have a job open for a secretary position for me. I mean the position is to be my secretary. Your mom was unsure if you'd be moving back home, but she thought you might want the job, or at least fill in for a bit while you're home until I can find someone."

Annabelle didn't know which was worse that her mother would try to set her up with complete strangers whenever she wanted, or that she would try to coerce her into staying here with the promise of a job. She needed a job desperately, but she didn't want one like this. She didn't want her mom to win. Her mom hadn't even asked her. She'd just talked her up to them. What had her mom told them she'd being doing for work? Annabelle wondered. It's not like she could tell this man the truth without embarrassing her mother. Her mom always acted embarrassed whenever her occupation came up in conversation.

"It's true I will be in town for a little while during the time my dad is recovering, and while I'm needed. However, there was never any talk of me moving home." Annabelle said as she gave her mother a stern look then continued, "I will think about your request, and I will consider helping you out until you can find someone permanent."

"That's wonderful" Charlie said excitedly.

That was the thing she realized she couldn't help but like about Charlie. He wore his emotions out in the open where everyone could see them. She felt drawn to him because of it. In the small time she'd known him, she could already tell he was bursting at the seams with energy and life that flowed abundantly. She was assuming this caused others to be drawn to him as well. She imagined he was probably a great preacher. Yes, you had to know the Bible and be able to interpret it, but there was more to it than that. People had to be able to believe and trust you. They were letting you oversee guiding their souls. There was a lot of responsibility in that job that couldn't be taken lightly. She hoped he understood that. She couldn't help but feel a little excited to get to work closely with him and spend some time with him. She was hoping maybe she would get caught up in some of his positive energy, and it would rub off on her. She could use all the positive energy she could get right now.

"So, you can think it over and give me your answer Sunday After the 11 0'clock church service ends." Charlie said as he walked across the room to sit in the chair by her father's bed.

"I probably won't be there to…" She started to say, but then realized he wouldn't hear her. He was engrossed in a sports conversation with her dad. Sports conversations with her dad lasted for hours. She knew it was a hopeless battle to fight. She thought to herself, "Sunday I will be in attendance at church." When was the last time she'd stepped foot into a church? She honestly couldn't even remember right now. It was probably the week before she'd left home for good. The week before everything went wrong. She hoped she'd be ready to face whatever would be awaiting her there. The wrath of God perhaps?

Ch. 6

Charlie had to admit he was very intrigued by Annabelle and her entire family. They could hold it together and cohabitate peacefully when in a social setting, but he had a feeling once they were out of the public eye things would change. As he was listening to David talk, he bowed his head for a quick word with God.

"God, I'm here, and I am ready. Point me in the direction you want me to proceed, and show me your will, so I can fulfill it. I am ready to do whatever is necessary to help this family and the grieving souls in this room. In your loving name, I pray. Amen.

< < > >

Annabelle watched her mom walk across the room and stop to talk to Pastor Maxwell. She didn't want to be in anyone's way, so she moved across the room to sit beside her sister who was still peering out the window as though she was studying something intently outside. Her sister had been weird this entire time, and something felt very off about her. Annabelle had kept in touch with her through phone calls here and there, but she hadn't really made it much of a priority. Deep down she loved her sister, but she also envied her. Jill got the best grades, had the best luck and got all the adoration her parents didn't want to waste on her, the screw up. Jealousy had been a hard thing to make room for in their relationship. She hadn't even realized it had moved in until it had taken over the bedroom and kicked her out to sleep uncomfortably on the sofa in her mind. She felt its presence everywhere in their relationship now. It was lingering behind every word in every conversation and at the forefront of every thought in Annabelle's mind. She honestly wasn't sure it would ever leave at this point.

Jill was staring intently into the nothingness before her. She wanted to leave this place. She had an overwhelming desire to jump up and race out of here as fast and possible and never come back. She had played the role of the perfect one for so long now that she didn't know how to be anyone else. How could she be expected to put on a brave face and act like everything was fine when her world as she knew it was crumbling all around her? Her dad was upset with her. She could tell. He might be pretending like he doesn't remember what happened, but that's all it is, pretending. Her poor, sad mom was so driven to please and make sure everyone was happy and content that she hardly saw what was right in front of her. This was one of those times. She was oblivious to the decline and fall of her own flesh and blood. More than anything, though, she was just so angry and upset with herself. How could she be so stupid! She knew better. She knew how she was supposed to act, what she was supposed to say, wear, and which people to hang out with. She had never once stepped out of line. The first time she did, God decided to punish her. How was that fair? She knew people who constantly were making bad choices and doing the wrong thing, and they never got punished. All these years of being the best and brightest had all dissipated and what she was left with was her sad, pathetic self. She was so full of raw emotion she wanted to burst into tears, and she probably would have if she hadn't felt a hand on her shoulder.

Jill was suddenly hyper aware of Annabelle's presence on the couch with her. She held back the tears, plastered on her best smile, and turned to face her sister. Annabelle was sitting there watching her. She became nervous. She didn't want to give anything away to Annabelle who had been the black sheep for so long that she'd probably love nothing more than to see her sister's fall from grace. She couldn't give her that satisfaction. She averted her eyes and took in her surroundings. Her father, who could barely look at her, was droning on and on about sports to a guy he had only recently met. He was some new hot shot pastor at their church with charisma and a personality bigger than life itself. She had gotten the impression from hearing her mother talk about him that she wanted nothing more than for one of her daughters to be with him. Jill knew her mother was always trying to match them with someone she deemed to be superior to them in some way. She assumed her mother had chosen the new pastor for Annabelle, because her mother probably assumed, he could save her from her wild and crazy ways. She knew her mother didn't know anything about her wild and crazy ways, so she was safe for now. She thought about having to break the news to her mother. It would crush her. How would she be able to do that to her? She could feel the tears welling up and pressing against the back of her eyes with the force of flood waters on the walls of a dam. They were about to break loose when she heard her mother's voice, and it brought her back to level ground.

"Annabelle, where are the drinks dear? Weren't you able to find the snack machines?"

"Yes, but all of them are messed up except for the ones on the first floor, and when I tried that one, it ate my dollar."

"Oh, well, what about the cafeteria?"

"I asked about it, but the lady I spoke with said they have one of those crazy soda dispensers to make a lime coke, and they don't carry dad's favorite Fanta flavor in the vending machine."

"Well, I guess someone will have to go out and get some drinks and probably some dinner."

"I will!" Jill shouted and jumped up so fast she surprised even herself. She's been waiting for an excuse to get out of here. She just hoped her mom wouldn't try to make Annabelle go with her.

"Alright Jill, because of your enthusiasm you can go. Take someone with you, so that we can make sure to have a car here in case we need it for some reason."

Jill nodded and grabbed her purse she didn't make eye contact with anyone as she headed toward the door. She had already seemed weird enough jumping off the sofa and shouting. She didn't need to draw any more attention to herself. She just hoped no one had noticed. She was almost to the door when she heard a man's voice announce he would go with her. She knew it wasn't Pastor Maxwell, which was a relief, but she wasn't sure how she felt about being joined by Pastor Cochran. She technically didn't know him, and the last thing she needed right now was to be trapped in a car with a pastor when she was feeling like this. God had a sense of humor, but it always felt like he never took her feelings into account. This also made her want to scream out in anger and fall apart in tears all at the same time.

Jill glanced back at him before she left the room to make sure he was following. When they were in the hallway she stopped and waited on him to proceed.

"Is something wrong?" He asked curiously as he stopped and stood near her.

"No." She said matter o-factly. "I'm just waiting on you to lead the way to your car. "

"Oh. Right!" he said and started walking again.

They hadn't gotten very far down the hallway before Charlie glanced back over his shoulder at her. He knew her wanting to go and grab dinner was just her way of getting out of there. Maybe the tension hadn't all been surrounding Annabelle. Maybe Jill was part of the tension too, or maybe she had her own. He wasn't sure yet. He did know this was an interesting family with an interesting family dynamic.

Jill noticed him glancing back at her and knew in true pastor fashion he was going to want to carry on a conversation with her. She hoped and prayed she was wrong. Now was not the time for her to be talking to anyone. She just wanted to get out of this hospital and into the fresh air where she could breathe again. That seemed like such a small request after all she had been through.

"So, your mom tells me you're at sophomore at the state school." He said trying to ease some comfort into the awkward situation.

"That's right. I 'm halfway through my 4th semester. This whole "dad in the hospital" situation will add some unwanted stress to this semester, but nothing I can't handle."

"I'm sure the professors will understand and let you make up anything you miss. Your mom was talking about how smart you are. I'm sure it won't be hard for you to catch up."

"Maybe"

"What does Maybe mean?" He asked as they got on the elevator, and he pushed the button marked "P" for Parking. The irony of this situation hadn't eluded him. He'd just been on this exact same elevator earlier with the sister of his current elevator mate.

"Maybe means that even though everyone tacks on a smile and says they want to help in any way they can. What they really mean is I want to help you if you don't inconvenience me or make my job difficult. This whole situation" She said moving her hands toward and away from each other in a fanning motion that she was using to encompass everything around them, "all of this is going to cause inconvenience to me and my professors. They aren't going to like that."

"Has that been your experience so far at the college you're at?"

She laughed. "That's been my experience with life in general. The less issue you cause people and the more you just do what they say and stay out of the way, the better off things will be for you."

"Maybe but living life in the shadows of everyone else is no way to live at all. I don't know if I'd even call that living."

"It worked pretty well for me."

The elevator stopped, and they both stepped off into the basement parking garage. Charlie took out his keys and they walked a few aisles over and about halfway down the row before he stopped in front of a black jeep. He unlocked the doors and they both climbed in. He had been thinking about what Jill had said all the way to the car. She needed something bigger than anything he could give her. He knew God would allow him to be the vessel to deliver his message of love and healing, but he wasn't sure she was ready to hear or accept it yet.

"Why are you saying worked like past tense?"

"Well, everything was going great until things finally came to a head with Annabelle, and she moved out. Growing up with a sister like her, you couldn't help but fade into the background. She is so full of energy and life, and she isn't afraid of anything. She was constantly pushing the boundaries in our home. All the attention was always on her. My parents were constantly helping her clean up her messes and getting her out of jams and always focused on her. It was easy for me to do my own thing. I really like doing my own thing and not being noticed. I got good at things like sensing when something big was about to go down between Annabelle and my parents. I would sneak off to my room and escape into an awesome book or study. That's why I'm supposedly so smart. I had nothing better to do. Life was moving along this way, and I was fine with everything until one day Annabelle said she couldn't take it anymore, and she moved out. Once that happened, my mom focused all her "fixing" energy on me. You know, she couldn't fix Annabelle and keep her under control, so she had to make sure she could do it with me. "

"Okay, and how did that go for you?"

"It was horrible. I took it as long as I had to, and when the opportunity to move away for college came, I took it. I told my parents I wanted to be completely immersed in college life, but really I just wanted things to get back to normal."

"Did they?"

"Did they what?"

"Did things go back to normal once you moved away?"

"Not really. It was just a new place with new routines and new people. I think it was too much freedom. I've made some decisions that are so unlike me, and now, I'm just trying to move forward and figure out if this is the new me or not."

"Are you really moving forward if you're just lugging the past around everywhere you go?"

"I don't think I'm lugging it around as much as I think it is stalking me. Lugging it around implies I am the one keeping it there, but it's the opposite. I don't want it everywhere I go."

Charlie pondered this a moment as he started the car and pulled out of the parking garage. Once they got out onto the main street, and he started heading in the direction of food, he felt compelled to finish the conversation.

"I think you're carrying it around, because you can't let go of it."

"I can let go. I have let go." Jill said defensively.

"Have you asked God to forgive you?" Charlie asked already knowing the answer.

"Well, no, but that doesn't mean I haven't let it go."

"It does. God will wipe your slate clean if you just pray and ask his forgiveness. It's the easiest thing, but it always seems like the hardest thing for people to do." He said more as an aside to himself than to Jill.

"God doesn't want to hear from me about that. Trust me. I've done everything I can to make it up to him. I still feel like he's disappointed in me."

"Jill, you've got it all wrong." He said sincerely. "You can't put God into the mold of an earthly parent. He's nothing like an earthly parent. His love is unending and limitless. It doesn't matter what you do. He will always forgive and love you no matter what. Humans just aren't capable of the capacity of love Christ is capable of. I'm sure your parents are great people, but even the best parents in the world don't compare to Christ. You've got to stop thinking he sees, thinks, and feels about you the way you would assume your parents do. When you do that, you're missing out on so much love and joy that abounds."

"Hey, there's a burger place up ahead on the left. Let's grab some burgers there and take them back to the hospital. My mom didn't give me any money, so we need to make this run cheap." She said not turning to face him or acknowledge him.

"Okay" he said feeling a little defeated as he assumed, she just wasn't ready to hear everything he had poured into her.

"For the record", She said, "I've really enjoyed talking to you. I feel like even though I haven't made any major changes in the past few minutes, I do feel better. I'd like to do this again sometime. I mean in a completely innocent way. Do you possibly ever counsel people? If so, would you consider counseling me? I think it would be good for me, and I would really appreciate it."

"Yes. I can do that. We can work out all the details and set up a time and place to meet. If that's okay with you?"

"We can't meet in your office?"

"We might can. I have to check. I usually let other groups use it after hours. If not, I'm sure we can find somewhere. It won't be a problem."

"Good to know." She said sounder happier already. "Now, let's get this food and get back to the hospital before my parents and sister have a throw down in the room. They have a volatile relationship that I can't even begin to get into right now."

"What's the deal with your sister?" Charlie asked after they had placed their orders and were waiting for the food. "She seems very, ummm tough. Like she's really closed off and guarded."

"That's because she *is* closed off and guarded." Jill said while grabbing the takeout food bags from Charlie who had just gotten them from the drive through window.

"Okay, so why is that?" Charlie asked as they drove away.

"I can't say." Jill said still looking down.

"Oh, you mean you don't know?"

"No, I know why she is like that, but it's her story to tell, not mine. If she wants you to know, she will tell you."

"That's very admirable of you to protect her like that. Y'all must be really close."

"Once upon a time we were, but things have changed since then. I like to hope we will be close again one day. We just have a difficult dynamic in our relationship."

"So did Joseph and his brothers, but it all worked out for him in the end."

"I wasn't trying to paint my sister as the type of sibling who would push me under the bus as long as it benefits her."

Once she said it, Jill stopped and really started thinking about it. Isn't that how her relationship with Annabelle had always been? It was always a relationship based on convenience for Annabelle. She had always used Jill in whatever way would benefit her the most. Jill thought she was doing a good thing by keeping in touch with Annabelle and trying to talk to her about God and keeping her informed of things going on within the family, but Annabelle didn't see it that way at all. Jill bet that she had a hidden agenda and somehow all the information Jill had given her over the past few years was benefitting her somehow. She felt like such an idiot. All this time she had prided herself on being a great sibling and friend, but she was really nothing more than a chump. Annabelle had been using her all this time, and Jill had taken the bait and fallen right in her trap. She was getting angrier and angrier the more she thought about it until Charlie broke her out of her trance.

"I didn't mean that at all. You're looking at the story and dwelling on what Joseph's brothers did to him. Instead, you should see how God blessed him for being a good and faithful servant, and Joseph turned around and blessed his brothers as soon as he had the ability. Joseph even tells his brothers he was meant to go through all the bad, so God would bring him to the place he ended up where he was in a position to save his family from a famine. It isn't always about actions and what people have done to hurt you. Sometimes, it's about the way you handle the actions and the hurt that truly defines you."

Jill let his words wash over her and push her anger and negativity towards her sister out of her mind. She feared she had always known in the back of her mind that Annabelle had a knack for getting people to do whatever she wanted them to. Jill stared out the window and smiled, because she knew that no matter what she wouldn't change the way she'd handled things all these years. She was being the person God wanted her to be. She didn't know any other way to treat someone than to follow the example Jesus set by the way he treated everyone he met. He never worried about their intentions or what kind of person they were. He did it because it was what God had instructed him to do. Jill felt a wave of peace wash over her as she realized she was also following God's commandments for her life. She didn't need answers or information from her sister. She just needed to love her unconditionally no matter what, because God instructed her to love everyone. In such a small amount of time, all the dread Jill had been feeling about returning to the hospital and facing whatever situation they would come back to had vanished and a calm peace was in its place. As they made their way back to the hospital, Jill took in a deep breath and prepared herself for whatever they would find behind door 735.

Ch.7

When they got back to the hospital, Charlie asked Jill if she would be okay if he prayed before they went inside. The request surprised her at first, but then she realized it was exactly what her soul needed. She looked at him and nodded in agreement. Then they both bowed their heads, and Charlie began to pray.

"Gracious and heavenly father, one of the greatest gifts you've given to us aside from the gift of salvation is the bible. You have given us stories and promises straight from you, so we would have some instruction on what to do in every situation. God, sometimes our situations aren't easy, and although we know where to turn, we can forget and easily lose sight of your path and the bigger picture you have set for us. In those moments, it is important that we remember that your love will never fail us, and you are always here for us. You are always covering us in your love and protection. You show us time and time again throughout your word relationships are so important. It is so important that we nurture those relationships and keep connections with others. We are meant to be a people who do life together and love and comfort each other through the ups and downs of life like you do for us. We are your hands and feet, Lord. We are the ones who are meant to show the world your love and compassion. Right now, I lift up Jill to you, God. She wants to follow your commandments, and she wants to be a good daughter and sister right now, God, but she is finding it to be difficult because of some hurt feelings and past situations that are arising within her. We know the Devil is responsible for bringing doubt, shame, anger, and all negativity back into the light to show us, God. Please protect her and shine your light through her as she learns to interact with Annabelle again, and please bless both of them by allowing them to have a renewed relationship and a renewed spirit in you. We know you are the only one who can bring forth this blessing, and we know all that you promise in the bible for us. We love you, and it is in your holy name we pray. Amen."

When Jill opened her eyes and looked at Charlie, his face was completely at peace. She nodded a thank you to him and took in a breath. She did feel rejuvenated, and she now had a mission to try and set things right with Annabelle. She knew it would be hard, and she honestly wasn't putting much faith into believing it would happen, but she was willing to try. She opened her door and heard Charlie open his and the two of them headed back inside with food.

Annabelle had spent the last 10 minutes sitting in an awkward silence in the hospital room. Her father was watching a baseball game on the television, but every commercial break, he seemed to be making it a point to glare at her and grunt with dissatisfaction. She had also noticed her mother had been exchanging knowing glances with Pastor Maxwell and then turning to glance at her. This was madness. She felt like she was going crazier by the second. She couldn't wait for Jill to return, so she would have an escape from this place. This was one of those moments that was making her wish she had a car. A car meant freedom and independence just like it had all those years ago when she received the keys to her first one in a little white box with a big delicate pink bow on her 16th birthday.

The party had been a huge event at the local country club complete with a DJ and a huge cake. Annabelle remembered how much her mother had agonized over making sure every detail was perfect which it was. Her mom had gotten her favorite restaurant to cater the event, and all of her friends couldn't stop talking about how she had the best food and music. She didn't honestly remember much about the food now. In fact, she couldn't even name 3 of the menu items. She did, however, remember what it felt like to be in the spotlight and have all eyes on her. That was the moment she really got addicted to that feeling.

That night changed everything in her life, and it sent her in search of something she had never even realized she wanted.

Annabelle remembered loving that all eyes were on her for her special sweet 16 dance with her high school boyfriend, Brian, as well as the moment her father presented her with her gift. She remembered being slightly disappointed at the size of the package, but once she opened it, her opinion completely changed. She remembered rushing outside with all the other guests as though she was cattle being herded through the twists and turns of the catch pen. She remembered seeing the car and the pure delight she felt when she realized her mother and father had gotten her dream car. It was a beautiful white sports car with a tan leather interior. She also remembered how jealous everyone had been of her gift. People at school talked about her car for years, and she realized deep down she loved knowing people were jealous of something she had. At first, she had been afraid of that feeling, but once she realized she could use it to push herself to succeed, she couldn't get enough of it. At first, she tried to harness the feeling for good and only use it to push her academically to be the best in the class, but arrogance is a tricky thing. A little really goes a long way. Eventually, she found herself consumed by it, and no matter what she did, she couldn't get enough of it.

Annabelle thought about that now as she remembered the way it felt to have people wanting to be her and wanting everything she had. The way it felt to be adored by everyone. She glanced around the room and took in the full picture. She was in a private hospital room in an old 3 seasons ago sun dress that she'd been hanging onto for dear life to help maintain an image that she hoped would help her get booked for gigs and wearing very worn cowboy boots. The dress was a beautiful mint color that really helped illuminate her skin tone as well as brighten her mood. The boots were ones she'd found in a thrift store and then lied and told everyone she'd had since high school when she knew they'd noticed the wear and tear on them. She kept her brown hair long, so she wouldn't have to do much to it in case she couldn't pay her water or electricity bill one month. She would let it start growing out until she could scrounge up the money to pay for an appointment at the hairdresser. She breathed in deeply and let her assessment of herself sink in. She had come here because she honestly had nowhere else to go. She was dressed to sell the façade she was hoping everyone would buy into. Would people honestly be jealous of her now? Would anyone wish to be her? No, definitely not if they knew the real Annabelle and how much her life had turned into a miserable existence as it had begun to spiral in a downward motion and was dragging her along kicking and screaming. She realized then how important it would be to make sure no one found out. She would be able to stay with her parents as long as her dad was in the hospital, but how long would that be? He wouldn't be there forever. Soon, he would be discharged, and she would be out with nowhere to go. She needed a plan. Suddenly the words to an old song she hadn't heard in years crept into her mind; "I am pressed but not crushed, persecuted not abandoned, struck down but not destroyed. I'm blessed beyond the curse for His promise will endure that His joy's going to be my strength. Though my sorrows may last through the night, His joy comes with the morning."

Annabelle could hear the words as audibly as if someone was speaking them directly to her. She glanced around for a moment to see if anyone else heard them. Her mother and Pastor Maxwell were still sitting off to the side quietly, but they were now whispering to each other. Her mother was still glancing in her direction. She assumed her mother was undoubtedly recounting her whole tragic tale to the Pastor and asking him to pray desperately for her. Annabelle thought the entire scene was a bit tragic. Here she was trying to come up with a plan one minute and realizing in the next minute she's probably going crazy due to the number of voices she'd been audibly hearing in the past 48 hours, and her mother is under the impression a few well-placed words out of the pastor's mouth will skyrocket straight to Heaven where God will rain down blessings on her. Yeah right. It was sad her mother believed that, tragic even. Her mother was like a lost puppy following whoever gave out the best food. Pastor Maxwell must have the best chow in the neighborhood the way her mother was hanging on his every word.

Then there was her father sitting there ignoring her and probably wishing she would just vanish off the face of the earth in the next second. If looks could kill, she would've died a long time ago from the looks her father was throwing. Yeah, if God existed and he had a plan, it must be to torture her by allowing her to be stuck in a room with these people while she started the steady decline into crazy land.

"You don't have to sit there taking up space. You could make yourself useful and get me a drink. I'm extremely thirsty over here."

Annabelle was playing with a loose thread on the bottom of her dress when she heard her dad speak. She knew he was talking to her mother, but there was a hardness in his voice that was so unnatural. He never talked to her mother that way. Something must be very off between them.

"Hello!" He said louder with a chill in his voice.

Annabelle looked up only to realize he was staring right at her. She glanced over towards her mother to see her still engaged in deep conversation with the pastor. She looked back at her father in disbelief. Was he really talking to her? He usually tried very hard to avoid speaking to her. Why would he be doing it now?

"Are you talking to me?" She asked him.

"Who else would I be talking to?" He responded with the chill still there and just as chilly as it had been the first time.

"Mom. You obviously could be talking to mom." She said with her own version of chill in her voice.

"Your mother has done enough, but I haven't noticed you do anything except just sit there taking up space on the couch, so make yourself useful and get me something to drink."

"Did it ever occur to you that people might be more willing to do things for you if you ask, oh I don't know, *politely*?"

"Hmpf" He said with a loud grunt. "Did you ever think I might be thirsty? No, you didn't, because you never think about anyone but yourself."

"You're right. I'm just the most selfish person on the planet. Too bad I haven't learned to read minds yet and become perfect like you", she said sarcastically. Then, without another word, she stood and began walking to the door.

"Where are you going? The water is that way", he growled pointing toward the sink on the far side of the room.

"I'm not getting you water. I'm leaving. I don't have to take this."

"That's fine. Leave. That's what you're good at. You're good at leaving and shutting everyone out."

"I know. I learned it from you." Annabelle said as she walked through the door and let it close with a loud thud behind her.

She knew there was a possibility that things would be bad if she came back and had to face her father, but she didn't know they would be that bad. How was she supposed to deal with that? She stopped outside the door and faced the wall. She put her arms out in front of her bracing herself against the wall. She let her body fall forward until she had her head on the wall in her hands. This had all seemed so much easier in her head. How in the world was she supposed to do this? She just wasn't strong enough to take this. It was obvious to her and probably everyone in the room that her father wanted nothing to do with her. How was she supposed to accept that and move on?

She stayed leaned up against the wall that way for a few minutes until she heard the door click. She tensed and braced herself for anything. She felt a hand on her shoulder, and she opened her eyes just enough to see the shoes standing next to hers. They were ballet flats. She knew instantly it was her mother. Annabelle lifted her head off of her hands and turned to face her. She didn't know what she expected to come of this, but maybe having no expectations would be a good thing.

"Oh Honey," Her mom began, "He doesn't mean any of those things. He's on a lot of medication, and it makes him lash out and be irritable. Just ignore him."

Annabelle was stunned. Did her mother actually think this was caused by medicine?

"How am I supposed to ignore him when he's constantly reminding me of what a disappointment, I am to him?"

"He doesn't mean it, Honey. He really doesn't."

"Yes, he does! Don't you get that!" Annabelle hissed at her. "Why do you always choose his side?" She said and began to shake her head in disbelief.

"It's not about sides, honey. There are no sides."

"Yes, there are. There has been a dividing line for years, and you've always been on his side and defended him. I don't understand why."

"No, there are no sides. When it comes to family, there are no sides and no lines. Families fight, argue, cry, and love, but at the end of the day we're still all family. That puts us all on the same side."

"No, mom, it doesn't! For as long as I can remember you've lived in this fantasy world where everything is always good and wonderful and happy but guess what? Our reality isn't like that. Our reality is broken. It is broken and shattered into a million tiny pieces, and when he says things like that, it breaks even more! When you come out here and defend him, it breaks again and again every single time! At this point we're probably beyond repair!" Annabelle was shouting now, but she didn't care. Her mother needed to hear this. Her disillusioned mother needed to wake up and see what was right in front of her and what had been right in front of her now for years. She needed to realize the role even she had played in the destruction of their family. "And the thing that cuts even deeper with dad's words and my being on the other side of the line alone is that you don't even act like you care, or that it even bothers you at all. You just can't stop the delusion long enough to see how fragmented we all are!"

"I do see the cracks. Trust me, I do."

"Then you just don't care? You're not worried that we will become so far gone, nothing will help us?"

"No, I don't worry about any of it."

Annabelle stared at her for a long time in stunned silence. Was this the moment her mother would tell her she didn't care if she ever saw her again, or that she wished she hadn't come here? Annabelle didn't know what more her mother could say, or if she would even want to hear anything she had to say, but Annabelle willed her to speak and explain. She willed her with every fiber of her being to stop and explain everything that Annabelle just couldn't seem to fit together on her own. She felt like she was putting together a 1,000-piece puzzle, but only half the pieces were the correct ones. She was trying to place the extra pieces into the empty slots in the puzzle, but no matter how much she turned them and pushed and wiggled them into the spots, they absolutely refused to fit. Finally, her mother spoke, and the remaining puzzle pieces appeared.

"I don't worry about any of this, because it isn't my job."

"You're job?" Annabelle asked bewildered.

"Yes, my job is not to worry. My job is to hand over every situation in my life to God and let him take care of it. You see, I don't worry about our family's relationship with one another, because I frankly don't have time. I have spent every free second of the past 3 years since you left wearing out my knees praying."

"Praying?" Annabelle asked not quite believing what she was hearing.

"Yes, praying. I pray for guidance to know what to do to lead this family in the right direction. I pray for you, your sister, your father…"

"Do you pray for God to soften his heart, so he wouldn't be so horrible anymore."

"Not exactly. I pray that God would heal his heart."

"Heal him? You mean like right now with his heart complications?"

"No Annabelle, you might not want to see it, but everything that happened between you and your father that lead up to you leaving us really, really hurt him. He hasn't been the same since. That's why I pray for God to heal his heart and the pain he feels. I think that's one of the only ways things will get better."

"What's the other way?" Annabelle asked sure the answer would have something to do with her marrying a nice Christian boy and settling down and leaving behind her wild ways, but her mother once again surprised her.

"I pray God would mold and shape your heart to be on fire for him, and that it would burn bigger and brighter for him."

"So, this doesn't have to do with me getting married to a nice Christian boy?"

"No, I'm done playing matchmaker. You're not ready for someone right now. You're still raw material in the hands of the Lord, but when he is finished with you, I just know you will be a pillar for The Lord." She put her hands on Annabelle's shoulders and looked her straight in the eyes. "God has big, big plans for you, and if you let him change you, he will show you things, you didn't imagine could be possible for yourself."

Annabelle looked at her mother and nodded. She wanted desperately to believe what her mother was saying, but she had been down this road before. She had been a devout Christian, and that had only brought her to this place. Three years later, and she was back at square one with no job and nowhere to go. She just couldn't believe God would choose that for anyone he loved so much.

"I know you probably don't want to, but I hope you will stay. You can stay at the house as long as you like, and I promise to keep dad at a distance. Just promise me not to get him riled up. I'm afraid his heart won't be able to take much more of that."

Annabelle wanted to protest and try to explain that it was all him, and it wasn't her. She wanted to, but after the talk they'd had, it seemed like a moot point. What was the use in insisting on disagreeing with her mom? Now just didn't seem like the right time, so she nodded instead. Her mom reached forward, and Annabelle moved towards her at the same time. In an instant, they were locked in a hug. Annabelle had forgotten how great it felt to be held by someone who truly loved you despite all of your faults. She had allowed herself to get so caught up in the drama and had allowed it to really cloud her vision of what was here right in front of her. Her relationship with her sister and father were far from perfect, but for now, she would work on the one with her mother. She just hoped her mother would come to accept that she wouldn't be the good little Christian girl she'd once been. She didn't know how to tell her mother without disappointing her and ruining the moment, so she decided that would be a conversation best saved for another day.

"What happened? Is dad okay?" Jill asked breathlessly as she came running down the hall towards them. The sight of her mother and Annabelle in a hug must mean something terrible had happened to her father.

"Nothing, dear. Your sister and I just had a lovely chat, and we put some things behind us, and we've agreed to start fresh. That's all." Her mother announced proudly.

"What'd I miss?" Charlie asked as he strode up behind Jill carrying a bag of takeout burgers, fries, and a full drink carrier. He looked at the 3 women before him questioningly.

"Nothing except apparently a kumbaya moment between my mom and sister. Weird, but I'll take that over something else happening to my dad any day." Jill announced over her shoulder to him as she surveyed her mother and Annabelle suspiciously. It was incredibly hard to believe they were making amends. Jill knew the pain Annabelle had caused her parents, and even though her mother was a kinder soul than her father, no one made up and moved on that quickly. Something was going on here.

"Well, let's head inside and pass out the food and break the news to your father that he's only having a salad for dinner." Their mother said and started towards the door.

"Actually," Annabelle said tentatively, "I think I'm going to skip the whole 'going back inside moment'. I probably need to head back to the house and get some things figured out concerning my staying in town a little while."

"Yes, that's a good idea." Her mother said. "You should head home and get some rest. Tomorrow we can look over the classifieds, and I will make some phone calls, and we will see if we can't line up a job for you."

"Actually," Charlie said before Annabelle could protest about not needing a job, "The church has agreed that I can have a secretary remember. I was hoping you would be interested in that?"

"You're serious about asking me to work at the church?" Annabelle said with a questioning look on her face. "You do remember my stance on God, right?"

"Yeah, but I don't think anyone is worried about that. Besides, you make me laugh, and it's very important to keep someone around who keeps you laughing and on your toes. You do both of those things, so what do you say? Will you take the job?"

"Okay." Annabelle said tentatively. She desperately needed a job too much to turn this opportunity down, but she just hoped her mom hadn't orchestrated this somehow as a way to get her back into church.

"Here," Charlie said passing by Anna's mom and sister, "let me just set this inside, and I will give you a ride back to your parent's house. That will give us a chance to iron out the details, and you can ask me any questions you have about the job."

He was gone before Annabelle could say anything. She glanced at her mother and saw how happy she was. She probably thought this was some kind of divine intervention, but Annabelle knew working in a church did not make someone a Christian. She had seen plenty of hypocritical Christians in her day, and most of the time, they were the most devout of everyone in the entire congregation. She was surprised when she glanced at Jill's face. Jill had a look hes couldn't quite place. Was it jealousy? She didn't know why Jill would be jealous of this opportunity unless Jill liked Pastor Cochran. She definitely had to sit down and talk to her sister, not tonight, but at some point, in the near future, they needed to have a talk. Jill had been acting strangely all day, and she hadn't been able to figure out what was going on with her. Annabelle knew after she'd left home, Jill had become their dad's favorite. Jill should be so happy to see him awake and doing better, but Annabelle had noticed Jill had been distant and withdrawn when it came to their father today. That was very strange.

Annabelle didn't have time to process much more to add to her mental 'To Do' list before Charlie came back to take her to the car and back to her parent's house. They said their goodbyes and she walked away from her family for the second time in 3 years, only this time, she was walking away with an assurance to see them soon, and the knowledge that tomorrow was a new day full of surprises. She had a job and the possibility of putting down some roots this time as long as her father didn't have anything to say about it. Maybe home wouldn't be as bad the second time around. She took a deep breath as she followed Charlie down the hospital hallway toward the elevator. The weight that had been on her chest had lifted some. It wasn't entirely gone, but there was the lingering possibility that with more days like today, it would be.

Ch.8

On the way to the car, Charlie sent up a quick prayer to God about Annabelle and the time they were about to spend together.

"God, please let your will be done here. Please give me the ability to be a positive influence in her life. Please give me the right words to say and help me know how to help her with whatever she is going through. She obviously has a lot of hurt and anger inside of her, and I want to help her so much. I know what it is like to live a life when you are eaten up with hurt and anger. I remember how it feels, and I want nothing more than to save her from that life. Please God, work through me as I show her how amazing her life will be if she follows you. Amen."

< < > >

Once Annabelle and Charlie were both seated comfortably in Charlie's Jeep, and she had given him directions to her home which was not far from the hospital, she turned towards him.

"Thanks for what you did back there. You really saved me from my mother's inability to stop trying to fix everything."

"Annabelle, I was being completely honest. There is a job at the church, and it's yours if you want it. You don't have to fill out a resume or come in for an interview. You just have to show up tomorrow morning at 9:00 at the church offices ready to work. I promise not to be a demanding or impossible boss, and I will always do my best to make your day as pleasant as possible."

"Thanks for everything you've done for me so far, and I'm sorry I was crazy earlier at the vending machine. I was nervous about seeing everyone and dealing with my dad."

"Yeah, I could tell there was some definite tension between y'all. I don't want to pry, and you don't have to tell me if you don't want to, but what happened between y'all?"

"He's mad at me, and when I say mad, I mean words like furious, enraged, and tempestuous."

"Tempestuous?"

"Yes, it means..."

"I know what it means, I was just surprised, because I rarely hear people use words like that in their everyday conversations."

"I use my extensive vocabulary when I need to impress people." She said with a smile.

"Oh, I see." Charlie said with a nod of understanding.

"So, anyways my dad has actually been mad at me for the past 3 years."

"Why is he so mad at you? What happened?

"The short answer is, because I fell out of love with…everything: soccer, my high school boyfriend, life. In his mind, I had everything going for me. My senior year, I found out I got into Clemson, and they offered me a full ride soccer scholarship. He was thrilled. It's probably the happiest I've ever seen him. It's like all of his plans for our life were finally happening. My high school boyfriend also got into Clemson, and we had big plans to go to college, graduate, and get married. Like I said, everything was perfect at least from the outside, but on the inside, nothing was perfect. My dad kept telling me stories about this girl who graduated from my high school and went to Clemson with the same scholarship. According to my dad, she moved back here after graduation, and she now teaches P.E. and does private soccer lessons. He was so proud when he would talk about her. His eyes would light up, and I could see the wheels in his brain turning and creating visions of a life just like that for me. I knew he wanted the exact same life for me, except it would include marrying my high school boyfriend, Brian, settling down, and having children."

"That doesn't sound like a bad life."

"No, it doesn't. It sounds like a great, comfortable life if that's the life you want."

"Let me guess. That's not the life you wanted?"

"At first it was. I was happy hearing about it, and I would have little daydreams and imagine all of those things happening in my life. I had even decided that Brian and I would have 3 children 2 boys and a girl, and I had their names picked out and everything. Then, one day, I started to see the holes forming."

"The holes?"

"Yes, I would start thinking of a scenario for the future, and suddenly, something about it wouldn't be picture perfect anymore. One day, I woke up and realized my father had mapped out my entire life without even asking me what I wanted, or what I saw for myself in the future. That's when I finally started letting myself have dreams for my life that only included me. Then, one day my dad was going on and on about my future and this beautiful life I would have, and suddenly, I could feel the walls closing in all around me. That's the day I decided to leave and pursue the life I wanted for myself. Unlike my dad, I had big dreams for myself. I started dreaming big, and I continuously pushed the limits of my dreams until they were limitless. It was so exhilarating and refreshing to be in charge of my own life and future. I wanted it all."

"It sounds like you had big plans for yourself."

"Yeah, but I still ended up back here. Only in this scenario, I'm unemployed, unmarried, and I'm back to living with my parents. Only one of whom actually speaks to me. What kind of life is that?

"Sounds to me like God gave you a clean slate."

"None of the pieces of my life can actually sound appealing to you."

"All I'm saying is that you can be thankful you aren't married to someone you don't love, and you aren't working in a job you hate. You dodged two bullets. There were most likely much easier ways to go about getting that life like maybe talking to your dad and telling him what you envisioned for yourself."

"Trust me. He wouldn't have listened."

"How do you know? Did you ever try?"

"No, I just know how he is. He was so excited about the future he had planned for me, and he couldn't see anything else outside of his plan. I think the hardest loss for him was when I dumped Brian. That was when reality came crashing in on him, and he realized he wouldn't be gaining Brian as a son one day. I don't know if you know this, but he and Brian still hang out a lot. They go fishing and watch sports together all the time. Losing Brian was worse to him than losing me."

"You don't know that."

"Yes, I do. He couldn't bear to lose Brian, so he found ways to keep him in his life. He could manage to lose me. I left 3 years ago, and he never went out of his way to try and get me back in his life, and I'm his own flesh and blood. What does that tell you about how screwed up our relationship is?"

"Well, it tells me he was definitely hurt by what happened and losing you. It also tells me how important it is that the two of y'all sit down and have a talk."

"You heard me talking to my mother about what happened tonight. How am I just supposed to sit down and talk to him? He can't even stand being in the same room as me."

"You need to pray for strength and for God to make it okay."

"Right…I should've known your answer would be about God or Jesus or prayer. I guess I'll have to get used to hearing churchy answers from now on."

"Yes, prayer is powerful. You must pray without ceasing. You pray and pray and pray until you're certain you've given it completely over to God, and then, you pray some more as you watch God take control of the situation and transform it right before your eyes."

"If prayer were so easy, everyone would do it."

"That's not true at all. Prayer is easy, but it takes time and patience, and you have to relinquish control of the situation and give it completely to God. That's a powerful combination of things people have trouble with. People are selfish by nature, and they always think they know the best answer, or they can do it better. That's why even though prayer is free and easy, people aren't lining up to do it.

"Everything you're saying sounds great and wonderful, and I really want to believe you, but I know life isn't really like that. Life isn't great and wonderful. Life is hard, and it will knock you down more times than it will help you up. I've learned the only person you can really depend on is yourself. It's a sad fact, but it's true."

"I understand why you feel that way but believe me when I tell you that God has been there for and with you every step of the way. You might have felt alone, but you were never alone. God never left your side or abandoned you, he has always been there just waiting for you to reach out for him."

"How can you believe that?"

"Because God does that for everyone. No one is so enveloped by sin that God doesn't love and protect them anymore. He does it for everyone. He gives us his promises in The Bible, and one of his promises is that he won't forsake us. Do you remember the parable of the prodigal son?"

"Yeah, I think so. Didn't the son leave and end up eating with pigs or something? Trust me, I might be in a bad place, but I'm not that bad off."

"Those are pieces of the story, but you're missing a lot. The son wanted the fortune he would inherit once his father died, but he didn't want to wait for that to happen. He went to his father and demanded it. His father obliged him and gave it to him. The son took it and left to start his own life in the world. He got completely tangled up in the world and ended up spending all his money, and yes, he became so poor he was starving and wanted the slops he was feeding to pigs. He decided at that point to go back to his father and try to get a job as a servant. His father was overjoyed to see him and welcomed him back with open arms and a party. His father didn't care what he had done. He was just glad he had come home."

"Wow, I wish I had a father like that. My father wasn't even excited to see me at the hospital. I wish he was capable of forgiveness like the father in the story. I'd give anything to have what the prodigal son had.

"That's just it. You have everything he has. You have a father who, at any moment, will welcome you back to him with open arms."

"That's not true. You didn't hear the things he said to me tonight." Annabelle could feel herself getting angry. Why wasn't he listening? Why was this so complicated for him to understand?

"No, your earthly father isn't there yet, but your heavenly father has been waiting with open arms for your return every day since you left. On the day you do decide to return, he will still be there waiting to greet you with open arms, and the heavens will rejoice over it."

Charlie made the last turn into her parent's neighborhood. He wanted to let his words sink into her heart and break through the darkest places of anger and hurt she had sitting inside. The silence wasn't tense or unbearable like it sometimes can be. Instead, it was peaceful, and Charlie knew it was God. God was using him to relay his message to Annabelle. Charlie was proud to be a vessel for God's word, because that meant he was really working on her. Charlie had only known her for a couple of hours, but he could already tell she was special, and she had the potential to do great things, if someone would just direct her on the right path. That was his job. God had wanted him to offer her that job for a reason. He had felt a tugging at his heart when the opportunity presented itself. He knew beyond a shadow of a doubt that job had always been meant for her, and he was to be the one leading and guiding her towards the right path. He knew he would have to explain things to Pastor Maxwell in the morning as soon as he showed up to the church. Pastor Maxwell had gotten a bunch of resumes from church members, and he wanted the two of them to go through them tomorrow and pick a good candidate from the list. He was probably shocked Charlie had offered

Annabelle the position right on the spot, but he had been too kind to make a scene in the hospital room about it. Charlie hoped he could explain the tugging he'd felt on his heart, and the pull from God that this was exactly what he was supposed to do. He hoped all of that would make the difference.

Once the car was stopped, Charlie looked at the house. It was a big Southern Farmhouse with a huge wrap around porch with porch swings on both sides. He could imagine Jill and Annabelle sitting and swinging and talking about things in the swings on warm summer nights. It was a nice thought, but he wasn't sure they'd ever had long talks in the front porch swings. In fact, he really didn't know if they had actually been close enough when they were growing up for anything like that to happen. Jill seemed to allude to the fact they'd been somewhat close, but he wasn't sure exactly how close. Charlie had noticed that Annabelle seemed guarded with everyone in her family. She didn't seem close enough with anyone to just open up and let them in without worry. He shrugged off his concerns and decided he would find out the whole story later if she would tell him, but she'd had a long day, and she'd already divulged so much about her relationship with her father that he didn't feel like prying any further into her life. He turned his attention back to the house and noticed there were many windows spanning the front of the house. He could only imagine how natural light it would bring in during the daytime. Even though he knew no one was home, he could see there was a light on somewhere inside the house on the main floor.

Charlie turned toward Annabelle and smiled. She looked tired sitting slumped forward in the seat. At the hospital, she'd spent so much time on the defensive it must have worn her out. She didn't look as tough and confidant as she had then. Now, she looked like a young girl in her twenties who was wearing the weight of regret and disappointment, her own or everyone else's he wasn't sure, but he could definitely tell she was wearing it like shackles chained to her legs that were immovable. He hated leaving her alone like that, but he knew she was probably tired.

"Will you be okay by yourself?" He asked her with kindness in his voice.

"Yeah, I'll be fine. My sister and maybe my mom will be home soon. I won't be alone all night." Annabelle said trying to muster a little confidence back into her voice.

"Okay then" he said as he heard her open the door, and she jumped down to the driveway.

Annabelle thanked Charlie for the ride and waved at him as she closed the door. She turned toward the house and started walking toward the front steps. Thankfully her mother had never gotten out of the habit of leaving a light on in the hallway, so they never had to enter a dark house. That made her feel a little better about being here alone. Annabelle walked up the steps of the front porch, and just before she got to the door, she knelt down and started feeling around inside the plant on the left side of the door. Almost instantly, she pulled her hand back to reveal the shiny, silver object she was holding. She stood up and used the newly retrieved key to unlock the deadbolt and the lock on the front door. Once she unlocked it, she pushed it open and stepped inside the house. Once inside, she turned and waved to Charlie letting him know she was inside and safe. She closed the front door, and as she was locking it back, she heard his car backing out down the driveway.

Annabelle stood in the entryway for a moment and allowed the sweet hint of lavender wash over her. Her mother was always diffusing some kind of oil when she was at the house, and she did it so often the smell seemed to linger long after there was any oil left. Annabelle loved the smell of lavender, so she didn't mind. She made her way across the entryway to a table on the far side of the small room. The table was lined with frames of every shape and size and smiling faces stared back at her from the top of the table. She started looking at each one and taking in every scene and memory. It had been a long time since she'd been able to see these pictures. Most of the pictures were from family vacations over the years: She and Jill having a picnic in Washington, D.C. with monuments in the background, She and Jill posing at the top of a mountain they had just conquered together with a breathtaking view stretched out behind them, She and Jill in mid jump at the beach while the ocean waves rippled in where there feet would've been had they been standing, and she and Jill arms around each other in front of a huge facility that read Riggs Field, the place she was supposed to happily play soccer for the next 4 years before finally graduating, marrying Brian, and moving home to start a family. She surveyed each picture closely. She noticed how bright her eyes were shining in the first 3 pictures. She remembered so well how happy and full of life she had been. Each day seemed like an adventure she had the pleasure of conquering, but when she looked at the picture taken at Clemson, she saw something different. Her eyes were dim, and although she had a big smile plastered on her face, she looked exhausted. She searched her brain for the memory of that day. Little by little the memory came flooding back to her.

First, she remembered the feelings she felt that day. In a rush, the anger, hurt, disappointment, and betrayal washed over her. She could feel all the feelings she felt, but she was having a little trouble connecting the feeling to any specific event that had taken place. What had caused her to feel those things? Slowly she searched her brain for all the pieces of the puzzle. She knew they had gone there for a campus tour. She had just gotten her acceptance letter, and the trip had actually been her dad's idea. She remembered she was upset, because there was something going on that weekend that she had planned to go to, but she had to cancel her plans for this visit. Annabelle searched her brain, but she couldn't remember what she had been planning to do. She could only remember that it ended up not happening. Once again, everyone had to drop their plans and do whatever her father had planned for them to do. He could be very selfish like that. Just thinking about this was starting to make her angry. She thought about putting the picture back on the table and forgetting about trying to dredge up this obviously painful memory, but when she started to move toward placing the picture back on the table, she paused. She felt overwhelmed and consumed by a need and desire to explore further and remember everything. She knew this was unhealthy, and she should walk away and leave it alone. It had happened in the past, and there was nothing she could do to change it, but she just couldn't let go of the emotions that were wrapping themselves tighter and tighter around her every second until she felt like she'd be strangled by them.

She kept the picture in her hand, and she moved it closer to her face until she was staring back into the face of her 18-year-old self. Okay, so she had remembered not being able to do whatever it was she'd wanted to do and having to go and visit Clemson on a campus tour with her family, but there had to be much more to the story to create the expression she saw staring back at her. She searched and searched willing her brain to unlock and upend the contents she had locked and filed away long ago.

She stared at the picture until suddenly pieces of the puzzle started falling into place. The memory was so vivid, it was as if she was there reliving it all over again. She remembered her father had started learning everything about the campus when she had first shown an interest in going there. The two of them had sat and talked about the school, the campus, and the soccer program on multiple occasions. By the time the trip came around, Annabelle felt like she already knew everything there was to know about the school and their soccer program. It seemed only natural her father would insist on being their tour guide. Why would he want someone else leading him around and telling him things he already knew?

"He should've been happy about being the tour guide." Annabelle thought. She tried to remember what it was that had upset him. Suddenly, she remembered everything.

They had been walking down the path that led to Riggs Field after having toured the rest of the campus. She remembered the tightness she'd started feeling in her chest throughout the entire campus tour. She started feeling overwhelmed by it all and as though she would at any moment be engulfed by all her emotions and unable to breathe. She slowed her steps and started taking deep purposeful breaths.

"Breathe In. Breathe Out. Breathe In. Breathe Out." She told herself as she did just that. Her breathing was steadying, and she was solely focused on addressing the enormity of the emotions within her. She was trying to figure out what was causing her all of this grief. She started reflecting back on the past month. When had she started feeling this way? The more she thought about it, the more she realized she'd been feeling a small amount of this every time she'd stepped foot on a soccer field or anytime her father made mention of her future. She could feel the anger welling inside of her. Each step she took closer to the soccer field made her anger intensify. This was her life wasn't it? Had anyone asked her lately what she wanted? What if she didn't want to play soccer here, marry Brian and move back home to start a family? Her parents had always told her she could do anything she wanted, and she could grow up to be anyone she wanted to be. Why had that changed now? She was so caught up in her own thoughts, she didn't realize she'd caught up with the rest of her family who was standing right outside of the stadium.

"Annabelle isn't this great? This is where you will win championships, set new records and lead your team to victory. Can't you see it? It's going to be incredible. This is everything we've been working for." Her father was talking in a loud, proud voice as he made his announcement and came over to put his arm around her and hug her tight.

"Wait what do you mean *we* worked for? How is this we?" She asked in a distracted voice. She looked around sure to find someone who agreed with her, but her mother and sister were both smiling and nodding their heads along with everything her father was saying. Annabelle started to feel a panic rise within her. She was trapped. She was trapped in a life she didn't want, and the rest of her life, which had already been planned out for her. How could she escape all of this? She didn't know what to do. Her dad was going on and on about *their* dreams coming true while she was falling apart inside. Her mother and sister were completely oblivious to anything happening around them, but Annabelle wasn't. She had given up so much of her life for a dream she hadn't wanted, or had she? She thought about it for a minute. There were obvious points in her life when, yes, she had very badly wanted this dream to become her reality, but now that it was here, it was too much to bear. The scene going on around her was surreal, and she felt like an onlooker surveying the scene from the outside. She wanted to be excited and revel in this, but she just couldn't shake the way she felt. When she felt everything within her rise to the surface about to burst forth, she heard her father 's words, and like a balloon releasing air from a single pin prick, everything came bursting out of her.

"It's a shame Brian couldn't come. We could've taken y'all's picture here in front of the stadium. The next four years of both of your lives will be spent making memories here." He said with a twinkle in his eyes.

"Oh, that would be a lovely picture to show the kids one day. We have to remember to get one during move in day." Her mother said with a sing song quality to her voice.

"Are you people hearing yourselves?" Annabelle yelled, "There are no kids! I don't have kids! I'm not married to Brian! I am an 18-year-old girl who is about to graduate from high school! Why is everyone forgetting that?"

"No one is forgetting that, Champ" Her dad said in a calm, but serious tone, "Everyone is just excited for you and the opportunities you have laid out ahead of you for the rest of your life."

"What if I don't want those opportunities? What if they don't seem like opportunities at all?"

"They are *wonderful* opportunities, and you will remember that and everything we've sacrificed to get you to this point."

"You haven't sacrificed anything to get me here except maybe some gas and time off of work. I did all the hard work and gave up all of my time playing in games and tournaments and letting you control my future, but I'm not letting you control it anymore!" She seethed. She had let the anger take over, and now she had relinquished control to it. The power of the anger was intense, and she liked it. She felt herself yearning for more.

"We have sacrificed our whole lives and our identities to get you to this point, and you will be quiet and grateful to be here. Now, go stand over there with your sister while I get a picture, and then, we will leave. I don't want to hear another ungrateful word out of you for the rest of the trip."

She wanted to scream at him and tell him if she'd been such a burden then he needed to let her go, and he shouldn't have let her ruin their lives. She was ready to say it, and she could feel the words rising up to spill out, but she looked over at her mother and sister who were standing there just watching the exchange. She saw hurt in her mother's eyes, and she wasn't sure if she had caused it, or her father. She started letting the anger subside to guilt, and she walked over towards her sister. As she was smiling for the camera, she vowed to remember this day and the feelings of suffocation she was feeling. She vowed to press forward and come up with a way to get out from under her parents and the enormous stress of the life they'd built for her. Most of all, though, she remembered the intoxicatingly delicious hint of anger that still lingered within her.

Annabelle became fully aware of how hard she was gripping the frame in her hand. She released her grip a little, so she didn't end up breaking the glass. She sat the picture back on the table, and she studied it from a distance. She had forgotten so much about that moment. It was the moment that changed everything. The week after that, she had graduated, left home suddenly, and instantly changed any and every dream and ambition her parents had ever had for her life. Why would her parents keep a snapshot of that moment framed and sitting out for everyone to see? Did they not understand the significance it held? She must've spent a while standing and looking at the pictures and reliving the memory, because next thing she knew, she heard a key in the lock and the door swung open. She looked back towards the door and Jill was standing there looking tired and downtrodden. She could tell something was off about Jill. She hadn't seen her in a long time, but she knew when the twinkle in her sister's eyes was missing.

"Hey!" Annabelle said cheerfully hoping to awaken whatever was shut down inside of Jill.

"Hey." Jill said without an ounce of emotion.

"You look tired. Do you want me to get you a drink, or make you some tea or something? I'm sure I can still find my way around the kitchen." Annabelle said, and again she tried to add the cheer back to her voice.

"That's okay." Jill said, "I'm just going to go upstairs and go to bed. I'll see you in the morning,"

"I'm headed up in a minute to take a shower. I probably won't see you in the morning unless you've become an early riser. I'm starting my secretary job at the church tomorrow, remember?"

"Lucky you", Jill said sarcastically.

Although Annabelle had noticed the sarcasm in Jill's response, she was certain there was another emotion lingering there as well. She couldn't quite place it, but she was thinking it seemed like resentment or jealousy, but that couldn't be right. Jill had never had those emotions towards her before, and why would she start now?

"I'll stop by your room and say goodnight before I turn in." Annabelle said sweetly.

"Don't worry about it. I'm already going to be asleep." Jill told her.

Before Annabelle could protest and tell her she was going to worry about it, because she was worried about her, Jill was already making her way upstairs. Annabelle shrugged it off, and she figured there would be time later for them to talk. She took a quick shower to wash off the stress and tension from the day, and then, she went around collecting sheets and all the things she would need to make her room seem more like her room and less like the office her parents had converted it into. She didn't even see a single sign of her old life in there except for her bed in the corner.

Before she laid down, she walked quietly down the hallway and over to Jill's door. She rapped lightly on it, and then, she pressed her ear to the door to listen for signs of life. The wood felt cold against her cheek and made her shiver. When she didn't hear anything, she pressed her palm to the door and whispered, "I love you." Then she quietly crept back down the hall to her room. She made herself cozy under the covers and turned off the lamp next to her.

The house was so quiet at night. Annabelle realized; she'd forgotten all these things that had been normal parts of life to her in the past. As she lay there thinking, she felt her eyelids getting heavy, and right before sleep had overtaken her, she realized a new feeling had engulfed her. It was excitement. She was excited to see what tomorrow would bring, and she was excited that tomorrow promised to be a new day with a new adventure.

Ch.9

Charlie woke full of excitement for the day. He was excited Annabelle had agreed to take the job as his secretary. He knew God had big plans for her, and he felt honored to have been chosen to walk alongside her as he showed her everything God would bring to her life if she would just let Him into her life. He knew this would be a big job, and he wouldn't be able to do it on his own. Before his feet even hit the floor, he was ready to talk to God and start the day off on the right foot.

"God, thank you so much for granting me with such an important task as bringing Annabelle back to you. Please help me and guide me in this task. Help me to show her your promises and all the things you want for her in her life. Help me to guide her on the path you have set for her that will ultimately bring her back to you and help her to fulfill her purpose. Please give me the tools necessary to fulfill your purpose. Help me show her that no matter where her life had led her, you are here waiting for her whenever she is ready. Let me show her your unconditional love that is always waiting for her whenever she is ready to accept it. It's in your heavenly name I pray. Amen."

< < > >

When Annabelle opened her eyes, she was aware of two distinct things. The first was the beeping sound coming from somewhere nearby, and the second was that she was in a bed in a room that seemed oddly familiar. She lay there for the next few minutes trying to sort through the muddled, foggy thoughts of her mind as her eyes darted back and forth around the room taking in all the things the sunlight peeking through the curtains would allow her to see. She willed her mind to remember the events from yesterday, but it was so hard to think about anything with the incessant beeping. Suddenly, she realized it was an alarm, so she set up and followed the sound to the bedside table where an alarm was busy yelling at her to wake up. She studied the contraption for a minute until she realized how to turn it off.

Once the beeping was gone, she felt instantly better, and her mind wasn't quite as foggy as before. She still felt groggy, but at least she could process some thoughts. It took a few more minutes for the groggy, cloudy feelings in her mind to dissipate. Once they did, she began to register some new thoughts and observations. Everything from the previous day flooded back to her, and she remembered she was in her childhood bedroom in her childhood home waking up to start her first day at her new job as secretary of her childhood church. All of this would have been amazing, but she wasn't her old childhood self. She had changed, grown, and matured in ways she didn't think the church would agree with. She only hoped she wouldn't receive too much judgment once her entire story came out into the open. She knew church people weren't supposed to judge others, but she also knew they didn't all follow that rule.

As she was processing all her newly acquired information, her nostrils acquired something new as well. The sweet scent of cinnamon had wafted up out of nowhere and was now permeating her entire body through her nostrils. She lingered for a while in the bed letting the delicious aroma fully encompass her. As she was imagining what had created the smell, she heard a sound and realized her stomach was growling. She got out of bed, put on her house shoes and trudged down the stairs toward the smell.

She was halfway down the stairs when she realized something was wrong. It smelled like something was cooking, but she couldn't hear anyone moving around or any pots or dishes clanking together in the kitchen. That couldn't be right. Her family had always been loud and noisy in the kitchen. When she reached the doorway of the kitchen, she was surprised to see the room was almost empty. Jill was sitting at the bar drinking a cup of coffee while staring at her laptop.

Anna tiptoed in quietly trying not to disturb her. As she was coming around the island past the oven, the smell grew more intense. She looked down to see the flame of a lit candle dancing to and fro from its little glass sanctuary. She lifted the candle to examine it and written across the front were the words Cinnamon Roll. Disappointment instantly washed over her. She had come down here in the hopes of finding tangible cinnamon rolls she could eat, not just the scent of a cinnamon roll. She slammed the cinnamon roll candle back onto the counter and cursed. The commotion startled Jill, and she jumped. Anna looked at her, and she could see Jill breathing deeply with her hand over her heart.

"You startled me. I didn't even know you were awake." Jill said with a wide-eyed look.

"Sorry about that. I was just so disappointed when I came down here to fill my stomach with whatever was making that delicious scent, and I got down here only to find out it was a candle. Such a letdown." Anna said still visibly disappointed.

"Oh yeah, sorry about that, the smell of cinnamon helps me think, so I lit it while I was working on something." Jill said returning her attention back to whatever was on her laptop screen.

"Are you working on something for school?" Anna asked curiously. She hadn't heard Jill mention school or say anything about school in a while. Anna found that concerning since Jill had always been the studious one, and Anna suspected her confidence always came from her natural abilities in school.

"Kind of. Not really." Jill said very quickly.

"Well, either you are, or you aren't."

"I'm not working on anything. Don't worry about it." Jill said nervously as she quickly shut the lid of her laptop.

Anna studied her sister. She could feel the nervous energy radiating from her. Something wasn't right with her. Anna had been sure of that since she'd arrived home. Her sister's eyes hadn't looked the same either. They were wild and frenzied, darting back and forth towards Anna and back to her hands on the bar top. Anna also noticed the dark circles that were forming under Jill's eyes.

"What is going on with her?" She thought to herself. She studied Jill, and she noticed she looked thinner than she had remembered her being. Anna knew being thin wasn't an issue if you were thin, because you were athletic and eating right, but as she studied Jill, she realized that wasn't the case. Her arms had lost definition and tone, and they just looked like twigs sticking out from her body. Anna thought if someone ever grabbed Jill's arm hard enough, it might break off. Then, she noticed the thin, hollowed out look of Jill's face. The face that once held so much life and would light up with her smile was now just a shell with which to house her dormant emotions. Anna didn't know what was going on with Jill, and she really didn't want to find out right now until she got some food in her stomach.

"Hey, let's go grab some breakfast. It is obvious nothing will be coming out of this kitchen anytime soon." Anna said as she looked around the barren kitchen counters and then back at Jill.

"No, I'm okay with my coffee." Jill said.

Anna groaned in a hungry frustration and said, "C'mon, it's my treat. No one in this family can turn down free pancakes!"

"I really do have a lot to do today." Jill protested.

"Okay, so bring it with you, and we will work on it while we eat." Anna countered.

"No, I can't bring it with me."

"Yes, you can. It's obviously on your laptop. The beauty of a laptop is they are portable and can travel."

"No, I can't bring it with me. Just don't worry about it!" Jill said with a harsh tone sounding in her voice.

"Wow, for someone who is turning down pancakes, you sure are letting your hangry voice say a lot for you. Come eat then come back and work on whatever craziness is on there." Anna said pointing at Jill's laptop.

"Okay, fine! I will go to keep you company, but I'm really not hungry or hangry or whatever it was you called me."

"Awesome! I just need to run upstairs to change clothes, brush my teeth, and run a brush through my hair. Give me about 5 minutes, and I'll be back down."

"Okay" Jill said without the slightest hint of happiness while she turned back to whatever was on her computer screen.

Anna raced up the stairs to get ready. She made a mental note to check out Jill's laptop and whatever was on it. Apparently, that would hold the key to figuring out what was wrong with Jill, and Anna had to know what she was up against before she could fix it.

In about 5 minutes, Anna had returned downstairs dressed and ready to go and surprised to find Jill sitting in the same spot with her purse in hand, but the computer was nowhere to be seen. Anna didn't remember hearing Jill come up the stairs, so she wondered where she could've stashed it so quickly.

"I was thinking I should probably drive, so I can drop you off at the church afterwards." Jill said.

"Sounds fine to me." Anna said with a smile. She noted that Jill did not return her smile.

"Are you sure you want to wear that shirt?" Jill asked Anna with a questioning look while she she got up and headed outside.

"Of course! I love this shirt! Is something wrong with it? Did I spill toothpaste on it?" Anna said looking down and inspecting the shirt while following her sister out of the house.

"You didn't spill anything *on* it, but I'm afraid two very important things might spill *out* of it if you lean over to look for something." Jill said as she got to the car and pushed the button on the key fob to unlock the doors.

"Oh, don't be silly. This is the way everyone wears their shirts in the city. The trend probably hasn't caught on here yet, but maybe it's time *I* start the trend." Annabelle said as she and Jill slipped inside the car and closed their doors.

"Are you sure you're going to be comfortable wearing that inside the church?" Jill asked.

"God made every bit of me, so I'm not going to be embarrassed of his creation. Why should I be?"

"Because he didn't create you to go around showing off and flaunting his work."

"Then why would he have given me these if he didn't want people to see them?"

"He obviously thought you would be able to handle it better than you are. God created you for a purpose. You were created not to show off and bring attention to yourself for your body or your looks, but to bring attention to your devotion for him. He created you to be a bright light shining for him in a dark world."

"I really don't think it's as big of a deal as what you are making it into, but if it would make you feel better, I will go inside and grab a sweater." Annabelle said this with a calm little itch burning inside her. She was itching to go back in the house and find the laptop. Going in to look for a sweater was the perfect cover story. She was sure she would find the laptop and figure out what was wrong with her sister. This plan just had to work.

"It's okay. I have a tank top in the car, so you don't have to get out or anything." Jill exclaimed excitedly while reaching in the back seat and fumbling around for a minute until she brought her hand back up, and it was clutching a tank top.

"It even matches your outfit" Jill exclaimed happily. "That is definitely a sign from God.

Anna had to look away, so Jill didn't see her roll her eyes. She was disappointed she wouldn't get a chance to go back inside the house, but she was also tired of having her sister shove God and all his beliefs and hopes for her down her throat. When would she understand that God had plans for her that were different than the plans he had for Jill? One day Jill would understand.

"Fine," Anna said as she grabbed the tank top from Jill. "I will put in my purse."

"That's fine. You can change at wherever it is we're going."

Anna ignored Jill's comment about changing, but she paid attention to the part about where they were eating. Anna hadn't thought about where to eat, she'd only been interested in eating. Anna tried to think of a place to go, but then she remembered she hadn't been here in years. What kinds of breakfast places did they even have now?

"You're driving, so you can pick. Anywhere that has good breakfast foods. I'd kill for some pancakes right now. I haven't had those in so long!" Anna said to Jill.

"Well, if it's good pancakes you want, we need to go to Kate's!" Jill started backing out of the driveway and heading down the road.

"Wait, Kate's is still around?" Anna asked.

"Yeah, it's still going strong, and it usually gets packed, so I hope there'll be seats left when we get there. You sure you don't want to think about slipping on that tank top before we get there? You'll probably recognize most of the people in there, and they will all know who you are."

"No, I told you before that I don't need a tank top. You and all the other Bible thumpers in this town aren't going to scare me into changing who I am. This is me and everyone just needs to deal with it and start worrying about their own problems."

"Fine, but don't say I didn't warn you."

They drove out of the subdivision and closer into town. Once they got to the square in downtown, Anna started to recognize everything instantly. Right in the center was the big, old courthouse that had seen everything throughout its 100-year lifespan. It had stood as their unwavering town symbol while witnessing years of history, triumphs, tragedies, and multiple generations of families that had walked around it. The square around the courthouse was packed with people shopping the local produce which farmers had brought out to sell. That was the benefit of a small town. You could get the best fresh produce whenever it was in season. You didn't have to hope what you were picking up in the produce aisle was fresh. Here, you knew you were getting it fresh, because you knew the people who were growing it. Knowing everyone, had its drawbacks and its perks. It was great to know everyone and be able to use your word and family name as collateral in business dealings, or when you needed to know you could trust someone you were dealing with. It was not beneficial, however, to know that your business would reach all the way to your house before you ever made it home. The telephone lines were always buzzing in little towns like this. You would never be the first to deliver good or bad news to anyone in your family, because someone else was already 10 steps ahead of you and knew who your parents were.

Anna looked out the window and watched the stores as they passed by. She was trying to locate stores she remembered and then trying to conjure up the old memories she had of that place. They passed Dragonfly Running Company which is where she went to be fitted for and buy a new pair of running shoes every time her old ones had hit their mileage limit. Her father had her running constantly to keep her in shape for soccer. She went through running shoes a lot. She made a mental note to walk in there at some point and see if the store still smelled of pancakes and maple syrup. They used to host a pancake run every Saturday morning, and they made the pancakes on a flat top in the store, so for the rest of the week, the smell of pancakes would linger in and around everything.

Next, she saw The Other Side of the Moon where her friend Becca had worked during high school. She remembered how much Becca always loved to tell people that she worked at The Other Side of the Moon. They would get a puzzled expression, and she would laugh a little and then explain what she meant. Anna had always thought Becca liked telling people where she worked a lot more than she enjoyed working there.

Then they passed Murphy's Florist, and Anna could swear the scent of fresh cut flowers filled her nostrils. She remembered going there with her friends countless times to pick out and place orders for boutonnieres for the school dances as well as the mums they needed for homecoming. She smiled thinking of all the good memories she had there, and she took one final, lingering sniff as they drove farther down the square and away from the store.

Jill found the first parking spot she could, and she pulled in and parked. Anna looked towards the next block, and she saw a sign all lit up that said "Kate's". Anna couldn't count the number of times she'd met classmates and teammates here before school or after a big game. Talk about memories, this place held more than any other downtown location. She let her mind wander for a moment, and she tried to think back to the last time she'd been here. Who had she come with? What had she eaten? Her mind was fuzzy, and she couldn't remember.

She was brought back to reality by the silence. She realized everything was eerily quiet. She turned around to see Jill staring at her.

"So, are you getting out, or are we just going to sit here and stare at it and imagine we're eating?"

"I'm getting out." Anna said. "I just haven't seen this place in so long."

"Yeah, going home does that to people. This is your first time back. The longer you're here and the more times you come back, will make it easier." Jill said it like she was a pro at this.

Anna thought about it for a second and Jill *was* kind of a pro at this. Jill had been in college for 2 whole years. She had come back for every holiday she could, and she came back every summer. Anna thought maybe she ought to listen to Jill a little more. Maybe she actually knew a thing or two.

Jill and Anna walked up to the café and opened the doors. The smell of syrup and fried food hit them like a ton of bricks. They each turned and smiled at each other. It was Kate's signature smell. They walked in and saw an empty booth in the corner at the other end of the café. Anna walked quickly to the booth while Jill went and retrieved menus from somewhere up close to the bar. Anna had just started studying the menu when a waitress appeared.

"Hey, I'm Mindy! Can I get you gals something to drink?"

Jill ordered water and Anna splurged and ordered chocolate milk. This was her first day having a job, she should be celebrating right? The waitress left to get their drinks, Anna continued to look over the menu until she decided to splurge again and get a pancake breakfast with pancakes, eggs, sausage, and grits. This was the first time in a long time she hadn't had to watch every single ounce of what she was eating. She was going to enjoy it at least for today.

Anna looked across the table at Jill and realized her menu was closed.

"You already know what you want?" Anna asked already knowing what the answer would be.

"I'm not really hungry right now." Jill said as she took a sip of her water.

"Not *really* hungry means you're at least a little hungry, so get yourself a little something to nibble on." Anna urged.

"Fine, I'm *not* hungry." Jill said glaring at Anna.

"You keep saying you aren't hungry, but then you keep using the hangry voice, so it makes it impossible for me to believe you." Anna said matching Jill's glare.

"What is your obsession with that word and making me do things I don't want to do?"

"First of all, it's an awesome word, and secondly, grow up!"

"Excuse me? How am I not being a grown up? I'm not the one sitting here with private parts of my body about to spill out everywhere."

"You're not being a grown up, because you clearly don't understand life. Life is all about making us do things we don't want to do. That's just part of it. Do you think women get married and then decide they want to push a baby out of their private area and go through extreme pain or have a c-section and be cut open and stitched back up while taking care of a new life? I don't think so. They decide they want to have a baby, and they accept the labor and delivery as something they will do even though they don't want to do it."

"I hardly think my choosing whether or not I want to eat breakfast is anywhere near the same thing as giving birth to and deciding to have a baby."

"True, but it helped make my point, so that's all that matters."

"No, you're point is moot. I'm not hungry, so I'm not going to eat. Drop it."

Jill glared at Anna, and Anna was surprised to realize she wasn't angry at her sister. Yes, she wished her sister would stop saying things about her shirt, but she could live with those comments. What she couldn't live with was seeing her sister eat only random meals like the burgers she'd hoped Jill had eaten the night before, but she now realized she hadn't actually stayed to see if she'd eaten. She couldn't live with watching her sister's light fade, because of something no one knew was going on with her. Anna hadn't the faintest idea what was going on with

Jill, but she wasn't going to let whatever it was win. Just by the looks of Jill, something was going on, and she wasn't taking care of herself.

The waitress came by to drop off their drinks. She asked if the girls knew what they wanted to order. Anna immediately jumped in and placed her order for the pancake breakfast with all the trimmings. She also asked for a bowl of oatmeal and some fruit. Jill told the waitress she was fine, and then, the waitress left to give their orders to the cooks who Ann could see were busy cooking eggs in multiple different ways, grilling bread, and tending to a flat top covered in bacon, sausage links and patties, ham, and steak.

Anna looked back at Jill and noticed she had taken her phone out, and she was typing away on it. Anna took that as her cue from Jill that there would be no more conversation. Jill was here to give Anna a ride to the church and that was it. Anna looked past Jill and started noticing the other diners. Jill was right about one thing. Anna did recognize most of them, but she couldn't remember exactly who they were. Some of them would catch her eye and smile and wave at her. She politely waved back even though she had no idea who they were. She assumed they were people she knew from church or school growing up, and she hoped they wouldn't come over to try and talk.

Anna's stomach seriously felt like it was going to take revenge on her lack of effort to fill it with anything besides chocolate milk. Anna feared her stomach would begin to consume itself for nourishment if the food didn't make an appearance sometime in the very near future. After what seemed like an eternity of waiting, the waitress reappeared, and plates started appearing all over their table. Anna only felt a little guilty knowing all the plates belonged to her. Now she knew how Tim Allen felt in *The Santa Clause* when he was turning into Santa Clause and eating everything, he could get his hands on. Once the waitress left, Anna pushed the bowl of oatmeal and the bowl of fruit over in front of Jill. Jill stopped whatever she was doing with her phone. She carefully placed the phone on the table next to the food and looked up at Anna with a tough, questionable look.

"This is all very healthy. I ate oatmeal and fruit a lot when I was modeling, and it never steered me wrong. I promise if this is about you thinking you're fat, which you definitely aren't by the way, this is a good, healthy breakfast you can trust."

"Why would you think I think I'm fat?"

"You aren't eating, and it is clear by looking at you that you've been missing more meals than you've actually been eating for a while now. I'm surprised no one has said anything to you before this."

Anna stopped for a moment and realized that was true. She was extremely surprised no one else had noticed. Her mother was normally very on top of things like that and making sure they ate everything on their plate. Then, Anna realized how scattered her mom must be right now. Of course, she hadn't had time to study and scrutinize Jill, she'd been worried about her husband and his heart attack and scrutinizing every doctor and nurse and whether or not they are doing everything they were supposed to be doing. Jill was just slipping through the cracks. Anna couldn't let that happen, not to Jill. She couldn't let Jill go down the same path she'd gone down. She had to protect her. She had to do whatever she could to make sure she was well taken care of.

Jill took in a deep breath and steadied her gaze on Anna before speaking in a steady voice. "I'm only going to say this one more time, so you need to listen. I am *not* hungry. I *will not* be eating any of this food no matter how much you put in front of me or try to force on me. The sooner you realize that, the better."

"I don't buy your 'I'm not hungry argument', so I suggest you either figure out a way to eat this oatmeal, or you come up with a better excuse. I'm going to the bathroom. You have until I get back to do one of those things. For the sake of your health and wellbeing, if I were you, I'd be figuring out a way to choke down the oatmeal."

Jill watched Anna slide out of the booth and walk across the busy café to the bathroom. Before Jill could turn back towards the food, her mother's friend, Judy Maroney caught her attention. Judy waved and Jill waved back at her and quickly turned to face the food hoping that would be the end of their correspondence. Jill liked Judy as her mother's friend, but both Jill and her mother knew Judy had a way of meddling in people's lives and trying to find out their personal business. Jill wanted to stay far away from someone like that right now. The last thing she needed was for someone to put their nose in where it didn't belong and figure out her big secret. Jill prayed Judy had gotten the hint, and she stuck a spoon into the oatmeal and started to mix it around. It was a trick she'd picked up somewhere to make it look like you were eating even when you weren't. Her stomach had been so knotted and torn up, she hadn't been able to eat hardly anything, and what she did manage to eat, she had to fight to keep it down. Just when she thought she'd dodged the bullet, she noticed brown leather flats appear beside her chair, and as they kept moving to the other side of the table, Jill's eyes moved from the flats up the length of the perfectly pressed khakis past the navy flowy shirt up to the face of none other than Judy Maroney. Jill stared into Judy's eyes for only a moment before a very distinct curse word popped into her head, and in that moment, she knew she was in trouble.

Ch. 10

Charlie arrived at work early excited to get things ready for Annabelle's arrival. He wanted to make sure her new office was welcoming, so she would enjoy her time there. He knew he needed more than just a few days to show her God's love. He stopped inside her office and knelt on the floor to pray.

"God, I come to you to ask that everything that happens within these walls shines a light on you and points people towards you, God. I ask that I fulfill my role, so Annabelle can see how abundant a life filled with you will be. Please guide her in the way she should go and show her your love. Help me to be a shining example to Annabelle. I pray that I constantly show her your love and compassion as others did for me during the times when I needed it the most. I know you were always there for me and waiting for me to find my way back to you. I want to be that beacon for her, so she will know she isn't alone in the world. Give me the tools to help guide her way back to you. It's in your loving name I pray. Amen."

< < > >

Annabelle was finished using the bathroom, but she was trying to take her time to make sure she gave Jill plenty of time to make the right choice. She didn't care if Jill didn't eat the oatmeal. She'd love for her to eat it, but what she really wanted more than that was for Jill to be honest and just let her guard down and tell her what was going on. She knew she wouldn't be able to help Jill unless she could get her to open up and be honest with her.

Annabelle slowly moved towards the sink and squirted some soap on her hands. She was rubbing her hands together and creating suds while singing a song in her head to mark the time when the door opened. She looked up into the mirror and saw a woman about her mother's age with a black wrap dress and leopard print high heels. She didn't recognize the woman and knew she couldn't be from around here, because no one dressed like that around here. Around here, everyone dressed in conservative pants and knee length skirts and got their color scheme and patterns from the same neutral shades of bland and blander. No one wore dresses during the day unless it was a sun dress, and absolutely no one would dare to wear animal prints.

The woman moved over to the sink next to her and started checking her make-up and her hair. Annabelle felt an instant camaraderie to this mysterious woman, because she too was an outsider. She wanted to speak, but she didn't know what to say. The mysterious woman broke the ice for both of them.

"So, you from the city?" She asked Annabelle.

"Yes! Well, no, not originally. Originally, I'm from here, but I moved to the city after high school and did some modeling. I just came back for a short time to help my family with some things, but then I'm definitely going back."

"I could tell by your shirt. No one around here wears shirts like that."

"I know. No one around here has any idea what it means to be fashionable or trendy. I'm hoping I can help make an impact while I'm here."

"That shirt is definitely going to make an impact on people around here. There's no doubt about that." The mysterious woman said.

"Oh wow. Thank you so much." Annabelle said beaming and glancing once more at the shirt her sister has said was too revealing. She knew Jill didn't know what she was talking about, but this woman did.

"Don't get ahead of yourself. I never said the impact was a good one. Fashion is about taking risks, but it's also about understanding your audience. You can't go all out and put everything you've got on your first round. You have ease people into it, so they aren't pushed into hating it for fear of the unknown."

"That makes sense." Annabelle said glumly as her fingers gently slid across the material of the tank top in her bag.

"Would you excuse me?" She said to the woman as she retreated into one of the stalls.

"Certainly" The woman said, as she too sauntered into one of the stalls.

She pulled the tank top out of her bag and stared at it for a moment. Something about putting it on felt a lot like admitting defeat, but at the same time, she felt like this mysterious woman had a point. She finally decided she had to put on the tank top, and she would use it as a point of persuasion in her argument with Jill. She quickly slid off her shirt, put on the tank top, and replaced her shirt on top of it. She exited the stall and examined herself one last time before exiting the bathroom. She looked more like one of them, middle class and boring. As she was leaving, she noticed the leopard print heels that were visible under one of the stalls. Annabelle smiled to herself as she realized there were ways to make a statement and be unique without having to be in everyone's face about it right up front. She would work up to her 'in your face outfits', but for now, she would invest in a few statement pieces to keep her personality alive and everyone's eyes on her.

She exited the bathroom and noticed Jill across the café. At first glance she seemed to be in deep conversation with someone. Annabelle couldn't see Jill's face, but she could see the familiar face of the woman she was speaking to. Although she hadn't seen this woman in years, she would recognize her face anywhere. It was Judy Maroney. Upon further examination, it was obvious Jill had been forced into what Annabelle could only assume to be an awkward conversation with Judy. She knew Judy was about as brash and, in your face, as they come. She had no doubt Judy was giving Jill the third degree and trying to find out every dirty little secret Jill was keeping.

She wanted to go and rescue Jill immediately, but part of her enjoyed watching Jill squirm. Jill had been hard on her for asking what was wrong and unsuccessfully trying to find out what was going on, but that questioning was nothing compared to the inquisition Jill was probably going through right now. She thought for a moment about turning around and going back into the bathroom and letting Jill squirm a little more before helping her, but she decided to go and rescue her sister. She did want Jill to understand how much worse it could be, but she didn't want to hear about what going on with Jill through the gossip grapevine.

Judy Maroney was usually successful in gleaning information from people and once she had it, she was relentless. It wasn't enough for her to possess everyone's secrets. She would have to tell a few select people who she knew would tell another few select people and eventually everyone would know. Judy had been responsible for some of the residents of the town packing up and moving away just to escape the embarrassment of everyone knowing their darkest secrets. Judy's husband Marty had been in the interrogation sector of the military throughout his entire career. Everyone suspected Judy had learned everything she knew from information she'd gleaned from Marty over the years. He thought he was having conversations and spending time with his wife, but in all actuality, he was teaching her the basics of interrogating. Annabelle was sure even to this day; Marty Maroney had no idea of the monster he'd created. Judy had put all of her training to good use, and as far as anyone knew, she'd never chosen a target she couldn't eventually crack for information.

"Today you will learn the sour taste of defeat", Annabelle thought as she walked across the café, her eyes on the prize.

"Hey, Mrs. Maroney," She said sweetly, "I don't think I've seen you since I've been back in town. How are you? How's Mr. Maroney?"

"Oh Annabelle, my, my, it's been a while. I am doing wonderful as you can see," She said with a twirl. "Marty is also doing very well, dear. He's off on a hunting trip with some of his old military buddies. I've never been one to hunt, but it does put some interesting food on our table."

"I'll bet it does." Annabelle said trying her best to sound sincere.

"You know, I was just telling Jill here that I am so sorry to hear about your father's heart attack. I've tried reaching out to your mother, but I haven't heard back. How is she doing?"

"She's holding up. She's been pretty much staying at the hospital with my dad and that is keeping her pretty busy. You should go by and see her. I know she'd probably love that. Here, I'll write down his room number for you". Jill grabbed a pen from her bag and scribbled a number on the napkin.

"Oh good, this will definitely help me. I will try to make it out and visit today. You know, I was just telling Jill, she might want to go see a doctor. She looks so pale and sickly. Is she sick?"

Annabelle hated when one person would talk about another person when they were sitting right there. She couldn't think of anything that was ruder than that right there. She gave her sister a quick "see, I told you so looks" and then she quickly patched an excuse together in her mind.

"Oh, yeah Jill hasn't been doing so well with Dad being in the hospital. You know she was there when he collapsed, so she's kind of responsible for saving his life. Seeing someone on the brink of death and being the sole person who yanks them back to the land of the living can really take a toll on you emotionally. Eventually, when dad is completely in the clear, I think she will start to recover too, but for now, she has to process it in her own way." Annabelle smiled, and she was genuinely happy. She didn't realize she would come up with such an elaborate excuse so quickly.

"Oh, you poor dear" Judy said walking over beside Jill and giving her a quick hug.

Annabelle took this opportunity to slide into her seat and pick up her utensils to signal that she was ready to eat, and Judy should make herself scarce. Judy noticed her and shifted her purse higher up on her shoulder to prepare for her departure. Before she could go, her eyes caught something or someone in the restaurant.

"Jill, just make sure you recover before you let yourself go and become a social pariah like that one there." Judy had said in a voice that could only be described a honey glazed snark.

Annabelle and Jill both turned and followed Judy's gaze until their eyes found a woman in a black wrap dress with leopard print high heels sitting at the bar. Annabelle noticed the woman's brown hair was cut into a sleek bob, and she had caramel highlights to accent it. She didn't wear much makeup, but it was still more than most of the other residents.

"I don't know who we're looking at" Jill finally said, "where is the social pariah."

"Over there, sitting at the bar." Judy said.

"Who is she?" Jill asked. "Are we sure she isn't just an out of towner stopping for some coffee?"

"Positive." Judy said. "Ladies, that is Alise St. James, or I believe her stage name was Trixie St. James."

"Stage name?" Jill asked confusingly.

"Stage names are names you use instead of your real name." Annabelle spoke up. This was an area she knew well. She thought the name Trixie St. James sounded familiar, but she couldn't quite put her finger on it.

"I know what a stage name is." Jill said. "What I don't understand is why she would need one. I've never seen her before. Is she an aspiring actress?"

"She's one who has brought shame to the name of our little town. She was a model, a nude model for that rabbit man. She was one of those rabbits that would get paid to take her clothes off. Such a disgrace to the name of our town and the name of our Lord. I thought she was long gone from here, but it seems she has returned to smear her rabbit shame all over this town. Terrible, just terrible." Judy started shaking her head, and to the girl's delight, she started to walk away.

Jill looked questioningly at Annabelle. "I think Judy Maroney has officially lost her mind. What the heck was all of that about rabbits?"

"I think she was meaning to say that Alise St. James was a playboy bunny for Hugh Hefner. She just didn't know his name or the name of what he called his models." Anna said as she continued staring at Alise. Suddenly it was all coming together. She had heard her name before. When she was hanging out with bunnies, she had heard them refer to a very well-known and very successful bunny named Trixie St. James. They would find out where Anna was from, and they would ask her if she'd been raised on the same bunny patch. Anna hadn't understood the reference at the time, but now it was all very clear.

Annabelle couldn't believe she'd run into one of the top names in the nude modeling world. That was the world she was just starting to find a way into. Maybe Alise was the answer to everything. She could help Annabelle into that world and out of this one. This had to be a sign that she was destined for bigger and better things. She couldn't hold back her excitement. She'd have to figure out a way to talk to Alise and get her to look at some of her most recent shots. Alise would have great insight and suggestions, and if she liked what she saw, she could give Anna a huge leap into that world she wanted so badly to be part of.

"Annabelle, please don't tell me you're considering talking to that woman. You heard what Judy Maroney said. That woman is a social pariah. Do you want to become a social pariah?" Jill asked.

"I don't care what these people think of me, and I'm sure Alise St. James doesn't care either. I actually had a lovely conversation with her earlier in the bathroom, and she's really a very nice woman. What does Judy Maroney know anyway?" Annabelle snapped.

"Everything! Judy Maroney knows everything about everybody. If she says that woman is a social pariah, she isn't kidding. There has to be more to the story that you don't know."

"No, I refuse to accept Judy Maroney's word as the end all and be all of people. She doesn't know anything. She thinks she knows so much about people, but really all she knows is surface level. She doesn't know anything about a person's heart."

"Thanks to you, she knows I was there when dad collapsed. I'm sure that will be all over town by the end of the day."

"What did you want me to do? I obviously had to give her something, so she would go away and leave you alone. It's obvious you're carrying around some big secret, and you look terrible which she even noticed. If I didn't give her that, she was going to pull something from you. I pretty much saved you,"

"You didn't save me. You gave her something to talk about."

"Did you want her to go around telling everyone how horrible you look? That's what she would've done, and you know it,"

"Stop talking about how I look. I look fine. I'm just tired and upset about dad. That's all."

Annabelle stopped and stared at her sister. Was this a breakthrough to the truth? Was her sister finally opening up, or was she just hanging onto the excuse Annabelle had so graciously offered up? Annabelle wanted to believe her, but there was too much evidence pointing at something else. There was obviously something on her computer. How could the thing on the computer be connected to their father and his heart attack?

"Do you promise this is all just about dad and his heart attack?"

"Yes! Now, will you please drop it?"

"As long as you promise, I will let it go."

"I promise. This is just about dad. I am worried about him, and I am nervous this could happen again,"

"You probably need to go by there regularly and check in on him just to show yourself he is doing fine."

"Okay" Jill said with a shrug.

Annabelle looked down at her untouched plate of food. She didn't have long to shovel it in before they had to go. She made quick work of tasting and eating everything in front of her. Some of the food had started getting cold, but it all still tasted really good, so she ate every bit of food on her plate. She was trying to focus on eating and not on the fact that Jill had lied straight to her face. She had known Jill her whole life, so she could tell when she was lying. Jill obviously thought she was more stealth than she actually was. She hadn't known Jill to be a fan of lying, so it really surprised her how easily it had seemed to be for Jill to just throw out a lie to appease her sister. That made her more worried than she had been before. If Jill was prepared to lie to keep this secret covered up, it must be a pretty big secret.

When Annabelle was finished with her food, they signaled the waitress for their bill. The waitress had pretty much stayed away since she'd seen Judy Maroney at their table. People pretty much steered clear of Judy because they didn't want their business being shared all over town. Annabelle suspected Judy didn't know that she was somewhat of a social pariah herself. Annabelle hoped that if Judy ever caught wind of her own social standing, she might actually change her ways. She doubted it though. The gossiping and mass quantities of information about everyone is what kept people interested in Judy Maroney. Without all of that, what did she really have to set her apart?

Annabelle and Jill paid their waitress and left a tip on the table as they got up to leave. They weaved through the crowded café back to the front door. Once outside, they could breathe in fresh air. They walked to Jill's car, and Annabelle slid into the passenger side as Jill unlocked the door and slid behind the wheel on the driver's side.

"Okay, ready to head to work?" Jill asked?

"Is anyone ever ready to go to work?" Annabelle asked in rebuttal.

"Good Point" Jill said, and she started driving in the direction of the church. The morning had already been exhausting for Jill, and she was ready to drop Annabelle off and head back to the house to hide until her mother needed something. She didn't plan on venturing out much today. She had a lot on her mind, and she had a big decision to make as far as school was concerned. She didn't want to get any more of her family members mixed up in her drama and bad choices, so she settled for keeping it to herself and working it out on her own. She'd just have to work hard to stay away from Judy Maroney and keep her nosy sister at bay to make sure her secrets stayed hidden and buried until she was ready to unearth and reveal them to everyone.

Ch.11

Charlie was leaving Annabelle's office when he heard a door open at the end of the hallway. When he turned, he saw Pastor Maxwell entering the youth building, so he started walking down the hallway to greet him.

"Morning Charlie. Is today the day Annabelle will start work?"

"Yes sir, thank you again for being so understanding when we talked last night. I really felt that nudge from God, so I had to listen."

"I completely understand. You got a chance to really meet more of their family too. What did you think?"

"Their family dynamic is a mess, and I've been in prayer for them a lot. I think they can work everything out." Charlie said hopefully.

"I agree. With some prayer and some guidance, I think they will be just fine."

"I do have to say I was surprised. I thought Annabelle was the one who would need the most prayer and guidance with her life and family situation, but I think Jill has something going on too which is causing her some pain and stress as well." Charlie said thinking back to their conversation in the car the night before.

"I picked up on that also. Maybe you can get her to open up and help her with whatever is bothering her."

"I think I can, sir, and I really want to help her. She reminds me of my sister, Maggie, so this will be healing for me as well. I'd like to pray for her sir."

"Sounds like a great idea." Said Pastor Maxwell as the two of them bowed their heads for prayer.

"God, today is a big day for Annabelle. Please help her to find a sense of peace and belonging here that will encourage her to stay and inevitably get to know you better, God. I also ask to wrap the whole family in prayer. There's so much hurt and pain in their family, and I know they can come back to a place of love and light with your help, God. I also want to say a prayer for Jill. She's obviously going through a lot and with her sister coming back and her dad's accident, it seems to be bringing a lot of her pain to the surface. Please God, help her heal old wounds and be able to work on new pains that have come up. I want to help her, God. I want to be faithful to your call. Please guide me as I do this. She reminds me so much of my sister, so I don't want to lose sight of my goal. Please help me to stay steadfast in this mission. In your loving and holy name, I pray, Amen."

The two men hugged before Pastor Maxwell left and Charlie went back to his office to prepare for the day.

< < > >

Annabelle waved goodbye to Jill as she watched her sister's car drive forward through the parking lot, turn back onto the main road, and disappear past some trees. When Jill's car was no longer in sight, she turned back to face the massive building that loomed in front of her. The church had originally been built in the late 1800's, so it carried with it a sense of architecture and style from that period. It was well crafted and made of stone. The church was gray in color which would seem like a depressing color, but it actually worked as a backdrop against the sky behind it and the trees that framed the sides and front of it. The front of the building was elevated with an iron staircase leading up to the two double doors. There were wide, rectangular windows on each side of the door. All in all, the church had a very inviting look. Annabelle had always felt it to be a place that appeared very welcoming and cozy. That was the thing about churches. The décor could be spot on. It could be beautiful, inviting, and wonderful, but if the people didn't match the description of the building, the church was in trouble. She remembered moments in her life when she had felt like the people really embodied the look and meaning of the church, but she could also pinpoint numerous times when she felt the complete opposite.

As she stared at the building, an odd feeling came over her. It wasn't that she was nervous or anxious. She had no doubt this job would be easy, and she could do it. She wasn't worried about that. What did send a shiver down her spine was the little twinge of excitement she kept feeling in the pit of her stomach. She didn't want to be excited about this new venture. She didn't want to be excited about anything that had to do with the church. She had left that life behind long ago, and she had no intention of giving that up and returning to it any time soon. For now, she would just think of this as a new adventure she was embarking on. The idea of an adventure held the thrill of possibilities, but it also brought the knowledge that disappointment in at least one area was inevitable. She would live with those standards. She was setting herself up for success, not failure. She was being smart and realistic. With her new confidence, she took a deep breath, steadied her shoulders and climbed the stairs one by one until she reached the very top. She took one more deep breath and reached out to grab the door handle and pull back.

Annabelle didn't know what exactly she had expected. She had at least expected the door to open or be unlocked. Was that really too much to ask? She decided to try the door again, so she grabbed the handle with both hands and yanked and yanked with all of her strength. The door eased a little back and forth from her strength, but it was still locked. She turned and looked around from the top of the stairs. She couldn't see anyone around, and oddly, she couldn't see any cars. Why hadn't she noticed before there were no cars? Was Charlie playing a joke on her? If this was his idea of a joke, it wasn't very funny. She could think of funnier jokes than this one.

She allowed herself a moment of self-pity before she decided to pull herself together and go look for people or an entrance or something. She stood a little straighter and descended the stairs quickly with a little energy behind her descent. She kept telling herself the same thing.

"You can do this. You are capable. You are strong. You are fantastic."

As long as she could keep her mantra circulating through her mind, all would be okay. She was sure of that. She kept repeating it to herself as she walked around the side of the building. She found 4 doors and tried them all. They were all locked. She resorted to banging on the doors and windows to see if she could get someone's attention. She couldn't even see a light on inside the building. She had the same luck when she went around the back and the other side of the church. She found herself back at the front of the church a little less confident, a little winded, and no closer to getting inside than she had been when she had first been standing here. She felt a little hopeless and defeated, and to be quite honest, she felt a little stupid. How was it that she couldn't figure out how to get inside the building? It wasn't like this was a military base. This was a church for crying out loud. She decided to take one more look around and assess her surroundings to see if she could come up with any other options.

"If God really wanted me to have this job, he wouldn't have me stuck out here." She was surprised to find she had verbalized her feelings aloud. She decided maybe it was time to admit defeat and call the church and find out where she was supposed to go. Charlie had given her a phone number before she exited the car last night, and she had remembered to pick it up this morning. She took her cell phone out of her purse with one hand, and she took the paper out with the other. She was beginning to punch some numbers in on her cell phone while staring intently at the piece of paper when a gusty wind came out of nowhere and blew the paper out of her hand.

"No! Wait! Come back!" She shouted as she started chasing the paper towards the back of the church. She trudged after it until it got hung up on some bushes that were flanking a breezeway she hadn't seen before. She ran up to the bush and grabbed the paper. She stared at the breezeway and noticed it was next to a parking lot where she was standing, but it led to another building that had the same design and colorings as the church. This building had the letters O-F-F-I-C-E on the side. She was so relieved and overjoyed to have finally found it. She put the paper back into her pocket and walked up to the door. She knew after her eventual paper chase, she probably looked like a sight to behold. Her hair was probably all blown about and starting to knot and nest in certain areas, and she knew her clothes had become disheveled. What she hadn't expected were the bits of leaves and tiny acorns she was freeing from the knots in her hair, and she grasped the door handle. She gave the door a tug, and this time, it actually opened.

As soon as she stepped inside, the warmth and the smell of freshly brewed coffee invaded every part of her. She breathed in deeply, and she smiled. This was that inviting feeling of warmth she'd been missing. She walked forward to the first office she could find. There was a woman sitting behind a desk typing away on a keyboard. The woman was older than Annabelle with white hair streaked with gray. Her hair was short and cut into a bob. She had a friendly face and smile, and Annabelle hoped her demeanor matched her appearance.

"Hi. Excuse me." Annabelle said with a voice that she didn't think sounded very confident.

"Oh, hey there!" The woman said looked up from her computer with a big smile on her face.

"Hey, I'm Annabelle. I'm supposed to be starting work today. I am the new secretary for Char…I mean Pastor Cochran." Annabelle said stumbling awkwardly through her words. She had to get a grip before everyone here got the impression that she was one of those ditzy, dumb girls who couldn't actually comprehend anything.

"I remember you." She said smiling.

"You do?" Annabelle asked a little unsure. She was starting to sense the direction in which this was headed. This woman obviously knew her from before, and Annabelle had no idea who this woman was. She was trying to place this woman in her mind, but she wasn't having any luck.

"Yes, you probably don't remember me, but I've watched you grow up in this church. It's so nice to see that God has brought you back here. I'm Gail Spencer."

"Oh! Your last name is very familiar." Annabelle said trailing off. Her mind was racing to connect the last name, Spencer, with someone she knew. Suddenly it hit her. She did know that last name.

"Are you related to Olivia Spencer?"

"Yes, I'm her grandmother. Do you remember me from family events?"

"If I am honest, I'd have to say only vaguely. Olivia and I were pretty busy playing or hanging out, and we really didn't spend much time with anyone else. I'm sorry!" Olivia and Annabelle had been inseparable growing up. They went to each other's family gatherings, spent holidays together, and even went on vacations together. They had lost touch after Annabelle moved away, and she hadn't realized how much she missed Olivia until now.

"That's alright dear. I completely understand. I was young and free once too!"

This made Annabelle smile. Gail Spencer was the epitome of a grandmother. She had that sweet, humble spirit that was infectious and made you want to spend time with her.

"How is Olivia? I haven't seen her in years."

"She's doing wonderfully! She's happily engaged and looking forward to a Fall wedding."

"That's so great. I'm glad she's happy!" Annabelle was truly happy for her friend. She knew marriage was not in the cards for her right now, and she was happy to find out her friend was ready and happily embarking on that adventure.

"I'm so glad you will be working here, and we will be seeing more of each other."

"Thanks! I'm glad too!"

"Let me give Pastor Cochran a call and let him know you are here, and he can come and show you to your office."

"Okay that sounds great."

She found a chair and sat down while Gail called Pastor Cochran. She didn't feel like she'd been waiting very long when Charlie strolled into the room.

"Hey! Are you ready?" He asked enthusiastically.

"Yeah, ready as I'll ever be!" She said trying to place enthusiasm in her voice. It wasn't like she was going to war or anything; she was just starting a secretary job. The first day, let alone the entire job, couldn't really be that challenging.

"Good to hear! Follow me." Charlie said as he headed back out of the office.

"Okay." Annabelle said jumping up, throwing up her hand to quickly wave goodbye to Gail and following Charlie out of the doorway.

She had to hurry to catch up to his quick step. He was either a naturally fast walker, or he was just incredibly excited to get started. She noticed they were passing multiple doors, but they weren't going in any of them. When they came to the end of the hallway and ran out of doors except for one that led outside, Annabelle became very puzzled and started wondering what was going on. Charlie walked up to the door and opened it to reveal another breezeway. This one connected to another big parking lot and she noticed a big warehouse style building on the other side of the parking lot. She was still very confused about where they were going. She felt her brows furrow in confusion, and she made a mental note to soothe her face, so she could avoid wrinkles. She followed Charlie across the parking lot towards the warehouse. When he got to the door, he produced a set of keys and unlocked the front door. She followed him inside, and her to surprise, he locked the doors behind them. Annabelle turned to him completely puzzled and apprehensive.

"I'm really a very trusting person, and I want to believe you have a great reason for locking us in a warehouse together, so please ease my confusion and let me know I'm right."

"Yes, you are right. You are a very trusting person." Charlie said with a chuckle.

"I'm about to die, right? I mean this is the perfect moment. This is exactly how and when it would happen in a movie or on one of those CSI TV shows. There's just one thing that doesn't make sense."

"What's that? "Charlie asked still chuckling.

"Gail. Gail knows I am with you, and she saw me leave with you. She will tell people if I go missing."

"How do you know she isn't on my side, or I won't kill her also."

Annabelle looked at Charlie, and she honestly couldn't tell if he was joking which started to make her more nervous than before. She stared at him, and she felt her head slowly cock to the side as she studied him. She quickly glanced around to assess her possible escape routes and started to back up until she could feel her back against the cold glass of the door length window.

"Relax. Charlie said calmly. You are so gullible." He said laughing a little harder this time. "Do I honestly look like a killer?"

"Well, I don't know that killers have a certain look. They're just killers. How do you pick one out of a crowd?" Annabelle's voice was calm, but she hadn't moved from the door. In fact, she had no intention of moving until she was 100% certain she wasn't going to die.

"Trust me. I'm not a killer. I promise, and I'm a man of God, so my promises are worth something."

"That's the perfect cover, being a man of God. People feel like they have to trust you, so you can easily lure them in."

"I wouldn't do that."

"How do I know that? All I know is that you and I are locked in this big warehouse thing alone out here at the other end of the parking lot. What am I supposed to think?

"Maybe you should think that the big metal letters on the top of the building that said, "Youth Center" were correct, and this is in fact the Youth Building, or the Warehouse as we call it."

"Oh, I didn't see those words."

"Well, it does help to pay attention and be aware of your surroundings."

"Yes, it certainly does, but that doesn't explain why we are here."

"We're here, because this is where our offices are."

"In the youth building?"

"Yes. We are in the youth building."

"Why?"

"When churches hire someone like me who is just working until, I complete my internship and can find a pastoral position, they put us in other positions that need filling. In the case of Grace Baptist here, they needed a youth pastor, so here we are."

"Whoa. You did not say dealing with kids was part of the job. I am terrible with kids. I cannot work with kids."

"Relax. We're not dealing with kids. We're dealing with a limited number of pre-teens and much larger number of teenagers."

"Yeah, that's really not making me feel any better." Annabelle's mind was spinning. It hadn't been very long since she was a teen herself, so how in the world was she supposed to be a mentor and a role model for a teenager. What was she going to have to offer and teach them?

"You'll be fine. I promise!" Charlie said smiling confidently.

"Why do you sound so sure?"

"Because I know people. I have a knack for picking out hidden talents and knowing what someone will be good at, and I can tell you will be great at this. If you let it, something like this can really get ahold of you and change you."

"I don't need to be changed." Annabelle said sourly, "I am very happy with myself just the way I am."

"See, there's that spunky spirit which will make you awesome at this." Charlie said as he turned and headed down the hallway turning on lights as he went.

Every light that came on illuminated a new color in the brightly colored main room and hallway. The main room was adorned with a pool table on one side of the door and a foosball table on the other side of the door. There were 3 couches and 3 armchairs set up around the main room and a handful of bean bag chairs strewn about here and there in every available space. Most of them were still holding their indentions from their previous occupants. There were different vinyl Bible verse stickers adorning the walls. She saw verses about God's plans to prosper and not harm anyone and how you can do all things, because of God's strength. She remembered these verses from her youth days. At one time, they had held so much power and meaning, but now they were just words someone had written, slapped together into a cohesive thought, printed, and stuck to the wall. As Annabelle started to leave the man room, she noticed a bar top connected to a kitchen on her right. She had no doubts this is where the kids would spend most of their time if food and sodas were made available. You should never underestimate the capacity of the teenage stomach when it came to unlimited junk food.

She followed Charlie down a hallway painted bright yellow and adorned with names, verse, thoughts, and sayings, penned in multiple colors, fonts and sizes and created with multiple mediums. The kids had obviously taken control of this area. It was a very cool and expressive space. Charlie passed two doors, one on each side of the hallway. One was labeled "Men" and the other was labeled "Women". He stopped at the next door they came to on the right side.

"This is your office." He said smiling and holding out his arm to gesture and maximize the emphasis of his words.

Annabelle leaned in the doorway to peek into the office.

"You know. You can go inside, right, or are you afraid the boogey man is waiting in there to get you."

"You know. You really aren't as funny as you think you are." Annabelle said as her hand found the light switched and she flipped it to illuminate the room.

"I'd have to disagree. I can be extremely funny when I want to be." Charlie said with a smile.

"Well, then you must not be trying very hard right now." She said.

"Burn!" Charlie said accepting defeat.

"Burn?" Annabelle asked looking at him with a questioningly concerned look.

"Yeah, that's what the kids say when someone burns you with words. I might not have been here long, but I'm already learning so much."

"Wow! I have no words." Annabelle remarked as she walked fully into her office.

"I bet that's a first." Charlie said laughing.

"Hey, now that is not true. I am not known for being verbose." Annabelle said a smile catching across her face.

"Burn. You are supposed to say Burn, remember. All those big words are clouding your brain, and it is clear you have learned nothing in your brief time with me."

"I won't be saying "burn", and yes, I like using big words every now and then. It keeps people on their toes."

"True Dat" Charlie said following her into the room. Annabelle could only turn and smile at him. She didn't know any other way to respond.

Annabelle was pleasantly surprised by the office. She was afraid it would be boring and resemble a white, walled square prison cell, but she was very wrong. One of her walls was mostly taken up with a big window that looked out into the gymnasium area. Another wall had bookshelves all along the back of it with a desk, comfy looking spinning chair, and a nice computer set up. The other wall had another big window that showed into the hallway. Only the front wall wasn't taken up by a window or bookshelf. Instead, there was a bible verse adoring the middle of the wall with 4 pictures surrounding it. Annabelle stood still taking in the bible verse. In a beautifully simple script it read, "The LORD does not look at the things people look at. People look at the outward appearance, but the LORD looks at the heart." 1 Samuel 16:7.

"You like that verse?" Charlie asked stepping up beside her to marvel at the verse as well.

"What?" Annabelle said with a jarring sense of the reality that she had been standing still as a statue and staring at words on a wall. "They're just words from an old dried-up fictional book" she told herself, but something about them pressed hard into the deepest crevices in the deepest corners of her heart. She couldn't shake the odd feeling they had been chosen and placed there just for her.

"The verse, do you like it?"

"It's okay" She said nonchalantly. "At least it's different than all the ones you normally see on walls.

"Yeah, I looked through tons of verses before finding this one. This verse really seems to encompass everything we stand for here. We have kids at a very pivotal time in their lives, and we want them to worry more about pleasing God and less about trying to look or act a certain way for other people."

"I guess that's a good lesson." She said. "But these kids are in middle school and high school. They are doing a lot of what they're doing to survive."

"To survive? We want them to be unconcerned with fitting in and trying to do and be whatever society deems to be *cool*." Charlie said.

"Why? Why are you forcing them to stand out and be ostracized just to believe in something that, in the end, won't mean anything?"

"And being popular will mean something in the end?"

"Well, yeah! They will have all those memories and friends and everything to remember those great years by. It's hard to explain," She said exasperated, "You're just not getting it."

He paused for a long second before responding. Annabelle realized she might have hurt him by making her brazen judgment that he clearly wasn't ever cool and wouldn't understand. She thought back through her statement and realized, she had judged him, and she really didn't know anything about him except what was on the surface. She didn't have any reason to judge him, but it was what she was used to doing. Finally, he spoke again clearly and with a twinge of sympathy in his voice.

"No, you don't get it. These kids have a war they are fighting every day for their soul. The war is between God and Satan. Satan is always trying to take control of them and get them to sin and do bad things and make bad decisions. Satan wants them to become followers of the crowd or leaders of likeminded easily influenced children they can lead astray, but God wants so much more for them. He doesn't want them to have to look back and have fleeting memories of things that seemed good at one time. He wants them to stand out and shine brightly for him and lead others to him, so they can lead a life that is filled with greatness, love, acceptance, and everything else God will give and fill them with. My job and your job, when you're ready, will be to keep their brains focused on the bigger picture, the war, instead of these tiny battles. It won't be easy, because these children are at a very young and impressionable state. They will resist and push back at times, but you just have to love them and show them all the great things God can fill them with and do in their lives."

Annabelle looked at Charlie square in the face. She locked eyes with him, and she saw the sincerity and truth behind his words. The power of his words hit her like a ton of bricks, and in an instant, she felt her eyes stinging as they filled with tears. She spoke slowly never breaking her gaze from his. "How do I show them something that I'm not sure I even believe to be real."

He smiled at her. It wasn't a smile to say he felt sorry for or pitied her. It was a reassuring smile to say he understood. He spoke softly and calmly. "I promise if you trust me, I will make all of those things known to you and possible in your life. One day, you will be ready to pass that knowledge on to someone else, and it will be the most incredible feeling when you can do that."

Annabelle looked at him while her eyes glistened with tears. She wanted so desperately to believe everything he was saying, but it just wasn't that easy. This *loving* God Charlie was talking about had abandoned her in important points in her life. When she tried to venture out and leave all the terrible things behind, God wasn't there to support her and help her succeed. Instead, he was there to cause her to fail. If God had his hand in everything, then he also had his hand in her failures. Didn't that mean he had been responsible for them? How in the world was she supposed to be responsible for filling a child's head with nonsense and setting them up for failure too? She just wasn't sure she could be part of that. She felt the hardness come back into her heart and radiate across her face. She couldn't let Charlie think he had gotten to her. She had to show him she wouldn't just fall headfirst into believing about *his* God. She looked up at him once more, but this time she was wearing her tough, hard expression.

"What if I don't want to do that?" She asked him with the chill back in her voice.

"Fair enough," He said with a calm expression, "What if you just work at being my secretary, and you perform secretarial duties and nothing more. I will leave you out of any of the trainings or interaction with the children unless you want to be there. How does that sound? Will you stay?"

She thought about it for a second. He looked so eager to have her there, and she did need a job. She would never be able to get out of this place without any money, so she conceded to stay and be a secretary as long as it would take her to earn enough money to leave. She promised herself she would leave as soon as she had enough money, and she wouldn't hang around a second longer. She knew there was nothing here for her.

Ch. 12

Charlie felt like he had been washed in God's blessings, so he could think of nothing better to do but pray and thank God for all the blessings he was feeling especially grateful for today.

"God, thank you for sending Annabelle to me. Thank you for preparing my heart to be ready to help her and work with her. We both know just a few years ago I was in no position to help or guide anyone to you, God. I was a mess, and you brought me back. I am excited to see Annabelle have the same transformative experience I had. I know how she feels, because I felt that way for so long when I was at my lowest and darkest moments. I'm still so thankful every day that I was given more time here on earth to correct my mistakes and set things right with the people I loved and hurt. I hope to be able to give her the same chance through you, God. Thank you again for this blessing. It's in your heavenly name I pray. Amen."

< < > >

Charlie had known since before he ever met Annabelle that she had baggage. He had gotten a very brief story from Pastor Maxwell. He had specifically asked for the brief version to keep from having his perception of her tainted in any way. Based on the brief account he had gotten from Pastor Maxwell; he knew she had some rough spots in her childhood that had come to a head her senior year when she had just taken off and disappeared. He knew there had been rumors and speculation concerning where she had gone and what she had been doing, but he really wasn't interested in speculation. He was living proof about how much speculation and rumors could haunt and destroy a life.

He knew in time she would tell him everything she wanted him to know. It was *her* story to tell and no one else's, so until then, he would be patient and show her how calm and happy her life could be.

He had spent the morning getting her set up on her computer and showing her how to set up appointments and activities on their joint calendar. He gave her a brief tutorial on their phone system, so she would be able to answer and easily move between calls. He also showed her the rest of the space and all the amenities like the kitchen, bathroom, and huge recreational area. He explained to her that sometimes students would stop by after school to hang out and play basketball, volleyball, play music, or just sit and talk. He told her he liked the area to be open and inviting, so he welcomed them to come until 5:00. He noticed that she seemed especially interested in the stage area, and he explained to her the students had a praise and worship band that would perform every Wednesday night and occasionally on Sunday mornings. There was no disapproval in the look on her face, so he assumed she had liked that idea. He told her Wednesday nights and Sunday mornings the whole building would be packed with people. Sunday School, Worship, and Bible Study would be taking up most of the time. He honored their agreement by telling her she could stay in her office and work if she chose to. He said they usually kept the doors closed during those times, so no one would notice her in there. She seemed to be okay with that idea as well.

Finally, the tutorials drew to a close, and they both looked up at the clock to see that it was lunchtime. Annabelle wasn't sure what to do, but before she could say anything, Charlie was on his feet and looking at her like he was waiting on her for something.

"Do you want me to lock the door behind you?" Annabelle said with a look of confusion as she stood.

"No, I thought we were going to lunch. It is time for lunch, isn't it?" He said looking back at the clock.

"Yeah, but we just hadn't talked about lunch or anything like that, so I didn't know what the plans were."

"Oh, yeah sorry about that. I tend to assume things without actually clueing people in."

"Like telling me we are having lunch together?"

"Yes, exactly like telling you that we are going back up to the main building where the entire staff usually meets every day and has lunch."

"That's nice, but I don't know."

"Why not? The food is cooked by some of the ladies at the church, and it is really good."

"I just…"

"Oh c'mon. It's your first day, and you really need to have this time to relax and talk and not be stuck sitting in here by yourself."

"Relaxing and talking does sound great, but I just don't know."

"Okay, if we don't go and have lunch with the other staff members, we can just go and visit your dad at the hospital."

"On second thought, lunch with the other staff sounds great! Lead the way!"

"I thought you would see things my way." He said with a chuckle as they headed toward the door.

Bethany Rodgers

Jill sat on the horribly uncomfortable couch next to the window in her father's hospital room and silently willed him to look at her. It had been 3 days without a glance in her direction, and the silence had become unbearable. Her mother had been running around and doing everything to keep herself busy and help her husband and acting like nothing was wrong. Jill didn't know how her mother could miss the thickness that was hanging in the air and making it hard to draw a breath. She didn't know how much more of this she could take before going crazy.

Without warning, Jill felt a painful stirring deep within her abdomen. In that moment, it was as if the world had stopped turning. She sat still and waited to see if it would happen again, or if there were any other familiar signs she could cling to for hope. It seemed like an eternity had gone by when suddenly, she another pang, this one sharper, sent the message of hope straight to her brain. She had tried not to panic too much when the normal day for her period had come and gone. She had hoped she was just under a lot of stress with everything going on with her dad and school, so maybe that had affected things. She honestly hadn't wanted to say anything to Jason, but she had broken down and texted him last night to let him know she was concerned. He hadn't seemed as comforting as she would've liked, and she hoped she was also just imagining that. Jill nervously jumped up off the sofa and announced that she needed to use the restroom. She walked across the room and through the open door. She was anxious and nervous and excited all at the same time. She moved towards the toilet, undid her pants and let them fall to the floor, and held her breath until she saw it. The flash of red that symbolized freedom. She wanted to shout it from the rooftops, but she decided a silent happy dance would have to suffice. She hurriedly finished what she was doing and exited the bathroom. She walked across the room trying to seem normal, but she felt like she was walking on a cloud. She got back to the couch and grabbed the phone and scrolled through her texts until she found the name, Jason. She quickly typed out her message.

Jill: Good News! I got my period today, so no need to worry anymore!

She glanced at the clock after hitting send and wondered if he would be out of class yet. Then she saw the 3 little dots appear below her text, and she watched them pulse one after the other until finally a response appeared.

Jason: That's great, but I wasn't worried. We would've taken care of it.

She stared at his choice of words in disbelief. Taken care of it? What did that mean? She hoped he didn't mean an abortion. She could never do something like that. She assumed she'd just misunderstood, so she replied as if he hadn't even typed out the horrible words.

Jill: To be honest, I was a little disappointed. It wouldn't have been a bad thing. It's a symbol of our love.

Jason: Symbol of our love? No, what would people think if we have a baby and aren't married. You know who I am. Something like that would ruin me.

Jill: Well, we're sleeping together, and we aren't married, so I'm sure it wouldn't be any more shocking that that.

Jason: Sleeping together and having a baby together are completely different. Although, I'd be scrutinized for either one.

Jill: So, does that mean no more sleeping together?

Jason: We obviously need to be more careful. Have you thought about what I said about taking some time off to stay home with your parents?

Jill: I thought about it a little.

Jason: And?

Jill: I haven't decided yet.

Jason: Did you at least drop the class like we'd talked about.

Jill: Not yet.

Jason: I promise it would be much better if you would just drop the class.

Jill: But I NEED that class to graduate.

Jason: We've already talked about this. There are other options like taking a course at a college closer to home and transferring the credits, or you can wait until you're ready to graduate and see if someone else is teaching it. Why don't you just trust me and drop the class. It would be a much better option than having to turn yourself in for plagiarism. They can expel you from the school for that.

Jill: I know! I've just been trying to forget about the whole horrible ordeal and hope it would go away.

Jason: Well, based on the note I received the other day, it isn't.

Jill: Note? What note?

Jason: A note from someone who knows and is threatening to tell. Please just drop the class before you get kicked out of school for good.

Jill: Fine. I'll do it when I get home and have access to my computer and some privacy.

Jason: Let me know when it's done.

Jill read Jason's last text, and she couldn't help feeling like a mobster or a hit man. Her stomach had stopped doing flips and now it was cramping and churning deep within her abdomen. She didn't know which was worse. This situation had gotten so out of control, and she wasn't sure if there was even a way to rein it all back in. She had decided to keep the news a secret until she knew what was going on, but based on Jason's text message, she had 2 choices: drop the class or admit to cheating and probably be expelled. Neither option was good. She couldn't figure out how she had gotten to this place. The plan had been foolproof, and it had seemed like everything was going on without a hitch. Obviously, something had gotten messed up enough for someone to find out. She was so mad at herself for whatever she had done to screw everything up. What was she going to do?

Suddenly the realization hit her, she needed to pray. She bowed her head and closed her eyes and began to talk to God.

"God please, please help me get out of this mess I've made. I've made some mistakes, and I've wandered from you. Please forgive me and let me know what to do to get back to the place I need to be. I want to be near to you always, but right now I feel so far from you. Please protect me and show me what I need to do." Jill stayed this way praying and seeking God's advice for the next few minutes.

When she lifted her head and opened her eyes, Jill could see her father was sleeping, and her mother was clutching his hand and smiling at her. Jill felt her face warm, and she was suddenly very aware of her mother's piercing stare.

"Were you praying?" Her mother asked.

"Yes, I was praying." She said with a mixture of hesitancy and relief.

"That's great, honey. Your father needs all the prayers he can get right now."

"That's exactly why I prayed for him." She said with a smile.

Jill watched her mother turn back to smile at her father, and Jill let the smile fall from her own face. This was crazy. She hadn't been successful in telling her dad what was going on, and now her mother was so consumed by her father's heart attack that she couldn't imagine anyone else would have something going on in their own life. Jill could feel the air becoming thicker and thicker until it was becoming hard to breathe. She had to get out of this place. She had to get out of here and go somewhere. Where would she go? She thought briefly about going to see Annabelle, but she knew that wasn't a good idea. Annabelle would love finding out her perfect little sister had been intimate with someone, thought she might be pregnant, and probably getting expelled from school. No, Jill could not go down that path. There had to be someone else she could talk to. That's when she remembered her conversation in the car with Charlie. She took out her phone and found his number. Her hands were shaking as she typed out a message asking him if they could meet later to talk about some things.

What was only about 20 seconds seemed like 20 years that she waited for his reply.

Charlie: Yes, I would be glad to meet. Do you want to come over here and talk?

Jill: I don't want to run into Annabelle. I don't want her knowing anything that's going on.

Charlie: Ahh okay. Do you want to meet at one of the restaurants? They shouldn't be very busy this early in the afternoon. We should have plenty of privacy, so we can talk about whatever is on your mind.

Jill: Can I meet you at the new Mexican restaurant downtown?

Charlie: yes, I'll see you there in 30 minutes.

Jill: okay see you then. Thanks for this.

Charlie: anytime

Jill hoped the new, Mexican restaurant, La Fiesta, was a good choice. She had heard it was owned by a family who was new to town. Hopefully they wouldn't be the type of people to listen in to what she was saying to obtain some local gossip.

Jill arrived earlier than she had planned, so she went inside and sat down to wait for Charlie. Ever since her text exchange with Jason had ended, she had felt like her heart was going to beat out of her chest as anxiety threatened to fill her every pore. She reached into her kavu to pull out her phone. When the phone was on the table, she stared at it in disgust. How could this tiny piece of technology be the messenger of so much heartache and bad news. She stared at the phone and her emotions tore at each other inside her. She hated the phone, but she also felt attached to it. She wanted to smash it and never look at it again, but she couldn't. It was her lifeline to Jason. She couldn't live without Jason. Suddenly she realized, she couldn't even move it off of the table. How had she let it have such a pull over her, and why? She knew the answer immediately, Jason. It had always been Jason. Everything had been going wrong since she had gotten together with him, but like with the phone, she was hooked. She knew deep down he wasn't any good for her, but still she kept hanging around and coming back for more. The thing she had chided and counseled her friends for the in the past, was what had ultimately become her addiction. It was a cruel twist of fate that she was now in a position with no friends. They couldn't hang around and be patient while they said she was "throwing her future away". She shrugged as she thought, "I guess they weren't really my friends. Real friends stick around no matter what." She had stuck around, so why couldn't they? If they had just tried harder to understand her feelings, then they would've been okay with everything.

Suddenly, the enormity of her solitude engulfed her to the point that it began to spill down her face in the form of tears. In a matter of only seconds, she was sitting in the booth with her head in her hands and crying. No, she was sobbing. She was releasing all of her anger at herself for the destruction of relationships she had caused between herself, her father, and even her sister. She was releasing fear that Jason would be so mad at her for not having already done what he wanted. She was releasing anger at herself for not being able to follow simple instructions without even messing them up. The truth was staring her in the face as a puddle in her hands and drops on the table; she was a disaster that created destruction wherever she went.

"Chips?"

Jill looked up and realized someone was standing there. She was staring at a young Hispanic woman with the most striking eyes she'd ever seen. They were a unique color combination unlike any she'd ever seen in the world. The woman's eyes were a concoction of blues and greens, and they looked like the colors of the ocean.

"Chips?" The girl said again this time gesturing by holding the chips out further towards Jill and nodding at them.

Realization began to hit Jill as she became aware, she had been staring at this woman probably with her mouth hanging open. She did a quick mental check and realized her mouth had that dry cotton feeling, so it had in fact been hanging open for an extended period of time. Then, she thought about the mess she must look like. The sloppy, wet mess girl with red, puffy eyes and a tear-streaked face. Just to add insult to injury Jill lifted her finger to her nose to find it unnaturally warm. Her worse fears were becoming reality, she was most undoubtedly looking like Rudolph. Whenever she cried, her nose would become bright red on the end. She found it to be extremely unattractive and wished it was a trait she didn't possess. She was also now aware of something else wet on her face around her nasal region, and as she sniffed, she realized, she also had a runny nose that was running uncontrollably all over her face. Once she became fully aware of her embarrassing reality, she felt her eyes water all over again as she turned into another blubbering mess.

"Are you okay?" The woman asked.

"Yyyyes" Jill replied.

"For some reason, I don't believe you." The woman replied while giving Jill a pointed look. "Now, tell me what's wrong. You never know. I might can help."

Jill doubted this, but she felt like she owed the woman something for being such a sight right in front of her. "Everything."

"Everything?" The woman repeated puzzled.

"Yes, everything is wrong. I have messed up everything, and no matter how hard I try, I cannot seem to do anything right or fix anything. I'm a worthless mess!" Jill could feel her cheeks burning under the realization at the level of drama she had just spewed all over this woman. This woman, who was simply trying to deliver chips, didn't want to hear about her dramatic crisis. Jill was about to start crying some more from embarrassment when she heard the woman speak.

"I don't believe that for a minute. I know someone who thinks you are amazing. Someone who thought you were so worth it, that he gave his son as a sacrifice for you."

Jill stopped sobbing and looked at the woman wondering who in the world she could be talking about. No one had loved her that much. "Who is that?" Jill asked.

"Your father"

"*My* father had a heart attack, because of me. That's how amazing I am", she said flailing her hands to emphasis the word "amazing".

"Sweetie, I'm talking about your heavenly father. The one who created you and loves you unconditionally no matter what you do."

Jill began to speak and spew all the doubts about God she had been keeping locked away, but when she looked at the woman, she caught her gaze. Jill held the woman's gaze and stared into her eyes. Her eyes held a realization, and at that moment, she was certain beyond a shadow of a doubt of God's love for her. The feeling that came over her was one of security, comfort, peace, understanding and love. In that moment, she realized everything would be okay. She wasn't sure how, but she just knew it would all work out.

The woman smiled at her as if she understood and could sense it all too. "Pray." She said. "You must continue to pray and ask God to intervene. He loves you and wants the best for you, but you have to choose to let him in and give over control to him."

"Okay." Jill said in a quiet voice. "I will pray."

"Do it now." The woman commanded. "There is no right or wrong time to pray. There is just time, and if you've got it, you need to spend it with the Lord."

Jill nodded, clasped her hands, and bowed her head to begin praying. It had been longer than Jill wanted to admit since she'd prayed for herself. She was always praying for other people, but never for herself. It always seemed selfish somehow, but right here, now, it seemed like a perfect place to start. Jill silently sent up a prayer to the Lord.

"God I am so sorry of the mess I have made of everyone's life. I have been trying to fix everything on my own, but I only seem to be doing more damage and affecting more of the people in my life whom I love. I am begging you to intervene in my life and help me know the right thing to do in each situation of my life. Help my father heal, so we can have the talk we need to have about everything that has happened. Please help me have the strength to be honest with him. I love him so very much. God please also help to give me the strength to be able to reach out to Charlie and let him know everything that is happening. Please help me be accepting of his advice. I know I'm not usually good at accepting advice from others, but right now, I really need to be."

She was about to continue when she felt a shift in the air around her. She felt a presence, but it wasn't like the presence she had felt with the woman standing there. Instead, this presence felt denser and almost as though someone was staring at her. All of a sudden, she felt a hand on her shoulder. She looked up immediately startled by whoever had touched her shoulder. She had to admit she was actually somewhat surprised to see Charlie standing there. She knew she was meeting him here, but somehow his presence still took her by surprise.

"Hey. Sorry if I scared you. I just wanted to make sure you were okay."

"It's fine. I think I just got caught up in my own little world."

"How's that going?"

"I can honestly say it is expanding."

"Really, how so?"

"Well, I'm finally going to let God had some control for once. I'm always one to try and fix things and do everything myself, but I think that's what has gotten me into this mess and so many others. I always think I know the right decisions, and the right things to do but the truth is…"

"Chips?" A young boy said as he came over carrying a basket of chips and a container of salsa to their table.

"Oh, we already have…" Jill started to say as she glanced at the table expecting the chips to be sitting right there, but they weren't. In fact, there weren't any chips on the table anywhere. Jill's eyes darted around the table and then around the dining room as she was vaguely aware of Charlie glancing her way as he accepted the chips and salsa from the young man.

"Are you okay?" He finally asked. It seemed to Jill like that was the question of the day for her today.

"Mmmm hmm." She said unconvincingly. "I'm just looking for someone." She said as an attempt to further explain what she herself really couldn't explain.

"You have a friend who works here?" Charlie said looking around now as well.

"Kind of" Jill said taking one last survey of the establishment.

Jill was starting to become aware of how odd she must seem to him with the vague answers, and her incessant searching she'd been doing since he arrived. She knew if he had any chance of helping her. He needed to hear the whole story from her. She just wasn't sure how much of the story she was ready to tell him right now.

"There was a lady I met when I got here. She was extremely helpful, and she encouraged me to pray."

"That's great!" Charlie said. "We need to do that as often as we can."

"Yes, but that's so much easier than it sounds." Jill said with a hint of defeat coming back into her voice.

"True, but if we stay conscious of it, that will help us to remember."

"It's just so hard for me to let God in, because I actually have to admit that I'm wrong, and I've done something wrong. I hate that. I am not used to being the screw up. Annabelle was always the screw up, and I was always the one who was nothing like her. I obeyed my parents, I accepted their plan for my life, I followed that plan to a T, and now, after all that, I have still turned out like Annabelle. I just don't understand how this happened." Jill realized she had an edge in her voice. The anger she had felt in previous years had returned. She grabbed a chip and dunked it into the salsa. She took a bit of the chip piled high with salsa, and she chewed and chewed as the peppers in the salsa began to release their oil and started burning her tongue, the inside of her mouth, and even her throat. She accepted and welcomed the pain. I helped fuel her rage even more.

"You need to take Annabelle out of the equation. It cannot be about being like her or not being like her. You aren't her. You are a completely different person who is responsible for your own triumphs and mistakes just like she is responsible for her own triumphs and mistakes. No one is perfect, but you have to stop beating yourself up by comparing yourself to her."

"It's just not fair. I worked so hard not to be her, and all of that effort did nothing. I am not the one hurting the ones I love and pushing them away. I keep feeling like things are already so bad that nothing I can do will fix them."

"That's not true! You already started on a journey of healing when you decided to pray. Now, you just have to continue praying for each specific relationship in your life. Be honest with God. Tell him what you've done, and how you would like those relationships to be mended. Tell him how you would like them to be in the future."

"I can try that." Jill said conceding to his plan. "Nothing I've tried has worked, so now it is time to try something new."

Charlie and Jill spent the next hour discussing her relationships with everyone in her family, and what she wanted them to be like. He explained to her the steps that might be necessary to growing those relationships and mending any hurt feelings or lack of trust that had formed. Jill listened and was open to all of his ideas, but she never brought up any of her troubles at school or with Jason. She wasn't ready to let him into that part of her world. As they were finishing up, they'd agreed to meet again at the restaurant when she was ready to discuss the progress she was making. Jill made Charlie promise not to tell Annabelle. She didn't want her sister nosing around in her business. Charlie agreed, and as they parted ways, Jill smiled. For the first time in a long time, things actually felt like they were going to get better.

Ch.13

When Charlie got back into his car to leave the restaurant, his chest felt heavy, so he knew the best course of action was prayer. Jill had revealed a lot today, and he knew she was on her way to getting the peace she desired as long she could stay the course. Praying and talking to God seemed so uncomfortable and foreign to her, and he hoped he could help change that. He knew the only way she could find the peace she was seeking was giving everything to God.

"Lord, I humbly ask that you protect Jill. Protect her heart and mind from the enemy who undoubtedly wants to sway her from her decision to walk with you through this life. He won't want her to be at peace, so I know he will stop at nothing to see that happen, but I also know you are greater than he, and you have already defeated him, God. With your help, Jill will be able to keep him from her life. I pray she seeks you, Lord. I pray that she prays without ceasing and allows you to work in her life. I know the peace she is seeking. I have found it, and I know it is such a beautiful thing. I want to help her, Lord. Please allow me to help guide her to you. I also know how she currently feels. I remember running from you and everything you stood for. I remember being broken and seeking something without knowing what it was, and I remember the day I stopped running and came back to you, Lord. I will always remember that day, and the way my soul finally found rest. I pray for that same experience for Jill today, Lord. It's in your precious and holy name I pray. Amen."

< < > >

Across town, Annabelle had finally started getting the hang of her new routine. She had successfully answered some phone calls and figured out the online calendar system as well as the filing system. Things were definitely getting easier. The day had gone smoothly except for the random moment when Charlie had announced he had to leave for a meeting that Annabelle noticed wasn't on his calendar. She had checked repeatedly, and the only meeting she saw wasn't for 2 more hours. She hadn't known Charlie long, but what she had learned about him today told her he was meticulously organized. It didn't seem like him to just run off on a whim when he had another meeting to prepare for.

Annabelle heard the door open and assumed Charlie had come back. She was typing up the following Sunday's sermon notes when a figure emerged into the doorway. She glanced up from her chair and had to do a double take. Standing in the doorway was a petite girl with long blonde hair and big blue eyes. A girl she would recognize anywhere. It wasn't Charlie. Standing in the doorway was her childhood best friend. The girl she had been inseparable with until the day she had left this town behind and headed out to "follow her dreams". Annabelle's excitement was beginning to wane and was being replaced by anxiety. What would she say to her friend? How could she apologize for abandoning her all those years ago?

"Olivia? Is that you? What are you doing here?"

"Oh my gosh, Annabelle. I didn't know you were working here. I'm kind of surprised. News usually travels much faster in this town."

"Oh. It only just happened yesterday, so the gossip lines haven't had a chance to catch up yet." Annabelle wasn't entirely certain, but she thought she detected a guarded tone to Olivia's words. She was growing curious, so she continued on with her questioning. "I'm assuming you didn't come to see me, so I'm guessing you are pastor Cochran's 4:30 appointment?"

"Yes, I am, or *we* are."

"We?"

"Yes, we." A man's voice said coming in and stepping into the doorway behind Olivia. Annabelle recognized his tall muscular frame, short cropped brown hair and the dimples in his cheeks when he smiled. He wrapped his arms around Olivia's waist and pulled her back against him as he rested his head on hers.

Annabelle felt like the world had stopped turning. She had to make a mental note to make sure to keep her mouth securely shut tight, so it wasn't hanging open. Standing in the doorway looking cozy with Olivia was Brian. Not just any Brian. It was her ex-boyfriend Brian. How had she not known about this? Surely her mother would've heard they were dating. Maybe it was new? Maybe they just started dating.

"Hey Brian." She managed to say. "Fancy running into you here and with Olivia too. I'm guessing y'all are dating now?"

"Engaged actually." Brian said as he lightly touched the ring on Olivia's left hand which seemed to shine, and glitter much brighter suddenly than it had before.

"That is just awesome!" Annabelle forced out through clenched teeth. "Why don't y'all have a seat and pastor Cochran will be back any moment to get the meeting started."

As she watched them find two chairs right in view of her office, she vowed to have some seriously strong words with Charlie once he arrived. How had she gotten so unlucky to have to suffer through this? This was completely unreal. It was like one of her worst nightmares come to life. She knew these people still lived and existed here, but she thought she could avoid them until she left again.

She tried to go about her work without appearing to be thrown off by the arrival of her ex-boyfriend and ex best friend and their announcement of an engagement, but she kept noticing that no matter how much she tried to force it into the back of her mind, it continued pushing to the forefront. The whole situation was incredible awkward, and the seconds seem to inch by at a snail's pace. The worst part about it was that she had a full view of them sitting together, bodies turned toward each other, holding hands, and whispering. She was sure she didn't have any feelings left for Brian, but she knew things with him hadn't ended well. There was so much left unsaid between them, and she would've liked to have a chance to say what needed to be said and clear the air instead of running into him with his fiancée. It was all too weird.

Annabelle felt as though one of them was looking at her, so she shifted slightly in her chair to shake the feeling off. She glanced up and caught Olivia's gaze as it suddenly turned away. She had been right. She wondered if this was as weird for them as it was for her. She noticed Olivia's legs were crossed, and her dangling foot was swinging. Although she hadn't seen Olivia in years, she still knew Olivia always moved her foot when something was bothering her. Knowing Olivia also found this situation extremely uncomfortable helped slightly, but not much. She wished she could cross the room and talk to them and sort out all the awkward, uncomfortable feelings, but she just couldn't. Once again, her pride was holding her back. She wouldn't even know what to say.

After what seemed like an eternity of waiting, the door finally chimed, and Charlie walked in. He walked past Olivia and Brian waving to them as he came towards Annabelle's office.

"As you can see, Brian and Olivia, your 4:30 are here." She said looking toward the area where they were seated.

"Yes, thank you." Charlie replied. "We will be in my office, and I'm closing the door, so if you need anything buzz me on the phone."

"Okay" she replied. She had been trying to get him to sense the tension, but he clearly wasn't picking up on any of it. As Charlie turned and walked out of her office, she caught a hint of peppers in the air. "Where in the world had he been?" She wondered to herself. She watched the couple follow Charlie down the hallway to his office, and once they were all inside, she heard the door close.

An hour later, she heard the door open and the clacking of Olivia's heels as she came down the hallway. Annabelle was surprised when she looked up and Olivia was standing in her office with Brian and Charlie out of sight.

"Annabelle?" Olivia began. "I think. Well, Pastor Cochran and I both think it would be a good idea if we got together in a neutral zone and talked things through. You played such a big part in Brian's and my life, so it would be weird to feel like we're tiptoeing around each other while you're here. This is a small place after all, and we used to run in the same circles, so running into each other is probably going to be inevitable. Can we get together for dinner tomorrow night at Brian's place? Does 6:00 sound okay?"

"Yeah, that makes sense. I guess." Annabelle said noting that Olivia had said "while you're here" as if she expected her to be leaving again soon. "So, is it going to be the 3 of us?"

"It doesn't have to be. You know, you should bring someone. That way it will be nice and even."

"Even" she thought to herself, "more like less chance for them to gang up on me." She kept these thoughts to herself and replied with a simple "sure".

Brian came up behind Olivia, and gave her a squeeze, and the two of them left. When Annabelle heard the door chime, she knew she could relax.

"What a nice couple" Charlie commented coming into the room. "Young and in love with their whole lives ahead of them. They don't make couples as compatible as that anymore."

"Why did you think it would be a good idea for her to ask me to dinner?" Annabelle asked while giving him an angry look. "You just created a very awkward and uncomfortable dining experience for me next weekend."

"I didn't tell her to ask you to dinner." Charlie said looking stunned. "The only thing I said was that for their marriage to be successful, they need to make sure everything is out in the open, and they embrace every aspect of each other's lives especially the ones they both know exist, but they don't talk about."

"That's exactly what I am!" She exclaimed. "I'm the piece of the puzzle that everyone knows is on the floor under the china cabinet, but no one wants to actually salvage and use it for fear that it is too damaged. Better to let the puzzle stay unfinished than face the mistakes that were made."

Charlie just stared at her for a moment. Annabelle could see something forming in his mind. The wheels were definitely turning, she just wasn't sure in which direction they were moving.

"Wait. How are you the lone damaged puzzle piece in their puzzle life love story?"

"Oh wow!" She said realizing that he truly hadn't put the pieces of the puzzle together. "Remember I told you I had a boyfriend in high school who my dad was crazy about, and our futures were all planned out?"

"Yes…"

"Well, his name was Brian. The same Brian that you met with today is the Brian I used to date."

"That must've been incredible awkward for you."

"Just wait. It gets worse. I had a best friend growing up that I was inseparable with. Her name was Olivia. The Olivia you met with today is the very same Olivia I was best friends with the entire time I dated Brian."

"That's what I love about life. So many twists and turns, never a dull moment. Television and movie writers try so hard to come up with storylines that are believable, but all we really have to do is just look at our own lives and the lives around us to watch the drama, comedy and mystery unfold before our very eyes. Life is the perfect improv routine."

"I'm glad my pain amuses you."

"I'm sorry. I didn't mean it like that. What I meant was that in a matter of seconds you went from the elephant in the corner to being out in the open, and this is the most exciting thing to happen today."

"So, I'm an elephant now?"

"Okay, bad choice of words. I was working with the phrase 'elephant in the room'. Like you were the thing everyone noticed, but no one wanted to acknowledge. Maybe your puzzle piece metaphor was better."

"Somehow, I definitely think it was."

"It doesn't matter. All that matters is thanks to you I'm stuck having dinner with them tomorrow night, and to make it even more painful, I'm supposed to bring someone."

"Wow, this wouldn't be the time to show up alone. Who knows what they want to talk about They've had 5 years to sort through and deal with their feelings of abandonment, but something tells me they just swept all of their feelings under the rug. Now, they just need everything to be okay, so they can get married. That would be a tough position to be in alone."

"I know. That's why I won't be going alone."

"Well, that's not much time to find a date to agree to go to dinner with you and your ex-boyfriend and your ex best friend who is also his fiancé. Somehow, I just don't see guys lining up for that drama filled evening. I really wish I knew someone to recommend."

"That's okay. I don't need any recommendations. I know exactly who is going with me."

"Who?"

"You! Technically. It's your fault I'm in this mess, so you can enjoy the drama filled evening you created right along with me."

"Technically, I think you created the drama by running away and leaving everyone. All I did was give sound marital advice. I really don't think they want to have dinner with their pastor/marriage counselor. Won't that be weird?"

"It doesn't matter if it will be weird. They decided on the dinner and having you there will keep them on their best behavior and allow you to take some notes on what to counsel them on. It's really a win win if you ask me. Plus, if you do this for me, I promise to help you ward off the casserole brigade as a token of my gratitude."

"Casserole Brigade?" Charlie looked confused like he had never before heard of this.

"The casserole brigade is the group of single women who begin coming around an eligible man like flies to honey. You probably have had a few already and just didn't notice. They can get a little crazy and forceful. It's not their fault. I blame it on two things: age and mothers. They can hear their biological clock ticking away the seconds while their mothers constantly point out all their friends who are getting married and having babies. Stress like that is enough to make anyone crack after a while."

"So, you're saying if I go to dinner with you, you will keep the "flies" away from me until the right one comes along?"

"Exactly" Annabelle said proudly while holding out her hand for him to shake it.

Charlie nodded and shook her hand. He wasn't sure he truly believed in this casserole brigade, but it couldn't hurt to have Annabelle on his good side. He knew she needed to be in the church and around Godly people as much as possible. He also wasn't entirely sure what her level of trust of Godly people was, so he didn't want to give her any reason not to trust him. He also had a lot to think about with everything Jill had told him earlier. For some reason, he had a feeling she wasn't telling him everything. He wished he could show her she could trust him, because he knew whatever she was hiding was eating away at her. He wasn't sure how he could expect anyone in this family to open up to him, if he wasn't telling them his entire story either. He wanted to tell them everything and gain their trust, but he didn't want their opinions of him to change.

That was the thing about choices. When you were making them, it was impossible to know all the ripple effects they could create. Years down the road you might think the ripples are over when all of a sudden you see another and another. The choices you make have a way of following you and staying just near enough to jump out when you least expect it. At least that's how Charlie's choices had been. They'd lingered long enough to ruin everything good for him. He was really liking this new town and the people he was meeting, and he didn't want everything here to be ruined by his past choices.

That was what he couldn't figure out about Annabelle. She had made some unflattering choices in her past. Some of them she was upfront and honest about, but others she seemed to keep to herself. He couldn't figure out how she went around always acting like nothing mattered and none of it bothered her. Almost like she was proud of her choices no matter what they had cost her. Maybe that was it. Maybe she hadn't realized just how much they had cost her. Maybe she wouldn't realize she had lost something, because she never knew she really wanted it. Charlie knew all too well that the heartbreaking time inevitably came for everyone where they truly did start wanting the things that were slipping away, but at the point you realize you actually want them, it's too late to change course and get them back. He knew nothing was harder than watching a dream you didn't even know you had slip away with no hope of return.

When the time was right, he knew he would share his story with them, and it would hopefully help to save some of their dreams. Both of the girls needed so much help, but he knew they each needed different things. It would require a lot of prayer on his part to make sure he was ready for whatever task God placed in front of him. He had felt God calling him to offer Annabelle the position at the Church, and he had followed God's command and offered her the job. He didn't want to allow any of that to have been in vain. God was at work here in their lives. He could see it. He just had to stay in constant prayer and ask God to show him what to do and how to help each of them. He just hoped he could fulfill what God had called him to do. He had failed God so many times before, but he couldn't fail him now. He couldn't fail God, and he couldn't fail Jill and Annabelle. He knew he had to do whatever it took to help them.

With his new foresight and knowledge about what might lay ahead, he left Annabelle to go back to her work, and he departed back to this office to begin praying for her, her family, and her sister, and all the members of the congregation. He was called to such a higher purpose here than he had ever been called before. He could feel the weight of the responsibility resting on his shoulders, and he wanted to make sure he was able to carry it all.

When Charlie had left, Annabelle went back to her office to begin typing up the sermon notes again. She was happy to have someone like him she could count on. It had been a long time since she'd had someone like that in her life. Most of the people in her life had always wanted and expected something from her, but not Charlie. She knew dinner with Brian and Olivia would be incredibly weird and awkward, but she hoped it wouldn't be so bad with Charlie there. She knew he had taken a big leap of faith in offering her the job, and she didn't want to disappoint him. She could feel the weight of all of the responsibility he had entrusted to her resting on her shoulders, and she just had to make absolutely certain she would be able to carry it all and not disappoint him like she had everyone else.

Ch.14

Charlie found himself up early again that morning. He had woken up before his alarm with so many things on his mind. He had a feeling something was about to happen for Jill like she would hit a turning point in her story soon. He only hoped when it came, she would make the right choice. He thought about his past and all the choices he had made which had inevitably led him to this place today. He wished it hadn't taken him so much grief, heartache and bad decision to reach this place, but he felt so blessed he had actually made it this far in his life and had gotten to such a good place. Finally, he thought about Annabelle. She was going through so much, and he wanted to badly to help her, but he knew she wasn't ready for anything big yet. He would have to offer his help in easy, subtle ways right now. With a heavy heart, he got out of the bed and knelt beside it ready to come to the Lord in prayer.

"Heavenly Father, I come to you today with a heavy heart and the witness of so much brokenness. I am worried about Jill. I want her to choose the right path, but I'm not sure she is ready yet, but I trust you, God. I know you will intervene in her life and point her in the way in which she should go. I hope she listens and follows your commands in her life. With Annabelle, I feel she is changing, and her heart is becoming more accepting. Please continue working on her, Lord. She needs so much truth in her life right now. She is so lost, and she is scrambling to find her way right now. Please let me know when the time to point her in the right direction will be. I don't want to be too direct and scare her away. Please give me the knowledge to discern the perfect moment. Please God, allow me to use the brokenness and healing in my own life to help those around me to start their own healing process. When it comes down to it, we are all just a bunch of broken people who are made whole in you. Thank you for all the blessings you have given me when I didn't deserve anything from you. Thank you for being there no matter how many times I had turned my back on you, Lord."

< < > >

Annabelle awoke suddenly to the sound of the alarm chirping a loud good morning to her. The room was dark, and she couldn't remember why in the world she would've set the alarm to go off so early in the morning. She got up, tuned it off, got back in the bed, and let her mind wander to all the places she might have stored the reason for this early morning intrusion. She laid in bed thinking for a good 2 minutes before finally realizing that it was Sunday. This, she decided, would be her least favorite day of the week. She knew her job required her to show up at church and help Charlie with whatever he needed, but she had already told him she would not become involved with any church activities outside of the roles of her job. They had agreed she could stay in her office and work while everything was going on outside of her office. Having a reprieve from church made the thought of facing the place more manageable, but it certainly didn't make getting up this early any easier.

She quickly showered and went back to her room to get dressed, quickly realizing she didn't have anything that would be deemed "appropriate" for church. She weighed the consequences of choosing one of her own outfits and just dealing with it or seeking out an appropriate outfit from somewhere else. She knew it wasn't likely she would be coming into contact with anyone, but she also knew how gossip traveled in their town. Her mother had enough to deal with at the hospital without having to hear about her daughter flaunting herself all over church in un-church-like attire. Annabelle decided just this once, she would do her mom a favor and not cause any type of controversy. She tiptoed down the hallway and into her sister's room.

Jill's bed was across the room from the closet, and Annabelle knew Jill was a very heavy sleeper. She assumed both of these would work in her favor as the tiptoed over to the closet and opened one of the doors. When she had been living at home, she remembered Jill was always organizing the clothes in her closet and making sure to keep all of her dresses and skirts in one end. She had hoped Jill was still doing that now, and when she pulled the door open, she was pleased to find that she was right. Thankful that in the past few months, she had been meticulous about her workouts and good eating, she was pleased to find a number of outfits in her size. She flipped through dress by dress until she found one that she thought she could stand. It was a light pink maxi dress with white flowers all over it. It really was very pretty, and it was extremely comfortable to the touch. Annabelle looked a little further into the closet and found a light white cardigan that she could wear with it.

Pleased with her haul, she closed the closet door and started to tiptoe out when a sound startled her. She froze in the middle of the room with a dress and cardigan draped over her arm, and she was very aware of her own breathing. She waited for a few seconds, and she realized her sister hadn't woken up. She started back toward the door, only stopping when she heard the sound again. She glanced toward her sister when the sound was coming, and she saw a glow coming from her bedside table. She crept closer and could see her sister was turned the opposite direction. Peering down over the table, she realized it was her sister's phone just alerting her she had a text message. Annabelle breathed a sigh of relief and started to look away, but something about the message had caught her eye. She glanced back at it. It was from someone named Jason. She thought for a moment, and she realized, she had never heard her sister mention anyone named Jason. She wondered if he was a new friend. When she read the message, her heart caught in her throat.

Jason: Trust me, there's life after being expelled.

"Expelled?" Annabelle thought. "What?" How could her brilliant sister be getting expelled? She decided she must've read the message wrong. Unfortunately, no matter how many times she brought the screen to light, the message remained the same. Confused and unsure of what to do, she left her sister's room and ventured back to her own room.

The entire way to the church was much of the same. She was unsure of what to think and even unsure of how to help her sister. *Her* sister would never do something like that. It had to be a mistake. Maybe this Jason kid had just sent the text to the wrong person. Maybe he didn't even know Jill. This seemed to satisfy Annabelle's thoughts until logic reminded her that his number was programmed into Jill's phone. Then she started thinking about how Jill had been so weird about her computer, and she had no appetite the day they'd gone to breakfast. There were a lot of things that Annabelle was realizing she'd witnessed lately that weren't like Jill at all.

When she arrived at the youth center, she found the door unlocked and Charlie inside with a bunch of kids all nicely dressed and playing in the game room. She figured they must have been waiting for their Sunday school classes to begin. She smiled at Charlie who nodded in her direction as she made her way past the hordes of teens and into her office. She slid inside carefully and closed the door behind her. It was instantly much quieter than it had been in the hallway although the occasional teenage girl shriek was clearly audible through the closed door. She turned expecting to go to her desk when she noticed a girl sitting in a chair on the opposite side of her office. Annabelle, stunned, just stared at the girl and watched her, compact in hand, applying some bright red lipstick.

"Pictures last longer you know." The girl said in a sassy tone.

"Personal offices are also off limits to students when an adult isn't inside" Annabelle sassed back. She was impressed that she hadn't lost any level of sass over the years, but equally unimpressed of how much she sounded like her mother. Groan! She made a mental note to watch some MTV when she got home in the hopes of reverse aging.

"I'm new here. Plus, rules aren't really my thing." The girl stated matter-of-factly. "Are you going to tell me to leave?" The girl asked.

"If I did, would you?" Annabelle asked already knowing the answer.

"Probably not" the girl stated.

"Then, I guess you're staying." Annabelle said noticing the sound of defeat in her own voice.

The girl had put away the compact and was eyeing Annabelle suspiciously. Annabelle determined the girl must be sizing her up, so she did the same thing. The girl looked clean and seemed to obviously care about her appearance. She wore a short white dress with leggings and combat boots. Anna thought the combat boots really matched her style as well as the bright pink in her hair. Annabelle could tell the girl was new, and she was probably having a very hard time fitting in with the people in this small town. She knew they didn't take change well, and she could see that this girl would scare the pants right off the women in this town. The girl must have already sized up the town as well, because she fixed her big green eyes on Annabelle and announced, "You're different."

"What?" Annabelle asked thinking she had heard the girl wrong.

"I said you're different. You aren't like them. You're full of life and experience. I'm Rayne." She said as she held out her hand. "Rayne Culpepper"

"It's nice to meet you Rayne. I'm Annabelle." Annabelle said extending her hand towards Rayne.

Rayne took Annabelle's hand, and they shook. Rayne seemed satisfied at that point, so she pushed back further into the chair and pulling out a book to read. Annabelle could see the bookmark dangling from the middle of the book where Rayne opened it. She couldn't read the title but judging back the shirtless long-haired man on the front and the very chesty half clothed woman, she could guess what it was about.

"Let me know if you need help finding your class when Sunday School starts. I'm sure I can find someone to help you find it."

Rayne lowered the book a little and let her eyes peer at Annabelle over the top. "I'm not going to Sunday School, so you don't have to worry about me."

"Oh" Annabelle said trying to be precise with her words and not sound like her mother. "Are you nervous?"

"No, I just don't want to go. I'm not into all this God stuff. He hasn't done anything for me, so I don't want to be dragged along on all of my mother's religious outings. This will be a regular thing for a while, then my mother will realize it isn't working, grow tired of it, and I'll be out of your hair. Same story different town. Is that enough of my life story to occupy your small-town need for some drama?" Rayne said with the sassiness in full force.

"I will have you know that I have been away from here pursuing my big city dreams for 3 years. I am not one of those small-town type girls."

"So, you failed?"

"Excuse me?" Annabelle said noticing she was starting to sound less like her mother and more like a broken record.

"You went off to the big city for 3 years, but somehow you ended up back here. All signs point to failure. Your dreams didn't pan out, things didn't work out, there was a job shortage, blah blah blah. No matter what you call it, it still means the same thing, failure."

"Actually, my father had a heart attack, and he is in the hospital right now. I came back to help my mother take care of him." Annabelle said. She realized it wasn't entirely true, but there was some truth sprinkled here and there throughout her answer. It was enough to satisfy her.

"Oh. I'm sorry" Rayne said backing down a little. "My dad left us when I was young, so I only know what it's like to be without a father."

"Yeah, what's that like?"

"It sucks, but you take the hand life deals you, and you do what you have to do to get by. I wouldn't want someone hanging around and spending time with me, because they think they *have* to. I want someone to do all of those things because they *want* to."

"The grass isn't always greener you know. My dad was always around and always doing stuff with me, but it was only stuff that had to do with soccer. He was just being involved in things that would help perpetuate his dreams for me. It was never about anything I wanted or cared about. Always what he wanted."

"My mom barely notices I exist, so I don't know what it would be like to have someone help me plan out a life and help me make goals happen."

As soon as she said it, Annabelle realized how different they really were. Annabelle had been brought up being constantly doted on and given so much attention it had actually started making her feel smothered. Rayne, however, had grown up invisible, and without knowing it, she had created a persona that forced the world to see her. Anna thought about how Rayne had sounded when she described being invisible. It was as if she hated it, but here she was shut behind a door forcing herself to be invisible. Annabelle wondered if it was easier for Rayne to be invisible, because that's all she'd known. There was a comfort in it somehow. She glanced above Rayne's head and re-read the verse on the wall about how The Lord was only concerned with what was on the inside of a person and not the outside like people were. She realized how true it actually was. She was seeing Rayne a whole different way than she had when she'd first met her. When they'd first met, she thought she was some spoiled punk kid. Now, though, she could see Rayne was just a girl trapped between the darkness and the light much like herself. Leaving the comfort of the darkness and stepping into the light where everyone can see the real, true you is a very scary thing to do. Annabelle was glad she had met this girl, and she hoped she would be back again, so she could gain some more insight into her world.

Rayne stayed in Annabelle's office hidden behind the door for the entirety of Sunday school and church that morning. She and Annabelle had made light conversation, but mostly Annabelle worked while Rayne read her book in the chair. Annabelle could tell church was over, because the rec room filled with the sounds of voices and teenage presence. Rayne must have sensed it was time to head out of the room and wait to be picked up. Annabelle stood to walk with her, and she saw Rayne look back, see this and smile. The two of them got to the door, and Annabelle opened it. On the other side of the door a little way down the hallway. Annabelle could see Charlie trapped in conversation with a much older, trying to look much younger woman. The woman's hair was styled, her dress was short and low cut, her heels were entirely too tall, and she was playing with the necklace around her cleavage in an all too enticing way. Annabelle heard a sigh and turned to see Rayne staring at the scene with a blaze set behind her eyes. She was staring at the woman while anger radiated from her in waves. At first, Annabelle wasn't sure where this sudden change in emotion had come from until she looked intensely enough at the woman to notice some of her features matched Rayne's features. Once she took that bit of information along with Rayne's animosity towards the situation, she realized this woman was Rayne's mother.

Annabelle could think back to numerous times in her life when her mother had completely embarrassed her in public, in front of her friends, in front of boyfriends, etc. She remembered going to the ice cream parlor with her mother after her first breakup thinking it was sweet that her mother had invited her. Then, from the time they arrived until the time they left, her mother spent the entire time telling everyone who would listen that her baby, Annabelle, had just been dumped. Annabelle remembered how horrible it felt to know that her misery was out on display for anyone and everyone to see it. She looked over at Rayne and realized that anything her mother had put her through was nothing compared to the embarrassment Rayne's mother had most likely unleashed on her.

Annabelle knew she had to do something to help Rayne and stop her mother from making a spectacle of the both of them. In the back of her mind, she also remembered promising Charlie she would keep the women away from him as well. This woman was more cougar than casserole brigade, Annabelle doubted the woman could even cook anything that didn't come from a box, but a promise was still a promise. She gave Rayne a promising look and walked over to where her mother and Charlie were standing. She put on her best cheery, southern smile, and she extended her hand.

"Well, hey there! I don't believe we've met. I'm Annabelle. I see you've already met my partner in crime Pastor Cochran."

"Yes, I have had the lovely pleasure of making his acquaintance." The woman said without taking her eyes from Charlie's.

"I'm sorry. I think I must've missed your name." Annabelle said sweetly like she genuinely thought she hadn't heard the woman say her name.

"It's Gayle. Gayle Martin." She said obviously annoyed by Annabelle's interruptions.

"Gayle. What a beautiful name. What do we owe the pleasure of your visit down here today?"

"I'm just here to pick up my daughter, Rayne, and to talk to the lovely pastor here about the programs offered for teens."

"Oh. I had the pleasure of meeting Rayne today. She is such a lovely girl!" Annabelle said actually genuine this time.

"Lovely and troubled" Gayle stated. "That's actually something else I wanted to talk to you about pastor. I was wondering if you ever have counseling appointments…"

"Yes, Rayne is welcome here anytime she'd like. Whenever she feels she needs to talk, she can come on by." Charlie said with a smile. Annabelle knew he meant every word, so she smiled at Gayle and then at Rayne who still hadn't gotten up the courage to cross the room and be seen in association with her mother.

"No, I meant counseling for the parents. Do you ever counsel parents with troubled teens to give advice or equip us to deal with them?"

"You know, that is something Pastor Maxwell would offer. Pastor Cochran here mostly deals with the youth and pre-marital counseling. Everything outside of those realms is Pastor Maxwell's territory." Annabelle said smiling again. Annabelle gave a sympathetic look towards Rayne, and the girl mouthed a 'thank you' in her direction. Annabelle noticed the expression on Gayle's face didn't resemble one of backing down anytime soon. Annabelle had one more trick up her sleeve. "Hunny, will you be a dear and go grab my purse and jacket from the office. We really need to get going, so we can stop by and meet my parents for lunch." Annabelle made sure to give Charlie enough eye contact for him to be sure she was talking to him.

"Of course." He said with a smile as he disappeared down the hallway, past Rayne, and into Annabelle's office.

"I'll walk y'all out. He has to turn out the lights and lock up anyway, so heading outside is definitely better."

"Fine" Gayle said with still at least an ounce of determination in her voice. Luckily, she picked up on the hint, and she gestured to Rayne for the girl to follow them out the front door.

"Rayne really is a lovely girl, and I really hope she will be back." Annabelle said her smile still big and friendly.

"Well, we certainly will be back for one reason or another. I'm sure. There's some definite potential in this place." Gayle said, and Annabelle couldn't help but notice she looked at Charlie as she said it.

"Well, y'all have a great rest of your Sunday. It was nice meeting you Rayne." Annabelle said. Rayne mouthed another thank you, and she looked genuinely happy for everything Annabelle had done.

When the car pulled away, Charlie came up beside Annabelle, and it was his turn to thank her.

"That woman caught me completely by surprise. I have no idea what she wanted. At first, she was inquiring after her daughter, then she was hanging onto my every word and complementing everything I said and did. It was weird. It was like she had rehearsed it."

"I don't think this was her first time doing that. From the looks her daughter was giving her, Rayne has seen this charade play out multiple times before. I wouldn't be surprised if this has something to do with the reason they just moved here and left their last place."

"Really, you think it's that serious?" Charlie asked completely shocked.

"Yes, one woman like that can do a lot of damage if given the right attention and resources. She's definitely a pro which means, she's done this before, and it's worked. We need to watch her."

"And pray for her daughter. What's her name? Rayne?"

"Yes, Rayne." Annabelle said not really sure how praying for the girl would help this situation. What the girl really needed was to get away from her mother. Then, she wouldn't have to deal with her mother's games and antics. That's what would really help her, not a silly thing like prayer. Annabelle thought about telling Charlie this, but she knew it was no use. He would only disagree which she would expect from him. She decided to let it go.

As she got into her car to go by the hospital, to check on her mother, not see her father, she was suddenly struck with her realization from earlier about being invisible vs being seen. Rayne was invisible, because her mother made her that way. Her mother paraded herself around a room in a way where she knew she would be clearly visible to everyone, and she made herself visible to everyone who tried not to notice. Annabelle was different, she wanted to be noticed only subtly and in the right places. Her mother was completely different than Gayle too. Annabelle's mother had a grace to her, and a spark that was noticeable when she was in a room, but it was in a subtle, not in your face kind of way. Annabelle was suddenly very appreciative and thankful for this. She didn't know how she would've turned out if she'd had a mother like Gayle. Annabelle made a mental note to remember to thank her mother for the little things she'd done to help make her life exciting in all the right ways.

Ch.15

Before heading to the hospital, Charlie decided it would be a great time to pray for Rayne. After what he had witnessed from her mother, he realized she probably needed a lot more than she was verbalizing. He saw Annabelle taking some time in her car as well, so he decided it would be the perfect time to get in a quick prayer.

"God, thank you so much for bringing Rayne to the church this morning. I know we can help her with her needs and guide her to you, so she can get help with her spiritual needs. Thank you for placing Annabelle in the right place, God. Rayne really seemed to connect with her. I could tell the two of them are already forming a bond, and I'm seeing how you have a plan already in motion to save them both. I know we don't always see your plan or even notice the pieces, and I know from experience how hard it is to trust your plan without being able to see it, but I do want to take a moment to tell you how truly happy I am that you believe in us, and you keep pursuing our hearts even though we don't always acknowledge it, God. You never give up on us, and I cannot wait to share your love and goodness with Rayne, Lord. I am so happy to be a piece of the puzzle that will help guide her to you. I know Annabelle will have a big part to play in this, Lord. I ask that you help guide her on this path to bring someone closer to you. Give her the strength and understanding to be able to take on this task and see it through to the end. She has a much bigger role to play than she will ever realize. I can't wait to see all the glorious and wonderful things you have planned. It's in your precious, holy name I pray. Amen."

< < > >

Jill thought she would feel more relaxed after texting Jason back that morning and telling him that she wouldn't be turning herself in for cheating. She thought that would be the end to all her troubles. Instead, it had only caused new troubles. Jason had told her turning herself in would be an easy way out of the ordeal, so she should take that route. He had explained if she didn't turn herself in, an investigation could be held which could reveal everything. He told her it would be much worse to be caught than to turn yourself in, but Jill decided to take her chances. With everything going on at home, she couldn't be back on campus to deal with everything that would come from turning herself in.

Once again, Jill found herself in her father's hospital room worried and anxious about so many things. Why was he acting like he had no idea about anything that had happened? It was driving her crazy. She had remembered his expression when he'd first woken up, and she had thought there was something behind it. Now, she wasn't sure. He didn't carry on a conversation or anything with her, but he did manage to speak to her a little. Jill had been so afraid of what he might say, she hadn't allowed herself to be alone with him. Instead, she had either helped her mother do things, or she had been the one to go out and retrieve supplies or whatever they needed. Jill had decided that morning that she couldn't take the stress coming at her from both sides anymore. It was too much. She had reached the point where she felt she might explode, so she had done what she thought she had to do to eliminate one of the obstacles from her life.

Jill kept telling herself Jason would calm down. She knew he was upset, but he would live. She had been texting him all morning, but she hadn't received a single reply from him since she had broken the news to him. Jill assumed he was going to be giving her the silent treatment until he calmed down. He was always the one telling her she needed to be more mature and able to handle more situations and things in their relationship, but she wasn't the one who went on a silent pout fest whenever something didn't go her way. She felt an urge to point it out to him right now, but she decided against it since he was already so angry. "There's no point in poking the bear" she thought to herself with a laugh.

Jill felt a presence, and she looked up to see Annabelle in the doorway. She knew Annabelle wouldn't actually come into the room. After the massive blowup Annabelle and her father had the first day he had woken up, she stopped by to see how she could help, but she never entered the room. Jill got up and walked out of the room. Annabelle was leaned against the wall waiting on her to emerge from the open doorway.

"Hey" Jill said

"Hey" Annabelle replied cheerfully. "Is mom in there? I was thinking the 3 of us could go grab some lunch and catch up."

"Yeah, she's here, but you know she won't leave dad alone."

"Oh, that's not a problem. I brought back up." Annabelle said as she turned to look behind her, and down the hallway where Charlie was headed their way.

"Oh, I see. You came prepared."

"Yeah, I saved him from this cougar at church. He owes me one. It's the least he can do." Annabelle said laughing as she thought back to the incident with Gayle.

"Cougar? I've got to hear about this." Jill said with a smile. "Let me go get mom and see if I can convince her."

When Jill went back into the room, she seemed to have a little more zing in her step. Annabelle was glad. Jill had been so down lately, and after reading that text this morning, she wasn't sure what version of Jill to expect today. Annabelle wanted so badly to figure out what was going on with her sister, but it was such a delicate line. She really wanted Jill to tell her on her own, but she was starting to think that wasn't going to happen. Annabelle had been back a week, and she and Jill's relationship had gone from somewhat nonexistent except for a few phone calls here and there to being cordial. She felt like they were working on having a relationship, and she was hoping Jill felt the same way. She didn't want to push too hard and mess any of that up.

Jill emerged with her arm linked with her mothers. Annabelle thought that was a good sign along with the fact they both carried purses. Both things pointed towards success. Annabelle smiled as she gave her mom a hug. While her morning of watching Gayle try in every way to come onto Charlie had been amusing, it had also really taught her to appreciate her mother that much more. On the drive over to the hospital, she had really begun to think about and list off all the things her mother did for them on a daily basis, and all the success in their lives she had been responsible for. The woman definitely didn't get enough credit. Annabelle was hoping with this lunch and the time they would have together, they could bridge some gaps and form some new bonds over the ones that had been severed years ago by her own choices.

They rode the elevator down to the hospital cafeteria mostly in silence. Their mother had agreed to go to lunch, but she was adamant about the fact she would not be leaving the hospital to do it. She had been right that the hospital had pretty good food options, but Annabelle thought her not wanting to leave the hospital was a bit much. Her father's doctor had been saying he was healing nicely after his surgery to fix some problems with his heart. They were aware that it was only a matter of time before he would be coming home. As far as Annabelle was concerned, that meant they were in the clear. Instead of sitting around and waiting for possible death, now they would be waiting for life. She just hoped her father was ready to go back to life and make some of the changes the doctor had talked about with regards to his eating and managing his stress levels. Those were two things that Annabelle knew would take all of them working together to accomplish.

When they stepped into the cafeteria, the smells were the first things Jill noticed. She glanced around and noticed the cafeteria had 4 stations set up, and each was serving a different style of food. There was a station serving hamburgers and French fries and pizza, the next serving southern home cooked fried chicken, pot roast, mashed potatoes, green beans, macaroni and cheese, fried okra, and biscuits, the third station had oriental style foods like big containers of ramen or chicken, noodles, and vegetables, and the final station had soups and sandwiches. Jill looked at each of them, and they agreed whoever got their food first would locate a booth and determine where they would sit. Jill headed off towards the Southern comforts section to retrieve some of the delicious smelling fried chicken with all the fixins, and she saw her mom head over to the sandwiches and soup section. Jill had known that was coming. Her mother was very predictable. Annabelle was the live wire, and everyone knew it.

Annabelle looked around at all of the options as she attempted to let her nose do the choosing. She settled on the oriental station. The smells reminded her of the things she had been able to get late at night in the city. As she passed the Southern Comforts station, the smell of fried chicken wafted out and her memories instantly turned to Sunday afternoon lunches. After church her father would drive through the Wings and Things parking lot and get a big bucket of fried chicken, mashed potatoes, green beans, biscuits, and gravy. As much as Annabelle loved reliving the memories, she knew she couldn't go down that road right now. She had good memories and bad memories all swirled together when it came to her childhood.

Once everyone had converged at a table in the corner, the awkwardness began to grow. The only sounds were of plastic being taken off of their utensils, paper being ripped from straws, and food being cut. Marianne finally broke the silence with a question that Annabelle herself had been dying to ask.

"Jill, how is school going?"

"Fine." Jill said looking up with a shocked expression like she had been caught.

"When are you going to have to head back?" Annabelle asked curious as to what Jill's response would be.

"Oh, you know whenever. My teachers have e-mailed me what I need to stay caught up, and they've been very understanding with the situation. They are okay with me staying as long as I need to." Jill said hesitantly without very much confidence to back it up.

"Well, you know dad is going to be going home soon, so I guess you could be heading back after that." Annabelle said pushing just enough to see how her sister would react.

"I don't know. Mom will probably need help with him once he comes home, so I'm thinking of prolonging my visit and just seeing how it pans out. I might not even go back until the new semester begins, or I might take next semester off and stay here and help. Then there's always the option of transferring somewhere closer to home." Jill said in a tone that was very rushed.

"Semester off? Transfer? Honey, thank you so much for caring that much about your father and me to do that, but it's really not necessary. We are going to be fine. I promise. I would feel much better knowing you are at school focused on getting an education." Their mother said in a sweet voice.

It took everything Annabelle had not to laugh. Jill was playing into her father's illness and trying to use that as her scapegoat for whatever was going on, and their mother just assumed it was because Jill loved and cared for them so much. After the lack of parenting Annabelle had witnessed earlier that morning, she could not just sit by and watch her mother be taken advantage of even if it was by her sister. When their mother excused herself from the table, so she could go and refill her drink, Annabelle took the opportunity to let her little sister know exactly what she thought.

"So, you're really thinking about staying?" Annabelle questioned.

"Yes. There's a lot of benefit to it." Jill said taking a sip of her drink.

"Helping mom and dad. Right?"

"That's right."

"So, this wouldn't help you in anyway? It would be a completely selfless act?"

"Annabelle, what is going on? I feel like you're interrogating me." Jill said looking helplessly at her sister.

Annabelle saw the helplessness in Jill's expression, and for a moment she forgot the severity of what they were discussing. She forgot how this was affecting her baby sister. For a moment, Annabelle forgot everything except her desire to be the sister she'd never been. All she wanted to do was take Jill away from all the bad and protect her from everything. She had forgotten for a moment, but then it started coming back to her. She started realizing what she was doing was for Jill's own good, and it was because she cared about her. Annabelle realized that for the first time in a long time, she truly did care about Jill, and she did want to help and protect her. She just needed to know what she was protecting her from. She took a calming breath, and then she spoke the words she knew would inevitably pop this happy bubble of safety she'd created just moments ago.

"I saw the text. The one from Jason."

"What text?"

"The one about turning yourself in for cheating. I saw it on your phone this morning."

"You were going through my phone?" Jill said angrily. "You had no right! That's my property. You can't just go through other people's things!"

Annabelle had a sudden flashback to childhood when she had taken one of the Barbies Jill had gotten for Christmas. She remembered having a similar exchange with her sister then. Jill was shouting "Mine. Mine. Give it back!" While Annabelle was holding it over her head just out of her reach. Annabelle couldn't help but note the irony in the similarities between one of their adult and childhood exchanges. Annabelle set her gaze straight on Jill and gave her the most serious look she could muster before speaking.

"I wasn't going through your phone. I was in your room borrowing clothes for church this morning when your phone went off, and I glanced at it. That's it."

"You still had no right to look at it or read anything on it." Jill said still irritated, but her voice a little calmer.

"Jill, please tell me if you're in trouble. I really want to help you."

"I'm fine. Everything is fine. Let's just forget about it and move on."

"We can't move on and forget that you cheated in a class and might get kicked out of school!"

"Yes, we can!"

"No! Please let me help you!"

"I don't need anyone's help, and I definitely don't need *yours.*"

"What's that supposed to mean?" Annabelle asked taken aback.

"It means that I know how much you'd love for someone else to screw up, so they can have all the negative attention on them and not on you."

"Wow! I can't believe you'd think that about me. I guess I have been a really crappy sister to you. Which I take full responsibility for. I want to help you out of this mess you're in. I don't want to see your future get messed up in all of this. I want your life to be happy and good, because you're my sister, and I love you. I don't want you to have mistakes and troubles in your life."

Jill looked at Annabelle with an expression that matched the shock Annabelle felt. She knew her feelings toward her sister had been changing recently as they had been spending more and more time together, but she hadn't realized she would end up vocalizing them like that. In fact, Annabelle was incredibly surprised to hear them come out of her own mouth. She was happy, and she did truly feel that way, but she hadn't ever said that out loud before. Her family never said they loved each other, so saying "I love you" to someone in her family was such a foreign concept to her. Annabelle knew it must have taken Jill aback, because it took her awhile to say anything else. When she finally spoke, her tone was much calmer and lighter than before.

"Annabelle, I don't need your help. There is nothing going on. Everything is fine."

"What do you mean everything is fine? I saw the text. Stop lying to yourself and to me and just admit you need help!" Annabelle said as she gave her sister a frustrated look.

"Annabelle, everything is fine!" She said again with hardness to her voice that was saying the conversation was over.

"How can you even say that?" Annabelle snapped back ready to continue the conversation no matter how upset Jill was.

"Because I didn't cheat!"

"You didn't cheat?" Annabelle said more from thinking out loud than actually asking the question.

"No, I didn't cheat at school, on games, or on my boyfriend. I've never cheated on anything in my life! Why, would that change now?" Jill said as she stood up with her gaze fixed on Annabelle. Then, after hesitating for a moment, Jill left the cafeteria without every looking back.

Annabelle was still stunned when her mother returned. Annabelle didn't want to alarm her mother after all the stress she'd been under, and she really wasn't sure exactly what had just happened. She decided it was best not to tell her mother anything until she actually had something to tell her. Annabelle covered for Jill by telling their mother she had left to go to the restroom and then go check on their father. Annabelle just hoped she would be in the room when they went back upstairs. As her mother continued talking, she realized she wasn't paying attention. Instead, she was thinking about all the things she could have and should have said to her sister. For instance, she could have asked her about what was going on without jumping all over her and backing her into a corner. She also could have followed the innocent until proven guilty method. Why had she been so quick to think her sister was capable of something like that? Was Jill right about her? Was Annabelle on a mission to prove her sister wasn't the goody two shoes everyone thought she was? If Jill was as innocent as she claimed to be, why did she get so fired up about the questions?

Jill pushed the bathroom door open with such force that it swung violently inward and hit the bathroom wall. She was so mad at herself, Annabelle, and the entire situation. How could she have reacted so heatedly and allowed herself to become that person she'd always hated? She walked over to the sink, balled up her fist and brought it down hard onto the counter. She grabbed the counter to brace herself and stared hard into the mirror. She took a few deep breaths and removed her hands from the counter. She rubbed them across her eyes as she tried to focus her thoughts.

"What would she tell Annabelle?" Jill wondered. She knew Annabelle wouldn't back off unless she got an answer, but Jill wasn't ready to give her the real answer. She wasn't ready to tell anyone the truth yet. Jill needed something, someone. She needed to go and see Jason and talk everything through and figure out this whole mess. She had no idea what she would tell her mom, but she knew she had to go, so she left the bathroom and thanked God she had the keys to her car in her purse. Annabelle had her mom's car keys, so she would let them figure out what everyone was doing tonight. Without another word to anyone, she walked out of the hospital, got into her car and started the long drive back to Jason.

Ch. 16

When Charlie saw Annabelle and her mother coming down the hallway without Jill, he saw the pink in Annabelle's cheeks and realized it wasn't a good sign. It was clear she had been upset with someone, and since Jill wasn't with them, he could only assume it was Jill she had fought with. As David grew quiet and focused his attention on the baseball game on tv, Charlie took a quick moment to pray.

"God, I have no idea what has just happened, but I am trusting it to be all in your plan. Please protect Jill wherever she has gone. Please let her see through the lies and deceptions of the enemy and realize her family does care about her. Please let her listen to you instead of her heart. You have told us the heart can be deceptive, and I hope she remembers that today. Please also protect Annabelle. Don't let her cover herself in guilt over anything that happens as a result of whatever happened between them tonight. I know guilt is a powerful thing, and it can drag you down to some pretty low depths, God. I don't want to see that happen to Annabelle or anyone in her family. I don't want anyone to have to go through what I went through. Please protect them from those things, God. It's in your precious, holy name I pray. Amen."

< < > >

When Annabelle and her mother returned to her father's room, she wasn't surprised to see that Jill hadn't made it back. She knew something was going on with Jill, and she had a feeling it wasn't good. She wished she could just get her sister to open up, but after what had happened during lunch, she knew it was going to take more time. Annabelle smiled a bit noting to herself that while she was lacking in certain areas, she definitely had an abundance of time. She had known it would take her awhile to figure out what her next course of action would be. She knew after being on her own the past few years that being impulsive could seem good at the time, but there would always be flaws in the plan waiting to reveal themselves. It was best that she takes her time and really plan out her next move.

Annabelle saw her father look away from his conversation with Charlie to glance her way as she and her mother came in view. Annabelle assumed her mother had caught his attention, but she was surprised to see his gaze had fallen on her. She didn't know how to feel about this. Would be erupt on her again, or would he be pleasant? She wasn't sure which would be worse. She didn't like when he was mean, but she expected it and knew how to deal with it. She would not, however, know what to do if he suddenly started acting cordial with her. Annabelle knew if she wanted to rebuild their relationship, it would have to start at cordial, but she still wasn't entirely convinced that a relationship with her father was necessary for her success in life.

Charlie turned in the direction her father had been looking, and he caught her gaze as well. He motioned her over, and Annabelle felt stuck. She really didn't want to be so close to her father so soon, but everyone had seen Charlie call her over, so there was no way around it. She felt like a small child walking across the room waiting to be scolded for something she had done wrong. She felt her shoulders start to hunch, and she forced herself to straighten up and accept whatever was coming. She reached Charlie, and she felt him put his hands on her shoulders. They both knew this would be a difficult moment for her, and she felt much safer under the weight of his hands. She realized how comforting it was to have his hands there for support and comfort, and she was pleased to learn that she had started to view him as less of a boss and more of a friend. She was glad to know at least one person was on her side.

"So, I was just telling your father here about the eventful morning we had." Charlie said.

Annabelle could hear the smile in his voice, and she didn't even have to turn around to confirm.

"Are you talking about how I saved you?" Annabelle said to Charlie while still looking straight ahead at her father.

"*You* saved him? From what?" Her father asked suspiciously.

Annabelle decided not to let the sting of his apparent insinuation that *she*, the girl he thought needed saving herself, couldn't possibly save anyone else, and she pressed on with the story. "Actually, I saved him from an older woman with some questionable opinions about younger, pastoral types in the church." Annabelle said vaguely.

"What does that even mean?" Her father asked while his eyes darted between the two of them. "Was one of the elder's wives trying to tell you how to run things? They can be very set in their ways and judgmental at times." Her father said with experience. Annabelle remembered that one more than one occasion he had been schooled by the elder's wives on how to properly conduct the Lord's supper, Deacon nominations, Deacon luncheons and many other things.

"No, these opinions were less judgmental and more romantic." Anna said.

Her father let this sink in before saying, "Oh, one of these women wanted to set you up with her daughter or granddaughter? That's nothing to be ashamed about. Things like that happen all the time. You just politely decline and then avoid that person for as long as humanly possible until you are happily married. Then, she will give up."

"That's great advice, and I'm sure in the context of the situation in which you are giving it, it probably would work really well." Charlie started to say, "But, this woman wasn't going to give up until she had what she wanted. Which was me. For herself." Charlie added very matter-of-factly.

The room was silent as everyone took in this new bit of information. Then, without warning, a loud belly laugh sounded from the hospital bed. Annabelle looked at his father, and she saw he was really, genuinely laughing. The next thing she knew, Charlie was laughing. She could feel his hands moving on her shoulders to the rhythm of his laughter. Then, her mother started laughing, and before she knew it, she was laughing too. It had been so long since they had all been under one roof and happy, let alone laughing together about something. Annabelle searched her mind for the last time this type of situation had occurred, but it must have been so long ago that she couldn't even remember it. She looked at each of her family members and studied their faces in this moment. This is how she wanted to remember everyone. When she left again, she wanted to take this memory with her and cherish it always.

"I'm glad to see everyone is in such a great mood." The doctor said as he entered the room. "I've gotten the test results back, and it looks like everything is good. That means you will be heading home tomorrow as long as nothing changes." He finished with a big grin.

Annabelle turned to look at her father, and she saw a mixture of happiness and fear wash over his face. The fear seemed to subside as happiness took over, so she assumed he was just apprehensive about what had put him here in the first place. Until her mother spoke up.

"Are you sure he should go home so soon? We really haven't been here very long, and after everything that happened, I'm not sure we're ready."

"Mrs. Ward…"

"Call me Marianne." She said interrupting him.

"Okay. Marianne, we had done everything here that we can do. We've run tests and even done surgery to make corrections. Now, all that is left is that Mr. Ward…"

"Call me David please, doc."

"Okay. Now all that is left is that David will have to rest and begin to start living life again, slowly at first. Those are things that can be done at home and don't require medical attention. Therefore, we will be sending you home, where you can be nice and comfortable."

Annabelle glanced at her mother and saw the panicked expression on her face. She knew the double life her mother had been leading, life in the hospital and life outside of the hospital, had to be extremely stressful. She thought her mother would have been excited and relieved to hear this news, but all Annabelle saw in her eyes was fear and unhappiness. It was so opposite of what she had just seen that it scared her. She had never seen her mother unpolished and shaken and seeing her mother like that now scared her more than she was willing to admit. Maybe it was a good thing she was here to help out since things were apparently about to get rough.

After the news of David's homecoming had worn off, everyone started to get restless as the inevitable waiting period set in. Discharge paperwork would have to be processed and brought in for signatures, David would have to be detached from his many tubes and machines, and he would be getting up from the hospital bed to shower, dress, and not return to it. When they walked out of the hospital in the morning, the newness would really set in. Annabelle was ready to get home and try to get some things taken care of to make sure her father's homecoming was as stress free as possible on their family. She knew she and her father weren't in a great place, but in the laughter that had taken place before, she remembered what it felt like when the tension was lifted, and she surprised herself by realizing how much she wanted to experience that again.

Charlie was making his goodbyes. He hugged Marianne and shook David's hand. He glanced over at Annabelle and noticed she had softened since they had been here. He was happy to see the change in her, small as it was. He smiled to himself as he noted how much better she wore the relaxed expression than the overly confident one she usually wore. He went over, hands in his pockets, and nudged her shoulder, and when she turned to look at him, he asked if she needed a ride home. She nodded, and the two of them finished their goodbyes and left the room. She wanted to leave her mother with the car in case she needed to leave and get anything.

Annabelle was silent in the elevator and the entire walk to the car still thinking about her mother's panicked expression while she tried again and again to get Jill on the phone to find out where she'd gone. She had been relieved when Charlie asked her if she'd like a ride back to her house. She wanted nothing more than to get out of that room and get some time to think. Out of the corner of her eye, she could see Charlie glancing at her. She knew he had noticed how quiet she had been. He obviously wanted to ask her, but he wasn't sure how he would be received. When they got into the car, she asked him if they could stop at a grocery store on their way home, so they could pick up some essentials for the house. Her father had doctor's orders for a diet change, and she didn't want her mother to be severely overwhelmed trying to get the bad food out and the good food in.

After they were finished at the store and back in the car traveling home, Annabelle realized she'd done enough thinking and mulling over what had happened. It was time to stop thinking about it. Honestly, she realized she didn't even know if there was an *it*, or if she was just paranoid. Either way, she had to find out.

"So that was weird back there." Annabelle exclaimed realizing a little too late that Jill had finally picked up the phone while she had been talking to Charlie and just letting the phone ring in her ear. Now, she was in a conversation with both of them, one in person and one on the phone. She put Jill on speaker, so the conversation could continue as a conversation between the three of them.

"What was?" Charlie said glancing over at her for a brief second.

"You know, the way my mom and dad were acting when the doctor said dad could come home in the morning. I don't think I've ever seen my mother look so terrified about anything in her life."

"She was probably just scared of having to do it all alone without any doctors." Charlie said trying to be reassuring. He did his best to try, but to Annabelle, it wasn't reassuring at all. Instead, it was making her wonder if she was in fact reading into something that wasn't there. She thought about this for a minute and decided that maybe it was the simple fact that Charlie really didn't know her mother all that well.

"No, I don't think that's it. I promise you if you had known my mom for as long as I have. You'd understand and be able to see what I'm talking about." Annabelle said confidently.

"Well, I've known her my whole life, and I have to agree with Charlie. I don't think it was anything more than a simple case of fear. I can't blame her. I'd be panicking in that situation too." Jill said.

"Jill, no offense, but I'm older, so I've known mom longer than you have. I've always had a good relationship with her, and I've never seen her back away from a challenge like that. Usually, she welcomes challenges and hurls herself at them."

Jill let these words sink in, and she tried to tell herself to stay cool and not get upset at Annabelle's accusations that she just didn't have a good relationship with their mother. Jill truly, honestly tried, but when she started speaking, she realized there was a sharpness in her tone that she hadn't meant to be there.

"That's actually not true."

"What's not true?" Annabelle said defensively.

"That you've known mom longer than I have. It isn't true."

"Well, considering that I'm older than you, I think that would prove that it has to be true."

"Well, it would be true, if you'd stayed close and kept in touch after high school, but those few years you were gone was enough to bridge the gap."

"Excuse me?" Annabelle said completely thrown off guard.

Jill could sense the anger from Annabelle. It was so palpable, she could feel it through the phone conversation, and she thought about backing down and giving her some time, but then she thought about all the times she'd had to play second fiddle to whatever Annabelle was doing. That's when she realized how tired she'd gotten of always being in Annabelle's shadow, and how wonderful it had been the past few years for all the attention to be on her. That's when she knew she couldn't and wouldn't back down, not this time.

"The years you missed while you were gone 'finding yourself' or whatever you want to call it. Not having you around allowed me to get closer to mom than you will ever be. Mom and Dad are different than they were before you left. You can't see that for some reason, but they've changed. Actually, everyone has changed except for you."

"Wait, is this about that conversation we had at lunch. Are you still mad about that? Is that where this is all coming from?" Annabelle said with anger still boiling inside of her.

The car was pulling into the driveway when Jill said "first of all, nothing that came up at lunch was any of your business, but how you would even know that. You're the same selfish girl you've always been. Everything has to always be about you, and you have to know about everything. I have my own life without you, and I love it. In fact, I'm living my life right now. I'm on my way to see Jason right now, and I don't care what you think about it. I cannot wait for you to be out of my life again. Don't even try to argue. We both know how you are. We both know when things get too real for you, you'll just take off again." Jill abruptly hung up as the last words hit Annabelle like a bullet in the chest and knocked the breath out of her.

"What the heck was that?" She asked looking around the car while her right hand was in the center of her chest.

"I think that was your sister letting go of some things."

"Couldn't she have picked a better time than now to do that."

"Maybe, but this is the one she chose, so you'll have to live with that."

Annabelle turned sharply and her glare from a few moments before landed on him. "What if I don't want to?"

"I really don't see how you have much of a choice." Charlie said, "It really seems to me the only things you can do are move on and pray."

"Oh my gosh! Are we back to the praying thing again? I am so tired of you shoving prayer down my throat. I get that it's your thing, but it isn't mine."

"It could be if you would just…"

"Listen." Annabelle said while her hand left her chest and went out towards him to indicate that he was supposed to stop and listen. "When I was young, I prayed all the time, and it never did anything, so when I got older, I realized I was in charge of how my life turned out and making my own decisions. That's when I took over, and I've been making my own choices and living life my way ever since."

"And how's that working out for ya?" Charlie asked with a grin. He meant it to come off as playful, but Annabelle didn't look amused.

"I'd say it's going quite well. Obviously, there have been some bumps in the road…"

"Bumps in the road? You call finding yourself homeless and having to come home with your tail between your legs and move back in with your parents, who you have a strained relationship with, while you work 9-5 at a job that you're obviously uncomfortable showing up to everyday a bump in the road? I think it's pretty obvious that you need help, and the best source of help you can get is going to come from God. You need to get off your high horse and realize you're not perfect, and you need some help."

"I don't need any help. Maybe if you'd stop walking around judging and trying to fix everyone, you'd be able to ask God why it is that every time you look at a person you see them as broken and an object that needs fixing. We are just people trying to make it through this life with as few bumps, bruises, and scars as we can. Ask God why your job is to make everyone's life more difficult."

Annabelle said this as she got out of the car and moved to the trunk to get the grocery bags. She wasn't sure that Charlie would open the trunk, but after she smacked it twice, he realized she was waiting and popped it for her. She retrieved the bags quickly and angrily and went inside to put the new groceries away. On her way inside, she was surprised to find that she did say a prayer. She prayed with all of her heart that she wouldn't hear from her sister for the rest of the night. She concluded later that

God must have really felt bad for her, because she hadn't heard from Jill again before she went to bed. It wasn't extremely profound and earth shattering, but in a small way it was to her. For the first time in a very long time. God had actually answered one of her prayers.

< < > >

When her car turned onto University row, the street that ran parallel to the one the university was on, she turned off her music and steadied herself. This was it. This was her moment to take back all the happiness and all the things she had dreamed for her future when she was a student in one of these dorm rooms not long ago. The car stopped in front a big Antebellum home complete with the large columns in front, and she remembered her stolen moments in this house. Her cheeks burned red with some of the memories, but she assured herself the driver had no way of knowing what she was thinking. She got out of the car and grabbed her small weekend back out of the seat next to her. She smoothed out the skirt of her black dress before lifting the bag and closing the door. She waved goodbye to the driver and started walking up towards the front door. She took one last steadying breath and then rang the doorbell.

She had seen a few lights on in the house, so she wasn't surprised when she heard footsteps and the lock clicking open. As the door opened, she was surprised to see the person standing on the other side was not Jason. Instead, there was a petite girl with short brown hair, large oval wire framed glasses wearing jeans and a university t shirt and holding a book. Jill mentally noted this girl was probably only a few years older than her, more like Annabelle's age, but she was strikingly beautiful. Even with her relaxed clothing choices, it would've been hard to miss her beauty.

"Can I help you?" She said staring at Jill questioningly and making her realize she hadn't said anything.

"Oh yeah, I was actually looking for um professor Richmond. I think this might be his house. I'm one of his students." Jill said starting to think she hadn't remembered his house as well as she'd thought.

"Oh. He's not here right now, but you know he has office hour sign ups at school. It's not very common for students to come to their professor's homes. Is there something I can pass on to him?"

"It's very important, and I needed to tell him right away, so I just walked over. Who are you anyway?" Jill said feeling herself getting defensive at this woman's accusatory words.

"I'm Julie Richmond, his wife." She said matter-of-factly.

"Wife?" Jill heard herself mutter quietly as the gears in her brain started turning while she simultaneously felt like the wind had been knocked out of her. Of all the scenarios she had played over and over again in her mind, the idea that Jason was married had never been one of them. She suddenly felt a sense of panic that this just couldn't be real. "Well, it is extremely important that I speak with him, now more than ever. Do you know where he is?"

"He's at a student ethics board hearing for one of his students. What is this about?" She asked.

"He's already there and starting the process? What? I thought I had more time. Do you know which building they hold the hearing in?"

"Seriously, not another one. Listen, let me give you some free advice. I don't know if you just thought you could get away with it, but my husband double and triple checks everything. You're not the first girl to try and get away with plagiarizing your exam paper. It happens all the time with his students, so don't feel bad you got caught. When you have your hearing, just do what the girl tonight is doing. Just own up and admit to what you did. Do *not* do what the girl did last week."

"Last week?" Jill said a panic rising in her voice as the pieces started to fall into place.

"Yeah, last week that girl tried to say she didn't do it, but Jason, I mean Professor Richmond, had all the evidence, and it looked so much worse for her in the end. If she had just been honest and admitted what she'd done then it would've gone better for her, but now she's expelled."

"How many girls have gone to ethics hearings?"

"There's always at least 1 or 2 each semester. This year, including you, there's 3."

"Three! Three girls? Wow! How did he find the time? Wow!"

"Excuse me?"

"Let me start over. Hi. I'm Jill." She said sticking out her hand and trying to build up the nerve to put everything she was feeling about all she had just found out down inside of her. "Do you think we could go get a cup of coffee and just sit and talk for a minute?"

Julie looked at her skeptically for a moment and searched her face. She must have seen something there that looked genuine because she nodded quietly. She put up one finger to indicate to Jill that she needed a minute. Then, she pushed the door to and disappeared behind it. When she re-emerged only a minute later, she had her shoes on, a purse over her shoulder, and no book in sight.

The two of them walked down the street to the local coffee shop that was frequented by both faculty and students. It was not packed tonight, and they were able to order drinks and find a table easily. As they sat down and waited on their drinks to be ready, Jill was very aware of the anxiety she was feeling. She didn't know how to say all the things that Julie needed to know. There wasn't anything she was going to tell her that wouldn't shatter and upend her world, and what if Julie didn't believe her and thought she was a liar? Jill had no idea where to start or what to say, but when they're drinks arrived, she knew they couldn't just continue to sit and smile at each other the whole night. Luckily, Julie broke the ice first.

"So, what is this about? I just have to tell you, if you want to plead your case or get any sympathy for cheating, you came to the wrong person. My husband is the one who really holds your fate in his hands, so he's the one you'd have to talk to, but just know, I've never seen him excuse or go easy on anyone in the past."

"This is about your husband, but it isn't about cheating. Well, I guess it is about cheating, but not how you think."

"Okay." Julie said already sounding confused.

"So, I met your husband last semester as a student in his introduction to economics class. The class was listed as one of the courses I was required to take, and his class fit perfectly into my schedule with everything I had to take. After the first two papers, he asked if he could essentially tutor me and look over my papers and help me with them."

"So, he was helping you pass the class?" Julie asked.

"I wasn't doing bad in the class, and I was getting B's on the papers, so it was less about keeping me from failing and more about, well, I guess trying to get closer to me. I guess what I am trying to say is that he sought me out. He started saying his office was messy or being cleaned and making excuses to take our meetings outside of the office to restaurants and coffee shops like this one."

"Why would he do that? Wouldn't that have looked like something else?" Julie asked.

"I think he wasn't worried, because at that time nothing was going on, so it wouldn't have been a lie to say that if someone questioned it, and there was no evidence of anything."

"What do you mean 'at that time'?"

"Julie, what I'm trying to explain and maybe not doing the best job is that I spent most of last semester having an affair with my professor, who I honestly had no idea until I showed up at your door is your husband." Jill said and searched Julie's eyes for some kind of glimpse into what she was thinking.

"You're kidding right?" Julie said with a laugh. "Is this your cover story for cheating?"

"Julie, I didn't cheat. He is saying I did, because he doesn't want me to be able to come forward with this story, and he knows this story will come out."

"Why would he think that? Did you try to blackmail him by coming up with this lie?"

"He was afraid I would come forward, because I was afraid, I had gotten pregnant, and he knew that people would question that since I'm unmarried."

"Yeah, but you're a college student. Everyone knows that's like the perfect equation for being loose and free on the sexual front."

"Not every girl in college is like that, and I assure you I'm not."

"Well, apparently, you're sleeping with married men and professors, so what do you think that says about you?"

"Like I said before, I didn't know he was married until I met you, and yes, sleeping with my professor does make me seem loose and free with my sexuality, but I promise you, I have never done anything like this before in my life. In fact, if this came out, it would really change the opinions of everyone who knows me. I'm just as much at fault as he is for the affair, but I had nothing to do with the lying. That was all him."

"So why tell me about it?"

"I'm not going to lie. At first, I didn't know if I wanted to tell you. I could've easily walked away and not stayed to talk, and I really considered doing that."

"So, what stopped you?"

"You started talking about all of these other girls, and it really made me start thinking this isn't the first time he's done this. He has been doing this for a while and getting away with it, and I can't sit back and let this continue to happen to these young, vulnerable college students like me."

"Why would I believe this crazy story and your crazy theories? Do you have any proof?"

"I have some texts, so I can prove that we have been communicating via text. I also would be willing to bet he never has any male students who plagiarize, and I'm also thinking deep down inside you know something is going on, you just aren't sure what it is."

"Okay, so let's say this is true. Where would he have gotten the time? He is always busy with something."

"I saw him almost every day during our affair, so if he was making time for me, I'm assuming he was making time for the other girls too. I bet they have similar stories if they knew someone was willing to listen."

"Well, I'm not saying I believe you, but thank you for telling me. I will think about everything you said and see what comes of it."

Jill nodded and the two sat there for another minute sipping coffee until Julie said she had to go and excused herself. It was then that Jill realized it was over. Everything she had wanted to come back to and thought she was had waiting on her here was now all gone. She could feel her heart aching and tears stinging her eyes. She left the coffee shop and stood outside trying to decide her next step. She dug around and found her keys to her dorm room which was hers for a few more days until summer semester rolled in. She decided to go and have a good night's sleep and she could get a good meal at the dining hall the next day with the last of her money on her student account. That was as far as her exhaustion would lead her brain to go, so she walked back to her dorm room thankful everyone else was gone when she walked in, and she collapsed into her bed and fell asleep.

Ch.17

After the argument with Annabelle and finding out Jill had run away, Charlie had a restless night of sleep. He had awoken every hour throughout the night worried about both the girls for different reasons. He didn't know who Jason was or what was going on there, but it was obvious Annabelle did, and she didn't seem to like whatever the situation was. That made him nervous too, and he hated seeing the girls fight. It was completely opposite of what he had wanted and prayed for their situation. He felt guilty he had lost his temper with Annabelle, and he felt like he had failed them both now that their relationship was in such disarray. He was wallowing in his emotions when he realized nothing he was feeling from God. All of it was lies from the devil, and he needed to be leaning on God's truths at a time like this. He knew some early morning prayer time and bible reading would put him back into a good place spiritually, and he needed that right now.

"God, things are such a mess right now. Please watch over Jill. I have no idea where she has gone, but she was very angry last night and conflicted and full of emotions. I wish she wasn't making decisions in that state, but she is. Please place a hedge of protection around her and let her know you're with her. I pray she is on your path for her life and not straying, but if she is, please nudge her back onto the path you had laid out for her life. I also pray for Annabelle, God. She is hurting right now especially after last night. I know you are the God who can heal all, and I humbly ask for healing for her soul. I know she has a lot to do, and a huge role to play in the lives of others. I pray she is up for the challenge ahead of her today. It's in your holy name I pray. Amen."

< < > >

Annabelle woke early the next morning and moved around the house as quietly as she could. She didn't want to risk waking anyone and having more of what she had endured last night. It's one thing to assume people are still carrying around hurt feelings and resentment, but to actually know it exists, because you've just had it all hurled back at you is a completely different thing entirely. She dug around her closet until she found something that would pass as presentable. It was a sleeveless, white cotton knee length dress. She had gotten it to wear under her white graduation gown. She noticed a jean jacket pushed to the back of the closet and grabbed that as well. That would help with the sleeveless part. She ran a brush through her hair, grabbed her cowboy boots, and tiptoed downstairs. She grabbed a set of keys off of the holder by the door and headed to the car in the garage. She knew her mother would be headed back to the hospital to get her father which meant she would need access to her car, but Annabelle reasoned that she could be back in time to pick her mom up and give her a ride.

Annbellea had successfully avoided dealing with anyone in the house, but she knew she couldn't avoid Charlie. He would be the one she couldn't get away from. She agonized over the impending awkwardness as she drove closer and closer to it. She hoped she would arrive first, but as she pulled into the parking lot, and saw the black Jeep wrangler parked in his spot, she knew that wasn't the case. She cursed silently to herself and pulled into her spot beside him. She shifted the car into park, turned the car off, and sat staring at the building with her hands gripping the steering wheels until her knuckles were white. She was not good at confrontation. She wasn't good at the awkward determining who to assign blame dance. She was programmed differently where she usually just avoided this part. With her family, she would've locked herself in her room until her mother came to get her for dinner. By that point, everyone would have been over it. Later, she would lock herself in her room and sneak out to go meet up with some of her friends to drink away her pains. After those trips, she returned home buzzed and not caring what anyone was going to say. Annabelle considered cranking the car and driving to the nearest bar, and she would have done it if Charlie hadn't emerged from the door right at that moment.

Charlie emerged from the building hands in pockets, looking like a scolded puppy. He was staring straight at her making her squirm and fidget a bit. Annabelle stared back until she was so unsettled, she had to look away. She covered it well by looking down and focusing on taking her key out of her ignition, finding her purse and unbuckling her seatbelt. Unfortunately, that only lasted for so long. She had to look up again once she'd opened her door and emerged from the car. She could feel how clammy and sweaty her palms were, and she hated this feeling. She hiked her bag up onto her shoulder, took a deep breath, and started walking towards him. She was thankful at that moment for her sunglasses. They helped mask the deer in the headlights look she was certain she was sporting. She was also thankful he was wearing sunglasses, so she couldn't see all the things his eyes had the ability to say.

"Listen, I'm really sorry about last night. All the things I said and implied. It's not any of my business to judge you or try to referee your relationships with other people. You were right when you said I look at people like projects needing to be fixed. That was completely 100% spot on." He said as their paths on the sidewalk converged.

"Thank you, but I had no right to say that to you. I know your job is to help people, and you are just doing your job. I got overly emotional, and everything spiraled out of control."

"Yes, my job is to help people, but that doesn't give me any excuse or right to go around trying to force my help on anyone within a 5-mile radius. That's not my job. My job is to help people who are seeking help. I really blew it with you last night, and I really hope this doesn't affect things between us. We make a great team, and I don't want last night to sever that."

"It won't. I promise. Once I get a cup of coffee in me, I will be back to the shotty, less than hard working teammate you know and love."

"I'm counting on it. Let's go inside and get you that cup of coffee."

Annabelle nervously poured herself a cup of coffee and after half of the cup was gone, she was already starting to feel better. The warm liquid was having a nice, calming effect on her. Charlie had been trying to make conversation to keep the mood light and airy which was working. Annabelle played her part and laughed at his corny jokes, but when they both went their separate ways into their offices, she just couldn't shake the feeling that she was the child with her face pressed up against the glass of a snow globe watching the little town on the inside getting dusted with snow. A part of her wished she could feel like she was part of this or like she fit in, but she just knew deep down that was never going to happen. She was never going to be like any of these people with their faith and unbridled happiness. She sat in her office looking around wondering how she had gotten to this place. She knew her wall had started crumbling. She had felt it being chipped away little by little over these past few days that she'd been here. She knew she was approaching a crossroads. She would either have to allow the wall to keep crumbling, or she would build it back up and move on. She sat for most of the morning and pondered which path she would take. She knew she would only be here until her mom called. Then she had told Charlie she would be heading home to take her mom to the hospital to pick up her dad. She only had to make it to that point.

< < > >

Jill woke up still a little shell shocked from the night before. She lay in the bed for a moment reliving the animosity from the night before. She grabbed her phone, saw the time, and realized Annabelle would have already left for work. She checked her texts and saw there were no messages from Jason. She wasn't sure if she was surprised by that at all. Maybe Julie hadn't told him anything about their chat over coffee the night before. Jill knew now that she had found out the truth about Jason, there was nothing keeping her here. She would have to head back home and start trying to put the pieces of her shattered life back together.

She pulled herself out of the bed, showered, got dressed, and realized how hungry she was. She hadn't emerged for any reason last night, and she had gone to bed without any dinner. By the time she made it downstairs, she had a plan. She would run out and pick-up breakfast before heading back. That would give her a minute to get out of the house and some time to herself before she had to go back and face everyone. She also had an entire car ride back to figure out what she would tell everyone. She hadn't texted her mom. Honestly, she wasn't sure her mom would even have noticed she was gone with everything she had going on right now.

< < > >

When Annabelle arrived back home, she saw her mom was sitting at the bar in the kitchen with a cup of coffee in her hands. She walked over and sat her keys on the counter.

"Are you okay, sweetie?" Her mom said.

"Not exactly. I had a long night. Everything will be fine."

"If you'd like, we can just go ahead and go. I just need to pick up something on the way to the hospital. I know I could really go for a cup of coffee."

"Mom, aren't you drinking a cup of coffee right now."

"Well, yes, this is coffee, but it is decaf, and I need something very strong. I might even need some special flavoring added if you know what I mean." Marianne said as she winked at her.

Annabelle was completely confused and a little put off. "Special flavoring?" What the heck? Was her mother trying to imply that she wanted alcohol to put into her coffee? When did her mother start drinking? What the heck was going on? Annabelle had the feeling something wasn't right. She could pinpoint small signs of trouble, but she couldn't pinpoint the one big thing that was the cause of all the problems. Annabelle was fine with her mother needing some liquid courage. She could justify that to herself. She could even justify all of her mother's odd sentiments and feelings about having her father come home, but she would not, under any circumstances, admit, for even a second, that any of this was normal behavior for her mother.

Annabelle left the house with her mother with the assumption they were headed to breakfast and then to the hospital to pick up her father, but in actuality, as she later learned, they were going everywhere except the hospital. She rode along as Marianne made pit stop after pit stop. Annabelle told herself it was because her mother actually needed those new sofa pillows to make her father feel more comfortable, or those new monogrammed tumblers, with only an initial for her first name, to keep his drinks cool. Annabelle told herself a lot of things, but deep down it really felt like her mother was side tracking to actually avoid picking her father up from the hospital. Well shielded behind the frames of her sunglasses, she allowed her eyes to scan over her mother while simultaneously scrutinizing and taking in every move she made. Annabelle felt like she was losing her mind. Surely her mother wasn't actually avoiding picking her father up. That wasn't like her at all. Maybe she had just gotten so worked up in preparing for his homecoming, she had simply forgotten about picking him up.

"Mom?"

"Yes, dear."

"Are we going to go and pick-up dad soon?"

"What, honey?"

"When exactly are we going to go and pick-up dad from the hospital? Don't we have to pick him up by a certain time."

"Oh. Yes, I suppose we do need to head that way."

"Mom."

"Yes?"

"It's going to be okay. Dad is going to come home, and he's going to be fine. I will help you, so you won't have to worry about trying to do everything on your own or getting overwhelmed."

"That's nice, dear." Marianne said as she placed her hand on her daughter's knee and squeezed.

Annabelle knew her mother's touch was supposed to be reassuring, but she had to admit it wasn't reassuring at all. Instead, it felt completely forced and fake, like there was so much behind it that needed to be said but wasn't. She decided to keep an eye on how things went at the hospital and decide what to do from there.

Once they stepped through the doorway leading into the main entrance of the hospital, Annabelle was once again overcome by the vastness of it. There was a section of various chairs and couches to their left. Some of them were unoccupied and other whole areas were full of people sitting and waiting. Directly past the "waiting area" was a big round information desk manned by two older women each equipped with a desk area and a phone. To the right there was a window and a wall of offices. The sign above it read "patient accounts". Directly in front of them were a set of elevators which were the portals to every area of the hospital. To the left of the elevators was a café and gift shop. The aroma of coffee and cinnamon rolls was spilling through the air acting as a panacea for the waiting room ailments that came from a good dose of waiting and worrying.

As they walked towards the elevators, Annabelle glanced over at the information desk, and a sign on the desk caught her eye. She couldn't make out exactly what it said, but she thought she saw the words "CPR" and "class". She tapped her mother on the shoulder and explained that she wanted to look at something, and she would catch up with her.

Marianne looked a little hesitant, but she assured her mother she would be right behind her and everything would be fine. She turned, packed the hesitant look away as being normal for her worry prone mother, and then, she headed toward the information desk.

When she got up to the desk, she was able to clearly read the sign. There would be a CPR class offered on Monday nights in a room on the level above the floor she was on now. Next to the sign was a stack of registration forms. Annabelle grabbed one and began filling it out. This would be the perfect reason to stay. She would say she was taking the class to help her dad out if something else happened. It wouldn't entirely be a lie, because, after this class, she would actually be able to perform CPR on her father if he ever had another heart attack. It would be perfect.

As she was filling out the form, she could hear various chatter and conversations happening around her. She was trying to block them out as she focused on what each question was asking. At one point, she noticed the room around her had grown substantially quieter. The chatter had become whispers. The women working at the desk were whispering as well, but Annabelle was close enough to actually hear their conversation. She kept her head down and continued filling out the registration form as she listened in.

"I can't believe that woman has the nerve to show her face here after what she's done." One of the ladies said.

"What did she do?" the other one asked.

"she's the one responsible for creating the rift in Grace Baptist. Don't you remember?"

"I remember hearing about a rift, but I don't remember hearing about the cause."

"Well, you're looking at it. That home wrecker had an affair and ending up ruining more lives and relationships than just the ones in her family. Her latest victim is in the hospital here right now."

"Her latest victim?"

Yeah, the man she is currently having an affair with."

"Oh, do you think she was here to visit him? Are they together?"

"I'm not sure. I know his wife is up here every day, so that woman would have to have some nerve to come in here and try to see that man while his wife could be coming around the next corner."

Annabelle was shocked. She knew the youth pastor had left the church after a rift had occurred within the church community, but she hadn't realized it was because of an affair. She couldn't think of anything more horrible. She felt sick at her stomach at the thought. She had the sudden urge to look up and see who this terrible woman was. She wrestled with the urge until her desire to look became too powerful. She looked up, and she had to admit she was surprised to see Alise St. James sauntering down the hospital corridor. There was a young petite woman probably in her early 30's who seemed to be hurrying away from Alise. Annabelle started to feel bad for Alise and the fact that people were clearly avoiding her, but then, she thought better of it. Alise had brought all of this on herself, and she deserved what she got. After a final glance, Annabelle turned her attention back to the CPR paperwork. Once it was complete, she walked to the center of the information desk, told the two women there what she needed, and she was able to get her paperwork turned in and her registration fee paid.

When Annabelle stepped into the elevator, she felt a sense of accomplishment. She was doing something proactive, and she would be able to help her father and possibly save his life if she needed to. She loved this new feeling, and she realized, she hadn't felt this way in a long time. Lately, feelings of confusion, worry and guilt had painted her everyday outlook, and she was starting to suspect self-pity and even some self-loathing were creeping in where her cracks were beginning to show through her façade. A happy feeling, any happy feeling was such a rare thing, and Annabelle realized how much she had missed having something like that in her life.

All of this and more was on her mind when she stepped off of the elevator and realized the closer, she got to her parents' room that she could hear raised voices. She assured herself it wasn't her parents and probably someone close to that room, but the more she thought about all of the inconsistencies in their behavior lately, the more she realized it could be them. When she got to their door, she didn't have to wonder anymore. It was her parents, and when she opened the door, she got a full picture of what people with dysfunctional parental figures must go through on a daily basis. Her father who had just suffered a massive heart attack was sitting up in the bed in an aggressive stance with his finger pointed at her mother and shouting something about how she had never loved him and had been waiting for something like this to happen. How she'd pushed for it to happen. Her mother, shoulders shaking as her body was wracked with sobs, managed to fire back a few shots about how he'd left her behind years ago, and she didn't care anymore, because it would be over soon. What did she mean it will be over soon? Was he going to die? Annabelle knew in the back of her mind that the things she was hearing shouldn't be leading her to having this conclusion, but she just wasn't ready to face the other possible conclusion.

"Mom, Dad, what's going on? Is everything okay?" Annabelle said stepping slowly into the room.

"No, everything isn't okay" Marianne said through sobs. "Your father has something he needs to tell you."

"Marianne, not like this" Her father was saying.

"You have one minute to start talking, and if you don't tell her, I will."

He looked from Marianne to Annabelle and then back to Marianne. His anger towards her was palpable, but so was the hurt and shame in his eyes when he looked at her. Each second of the 60 felt like an hour, and Annabelle could tell her father was really struggling with saying whatever it was needed to be said. She looked at him and tried to reassure him with her eyes that whatever he had to tell her; it would be okay. He didn't look like he was so sure, and that made her nervous. When it seemed like time was actually about to stand still, and Annabelle didn't know if she could stand the suspense any longer, her mother blurted it out.

"Your father has had an affair, and we are getting a divorce. There, now she knows."

Ch.18

After Annabelle had left the church, Charlie had thanked God they were able to reconcile with one another. He hated thinking he had hurt her. He was usually so good about staying in control of his emotions. It had been such a long time since his emotions had gotten away from him like that. He wanted Annabelle to know she could trust him, and that wasn't a good way to show her that. She had left to pick up her mom and take her to the hospital to pick up her dad. This was a time she would need prayer.

"God, I know you are the great physician, and you know the days and seconds of our lives. Annabelle needs healing today as she endures emotions and worries with her family as well as strength to be there for them while her sister is away. David is coming home today, and this is a time for reconciliation with his family. The family can choose to use this time to come together and heal old wounds. I pray they use this time wisely, God. You spared him for a reason, and I pray they realize that. It's in your precious name I pray. Amen."

< < > >

Annabelle stared in disbelief at both of her parents. Numbness took over her entire body except for her stomach which felt like it had been hollowed out instantly. She had never felt this way before. What was happening here? She reminded herself to take a few deep breaths to settle herself. Once she was calmer and settled, she realized her parents were both staring at her as well. They weren't looking at each other; they were just watching her as if waiting to see her reaction. Annabelle realized she wasn't sure how to react. She wanted to say something, but more than anything, she wished they would say they were joking and then they could all happily go home. She wanted so badly for this whole thing to be a big joke, but when she looked into her mother's eyes and saw the hurt, they carried and the shame reflected in the eyes of her father, she knew this wasn't a joke. She took a final deep, calming breath and mustered all the maturity her short 21 years would offer and insisted they should get her father's things and head home. Again, she registered the fact that both of her parents were staring at her, but she couldn't worry about that right now. She just needed to make sure her father got home alright. That was the only thing she could focus on right now.

"Annabelle, did you hear what I said?" Her mother asked.

"Yes, but I don't want to talk about that. I just want to get dad home and make sure he's comfortable."

"Comfortable? In my house? What if I don't want that cheater in my house?"

"Mother, can we *please* not do this right now? It's really not the time for this."

"Not the time for this? Well, then when is the right time to discuss how hurt and betrayed I feel. When am I allowed to say that I am hurt and enough is enough? When is it ever going to be about me?"

"I don't know, but not right now. Dad needs us to take care of him. He's recovering from a heart attack. I don't think that should be taken lightly."

"Well, if he needs someone so much, maybe he should call his *mistress* to come take care of him, or would that ruin all the romance for her to see you like this?" With this, Marianne turned and glared at David with a look of Disdain that would have killed him instantly if it was possible.

David without even taking a moment to think, puffed up his chest and in a moment of pure pride stated, "As a matter of fact, she was already here. She came to check on me and make sure I was doing alright. She left right before *you* showed up."

Marianne looked stunned and then hurt washed over her face before a red tint of rage took its place. "That's it! I've had enough of this. You're still seeing her! How could I have been so stupid to think your family would've been more important than that relationship? I have had it with you! Find your own way out of here, and you'd better find somewhere else to stay. Do *not* even *think* about stepping a foot inside of *my* house!"

"It's not *your* house! It's *our* house!" David bellowed.

"Well, we will just see about that, but I wouldn't hold your breath on getting the house!" Marianne screamed as she hurried through the doorway with such force and finality that Annabelle knew she wouldn't be coming back.

The air in the room was thick and seemed to hang in mass of curtains everywhere she moved. She noticed her father was still standing, and even though she was angry at him for the mess he had created, she realized she was still his daughter. She walked over, took his arm, and helped him to the sofa to sit down. Once David was seated, it gave Annabelle a chance to think. She took out her phone and texted the only person she could think of who would be able to help them out of this situation, Charlie. Within a minute, she had a return text that he would be on his way to rescue them. With that handled, she made a call to let the nurses know they were ready to leave, and she requested a wheelchair for her father and some help getting him to the Lobby. She then proceeded to make sure all of his things were placed back in his bag. Once everything had been done, she joined her father on the sofa. She knelt forward and put her head in her hands and tried her best to figure out how this had happened and how she had missed it. She knew her parents had started drifting apart when she left, but she had always assumed they'd mended all those broken fences all these years especially once Jill left for college and they had the house to themselves. They always appeared to be cheerful and happy when she'd spoken to them, right? Had she been so distracted by her own drama that she had completely missed the collapse of one of the greatest relationships she had ever known. Annabelle registered a touch and realized David was meaning to put his arm around her. She couldn't register her feelings for him quite yet, so she allowed impulse to take over, and she slid away from his reach in an effort to let him know she wasn't happy with him or okay with their relationship.

They sat like that in silence until the nurse arrived with the wheelchair. Annabelle helped get her dad into the chair, and she walked behind them in silence the entire way down to the lobby while her dad and the nurse chatted and made small talk. She was amazed at the way he could just switch everything off like it wasn't bothering him. Of course, it had to be bothering him. It was bothering her, and she hadn't even been the one responsible. The more he pretended everything was okay, the angrier she became. Once they finally reached the lobby and were seated by the door, Annabelle couldn't even stand to look at her father. She just hoped Charlie would hurry up, so she wouldn't have to sit in this cloud of awkwardness much longer.

Charlie wasn't sure what had happened before Annabelle called him and asked him for help getting her dad home, but based on the tangible awkwardness that hung as thick as molasses in the small confines of the vehicle they were all traveling in. He knew it couldn't have been good. He wanted to know everything and to help, but it didn't seem like the right time or place to start asking questions. If Annabelle wanted him to know, she would tell him.

They pulled into the driveway and Charlie helped Annabelle get her dad inside and comfortable in his personal living room or what he had always referred to as "the man cave". After they made sure he was comfortably inside and had everything he would need for the night, Annabelle and Charlie walked into the kitchen to talk. They had barely had a chance to speak to each other with all the drama and excitement surrounding David's exit from the hospital. Annabelle knew Charlie must know something was going on. She was sure he had to be wondering where her mom was, so she decided to fill him in on everything that had happened.

After she explained everything she had just been through and witnessed between her parents, Charlie agreed it was a good time to call off the dinner and reschedule. Annabelle agreed and knew Brian and Olivia would understand. She couldn't leave her dad right now, and with no one else there to help take care of him, she was the only candidate. Feeling exhaustion hit her as the events of the day started to draw to a close, Annabelle walked Charlie to the door. They said their goodbyes, and he headed out, but not before he told her to take the morning off the following day if she needed it. He knew she had no idea when anyone else would be back to help her out. With a wave, Charlie was out the door and Annabelle was left in the house with no one but the person who she felt liked her least of all but depended on her the most now. It was a tricky situation to say the least.

Annabelle picked up to phone to call someone, her mom or Jill and figure out what was going on with them, but when she did, she noticed an unread text on her phone screen. It was a text from Rayne telling her she had heard about her dad getting released from the hospital, and to text her if she could do anything to help. Annabelle had given Rayne her number, so the two of them could keep in touch if Rayne ever needed anything. Annabelle hadn't thought she would be the one needing something from Rayne, but she was glad to know someone else was there. She decided her first call would have to be to Jill. She couldn't call her mom and have no idea where her sister was in case her mom decided to ask her. She didn't want to add more stress on her mom right now. She scrolled through her recent call list until she found Jill's name. Before she could click on it, she heard the knob on the door turn and looked up to see Jill entering through the front door. Their eyes met, and Annabelle started to say something, but Jill held up her hand to dismiss her.

"Jill," Annabelle tried again.

"Not right now, Annabelle. Please, I can't handle it right now." Jill said with palpable note of sadness in her voice.

Annabelle backed off assuming Jill already knew about their dad and that's where the sadness was coming from. Jill walked by her and upstairs to her room where she closed the door. Annabelle was once again alone. She made her way to the kitchen and made herself a sandwich which she took upstairs to eat. This house with all its many rooms was feeling more cramped by the second, and she didn't know how much longer she could stand being in it. After finishing her sandwich, she decided to turn in for an early night, and when she turned off the light, she quickly prayed for an easy, restful night.

The next morning, Annabelle woke early, dressed quickly and came downstairs to find Jill nursing a cup of coffee. She really didn't want to get into it with her sister again, and she just wanted to be thankful she was home. She told her she was headed out to the church, and she would be home later. She had called Charlie that morning to let him know her plans and that was without a vehicle, so she found him parked in her driveway waiting to pick to her up. They drove to the church in silence, neither of them knowing what to say after the previous day's events.

Once they had gotten to the church, they had each gone their separate ways to catch up on work that needed to be done. Annabelle saw the calendar had been updated to show their dinner with Brian and Olivia had been rescheduled for that evening. She wasn't any more excited about it than she had originally been, but it couldn't be any worse than what she had endured between her parents yesterday. At least if the dinner went bad, she could walk away from it instead of having to spend the night in a house full of the tension. She also knew something was definitely still going on with her sister. She had meant to ask her how things went with Jason, bur the events of the past 24 hours had taken over all of her attention, and she felt at this point, she would have to pencil in a conversation with her sister to remember to have one.

Annabelle had just finished talking to Charlie about plans for the week to make sure everything was on the calendar. She reminded him they had the dinner that evening with her ex-boyfriend and former best friend, Brian and Olivia, who were now engaged to be married. She saw a playful smile creep across his face as he nodded that he remembered and would definitely be ready in time to leave for dinner. Annabelle realized he also must be thinking the dinner would be completely awkward and strange. That realization just increased the number of knots in her stomach, and pangs of anxiety began to wash over her.

Once, Charlie was back in his office, Annabelle took a quick stroll around the building to make sure everything was in place in case any students began arriving. Some of the students had half day schedules at the high school and half day classes at a college right outside of town. They would finish up their day at the high school and their college classes would be cancelled, instead of going somewhere where they could get into trouble, they would usually start descending on the youth building.

Annabelle also knew that Rayne would be showing up soon. She had been able to work out a filing job for Rayne to give her something to satisfy her work study requirement. All of the kids at the high school were required to take the course for one semester and learn what it was like to have a job in the real world. The filing gig barely paid anything at all, but Annabelle knew it would be good for Rayne. She'd spent enough time now talking with the girl to know that her mother frequently left her alone and didn't have much to do with her. Annabelle knew Rayne must be lonely and just too proud to show it. The two of them would chat daily about things going on in their lives, and Annabelle had gotten some big wake up calls to some of the things these teens were going through. She had always hated that her parents seemed *too* involved in her life, but she had never thought about the possibility of them not being involved at all. She wasn't sure what she would've done growing up like that.

The sound of a door opening pulled Annabelle away from her idle thoughts and back to reality. She glanced over to see a girl with electric blue hair coming through the door. It took her only a second to realize it was Rayne. Annabelle could feel her heart literally aching for this girl. Annabelle knew this was just another way Rayne was trying to get the attention she was desperately seeking from her mother. Annabelle knew Rayne must be hurting inside, and she just wished she would be able to break through the fortress she'd erected around herself. Annabelle felt camaraderie with Rayne, because she recognized some of the same defenses, she herself had put in place to keep people at bay. She couldn't say she had given herself over to the whole God and Jesus fantasy everyone here was always trying to talk to her about, but she did appreciate all the self-reflection this place had brought out in her.

"So, blue? I have to say I really like it. The color is striking with your eyes. It really makes them pop."

"Yeah, I was just feeling something different from the same ole thing."

"So, what color is your hair *really*?"

"It's *really* blue."

"No, I mean natural. What's your natural hair color?"

"Oh. It's brown"

"Seriously?" Annabelle said the shock clearly evident in her voice as well as on her face.

"Yeah, why? Do I not seem like I could have brown hair?" Rayne said almost seeming a little offended.

"No, it's not that. I just know the darker your hair is, the more difficult it is to make it take on brighter colors."

"That is true. I guess it just means I'm more dedicated to my cause." Rayne said with a smirk.

"What cause is that? The 'I'm against boring hair colors' cause?" Annabelle teased.

"No, it's more like the 'I'm going to be myself no matter what they say' cause." Rayne shot back.

"Touché" Annabelle said feeling the camaraderie again.

"Yeah, so I was hoping you'd let me duck out a little early today. I know you have a dinner thing tonight which I expect to hear all about on Sunday, by the way."

"You want to leave early because I have a dinner thing? I was actually hoping you could give me some pointers on how to wow everyone there into submission."

"While it is true that I have some unbelievable talents at wowing people, I also have my own dinner thing tonight."

"Oh yeah? With some of the girls here?" Annabelle asked as she started thumbing through some files in a drawer looking for the ones that needed to be stuffed with the short stack of papers sitting front and center on her desk.

"No, actually, I met someone at school, and he wants to take me out to dinner."

When the words registered in Annabelle's brain, she stiffened and stopped her search. She straightened back up in her chair and glanced up at Rayne. Annabelle knew she had to play it cool and not seem as alarmed as she actually was. Annabelle wanted desperately to be happy Rayne had found someone to spend time with, but she was afraid this was just another ploy for attention, and this time, someone might have actually followed the bat signal back to its source. Annabelle wanted to be wrong, but she knew in her gut she wasn't. She also knew she had to play this smart, or she would risk damaging their friendship and the trust that had been formed as well.

"There's a lot to be done, so we will have to see about you leaving early. I just don't want to promise you something until I know it can actually happen." Annabelle said with a smile. "So, tell me about him. Is he from here? Do I know him? Are you going to bring him to church to meet everyone?"

"Wow, that's a lot of questions." Rayne said with a smile on her face to show she wasn't really as annoyed as she sounded. "I will now attempt to answer them all with three simple words, I don't know."

"You don't know?" Annabelle said puzzled.

"Yeah, I *just* met him, so I don't know if he's from here or not or if you do or don't know him. I also don't know that I would bring him by here since I'm not the biggest fan of this place myself. Why would I want to subject him to something I can barely tolerate? Besides, this is very, extremely new, and I don't want to jinx it by making any big future plans."

"And meeting me would be a big future plan?"

"Yes, I believe that would constitute as one. Besides that, he is taller than me, thin. He has dark hair that's pretty shaggy, which I love. He has a few piercings. I think maybe both ears, eyebrow, and lip. He also has this awesome tattoo on the top of his arm. It's really cool and artsy. I think you will really love it if you ever see it. He has a really cool story about how he designed it, too."

"Wow, I'm sure he does. A tattoo? If he's old enough to have a tattoo, that means he's…"

"Yes, He's 18, but before you go trying to become all motherly and worried and everything, don't be. He is totally cool. I promise."

"Does he have a job or a plan for his future?" Annabelle asked pointedly.

"I don't know since I *just* met him. I'm not going to interrogate him and scare him away right off the bat. I'm pretty sure he plays lead guitar for this band I saw once, but I'm not really sure since that night was kind of a blur for me."

"Wait What?" Annabelle said with a look of shock spreading across her face.

"Well…" Rayne started to say before she was interrupted.

"No, nevermind. I changed my mind. I don't want to know. I just want you to be careful. Don't be afraid to ask questions. It's your life, and you don't want to get too far in before you find out something that might be a deal breaker."

"Annabelle, I'm only 16. I don't have to be worried about all of that right now. I have everything I need." Rayne said with a sigh as her shoulders slumped and she slid further into the chair.

"You might have everything you need for basic life survival, but I want you to have so much more than that. You deserve to be happy, and you deserve to find someone who treats you well and loves spending time with you, and…"

"Someone who's unlike my mom, right" Rayne said without looking up.

"Oh, I didn't mean that." Annabelle said crossing the room towards her.

"Yeah, but it's what you're thinking." Rayne said still unable to meet Anna's eyes.

"Rayne, listen to me. You are beautiful and smart, and I for one feel so lucky to have met you and have you in my life. I know you are truly one of a kind and someone who has made my life better by having you in it. I truly only want the best for you, and I want you to be genuinely happy." Annabelle said as she slid into the chair beside her and put one arm around her shoulders and drew her close.

"Well, right now, he makes me happy."

"Well then, that sounds pretty good to me."

< < > >

Charlie stepped outside of the youth building in time to see Rayne getting into a car with a taller male driver and driving away while Annabelle stood at the door and waved. Charlie could see she had a worried look on her face, and he couldn't help but think how much her expression reminded him of his own mom's expression when boys would show up to take his sister somewhere. He could tell Annabelle really loved Rayne and was nervous for her. The two of them had an obvious special bond. Charlie knew God had sent Annabelle to Rayne for a reason, and he just prayed Annabelle would listen to what God wanted her to do for the girl. He also spent a great deal of time praying that Rayne would be receptive to Annabelle. The relationship web they were weaving had obvious areas of missteps and tangles seemed to be imminent.

Annabelle smiled when she saw him. She turned and locked the door behind them, and they headed to his car. He noticed she had an ease about her that hadn't been there before. She was letting herself settle into a good and steady routine. He knew she would never admit it, but he could tell she was relaxing more and actually enjoying life. Her eyes held a brightness that had previously been dim, but now it was actually starting to shine. He hoped that light would continue to brighten until it shined so brightly everyone could see it. He would continue to pray for her and pray for that to happen, but until it did, he would make it his mission to protect the little light she possessed to make sure it didn't get snuffed out.

The door flew open, and he was suddenly brought back to his senses. Annabelle was in the seat next to him before he even realized what was happening. Gone was her worried expression, and in its place was a thick cloud of anxiety which he knew was caused by what was to come and not by anything that had previously occurred.

He leaned closer to reassure her with his presence. "So, you ready for this?"

"Definitely not!" She said giving him a seriously look. "I'm just happy to have someone there in case things go south. I hope you know the potential for things to go south is very real."

"No, you're just worried. When I talked to them, they seemed completely open to the idea. I didn't know them when they were younger, but they seem to be levelheaded, mature adults. I don't think you have anything to worry about."

"Right" Annabelle said slowly drawing out the middle of the word. "Having dinner with my scorned ex-boyfriend and best friend and their pre-marital counselor couldn't possibly blow up in my face. Gosh, what was I thinking?"

"See, now you're seeing the big picture." Charlie said as he pulled out onto the road towards their destination.

Ch.19

When the car pulled into a driveway and came to a stop, Annabelle thought they couldn't possibly have traveled long enough to already be there. She had anticipated more time to analyze and plan out the evening and what everyone could say and her potential responses. A wave of panic washed over her, and she was sure she wasn't ready to face whatever was on the other side of the door. Somehow, she managed to keep her exterior calm and cool while it felt like a barrel of wild monkeys was raging inside of her.

Before exiting the car, Charlie glanced at Annabelle to see where her emotions were. He could tell she was a ball of nerves, and he hated seeing her so worried and anxious about something he had no doubts would turn out alright. He asked her if they could pray before they went inside. He wasn't sure if it was her nerves or something else that made her say yes, but whatever it was, he was thankful for it. It gave him hope she would continue down the right path.

"God, we humbly come before you today about to embark on something that is scary. The unknown is always a bit scary, but we know with you guiding our way and going beside us through life, things aren't so scary after all. We ask for that today, Lord. Please give us a peace that will stay with us throughout our visit, Lord. This has been ordained by you, and we know you tell us to forgive ourselves and others, and that, Lord, is what we are doing here tonight. We are practicing the forgiveness we learned from you when you gave your life to forgive us when we didn't and still don't deserve it. Please lead us in the way you would have us go tonight with our words and our actions, Lord. Please let this be a beautiful time of fellowship and peace. It is in your loving name we pray. Amen.

After the prayer ended Charlie was at her door in what seemed like a matter of seconds. He opened it for her and held out his hand as a peace offering to let her know he would be there to help her in any way he could. She accepted it, and once again, the trip up the remaining portion of driveway to the front door had definitely not been long enough. Before she could take a few steadying breaths, Charlie had knocked, the door had opened, and Brian was standing on the other side grinning at them both. Staring into the face of someone she had loved and abandoned, made her anxiety fill every nook and cranny of her being. She hesitated, took a slight step back, and steadied again when she was against Charlie. He reached up and grabbed her hand, giving it a gentle and reassuring squeeze. For a moment, all was right in the world, and she was finally able to breathe again. She dropped his hand and faced Brian as she had before, but this time, she did it as a more confident version of herself.

She no longer had feelings for Brian. She knew those had passed long ago. In fact, she wasn't sure she was ever really in love with him. She had always thought if she actually loved him, she wouldn't have left him and treated him the way she had. Brian and Olivia had both been such a big part of her life, and they had loved her for who she was and had understood her for all her quirks. She didn't know how it would be now that so much time had passed, and all three of them had grown into new people. Brian and Olivia had grown and blossomed together, but Annabelle knew her growing had all been alone and away from everyone else. With a deep breath, she gave Charlie's hand a squeeze and walked up the front steps into the house.

Once inside, the anxiety was palpable amidst the intoxicating scent of a chicken roasting away in the oven. Annabelle could feel the nerves and anxiety from everyone immediately, and she had to remind herself to stay calm, so she wasn't immediately on the defensive. When they got into the living room, Brian offered everyone a seat. Olivia came out, greeted everyone, and asked if they would like a drink. Charlie asked for sweet tea and Annabelle asked for water. When Olivia went back into the kitchen to make the drinks, Annabelle felt like that would be the perfect time to excuse herself and go help Olivia.

Olivia visibly stiffened when she saw Annabelle walk in the kitchen, but she pretended to be happy to see her. At first, Annabelle took offense to Olivia's obvious hesitation to being around her, but then she realized this was a situation that she herself had created. She was the only one who could really fix this. Without knowing why, she walked right up to Olivia and put her hand on Olivia's hand and looked her right in the eyes and said, "I'm so sorry." Olivia stared at her for a second before the words seemed to register, then she relaxed a little as she replied, "I'm sorry too!" With a hint of surprise in her voice, Annabelle couldn't help but ask Olivia what in the world she had done to be sorry for. As far as Annabelle was concerned, she had tarnished their friendship, and she was the one who would hand to pick up the pieces and make it whole again. She never expected she would have help from someone who she had betrayed and hurt so deeply.

"Where do I begin? Yes, I was hurt when you left, but I knew where you had gone, and I never once went to see you to convince you to come home."

"I know you called a few times. I ignored them, but I remember you did call."

"Yeah, but I also stopped calling. I could have kept pursuing our friendship and trying to talk to you, and I didn't. I let my hurt and my anger get the better of me. I let those feelings blot out an entire lifetime of friendship and great memories. Then, you did come home, and I knew you were back. My mom told me one day when she heard from your mom you were back, and I never once reached out to make amends. I was still too caught up in all the negativity to see clearly, and for all of that, I am so sorry! I don't know how to make up all the time we lost, but I would love for us to try. We might never be best friends again, but we can be more than what we are now."

"Olivia, I was horrible to you. You were one of my best friends, and I left without a word and stopped talking to you. I hurt you so much, and I don't understand why you are apologizing to me and being nice to me. I don't deserve it."

"I don't want to start a new life with Brian still hanging onto any negative, old feelings from the past. As a human, I can stew in those feelings forever, but as a Christian, I have the power and ability to forgive in the same way I was forgiven. I know how it feels to be extended grace when you don't deserve it, and I want to give you the gift of grace, so we can start fresh. I want this to be a turning point for us where we move forward from this point together. I want our paths to move forward together instead of apart. What do you say?"

"I say that I am so lucky to have a friend like you!" Annabelle said as she wrapped Olivia in a hug. Once the words had left her mouth, she realized how true they were. Olivia could've never spoken to her again, and no one would've been surprised least of all her, but instead, Annabelle couldn't get over what a great friend Olivia was to continue loving her in spite of her flaws and the past.

"Now, you and Brian just need to clear the air, and all will be well."

"Yeah, I really do need to talk to him." Annabelle said with a sigh. "I was horrible to you, but I was worse to him. He knew everything going on with me, and he had been there for me without hesitation. He thought we were going to get married, and next thing he knows I'm gone, never to be heard from again. I mean who does that to someone they supposedly love?"

"There's always time to ask for forgiveness, and there's no time like the present."

"There's so much history, I don't know if I can, I should've told him how I felt at the time, and as harsh as it sounds, I should've told him I didn't love him and didn't want to marry him. It would've been a little harsh at the time, but I think he would've gotten over it eventually, and it would've been a lot better than me just running away instead of just telling him the truth."

"Did you know it was the truth at the time," Olivia asked.

"No" Annabelle admitted, "I knew I didn't want to be married to him, and I knew my feelings for him weren't enough to sustain us long term. I just couldn't imagine telling him that, so I left."

"Well, the good news," Olivia said with a chuckle, "is I don't think he is going to be surprised to find out you didn't want to continue a relationship with him or be married to him. I think he has already figured that one out. Besides, I hear he is engaged to a fantastic girl," She said playfully.

Annabelle had forgotten how easy it was to be friends with Olivia. She had a way of alleviating stress and tension and putting her at ease when she needed it. "I'm so happy he has you!" she said to Olivia with a genuine smile while going in for another hug.

Olivia and Annabelle finally got the drinks ready and went back to connect with the guys in the living room. It was obvious by their fun, carefree nature that the girls had made up. It brought an ease into the air, and the tension started to dissipate. Once the timer in the kitchen announced it was time to eat, everyone had settled into an easy, casual rhythm with one another, and the conversation and laughter was flowing. The flow lasted through dinner and into dessert.

When it was getting close to time to go, and the dishes had been cleaned and put away (a great joint effort on the part of the girls), and the extra food had been packed up and sent home with Charlie (a joint effort on the part of the guys), everyone started collecting their things to head out. Olivia left first, stating she had an early morning work meeting. Brian walked her to the door, and he gave her a kiss on her way out. Once Olivia had left, Annabelle grabbed her things and headed in the same direction. When she got over to Brian, she stopped and sat her things down by the door.

"I had a really great time tonight," she said hesitantly unsure exactly what to say. "I am really glad we got the chance to do this, and I know this is so late, but please know how sorry I am for the way everything played out with us. I know I should've been more honest about my feelings, and I shouldn't have left you the way I did. I am so sorry! I want to be able to be friends with you with everything clear between us. Do you think that's possible?"

Brian looked at her for a long second really taking in her words and processing them before responding. "Thank you. I think if we were both honest with ourselves, we both knew we were drifting apart in the last few months before you left. There was something going on that was bigger than both of us could handle. I want good things for you, and I really hope you have dealt with and moved past whatever was going on back then, but if you haven't, I know a really great counselor you can talk to." With that, he looked behind her and gave a nod.

Annabelle followed his gaze and saw he was nodding at Charlie. She had to admit, she thought Charlie was crazy when he had set this whole thing up, but looking back now, he really knew what he was doing. Olivia had been right when she said it would be nice to proceed with their lives with a clean slate. Annabelle smiled and gave Brian a hug to say goodbye to what they had become and to show the hope she had for their future as friends. Then she looked back at Charlie and signaled she would be outside in the car.

Once Charlie opened the door and slid into the seat beside her, Annabelle turned and smiled at him. She didn't know how to thank him enough for creating this moment for her to reconnect and get some normalcy and structure back in her life. She hadn't even known how much she needed those things until now, so she could thank him for that too. Before she could say anything, Charlie started the conversation for her.

"Whew", he said blowing out a breath it seemed he'd been holding all night. "I am so glad that went as well as it did. I mean that could've been a huge disaster."

"Wait. What? You set this whole thing up. You knew it would go well. I'm pretty sure you even coaxed Olivia into approaching me first, because you knew I wouldn't be able to make the first move. You did all of that. That was all you!"

"I did set this up hoping it would go well and get rid of some long grudges and pain y'all had all been holding on to. I did encourage them to pursue wiping the slate clean for starting their lives together, but I did *not* instruct them on who should talk when and what they should say. Tonight, was a result of a little prayer and a lot of God."

"God? Seriously? What is everyone so quick to say God is the reason for everything that happens? You know sometimes things happen because they're meant to happen, not because God intervened and stopped something worse from happening."

"Annabelle, God is in total control, and he is the reason tonight went so well. I know you might not see it now, but in time you will see it, and it will make sense to you. Just have some faith. Can you just trust me on this one?"

"Trust you? About God?"

"Yes, I haven't steered you wrong yet, so I think you can give me this one."

"Okay, but I am not saying I believe fully in God doing all this. I'm just saying, I will keep an open mind and look for more of his weaving in my life."

"That's all I can ask for."

"Good, because that's all you're getting from me right now."

They drove the rest of the way back to the church with Annabelle recounting old stories of hers and Brian and Olivia's to Charlie. He listened to every word and laughed at every hilarious thing they had done. He had never realized how full of life Annabelle used to be before her light had been extinguished. He had seen some glimpses of it here and there, but he had never seen her the way she was right now. She was animatedly telling stories and smiling broadly and laughing big belly laughs. He was so thankful to God that this night had worked out, and she had been able to regain a piece of her past she thought was gone forever. Now, little by little he hoped she would be able to mend each and every relationship she had abandoned or destroyed by her escape. That would be his new prayer for her. He would pray that she would be able to recapture the person she had once been, not with all the stress and anxiety, but the one who was so full of life.

Annabelle had been having such an amazing time she hadn't even realized they were back at the church until she realized the car had stopped moving, and she looked up and saw the building. At the beginning of the night, she had been dreading it, but now she didn't want it to end. She felt so free and alive, and she hadn't felt this way in so long. She had Charlie to thank for everything. She knew he said it was God, but she wasn't in that place yet, so for now, she would just thank Charlie. She had really gotten to know him working alongside him all these weeks, and she was really starting to see his caring, helpful nature coming through. It was masked a lot by his humor, but she knew it always lay underneath just waiting for someone in need of his help.

She went to open her door, but Charlie stopped her before she could get it all the way open. When she looked up to meet his eyes, she saw something there that she didn't like. Somehow, she knew he was going to tell her something she wouldn't like, but she could also tell he felt like he had to tell her as a way to help her.

"What is it?" She asked cautiously.

"I just think you should know what you're about to walk into."

"Walk into?"

"I know you are hurting, and Jill is still hurting. Just keep that in mind in whatever kind of interaction y'all have tonight. She just found out about your dad, and that can't be easy for anyone to digest as quickly as she had to. Just remember you and Jill are on the same side, so work together in this, and kindness always wins, so be kind no matter what the situation is."

Annabelle nodded and walked to her car. Once inside with the car cranked, she saw Charlie pull away, and in that instant, she had never felt more alone. Whatever she was about to face, she had a feeling it wasn't something she wanted to go through alone.

Ch. 20

When Charlie got home, he wondered how things would go between Annabelle and Jill. Would they be able to work through their own issues to be there for their dad? Would they be able to help him right now knowing what they knew? Would there ever be peace in that family again? He knew he needed to pray for them and the entire situation.

"God, please watch over Jill and Annabelle and their entire family tonight. There is so much hurt, and grief mixed up right now in everyone's life. Everyone is feeling their own set of emotions, and right now, there's no right or wrong way to feel. Everyone has to work through things on their own, but I know you will be there right alongside them as they walk this course. I pray, God, that Jill and Annabelle can find a common ground here and walk this together. This should not separate them. They can work together in this and find a way to come together for their family. Their family needs them, both of them right now. I also pray Marianne finds the strength to face her emotions and come back home. I pray David is past this point in his life, and he can start to make amends where he has caused heartache. God, please wrap your loving arms around this family and bless them in this difficult and painful time. It's in your loving name I pray. Amen."

< < > >

Annabelle drove the entire way home in silence. Her mind had been racing over Charlie's words and every possible situation she could be walking into. When she finally pulled up the house and parked. She exited the car and slowly walked up to the door to let herself in. She knew it would already be weird inside with her dad being home since the entire time she had been back he hadn't been here. She hoped that was all she would feel, but when she came inside. She could already feel the tension lingering there and soaking into everything. She hadn't seen her mom's car in the garage, so she knew she was still gone, and that only made her more nervous about everything. She decided to take Charlie's advice and find Jill. She needed to find out what was going on with her, so she they could approach the situation with her father together.

After sneaking around the house for a minute trying not to be noticed by her dad since she wasn't sure exactly where he was at the moment, and their last interaction hadn't been so good, she finally found Jill standing at the kitchen sink. Upon first glance, Annabelle thought maybe she had been washing dishes from the day, but as she got closer, she realized she was just standing there bracing herself on the sink with her hands, her shoulders heavy with the burden of something Annabelle didn't yet understand.

"Go away, Dad. I don't want to talk to you." Jill said with a note of defeat in her voice.

"Jill, it's me." Annabelle said quietly. What's going on?"

"Everything" Jill said. "Everything is going on and going wrong, and everything is a mess, and I hate him! All this time, I thought I had let him down. I thought I was such a colossal disappointment that I had caused this, but really it was because of all *his* anxiety from sneaking around to see *her*."

"I know this is painful and hard to hear. I honestly don't know if I've processed it all completely myself."

"Do you know who he was seeing?"

"Yes, Alise St. James. I saw her at the hospital today, and the nurses said she was a home wrecker, and she was there to see her latest victim. Then, I saw her."

"Alise? Are you sure? I thought she was happily married. Everyone is saying she moved here to get away from all the scandal from the city. Are you sure it's her?"

"Jill, I know but it is her. She and our father and sneaking around and having an affair behind our mother's back, so you can go on loving her or hating her or whatever you want to feel towards her. I honestly have no idea how I feel right now, so that's the direction I'm choosing to go. I know this is all new to you, and that's why you're taking it so well. You haven't had time to really sit and process what this means, but I have had an entire day to have this hanging over me. I've been sitting and thinking about it all night, and I've decided after everything dad put me through, then he pulls something like this. I'm beyond angry with him!"

"You're right. This news is all new to me, and I haven't really had time to sit and think and cope with it, but I know what it feels like to find out someone betrayed you in the most intimate way. To think you have something special and beautiful and find out it was all a lie. Gosh, Mom must me really taking this hard. Has anyone reached out to her? Where is she?"

"I honestly don't know where she is. All I know right now is I need for today to never have happened, and for everything to go back to the way it was. That's what I need. I need to believe everyone is good again."

"Did you really believe everyone was good before though?"

"Yes, except…"

"Except me?"

"No, I was actually going to say except for me. Why would I think you aren't good? What have you done that was so bad? You're like little miss perfect, you always did everything right."

"I know it seems that way but trust me. I have done bad things too. Just because you don't know about my sins doesn't mean they don't exist."

"Okay, well tell me about them."

"I can't. This is all too much right now. I just need to go upstairs and get away from all of this. I was going to eat something, but I'm not even hungry. Dad is in the 'man cave' on his pull-out sofa bed, so if mom comes home, she won't have to see him. He has a glass of water, so hopefully he will be good for a while. I won't be going back into that room anytime soon."

"That's fine. I will check on him and take care of him tonight. If mom comes home, I will try to talk to her and work on everything going on there too. Just go get some rest. Everything will be better in morning."

Jill nodded quietly and retreated upstairs. Once she was gone Annabelle went to the study to check on their father. When she got there, the sight before her was something she knew she would never forget. He was laying back on the pull-out bed clutching his chest with his face torn in agony. Annabelle ran to help him unsure of what she could even do. She got over to him, and he clutched her hands tightly with a look of despair in his eyes. In all the scenarios and endings, she had meticulously thought through for them, this wasn't one. This wasn't the way it was supposed to end. She was full of so many raging emotions, and once she finally sifted through them all, she started to put a plan in place. She yelled as loud as could for Jill to come. Once Jill arrived, she told her to call 911. Annabelle had no idea how to do CPR. She had seen it in medical shows, but that was it, and she didn't know if you could do it with someone in a bed, or how many times you push on someone's chest, where to push, if you were supposed to breathe for them, etc. In that single moment, she realized she didn't know anything. She hurriedly started pushing on her dad's chest while her sister called 911.

By the time the ambulance arrived, and the paramedics rushed inside with a gurney, Annabelle and Jill had been alternating pushing on their dad's chest for more than 10 minutes. He had closed his eyes long ago, and his grip had gone slack, but Annabelle wasn't giving up hope now that the professionals had arrived. She and Jill moved aside and let them do their thing. They got him up and onto the stretcher, and a man jumped on the stretcher to continue pushing on his chest until they got into the ambulance. Both girls jumped in the back of the ambulance and rode to the hospital all the while watching tubes being inserted, and medicine, (something called epi) being placed into the tubes. The whole thing was a fast, harrowing ride to the hospital that was worse than anything she could imagine.

Once they got to the hospital, their dad was wheeled away, and they were left to go check in and wait for the outcome. That sat together holding each other for a long time until Jill suggested they pray. Annabelle didn't think it would matter, but she agreed and closed her eyes and silently pleaded in her head maybe with God, she wasn't sure who exactly she was reaching out to, but she let Jill's prayer wash over them both. When Jill said amen, and they opened their eyes, there was a doctor standing before them. They grasped hands a little more tightly and waited anxiously for the news. He looked at both and them and asked if there was anyone else, they needed to call to be here with them. They started to shake their heads no when they heard footsteps and someone rushing their way.

"I'm here! How is he? Oh my gosh? How is he?"

They turned and saw their mother making her way franticly over to them. They were stunned by her disheveled appearance, and her puffy eyes. The doctor probably thought she looked that way from the situation with their father, but the girls knew his infidelity had obviously wrecked her. When she finally reached the doctor, she sat beside Jill, joined her hand with theirs, and listened intently for the doctor's next words.

"Ladies let me start by assuring you we did all we could do, but we lost him. His heart was too damaged from the first heart attack and having this second one so soon after surgery just pushed his heart beyond repair."

"So, he's dead?" Annabelle asked quietly while looking into Jill and her mother's frozen faces.

"Yes" the doctor said matter-of-factly. He stood a moment longer. Then realizing they had no more questions, he nodded and walked away.

"So, what do we do now?" Annabelle asked looking at her mom and sister who both seemed completely in shock.

"We…we…I don't know." Her mom said still in shock. I didn't think this would happen, not in a million years did I think this would be how it ends.

"It's okay, mom. I'll make some calls." Annabelle said gently as she rose from her chair and walked off to call the only person she knew could help.

< < > >

Charlie saw Annabelle's name pop up on his phone and answered happily replaying the success of the night in his head. Once he heard her voice though, he knew something wasn't right. She told him simply that her father had suffered another heart attack and hadn't survived. She was at the hospital with her mom and sister who she thought were in shock. She apologized for the late call, but as she told him, she didn't know who else to call or what to do. He could hear the despair in her voice, and even though she wouldn't admit it to him or herself, he could tell she was lost in a jumble of emotions too. When he hung up, he called the pastor and relayed the message. From there the pastor would start the phone tree. He had a group of ladies, like all southern Baptist churches do, who could get anything done. By the time the pastor had hung up the phone, there was a meal train ready, the local funeral home had been notified, and the family minister was on his way to the hospital along with Marianne's closest friends to sit with her and do whatever needed doing.

Annabelle, Jill and their mother only had to wait about 10 minutes before people started arriving. Marianne's friends came in and all crowded around her. Jill and Annabelle were pushed to the background happy to not have to hold it together for their mother and grateful for Charlie setting this all into motion. Someone from the funeral home arrived shortly after and talked to the girls about setting up a time to come by and make some decisions about arrangements. It was a happy distraction. A hospital employee came by to ask if they wanted to sit with their dad for a minute and say their last goodbyes. They all looked at each other, but no one wanted to. Their mother was too hurt, Jill felt too responsible, and Annabelle felt too helpless like it would just remind her of the last time she had let her dad down by not being able to save him. Every one of them was fighting their own inward battle, and no one could face any of it at the time.

When Annabelle was sure her mom would be okay and was left in good hands, she and Jill went home to prepare for their meetings the next day with the funeral home. There would be a lot of decisions to make, and she needed to make sure she had a clear head to make them. She had tried to ask her mother about some of the decisions she knew would come up, but her mother was still mad, so she said she didn't care anything about the funeral. She said whatever the girls decided would be find with her. Annabelle didn't really want all the weight of every decision to be on her, but she felt like right now she was the only one who could handle the pressure, so she faced it head on.

When they got home, they went to their rooms without talking. After lying down for a bit without being able to sleep, Annabelle went to the study to tidy it up and make sure it didn't look reminiscent of the tragedy that had just occurred there. Once the room was cleaned, and the sofa bed turned back into a sofa, she suddenly felt really tired and sat down to rest. She must have fallen asleep, because next thing she knew she was waking up to the smell of brewing coffee and sunlight was streaming into the room.

Jill was sitting on a stool at the counter drinking hot coffee from a mug when Annabelle walked in. The two sisters eyed each other, but neither spoke. Both could see the despair and heartache in the other's eyes, but neither of them could even begin to understand the depth of the other's pain. Annabelle quietly moved around the kitchen getting herself some coffee and went to join Jill at the counter. They both knew they had a long day of decisions ahead of them, and both were aware by the empty hook on the wall that their mother had not come home yet. There was so much that needed to be said, but so much of it was being tucked away and secretly hidden inside both of them. Annabelle couldn't take the wall of silence adding brick by brick each second that dragged on without a sound. She opened her mouth to speak, but instead her attention was pulled away towards the front of the house from the sound of the doorbell. She glanced at Jill who shrugged silently noting she wasn't expecting anyone. Annabelle wondered if it was her mother being dropped off by a friend from church, so she went to answer it.

On the other side of the door stood a young woman who Annabelle noted couldn't have been much older than herself. The woman was very pretty with blond curly hair, high cheek bones, and big blue eyes. She smiled brightly at Annabelle which put her at ease almost instantly.

"Hi, I'm Ruby. I just stopped by to check in and see how everyone is doing after everything last night. Oh, you poor girls, and your poor mama. I really hope everyone is okay." She said her voice sweet as honey.

"Oh, um hi Ruby. It's nice to meet you. I'm Annabelle." She said extending her hand for a shake. "We're holding up as best we can right now, but thanks for asking."

"That's great. Listen, I also came by to get a few of your daddy's things to take to the um well you know…"

"The funeral home?" Annabelle finished questioningly.

"Yes, that's where some items are currently needed."

"Oh, well, we're heading that way soon. We can take them when we go if that would be okay."

"That's fine if you want to. It's just the ladies sent me to make sure the burden is off of y'all, and I really want to do my part and not have to come back empty handed. They're doing so much for your mama, so this was the least I could do."

"Oh. The ladies from the church sent you. I understand now. Okay, well, just tell me what you need."

"Anything your daddy used to wear like jewelry and anything he used to keep in his pockets. To make it as realistic as possible if you know what I mean."

"Okay, I can get his watch, and his favorite pen he used to always keep in his shirt pocket, and his cuff links. Everyone will recognize those 3 things as being his. Would you like to come in while I go and grab those things?"

"Oh, that would be lovely. Thank you!"

Ruby stepped inside the entry way and Annabelle scurried down the hall toward the office where her father kept mostly everything, he would have on him during the day. Annabelle carefully looked through the dish on top of his desk that help his rings and watch. She carefully selected a watch she had seen her dad wear a million times and a ring he wore on his right hand. She thought about getting his wedding ring, but something stopped her. It was a feeling she couldn't really explain. She decided it must have come from all the uncertainty about how her mother would feel after the news of the affair had surfaced. Annabelle returned to the door with a box with her dad's possessions from the office. She gave them to Ruby and thanked her for coming out to the house to get them, so she and her sister didn't have to remember to take them to the funeral home themselves. Ruby acknowledged the thanks and shrugged it off as being something helpful during this difficult time. She said goodbye and was out the door in a flash. Annabelle couldn't help but think about how nice Ruby was, and she wanted to really have a chance to thank her and the other church ladies after this whole thing was over. Annabelle thought about how much it really meant to her to have people reaching out to help them even when she hadn't been a very integral part of the church in so long. For all of her time working with Charlie at the church, she still hadn't been able to set foot inside the sanctuary. To see all the help and kindness coming their way even though she knew the women in the church most likely all knew her past and didn't agree with it, she thought maybe she could give something back and at least attend one sermon aside from her father's funeral. She made a deal with herself that she would attend at least one sermon after her father's funeral. With that thought she made her way back to the kitchen where she saw Jill still sitting at the bar with her coffee mug, but this time, she was playing with her phone. Annabelle could tell by the look on Jill's face that something was wrong. She took in a breath and steadied herself. She had to prepare for bad news, because she really wasn't sure if she could take anymore at this point. She stepped over the threshold into the kitchen and was about to say something to Jill when she heard her own phone start ringing in her pocket. She plucked it out and saw Charlie's name on the screen. As soon as she brought it to her ear and said hello, Jill looked up her eyes swimming with tears. Annabelle regretted answering it immediately and not first talking to her sister. She gave Jill a sympathetic look as she stepped backwards out of the room and went to see what Charlie needed.

Jill sat heavy hearted staring at her phone. Jason still hadn't responded to any of her texts lately. She didn't know what to do. She really wanted to talk to him and let me know everything that was happening. She knew deep down inside he still cared about her. She just needed to talk to him and sort everything out, and then everything would be okay. Right? She needed to tell him about her dad and how much she wished all of this was just a bad dream. After a few minutes of thinking about it, she knew deep down that everything she found out had been real. She didn't want to believe it all, but she knew it was real, and the pain from that coupled with the pain of losing her dad was almost too much to bear. She felt like she was breaking inside.

All of the memories of everything they had been through suddenly became too much for her. She didn't feel like she could hold all of those feelings inside when so many others were racing to get out. Before she knew it, she could feel tears stinging her eyes. She started having a feeling of being watched. She didn't have a chance to turn and check before she heard a phone ringing and looked up to see Annabelle with a phone to her ear giving her a pitying look. The look was almost too much to bear, and luckily Annabelle walked out of the room to have her conversation before Jill had to turn away. She knew from the look on Annabelle's face that she had seen the tears in her eyes. She knew her sister well enough to know she wouldn't let this go without asking about it, so that didn't give Jill much time to come up with an excuse. She still didn't feel ready to confide in her sister or anyone else about what she had done and what was going on.

When Annabelle had made it into the living room, she visibly calmed. This house was too quiet and emotional right now, and she couldn't stand being in it for much longer. Hearing Charlie's voice on the other end of the phone was a welcome comfort she didn't even know she needed.

"Hey, I know things are probably crazy right now, but I was just calling to make sure everything was going okay and see if y'all needed anything."

Annabelle took a steadying breath before answering. Her emotions felt like tiny pinballs shooting all around inside a pinball machine hitting targets left and right. "Honestly, things aren't really crazy just different and weird. No one is acting like themselves, and it is unnerving." She hadn't realized how true that was until she put that statement into words and heard herself voice it aloud. "My mom hasn't been home all night. I really hope she's with her friends from church, and something is going on with Jill, but I know she isn't going to let me in and tell me about it, and honestly, right now, I don't even have the energy to try and figure it out."

"Yeah, that sounds like a ton has been heaped on your plate. What can I do to help?"

"Well, I have to be at the funeral home in an hour to help get arrangements underway. I don't know if you're busy, but…"

"No, I'm not busy at all. I'll be there. Annabelle?"

"Yes,"

"How are *you* doing right now?"

"Honestly, I haven't even had time to think about it, so I have no idea. Ask me again when everything calms down."

"I'll see you at the funeral home in an hour. Just make sure you are taking care of you. Don't lose yourself in all of this."

"Thanks. I'll try not to." Annabelle said before hanging up. Knowing Charlie would be meeting them at the funeral home made it bearable to even go there. If he had said no, she wasn't sure she would've been able to muster enough energy to actually get herself and Jill there in time.

When Annabelle rounded the corner and stepped back into the kitchen, Jill wasn't sitting at the bar anymore. She was now up rinsing out her coffee cup in the sink. Her eyes and face showed no signs of tears or emotion. For a moment, Annabelle convinced herself she had imagined it. She could almost let it go, but there was a nagging from somewhere deep within her telling her that whatever was going on with her sister was not to be taken lightly. Annabelle started to walk towards Jill, but before she had gotten to the bar Jill had excused herself saying she needed to run grab her stuff to be ready to head out. Then, she had run off towards the stairs taking them, what sounded like, two at a time all the way up. With the sudden departure of Jill, Annabelle felt the weight of the stress and tension of the past few hours crash over her again like a heavy wave. She was standing and not giving into the waves, but she didn't know how long she could hold them off before she was taken down with them.

Ch.21

Charlie knew the weight of the past 24 hours was taking its toll on Annabelle. He had been able to tell from her phone call. He knew from experience that grief could take you under if you let it. He wanted to make sure that didn't happen to her. She had a spark he didn't want to see diminished by this, and he knew God had big plans for her. Charlie remembered the years he had spent questioning God when he was in the midst of his own grief. He didn't understand why God had chosen to take David now, and he knew he might never understand it, but he knew this was all part of God's plan, and it was much bigger than he could ever imagine. Before getting ready to go meet Annabelle and Jill at the funeral home, he said a prayer.

"God, I come before you today confused about the situation I'm facing, but also accepting of your decisions. I have learned your plans are bigger and greater than the ones we make for ourselves, and I am coming to ask you to bestow that same understanding on Annabelle and Jill today, Lord. They are hurt and confused, and they are about to have to make a lot of decisions. Please be with them and guide them through this process. Please give them peace during this difficult time, Lord. I know you can pull us from the depths even when we think we are too far gone to be saved. You saved me, and I know you can save them too. Please instill in them the ability to trust you, God. It's in your precious and holy name I pray. Amen."

< < > >

Annabelle had decided to try and talk to Jill on their way to the funeral home since something would need to fill that space, but Jill had other plans and used the radio to cancel out the silence instead. Annabelle had tried to turn down the music a few times, but every time she tried to touch the radio, Jill had told her to leave it alone claiming every song that came on was one of her favorites. Eventually, Annabelle gave in and just gave up trying to talk to her. When they pulled up at the funeral home, Jill even exited the car more quickly than Annabelle in a desperate attempt to find another person and to keep her from having to be alone with her sister. It became clear to Annabelle this conversation wasn't going to happen anytime soon.

Once Annabelle got inside, she saw Jill already inside talking to Charlie. One of them must have said something funny, because they both were laughing. Annabelle thought for a moment that this did not seem like a place for laughter or any kind of happiness. This seemed like a place where all the happiness had been sucked away, and she initially wanted to retreat through the front door to a much happier world than the one found in here. She wanted to so badly, but she knew she couldn't. She had to stay and face this no matter how hard this would be.

By the end of it, she was more exhausted than ever. Annabelle and Jill had sat at the funeral home and made decisions about everything from flowers, song choices and grievance brochures to what would be said at the graveside and what he would wear. Luckily, at the last minute, she had remembered to grab his favorite suit from his closet, so she was able to give it to the funeral home director. Her mother finally strolled in with some friends when they were wrapping things up. Annabelle and Jill tried to talk to her about their choices and make sure they were okay, but their mother made it clear she couldn't take on that burden right then and didn't care what they had chosen.

As they were wrapping things up, the funeral home director asked for any personal effects of her father's that he would need to have on him when buried. Jill looked to Annabelle and Annabelle looked to her mother. Everyone looked questioningly back and forth at everyone else, but no one said anything. Finally, their mother spoke.

"I guess we can get some of his things from the house and bring them up here."

Annabelle and Jill looked at their mother with puzzled expressions before Annabelle clarified, "you mean his wedding band? I really wasn't sure what to do with it, but I did bring it with me if that's what you're meaning."

"Yes, well, I mean his wedding band, and he had that really nice, expensive watch he was always so proud of, and his cuff links. Did you remember to bring those?"

Now Annabelle and Jill looked at each other for a long moment to ensure they had both heard their mother's words correctly. Then, Annabelle spoke slowly, "No Ruby came by the house and got them and brought them to y'all already."

"Wait. Who is Ruby?" Her mom asked turning to look at the older ladies all gathered around her. "Do y'all know anyone named Ruby?"

They were all shaking their heads looking from one to another. Annabelle could feel the panic rising inside her like an angry wave, and she knew this must be a misunderstanding that had to be sorted out. Maybe the women were just confused, or someone had sent her without telling the others.

"Someone sent a woman named Ruby to the house today to collect some of dad's things to bring up here. Doesn't anyone remember doing that?"

"Honey, no one here knows anything about that." Her mom said.

"Maybe you can describe her to us honey." One of the women towards the back said.

"Oh yeah, I can do that. Well, she was petite, about this tall." Annabelle said as she held her hand up to show everyone the height of the infamous Ruby. "She had long blond hair, and she was tan like she spends a lot of time in the sun. She looked to be about my age, but I can't be certain, and…" Annabelle trailed off as she heard a gasp and realized all the women were looking at my mom all with shocked expressions on their face. "What's wrong?" Annabelle asked innocently and glanced at Jill. Jill just shrugged, and they both returned their gaze to the group of shocked women before them.

"Oh honey." Her mom said with a sigh. "Ruby is the girl your father was having an affair with. I didn't know her name until now, but based on your description, that was her."

"No, that can't be right." Jill said. "Dad was having an affair with Alise St. James. The ladies at the hospital were talking about it, and she was the one standing there. Annabelle told me. She saw her there."

"Alise? No, honey. Alise must have just been there visiting someone else. She is happily married. I can see how you were confused, but no. I didn't know a lot about your father's mistress, but I did know that she was young and blonde, and since no one here knows this girl or sent her to the house. I can only assume it's her."

"She had some nerve coming to our house like that, and just requesting dad's things." Annabelle said anger sprouting in her voice.

"I don't think nerve was ever something she was lacking." Her mom said with a small laugh.

"How can you laugh about something like this? This was horrible! This girl came to the house and lied to us and stole from us! There's nothing funny about this!" Annabelle said her voice full of anger this time.

"Well, I don't know what else to do. It's really pretty funny if you think about it. I mean, your father chose her over everyone, and what does she do the second he is out of the picture? She steals from him! Your father's mistress who took everything from me, took so much from him too, and he was too blind to see her for who she really was. Yes, I find that funny. Don't you?"

Annabelle and Jill both looked at their mother solemnly. Neither of them wanted to put their feelings into words, because they knew their feelings weren't the same as their mother's. Both girls were conscious of their own feelings and looks, but within seconds, they knew by the change in the air around them that everyone else was casting the same solemn look their mother's way. Annabelle didn't even want to turn and see in their eyes what she already knew was reflecting in her own. It was quiet for several long minutes before anyone spoke.

"No," Jill finally said speaking everyone's feelings aloud. "I think it's sad."

"Sad? How can you think it's sad? He's just getting done to him what he did to everyone else. There's nothing sad about that. It's just poetic justice." Their mother said disdainfully.

"I agree. The reciprocation of the behavior is uncanny, but to put yourself out there and make yourself vulnerable only to be embarrassed and made a fool of is never funny, no matter the circumstances of the situation. It's always just sad even in this situation." Jill finished and looked at her mom with a sad pitying look, and she watched as her mom's smile fell on her face.

"I know..." Her mom started in a small voice. "What it is to be embarrassed and made a fool of by someone you thought loved you and would never do that to you. I know because that is what he did to me.

Once again, he gets to only be made to look stupid here in front of just these people," she said gesturing to everyone gathered in the room. "While I have to walk around every day in front of everyone who will know what happened. I have to play the part of the grieving widow who wasn't even good enough to be able to hold onto her husband and keep his eyes from wandering. That is the role he has left me to play! Don't tell me you feel sad for him, because his infatuation with *Ruby* wasn't returned while my *love* for him has been blazing our whole marriage and not mutual even half of that time. I loved him without wanting anything in return for so long, I don't even know what it would feel like to be loved back, but I did it, because that's what you do in a marriage. I did it for him, and he repays me by going out and finding someone else to give it to. Do you know how that feels?" She said leveling her gaze and pointing her finger at Jill while her best friend, Mary, came up to hug her shoulders. "No, you don't! Don't you dare try and tell me about how sad you are for him! You have *no* idea what this has been like for me, or how horrible and stupid I feel!" With that, her mother turned into Mary's arms and started to sob.

"I do" Jill said almost inaudibly. She hadn't realized she had even said it out loud until she noticed Annabelle turn to look quizzically at her. That's when she realized she had given more away about her past than she had ever intended. Jill was hoping Annabelle would realize she had her own secrets she wanted to keep quiet, so she wouldn't try to pry, but she had no way of knowing for sure.

After thanking the funeral home director and getting Marcie set up to alert the phone tree about the date and time of visitation the following night and the funeral the following afternoon, Jill and Annabelle left without a word or glance in the other's direction. They rode the whole way home in awkward silence. They spent the rest of the day avoiding each other and greeting guests who came to pay their condolences and drop off a casserole. It wasn't until later around dinnertime that Charlie stopped by.

Annabelle had been busy arranging casseroles in the fridge for storage until the freezer could be cleaned out enough to make some room. She was elbow deep in the refrigerator when his smiling face appeared from around the corner and made her heart leap into her throat.

"Oh my gosh!" she exclaimed and clutched at her chest trying to get a steady, calming breath. "I wasn't expecting you to be here. I didn't know you were stopping by."

"Yes, that would explain the look on your face and the squeak you made when you saw me." He said with a laugh.

"I don't squeak!" She said seriously.

"Umm okay, but I heard it, so…"

"You heard nothing. I do not and have not ever squeaked. End of discussion." As she said this, Annabelle slammed the fridge door and flopped herself down in a chair at the kitchen table. She had been trying to ignore the exhaustion she knew was taking over, and there was another emotion she couldn't place that was fighting for space inside her as well. The space inside of her at this point was quickly running out, and she needed her new emotional tenants to vacate the premises as soon as possible.

"So, how are you doing?" Charlie asked her and he sat across from her.

"I'm good. I'm just tired. Who knew there was so much planning that had to go into all of this, and you know with my mom playing the 'I don't care anything about your father' role, it has left a lot of things on my plate. I'm just trying to get through the next 2 days, so things will get back to normal."

"I get all of that, but how are you emotionally?"

"I told you. I'm fine, just tired."

"Annabelle, I hate to be the one to point this out, but tired isn't an emotion, so let's pick a word that is actually an emotion like you can be sad or even angry."

"Angry? Why would I be angry? My dad died. That's it. He died. Yeah, it's sad, but I haven't really known him in a while, and before that, the man I knew wasn't someone I liked very much, and I think that feeling was mutual."

"Hmmm. So, you're not angry?" Charlie looked at her with a piercing stare that she felt all the way into her core.

Annabelle let his words sink right into the very center of herself, and she thought about her own words. Was she angry? She really wasn't sure. On the one hand, she'd had a father who was there throughout all of her childhood years, adolescence, and he would've been there even into young adulthood, but she pushed him away and severed her tie with him. She had never really known how she had felt about that. She hadn't ever really been able to square up who should take the blame. She felt like they were both at fault for different things. Her dad had pushed her too much without stopping to consider her needs, and she was ready and willing to walk at the first sign of escape instead of staying and trying to work it out. On the other hand, her dad didn't follow after her to help work out anything between them either, so didn't that make them even? Annabelle could honestly say she wasn't sure, but someone who might have some good insight was sitting across the table and looking at her with eyes filled with concern. She wanted to tell him so many things, but she just couldn't tonight. That emotional wave was one she didn't have the strength to ride right now. If she let it out, she was afraid it would swell and collapse taking them both down with it.

"I'm fine." She said with a weak smile. She tried to make herself sound convincing, but she knew by the look on his face that he hadn't believed her. Instead of dwelling on the overwhelming feeling growing inside of her, she suggested they grab some dinner in an effort to spend some time away from seclusion where others would be present. She hoped that would steer the conversation away from herself and her feelings.

Annabelle, Jill and Charlie heated up some servings of a casserole that had been dropped off and all sat quietly and ate. When they finally did start talking, it was mostly about superficial things. There were no more piercing stares or probing questions, so Annabelle locked her feelings away and shut them up tight inside of her for another day.

Before leaving, Charlie asked about work and told Annabelle to take some time after the funeral. The more she thought about it, the more she felt like she didn't want any time away from her regular schedule, and she told him as much. He nodded and went on his way leaving behind two sisters full of words and wounds. Annabelle and Jill both had a night full of restless sleep.

Jill woke up first thing the next morning with a plan. She was going to clean out her father's side of the closet and pack up his things, so her mother didn't have to. She had tossed and turned most of the night, so she knew her mother hadn't come back home, but as she entered her parent's bedroom, she could hear someone rummaging around in the closet. When she pushed the door open, she could see Annabelle sitting cross-legged on the floor in some black leggings and a blue tunic surrounded by piles of her father's clothes and an empty box in front of her. Apparently, they had the same idea, but Annabelle had gotten there first.

Jill entered the walk-in closet hesitantly not sure if she was welcome. Seeing all of his clothes and his things made it seem like a sacred space, and for a moment, she wanted to put everything back where it had come from. Annabelle looked up and smiled softly at her as she entered and crossed to the other side of the pile to sit down. She saw Annabelle was folding the clothes and putting them in a separate pile, so she grabbed a shirt and started to do the same. They worked that way in silence for what felt like a long time until Annabelle finally spoke.

"So, how are you doing with all of this? I know I should've asked earlier, but there has just been so much going on with mom and everything else."

"I'm fine. I mean, it's sad, but I'm holding in there, and I'm trying to stay busy."

"Yeah, that's how I feel." Annabelle said with a sigh "Hey, can I ask you a weird question?"

"Yeah, I guess so."

"Are you angry?"

"Angry at whom?" Jill asked surprised, but also with a little worry that Annabelle noticed creep into her answer.

"I don't know. I guess angry at dad. Charlie asked me if I was angry last night, and I didn't know what to say. I had honestly never thought about it before." She said clutching the shirt she was holding tighter to her chest in an almost hug.

Jill really thought about it for a minute before answering, and when she did, Annabelle could tell she was serious. "I'm mostly just sad when I think about dad and everything that has happened. I'm angry with the way he treated mom and how he lied and deceived us for so long. Oh, and I'm also extremely angry at Ruby for her part that she played in all of this mess and for stealing from dad, so yeah, I guess I'm angry at a few things."

"Yeah, I'm mad at Ruby too, but I also see mom's perspective that he deserves it for what he did."

"Does he though?" Jill said quietly looking straight at Annabelle "Do people deserve bad things to happen to them for the mistakes they make?"

"I think they do. I mean we get to choose to do the right or the wrong thing, so being punished for making the wrong choice makes sense."

"Yeah, but that's not how God works. No matter how many bad things we do, he continues to pursue us and love us no matter what. Don't you think that's how we should be?"

"I think we aren't God, so we can't be expected to do everything he does."

"He sets the example for us to follow, so how can we not try to follow his example?"

"Look, I don't know. I do know that we have had a lot of bad things happen recently, and we can't say we didn't bring it on ourselves, or at least, I can't say I didn't. I did a lot of bad things, and I came home broke and homeless just in time for my dad to die. There's got to be a reason for that, and you can't tell me it was part of some bigger picture."

"But what if it was?"

"Someone dying? Part of a bigger picture? Really?"

"Yeah, I mean I don't think it happened as a result of sinfulness."

"Of course, you can't, because you're perfect and always make the right choices and never do anything wrong. Listen, it's not because of anything you did, so don't worry about it."

"I'm not perfect. I do make mistakes, and actually, I've done some pretty horrible things okay."

"Yeah right! You are miss perfect, and you always have been. What did you do that was so bad?"

"It doesn't matter what I did. I did something, and it was really bad, and I can't sit here and listen to you talk about how people are getting punished for their sins by horrible things happening to them! So just stop!"

"Why not? If it's true, why does it matter that I say it? It's what I think, and what I believe, and I have every right to say that. You can just not listen and believe whatever you want, so I don't know why you're getting so upset about anything I say. You've never cared much before."

"Well, I do care, because if you're right then dad died because of me and the horrible things I did, and I refuse to believe that and live like that." Jill said as she jumped up, threw down the shirt she was holding and stormed out of the room.

Jill moved as quickly as she could across the house and down the stairs to where her keys were on the counter. She snatched them up and grabbed her shoes. She never even looked back to see her sister's face after her revelation. She was in the car and backing out of the driveway when she glanced up and saw the door opening and Annabelle's face emerging. She couldn't take a good look though. She didn't want to see anything that was on it. She just put her hands on the steering wheel and started driving.

Annabelle sat in the closet momentarily stunned at her sister's revelation. She had no idea what her sister was talking about or why she thought it was her fault her dad had died or even what in the world she could've done that was so bad. She knew her sister had been going through some things, but she had no idea how bad it was. Once the statement had taken root, she realized she had to do something. She needed to talk to her sister, so she got up and raced across the house after her. She reached the garage door just in time to see her sister backing out of the driveway and then she was gone, and Annabelle was alone once again.

Annabelle knew how it felt to want to run away from everything and just be alone, and right now, she had too much to do to fight with her sister over something she didn't understand. She knew and had known Jill was going through something, but it had been made obvious to her that Jill hadn't wanted to let her in and confide in her. At the time, Annabelle had been fine with that, but now she knew that next time she saw Jill, she would have to get her to talk. They had lost their father, and she didn't want to lose her sister to whatever all-consuming emotions were currently eating her alive.

Annabelle spent the next two days alone in the house going through and packing up her father's things. Her mother was still staying at a friend's house and Jill hadn't come home yet either. Annabelle had been alone in her endeavor, and she preferred it that way. Rayne had texted her a few times and even stopped by to share some casserole. Annabelle enjoyed her company and having someone to talk to. She hoped forming a bond with Rayne would be good for her and not drag her down. The best part about having Rayne visit is they didn't talk about her dad at all. Instead, they talked about Rayne's new boyfriend, his band, and other areas of Rayne's life. Other than those few times she had seen Rayne, she had been alone. It was nice to be able to go through her father's things and work through her emotions and memories by herself instead of having to share her memories with someone else. She paused occasionally for food and bathroom breaks, but she spent the majority of her time focused on her task.

About midway through the second day, she had finally finished. She packed up the last box and felt a sense of peace and closure. After that, she headed to her room to pull together her outfit for the viewing that night. She knew she would be seeing her mom and her sister which would be nice, but she would also have to see everyone who she could only assume had judged her after she had abandoned all of them and left. She would have to see everyone and put on a fake smile and graciously accept their sadness and remorse for her situation all the while wondering how much they knew about her mother and father's situation and if they were judging them too. The thought of it exhausted her, and before she realized it, she had fallen asleep.

Annabelle woke up and could tell the day had progressed some during her nap. It took her a second to remember where she was and what had happened. She glanced over and saw the outfit on her closet door and remembered suddenly where she had to be. She checked the time on her phone and realized she still had an hour before she had to leave. She got up to start getting ready and stopped suddenly. She had forgotten that she had no car and no way to get to the viewing. Her sister leaving had been unexpected, and she hadn't realized at the time that she wouldn't be coming back home, so she hadn't made arrangements to get to the viewing. She grabbed her phone and called Charlie, but he didn't answer. She quickly sifted through people in her mind deciding who to call next. Finally, she thought of someone. She made a quick call and felt an instant sigh of relief when she realized she had her ride situation taken care of. She moved onto getting ready and hoped nothing else disastrous would happen before this night was over.

Thirty minutes before she was expected to arrive at the funeral home, a car pulled up in her driveway and a text appeared on her hone to announce its arrival. She grabbed her purse and ran downstairs. She went outside and opened the back door of the black 4 door sedan and slid inside ready to head to her next destination. When she closed the door, she looked up and smiled at the two faces looking back at her. They had been with her through so many important periods of her life, and it seemed only fitting they would be here for her in this moment too.

Brian and Olivia both had sad smiles on their faces that she felt matched hers and most of the ones she would see that night. She thanked them for rescuing her and agreeing to come to something she was sure they would rather sit out, but her to surprise, they said they were already planning on attending the viewing. Annabelle knew Brian had kept in touch with her dad even after she'd left, and her dad had thought of him like the son he never had. Olivia had been a constant in Annabelle's life growing up until she had left, and now she was a constant in Brian's life. Annabelle suspected they had both spent a lot more time around her father than even she realized. She knew this would be hard for her, Jill, and her mother, but she hadn't stopped to consider what this would be like for other people. Her father had friends who would suffer from his loss, and Brian would have to navigate a world without his mentor. Although she suspected he had no idea about the infidelity, or he wouldn't consider him to have been the mentor he thought he was. Annabelle thought about telling him, but she didn't have the heart to shatter his image of a man who had been so present throughout his life. Brian's own dad had left his mom when he was young, so Annabelle's dad was really a father figure for him. She realized he should have a spot standing with the family tonight too. She wanted to ask her mother about it when she got there and see what she thought.

When they arrived at the funeral home, everyone rushed inside to go over one more time what their roles would be for the night and ask any questions they had before people started arriving. Annabelle fell in step with her mother and sister as they got a chance to view their father privately before anyone else showed up. After standing in silence next to her mother, who Jill had been sure to position in between them, for a good while, the funeral home director came back and gave them directions on where to stand. Annabelle saw her chance and asked her mother about Brian standing with them. She had a whole speech prepared to persuade her mother, but to her surprise, her mother willingly agreed without hesitation stating that she thought that was a fantastic idea. Annabelle immediately let Brian and Olivia know, and by the tears in his eyes, she could tell Brian was thankful and excited to get to play a part in this moment.

The viewing went by quickly, but at the end of the night, everyone was exhausted. Annabelle had no idea it could be so exhausting to shake hands and receive condolences. It seemed like the whole town came out to see them. Annabelle wasn't sure if it was truly just to leave their condolences, or if they were hoping to get a glimpse of her and see how the estranged daughter was doing. At the end of the night, they reviewed their plans and times to arrive for the funeral the next day, and then they all left and headed back to the house. Everyone had agreed to stay at the house that night. After they got home, everyone went their separate ways and went upstairs claiming exhaustion and agreeing to talk the next day.

By the time Annabelle woke up the next morning, everyone was gone. She was once again alone. She wasn't surprised Jill had bailed. She knew she didn't want to get stuck in a situation where she would have to talk and come clean about whatever was going on. She was going to have to start getting ready for the funeral, and she knew she was going to see her mom and sister there. She decided this would be it. Before the day ended, she was going to confront her sister on whatever was going on and get to the bottom of this whole thing. She knew today was already going to be tough, but for some reason, she had a feeling she needed to go ahead and have this conversation because the chance wasn't going to present itself again.

Annabelle got ready and made some calls, and by lunchtime, she had secured a ride to the funeral home again. This time Charlie was answering his phone, so it was easier to get a ride. Her whole body felt like a butterfly house wanting more and more to take flight every inch the car progressed closer to the funeral home. She wanted to talk to her sister, and she was ready, but she knew she would be a bundle of nerves until it happened.

Once they arrived at the funeral home, Charlie got out and escorted Annabelle inside. She knew he could sense some tension brewing inside of her, but he was being respectful of the day and hadn't mentioned anything about it. Annabelle met up with her mother and Jill who were talking to the funeral director going over the last of the details. Annabelle glanced over at her sister and tried to make eye contact, but she couldn't ever get Jill to meet her eyes. She was staring intently at the funeral director and nodding at all the appropriate times. To a watchful eye, she would seem fully engrossed and in tune with the conversation ahead of her, but Annabelle knew better. She knew Jill felt the same tension she could feel in the air, and Jill wasn't about to make eye contact with her and have to face any of the tension.

The funeral was lengthier than Annabelle would've liked. She was so nervous and anxious about the impending conversation with her sister that it was hard for her to pay attention to everything being said about her father. She had already worked through her emotions during her packing spree, and she didn't feel like revisiting all of the now here in front of most of the whole town. Her sister was silently weeping beside her mother. She kept sneaking sideways glances at Jill and noticed the tears rolling down her cheeks. She found a tissue packet in the side of the pew, and she casually and covertly handed one to her. Then, she glanced at her mother to gauge whether she needed one as well. She determined it couldn't hurt, so she offered one to her mother, but she held her hand up to decline it. Annabelle knew her mother had a lot of conflicting emotions about everything that had happened, and the way it had all played out. She wished her mother would be honest with herself and just let herself grieve. Yes, she was mad at her late husband, but she could grieve for the love lost, life lost, deceit, etc. There was plenty to choose from in this situation.

The funeral finally ended and after a very awkward procession back out of the funeral home with her mother and sister, they all headed back to their house where they would welcome guests into their home to mingle and give their final condolences. As Annabelle and Charlie headed back to the house, she tried to gather the last of her nerve that she had left to be able to see everyone and put on another round of fake smiles and greetings. She kept reminding herself this would be the last time, and she wouldn't have to do this in the future.

When they got to the house, she was happy to see some of the women from the church were already there setting up plates of food, drinks, and making the house feel happy and homey instead of the horrible loneliness that had been lingering there lately. Annabelle heard herself sigh audibly at the thought of not having to lift a finger to do anything to set up for this moment. Her mother and Jill ad come together in Jill's car, and it was parked at the top of the driveway. The prospect of Jill being blocked in and not being able to run this time excited Annabelle. She realized this would be the best chance she would have to talk to her sister without her having an easy exit strategy. She needed to make sure people had arrived and just go for it.

Once everyone had arrived, and the house was filled to an almost uncomfortable capacity, Annabelle knew her time had come. She heard Jill announce she was going to go and grab something from the garage, so Annabelle followed. Once out in the garage, she helped her sister look for the item she needed while working up the nerve to confront her.

"Jill, can we talk?"

"Annabelle, it's been a long day, and it's not over yet. Can this just wait?" Jill said already sounding exasperated.

Annabelle thought for a moment and then replied, "No, I have tried to be patient about this conversation, but every time we get close to this topic, you run away, and I don't see you for days. We need to have this conversation, and it needs to happen now."

"Fine, what do you want to know?"

"I want to know what the heck is going on with you, and don't tell me it's nothing. Something has been going on since you got back from your trip to see Jason. You've been moody, extremely weird and cryptic about your phone, and then the other day you told me you had done something so awful you think it killed dad. Just tell me what is going on."

"Nothing is going on. I was just upset and talking nonsense, and that's it. Nothing is happening, so you can just go back to worrying more about yourself than everyone else!" Jill spat angrily.

"Jill, I'm here for you, and I'm not going anywhere. I with you would just tell me what is going on, so I can help you. I know something is going on, and you don't have to carry this grief and worry and everything alone. I'm here for you just please tell me what is going on, so I can help you."

"Here for me? That's a joke! You haven't been there for anyone but yourself in years. Once life got too tough for you, you bailed and didn't confide in anyone."

"I know!" Annabelle cut in. "That's why I'm begging you to confide in me instead of doing what I did. I promise I am here for you."

"No, you're not. Stop lying to yourself. You just want someone to have messed up more than you did. Guess what! I did! Is that what you want to hear? I had an affair with my professor who I just found out is *married*, and I thought I was pregnant, and now he's insisting I drop the class and get an F, so no one will find out, and he won't get in trouble, and I told dad, and he had a heart attack. There! Is that what you want? I am a huge screw up just like you but probably worse." With that, she took off back into the house.

Annabelle stood silently fixed in place trying to process everything she had just heard her sister reveal. Sometimes, the bad things you made up in your mind weren't as bad as the truth. She had prepared herself for the possible scenarios, but this hadn't been one of them. She felt awful her sister had been carrying all of this around, and she wanted to make this right and talk to her, but she needed to sit her down and talk to her in an environment where her sister would feel safe. She went back inside and started searching for Jill. She walked through rooms and rooms of people grieving and wanting to hug her and talk to her, and eventually she ended up in the living room with her mother. She wanted to tell her mother everything that had happened, but she knew this wasn't the time. Her mother came up and gave her a big hug, and that's when she saw Jill tucked behind a door on the other side of the room crying.

Ch.22

Charlie saw Jill behind the door, and he went over to her. She was crying, and had her face turned into the doorway. He wrapped an arm around her and whispered a prayer over her.

"God, I don't know what is going on here, but you do. You know all things. Please send blessings and comfort to Jill right now, Lord. She needs it so much right now. This day has been hard on everyone, Lord. Please comfort her and wrap her in your loving embrace. In your loving name I pray. Amen."

Jill glanced over at him, and he wrapped her in a hug, and she cried on his shoulder. He maneuvered her into another room where he could deposit her away from all the wandering eyes and speculations of the crowd. He knew some of this was grief for her father, but he had a sense there was so much more going on here. He had no idea what it was, but he knew someone who would. He sat Jill on the sofa in an extra sitting room they had off of the main living room. He told her he was going to get her a drink and some tissues, but he was also going in search of some answers, so he could help her. Jill reminded him so much of his sister, Maggie. He couldn't argue that he felt protective over her like a brother for a sister. He wanted to find out what was bothering her and fix it for her right away.

< < > >

Annabelle gave her mother a tight squeeze as she and Charlie took her sister into her dad's old "man cave". She had learned so much in the past 24 hours that she'd need a lot more time to process and come up with a plan, but for now, she just needed to be here with these people healing alongside her mother. Most of her job might be forcing her mother to realize she needs to grieve and heal since it has been obvious that her mother wants nothing to do with grieving. When the hug ended, and her mother stepped away to talk to some more guests, Annabelle noticed Charlie coming her way with a concerned look on his face.

"I don't know if you know this, but Jill was just crying over there." He said pointing at the spot Annabelle had seen her. "She's pretty upset." He said the concerned look still there.

"Yeah, I actually saw her, but my mom needed me right then." Annabelle said as she pointed behind him towards her mom. He turned and followed her finger to see her mother laughing and seeming to have fun with her friends. Realization dawned over his face and then confusion.

"Do you know what's wrong with Jill?"

"Yes." Annabelle said matter-of-factly.

"Well, can you tell me, so we can help her?" Charlie said, and Annabelle could tell he was concerned.

"She's probably upset about our dad dying, and she told me some stuff and we just got into a big fight before this. That could have something to do with it." Annabelle said shrugging.

"About what?"

"Some revelations she had that were very personal, so I don't think she would want me to repeat them." She said seriously looking at him.

"Yeah, I understand that." He said nodding. "Seriously though, how can I help?"

"Just continue to be there for her, and knowing you, I'm sure you will be praying a lot. I guess prayer can really help."

"Right on!" Charlie said smiling.

"You're so lame." Annabelle said smiling at him.

They talked for a little while longer before she excused herself to the bathroom to check her own reflection and make sure she hadn't cried off all of her mascara. She returned to the main room feeling good, and upon seeing the room full of people still mingling around talking in low voices, the exhausted feeling from before started to creep back in. For a small minute, she envied her sister's escape from all of this and wish she could've pulled off the same thing, but then she saw her mom and realized she was needed here. She wasn't carrying all the shameful, unspoken baggage her sister had been carrying, so she didn't need an escape right now. She would get through this and everyone would be just fine.

Ch.23

Charlie had been praying for Jill and the whole family since Jill's reaction at the wake. He had never seen her fall apart like that even when her dad was in the hospital and going through surgery. When he had tried talking to Annabelle about it, she had seemed so calm. Come to think of it, she had seemed pretty calmed the whole day considering what was going on in her life. He had never really appreciated how strong she was until now. Inner strength is a gift, but he wondered if she had realized it herself. She had told him she would be back at work today ready for a bit more normalcy in her life. He was prepared to give her just that. He said a quick prayer at this desk before she arrived.

"God, thank you for every blessing you have bestowed on us. Thank you most of all for sending your son to die for us. I pray that Annabelle will find what she is seeking right now, Lord. She is on her quest for you, and I know if she keeps searching, she will find everything she is looking for in you. I know she has a lot of inner strength, Lord, and I pray she uses that to her advantage and realizes what a gift it is during times like these. Please send her comfort and peace and hold her during this difficult time. I can see the changes in her and know a breakthrough is coming. I know she is meant to do big things in your name, Lord. Please help me to be the vessel to continue guiding her to you. It's in your perfect, holy name I pray. Amen."

< < > >

Annabelle was feeling light, happy, and free as she sat at her desk at work and thought about how nice it felt to be back to a normal state of living. She hadn't realized how much she missed having a schedule and someone to escape to everyday. She had spent some time talking to her mom the night before, and they had made some good progress in their healing journey. Her mother had realized it was okay to grieve for the parts of her dad she would miss, and it didn't make her okay with anything he had done.

Charlie had been nice and welcoming this morning, and when Annabelle got to work, she was both surprised and excited to see Rayne in her office waiting on her. It had been so long since she'd seen her, and she really wanted to make sure the girl was doing okay. Annabelle smiled at Rayne as she entered. Rayne was draped over the chair in her office as usual in what looked like a very comfortable position. Annabelle dropped her stuff beside her desk and walked over and sat down in the chair next to Rayne ready to catch up and relax with one of her favorite people. Before she could say anything, Rayne started talking hurriedly.

"I heard your dad's funeral was really nice! I wanted to come, but it seemed private, and I didn't want to interfere with you and time with your family." She said.

"I completely understand why you didn't come, but I want you to know you're welcome to come and hang out with me and my family anytime you want. You will never be interfering." Annabelle said sincerely smiling at her.

Both girls smiled at each other, and Annabelle leaned in for a hug which was reciprocated by Rayne. Annabelle smiled to herself when she realized that for all of their relationship, she had felt like being older meant she had to be the authority figure, and she couldn't let herself go to fully connect, but for this moment, their age difference didn't matter at all. They were just two people who cared about each other and realized the comfort a hug could bring. Annabelle smiled to herself when she realized that she wasn't as alone as she had sometimes let herself feel like she was. She had her mom and sister which were two relationships she knew would really have to be worked on, but then she also had Charlie, Olivia, Brian, and Rayne who accepted her warts and all and loved her for all of it. Annabelle knew Rayne might never know how much this moment meant to her, but she would also treasure it. When Annabelle pulled back, she could see Rayne's eyes glistening with tears.

"So how have you been? How are things with your mom, and your new boyfriend? Sorry! I forgot his name."

"Oh, it's cool. Last time we talked about him, I didn't know his name, so you didn't forget."

"Good. I feel better then!"

"Since we talked last, I have found out his name is Rex, and he is amazing! Seriously, he has been awesome with everything that's been going on, and it's been nice to get away and get to go watch his band play at night, so I'm not alone."

"Alone? Why are you alone?" Annabelle asked concerned.

"My mom has a new boyfriend, so she has been MIA as usual."

"What? Your mom has been gone? I had no idea!"

"Yeah, it won't last forever, it will only be until they break up, and then I will come home one day and see her on the couch with a tub of ice cream eating it with a spoon. That's her normal routine."

Annabelle tried to keep a straight face as Rayne revealed so many pieces of her life. She hoped her face didn't portray how sad she felt for her and the life she was leading. Annabelle had the urge to just scoop her up and take her home and make sure nothing bad ever happened to her again, but she knew that wasn't completely realistic given the circumstances, so instead, she tried to be sympathetic and understanding to everything going on in Rayne's life. Annabelle suddenly realized Rayne had continued talking while she had zoned out, so she put more effort into listening to her friend.

"…so that means I don't know if I will be here Sunday or not for church. His show is kind of far, and they are playing Friday and Saturday, so I'm not sure I will be back in time. Then, they are also finding out about their tour." She said happily.

"Tour? What tour?"

"Well, their band has been invited to tour with another band this summer, so they should know the dates and everything this weekend and make all the final decisions. It's going to be so much fun. I can't wait for it!"

"Wait, are you going on tour with his band?"

"Yeah, I'm his girlfriend. It wouldn't make sense to let him go off alone with all those other girls. That's like asking him to cheat."

"Well, it's not, but we will get to that later. What does your mom think about all of this you going on tour with a guy you barely know and a bunch of other guys?"

"Seriously? My mom wouldn't care even if she was around to care. Hopefully this relationship lasts long enough that I can go and not have to worry about her at all."

"Listen, I know you really like him, but I think you need to really think about everything and make sure this is all what God wants for you and your life." Annabelle was stunned when the words came out of her mouth, and she had the urge to look back and the door and see if Charlie was standing there saying them. When she looked up at Rayne, she could tell that she was equally surprised to have heard the words uttered from the mouth of someone like Annabelle too.

"Since when did you get all holier than thou?" Rayne asked in a mocking tone.

"I honestly have no idea." Annabelle answered. "I think with everything that's been going on, I've been really thinking a lot about it, and seeing how much I'm missing in my life, and I've been trying to fill that void with everything but God. I think now he is trying to show me in several ways that he is the only one who can fill that void."

"So, you're like *them* now?" Rayne said sweeping her hand disgustedly around toward Charlie's office and in the direction of the church offices.

"No, I don't think I'm there yet. I feel like I'm on a journey, and I see my destination and how wonderful it would be, but I'm not sure the price I would have to pay to get there."

"I'll tell you the price." Rayne said angrily as she was getting to her feet. "You have to give up everything fun that doesn't conform to *their* ways, and you have to give up everyone like that too. You have to pretend to love and be nice to everyone and judge everyone behind their backs. There is no positive side to the people here. You were the *only* good thing about this place, and now they've gotten to you too!" Rayne spat. Angrily she grabbed her bag and headed to the front door. Annabelle wanted to follow her, but something stopped her. She had no idea what to say to Rayne. She understood everything she was saying, and not very long ago, she would've agreed with her, but after everything she had gone through lately and all the support she had experienced from these people, she was starting to think Rayne's opinion and even her own opinion were wrong. With a heavy heart and a desire to find a way to show Rayne all that she had learned and experienced lately; she went to Charlie's office to ask him for some help.

When Jill woke up the next morning, she could hear what sounded like someone knocking on her front door. She didn't think it would be for her, but she couldn't hear anyone else stirring, so she decided to go have a look. When she opened the door, she was surprised to see Julie standing on the other side. For a second, Jill contemplated shutting the door before Julie could do anything, but then she realized Julie didn't look angry or like she had any intention to do anything bad, so Jill stood with the door cracked and waited to see what Julie had to say.

"I went through Jason's phone last night. It isn't the first time I've done it. I've honestly suspected he was doing something since he was always so busy, but I didn't know what to look for until you showed up and gave me a missing piece to the puzzle." She said solemnly.

"What did you find?"

"I found out he's a good liar and good at covering his tracks, just not good enough. I looked specifically for the texts you showed me, and I found them under the name of Rob. Rob is a guy he worked with who he was always going to have drinks with after work or meeting for dinner. I tried to invite Rob over for dinner many times, but Jason told me Rob's wife had died recently, so he was not ready to be set up or become a third wheel."

"Wow! He put a lot of time into this."

"That's not all. When I realized you were Rob, I started thinking about all the other guy friends he has mentioned hanging out with and checking to see if they were in his phone as well. I remember him talking about Rob, George and Frank this semester, so I paid special attention to those names in his phone."

"And?" Jill asked wanting more information but unsure she was ready for the answer.

"More texts like the ones you got. He was trying to convince them to drop the class on allegations of cheating, so they could be together later. It was very surprising how many of the men in my husband's phone are sending him texts about how much they love him."

"Yeah, but remember they aren't men. They're all female students."

"I know, but I think either way we have a lot to talk about. I didn't know what to do with this information, and I found this address in his phone under Rob's name, so I got in the car and drove here hoping this would help."

"I'm so sorry this happened, and I hate this is the way you found out. I really hate this was going on and the part I played in all of it."

"I understand. I obviously wouldn't have chosen for this to happen, but I'd honestly rather know than to continue being left in the dark about everything. I feel like a fool for not knowing what was going on. I mean how could I not have known?"

"Sometimes we see what we want to see, and don't forget, the devil is good at deceiving us. It *is* his number one job, so he has had a lot of practice."

"The devil? This has nothing to do with him or God or any other made-up characters. If God was real and loved me, He wouldn't have let this happen, so I don't want to hear any of your lies about how God loves everyone, and if you are really someone who believes in God, shouldn't you not be sleeping with married men?"

Jill felt the sting of Julie's words deep into her core. She knew she had done so many wrong things, and she felt horrible, and she wasn't sure how long she would be paying the price for this mistake. She composed herself, so the sting wouldn't come out in her voice when she spoke again. "You're right. I haven't been a good Christian or doing any of the things God would want me to be doing. I am sincerely working on that. I'm really sorry, and I hope we can both move forward together.

Jill was sincere in her apology, but she wasn't sure what Julie would think. She was honestly surprised when Julies shoulders slumped, and all of her anger seemed to dissipate. Then, she shocked Jill even more by asking if she would come with her to an appointment, she had set up the night before with the Dean. It had been hard enough for Jill to have to come clean and admit her transgressions to her sister, her father and Julie. She wasn't sure she could open up and admit them to a complete stranger. Julie could sense her hesitation, and she was quick to reassure her that it would be okay. Julie explained about needing a witness and how much it would help to have someone come forward. Jill was raging on the inside. Her emotions were pulling her in all different directions, and she had no idea which parts of herself to listen to. Finally, she decided to go. She knew this had happened before her, and it would continue to happen after her if he wasn't stopped. She mustered all the courage she had deep down inside of her, and she nervously agreed.

< < > >

Annabelle was busily filing requests and making the schedules for the upcoming week when Charlie walked in. After the conversation she'd had with Rayne that seemed to explode and take off in a direction she couldn't have foreseen, she wasn't completely prepared to have another conversation today. She had gone to Charlie's office to talk to him after Rayne had left, but he hadn't been in there. Since then, she had just been avoiding her feelings and throwing herself into the work she'd missed during her leave of absence.

She knew Charlie had no idea what had happened, but that didn't mean she would excuse him for coming in with a cheery disposition and a smile on his face while she sat there feeling like her world was crumbling piece by piece and feeling confused by all the things she'd been feeling lately.

"Hey, I need your help with something." Charlie said happily as he seemed to bounce into the office with all the energy of a giddy two-year-old.

"Okay. What can I do for ya, boss?" Annabelle retorted trying to stay out of the trap of his happy disposition.

"I just got back from the main building and meeting with the pastor, and he told me he's going to be out the next two Sundays, and he wants me to preach in his place."

"Wow!"

"I know I'm excited and nervous, and I think I know what passage I want to use for next Sunday, but I want to run some things by you and see what you think. You want to go to lunch and talk about it over some chips and dip?" He asked eagerly.

"Sure." Annabelle said reluctantly. She couldn't imagine going over preaching notes for Sunday right now, but when she weighed that against her dread of sitting in this office all day trying to drown her worried in work, she realized it would be nice to get out of the office for a little while and focus on something else.

There weren't many people at the restaurant when they arrived, so they were quickly escorted to a table where an older man arrived shortly with a basket of fresh tortilla chips and a small bowl of salsa. They both had time to eat a chip before another man arrived to get their drink orders, and he left saying he would be back shortly with their drinks and to take their food orders.

"So you wanted to go over some notes for Sunday?" Annabelle said grabbing another chip and dipping it before taking a bite.

"Yeah, I've actually been thinking a lot about what I want to preach about Sunday, but I want to run some notes by you and see what you think."

"Okay. Shoot." Annabelle said grabbing another chip.

"I really want to talk about the dark vs light in Ephesians 5. I could do one sermon on the darkness and things that can happen when we're walking in the darkness and how we should avoid those things and those behaviors. The following Sunday I could do a sermon on what happens when we're living in the light and how we are changed."

"Okay, so the darkness is our sin?"

"Yes, the darkness is our separation from God, so living in sin or living without him. The light is when we have found him, and we're exposed in our darkness and strive to do better."

Annabelle had never remembered reading that specific passage, but the concept of light vs dark in the world and inside of everyone wasn't a new concept for someone like her who had grown up in church. In the past, she had always felt she understood the light, but in the past few years, she had been living in the dark. Although she knew she was digging herself out of the dark pit she had been living in, she felt an overwhelming desire to defense herself and her actions during that darker period of her life. She had done some things she wouldn't be proud to announce to everyone, but hadn't all of those things helped shape who she was? When she thought of some of her old actions, she felt a small flush rise up her neck and cheeks. The shame she felt made her want to defend herself more. Mostly, she was afraid of what Charlie would think if he found out? Would he look at her the same way? She had enjoyed being around him, and they had developed a nice friendship in their time working together. She would hate to lose all of that over something she had done long before she knew him.

"So, what do you think?" Charlie prodded with a look of excitement quickly fading into uncertainty.

"I don't know. Are you going to spend an entire Sunday telling people all the things they've done wrong and making them feel bad about themselves? If that's your plan? I don't think it's a very good one."

"No, it's not about what they're doing wrong or have done wrong. It's more about what Christ has done for them."

Annabelle picked up a chip and studied it as she thought about how to respond. "If you want my honest opinion, it might make people feel bad about themselves, and it might come out a bit judgy. I don't think the first sermon you give should be you judging everyone."

"Oh that's not it at all. I think you're misunderstanding. That's not where it would be coming from at all. Just wait and see. You'll understand once you hear the whole thing." Charlie said as he selected a chip to eat.

Just then the waiter arrived and took their food orders. Annabelle wasn't sure if she would be able to eat with all the knots in her stomach from the journey she'd just taken back through all of her own dark, personal memories of the past few years. Luckily Jill wasn't here to share any of her shameful memories with Charlie. Annabelle made a mental note to make sure Charlie never found out about her past.

"And what makes you think I'll be in the sanctuary to hear this sermon of yours?"

"Well, you have to be there." Charlie said seriously. The secretary to the pastor is always there to help if the pastor needs something for the service, and since I'm leading the service the next two Sundays and you're my secretary, you have to be there."

"Is that a rule? I don't remember seeing that in my job description."

"Well, I don't know if it's an official rule, but you have to be there. I can't do it without you there." Charlie said earnestly.

"I just really don't see any reason you can't do this without me. We both know you don't need me there to do a great job."

"You're wrong. I do need you there." He said smiling at her.

"Why?" Annabelle pressed.

Charlie stared at her for a long moment like he was about to say something important, but then he looked away for a minute. When he looked back, he said, "I might forget something. It would make the morning less stressful if I know you're there to help me if something goes wrong."

Annabelle didn't mind his answer, but she felt a twinge of disappointment she couldn't place. She wondered what he was going to say before he looked away. She had a feeling that response wouldn't have caused her any disappointment. She knew deep down she couldn't let him down, so she sighed and said, "Well, I guess I could be there at least for the first one." Seeing the smile on his face melted her heart, and she did her best to tamper her feelings. She was an emotional mess right now, and she didn't have time to get caught up in all the different emotions she was feeling right now.

"Yes, that's what I'm talkin' about!" Charlie said so enthusiastically Annabelle expected him to hold up his hand for a high five.

For the first time in a long time Annabelle was feeling wanted and needed. She couldn't deny how great of a feeling it was. There was so much going on inside of her, too many feelings to stop and name them all. She could tell she was changing, and she wanted to confide in someone, but she didn't feel connected enough to anyone right now to share this with except for Rayne who wasn't currently speaking to her. Charlie noticed her silence and suspected she was still dealing with a lot.

"So what's up with you. Have you talked to Jill lately?"

Annabelle snapped out of her trance and looked up to see him looking at her. "No, I doubt I will be hearing from her for a while."

"Have you let her know you're here and available for talking?"

"No, our relationship isn't like that. It hasn't ever been that way."

"Well, that doesn't mean it can't be like that now. I'm sure if you just reach out and let her know you're here for her that will mean a lot right now."

"No, I'm not going to be doing that." Annabelle snapped as she grabbed another chip.

"Well, why not?" Charlie demanded. "After everything y'all just went through, there's really no reason not to. You know as well as anyone that we all need someone to lean on."

"No, there's no reason for me to get involved and force myself into her life."

"I really don't understand why you can't just reach out and check in to make sure everything is okay. I mean she *is* your sister."

"If *you* care so much, why don't *you* reach out?"

"She isn't my sister. I think it needs to come from you, and I don't understand why you're being so resistant. You know that's what she needs. It would be the best thing right now for her to know someone is there."

"You're wrong!" Annabelle snapped. "Whenever I try to help, I always end up pushing people away. I do it with everyone. It's my specialty! I tried to help Jill and now she won't talk to me. I tried to help Rayne, and now she won't even come around anymore."

"Rayne? What happened with her?"

"I tried to insert myself in her life too much, and I think it freaked her out, and she ran away. She accused me of changing and becoming more like you and everyone at the church. She felt like she lost me." Annabelle feeling the anger dissipate from within her like a deflating balloon. In a wave, she felt a pang of grief for the loss of that relationship.

"Is she right?" Charlie asked simply.

"Of course not, she would never lose me?"

"Well, maybe you should reach out and tell her that, but I really meant is she right about you becoming more like me and everyone else at the church?"

Oh. I don't know. I told her I'd been thinking a lot about the things I'd heard, and I keep feeling like I'm searching for something, but I'm really not even sure what that is." Annabelle said with a sense of defeat. She wasn't sure why she felt like opening up and revealing this to Charlie, but she felt like something told her to open up and confide in him and it would be okay.

"So, Indy, you're finding yourself at the beginning of your quest." Charlie said with a twinkle in his eyes.

"What?"

"You know. Indiana Jones starting out on a quest for the truth."

"No, I have no idea what you're talking about."

Charlie's jaw dropped open, and he stared at her with a stunned look across his face. He didn't speak again until the waitress finished dropping off their food and left. Then he took a slow breath and started speaking. "So, you're telling me you've never seen an Indiana Jones movie?"

"That's right." Annabelle stated with a smile teasing her lips because she wasn't sure if she should be proud of this or not.

"Okay." Charlie said pausing while his thoughts and his words caught up to one another. "We will have to do something about the fact that you've never seen one of those movies. I mean I don't even know if we can continue to be friends if you've never seen an Indiana Jones movie."

Annabelle tried to keep her face impassive as he mentioned them being friends. She was glad to hear him say they were friends, but a piece deep inside of her felt like she wanted something more.

"Secondly," Charlie continued without stopping to gauge her reaction, "Indiana Jones always goes on a quest after some information has been presented to him, and it intrigues him enough to pursue it. I'm making the connection that you and Indy are one in the same right now. You've been presented with information that was intriguing, and now, you're wanting to pursue it and see where it leads you. Am I right?"

Annabelle took a minute to really let his words sink in. She thought about everything he had told her relating to the bible, everything she knew about God from her growing up years and every bit of information she had obtained from her own observations. She thought about all the kindness that had been shown to her even when she knew beyond a shadow of a doubt, she didn't deserve it and the support system that had surrounded her mother, sister and herself when everything had happened with her dad. She would be lying if she said she wasn't at least a little intrigued about where all this kindness, love and support had stemmed from. She knew she wanted to keep searching until she found an answer because honestly, after everyone she had been around for so long in the city, the genuine kindness she had felt here really baffled her. People were kind and loving without wanting anything in return, and if she was honest with herself, she didn't understand that kind of love.

When she finally felt like she had reached an answer, and she was ready to speak, she looked up to see Charlie looking at her expectantly. Of all the people who didn't have to be nice to her, he had been showing her kindness and support from day one when she had kicked him in the hospital. She felt a flush rush to her cheeks when she remembered even afterwards how unkind she had been to him. She had not deserved any support or kindness from him, but he had been there through everything to give it and offer advice even when she didn't want it. He had even helped her mend two friendships when there was nothing in it for him. She *had* to know where all of that came from.

"Yes, I suppose I'm starting my quest." She said a little embarrassed to say the words aloud.

"That's excellent news." Charlie said with genuine happiness on his face.

"I'm not sure where to start though." She said a little embarrassed.

Charlie looked at her unconvinced. "Really? Are you sure about that?"

"Okay well, I guess I could start reading the Bible. That seems like a good place to start."

"We have some Bible study groups at church. I could definitely hook you up with one of them. That way you can read and have discussions about what you're reading, and you have people to help you with any questions you have."

"Okay. That sounds doable."

"Oh, it's definitely doable for you. I suspect you can handle a lot more than you give yourself credit for."

"Really?" Annabelle asked intrigued by his statement. She wasn't sure what he meant by this, but she suspected she would like where he was going with it.

"Yeah, I'm usually a good judge of people, and I can tell that you, my friend, are tough with a deep to the core inner strength. I suspect there's not a lot that rattles you or throws you off."

"In the past, I would definitely have agreed with you, but lately, I'm starting to think that's not the case at all." Annabelle said with a hint of sadness in her voice.

"God has a way of coming in and blowing away everything you thought you knew about yourself, the world, others and everything. He is going to make you revisit how you feel about a lot of topics and even change your opinion on some of them. Just make sure you're ready for it because you will come out changed in some ways."

Annabelle thought for a second then nodded. "I think I can handle that."

"Good to hear." Charlie said with a chuckle. "Now how about we eat up and head back to work. I think you have a quest to embark on and maybe some relationships to mend."

"Will do boss." Annabelle said grabbing her fork and knife eager to cut into her enchiladas.

Ch.24

When they got back to the office, Charlie felt an overwhelming need to pray for Jill. He had no idea what was going on, but after everything he and Annabelle had talked about, he knew everything wasn't okay. He bowed his head and started praying.

"God, I know you know the entirety of my life and even know things that will happen that I cannot imagine or even understand. I know you love us in spite of every sin and every flaw and nothing we do actually surprises you. Jill is facing something right now, Lord, that is so much bigger than she is, but it isn't bigger than you are. She needs you right now. She needs to feel your closeness and your peace settle within her heart. Please give her the courage to do whatever needs to be done to combat the issues she is facing and please show her you are the God who stays and never leaves us and your love is everlasting. Amen."

< < > >

Jill wasn't sure if it was the slight chill in the office or her nerves that were making her feel slightly shaky. She wished she had grabbed a sweater, but in all honesty, if she did, she would probably be sweating through it right now from nerves. She had only been in the office a few moments before the dean had excused himself to take a phone call. She wished they could just get this over with and be on their way. She looked over at Julie sitting in the chair beside her. She knew she owed it to this woman and others like herself to come forward now before there were more of them. She had been going over in her mind how reckless she had been thinking he really loved her and all the other lies he told her that she believed. She was never this naïve, and she didn't understand why she had to become this person now. She silently wished she was more like Annabelle, Annabelle was tough, and she would never find herself in a tangled mess like this.

Suddenly, in the quiet still of the office, she could hear footsteps approaching. She felt fear creep up her spine for what they were about to do. She knew it was the right thing, but there was so much she would have to admit that she didn't know if she would be ready to admit to someone else. She heard the footsteps coming closer, and she heard Julie move only a second before she felt her hand close around her own. She did get a sense of relief knowing they were in this together. At least she had someone to back her up. When the door opened, they both turned towards the sound and saw the dean coming back in with a manilla folder in his hands. Directly past him in the waiting room, sat a very familiar face she hadn't seen in months, Jason. Jill instantly felt her blood run cold and wondered if Julie had also seen him. She got her answer when Julie squeezed her hand and looked at her with wide eyes. Jill knew he had seen them too. Both of them, here together in the dean's office could only mean one thing to him. She knew him well enough to know he wasn't going to go down without a fight, and a fight was what she was most concerned about. She didn't want her reputation to be dragged down along with him, but she had come this far, and it wouldn't make sense to back out now. She couldn't leave Julie hanging with no witnesses. He had done something awful to her, and she had helped him, so Jill felt obligated to make things right.

"So, ladies, what is this about?" The dean said looking intently at both of them.

"We would like to file a sexual harassment report against my professor." Jill heard herself say with as much confidence in her voice as she could muster.

She could tell when the dean removed his glasses and rubbed the bridge of his nose with his thumb and forefinger that this wasn't how he was expecting his morning to begin. He put up a finger to them, picked up his phone, and asked his secretary to join them with her computer. Jill and Julie sat quietly listening to the secretary move somethings around as they assumed, she was grabbing her laptop and joining them. She could only imagine what Jason was thinking. She was sure at this point; he would be starting to panic. She suspected he has most likely researched this enough to know the procedure and what would happen if someone came forward. She knew while she was giving a statement inside the room, he would be on the other side of the door piecing together a statement of his own. Both of their statements would be poised to destroy the other. She wondered if she would be automatically believed, or would there be a trial? She hadn't really thought all of this through. Was she prepared for everything that was about to happen? Her thought was cut short when the secretary entered the room and closed the door quickly. She took a seat next to the dean's desk and set her laptop on the edge of his desk. When she had it opened and ready, the dean looked up at them.

"Okay ladies. Let's start from the beginning. Tell me everything, and Carol here is going to keep a transcript of our conversation for our next steps in the process."

Jill was unsure who was supposed to speak first. She looked at Julie who had grasped her hand again. She felt like Julie needed as much encouragement right now as she did, so this time, she was the one who squeezed her hand. When Julie looked at her, Jill saw her give a slight nod and knew it was time for her to begin with her tale. Julie hadn't heard all of the details, and she felt sick inside about everything she was about to have to tell her.

"My affair with Professor Richmond didn't begin at the start of the term." Jill began nervously. "It flourished out of something innocent with him complimenting my work then leaving me notes to come by his office to discuss some of the points in my paper. The first time we ever crossed the line between teacher and student was when we were leaving his office after an exhilarating discussion on one of his lecture topics. He asked to walk me to my car since the sun was setting, and I agreed, because I didn't want to be out alone on campus in the dark. When I turned to say goodbye, he kissed me. I didn't know then that it would be anything more than that." Jill said trying to remove herself from the story, so she didn't get emotional.

"Was there anything more than that?" the dean asked with hopefulness in his voice.

"Yes, I started getting invited back to his office more frequently which turned into more kissing and sharing meals together which eventually led to the start of what I considered to be a relationship. The first time we slept together," Jill had to take a moment to prepare herself to air her shame and guilt in front of all these people, "We left his office, and it started pouring. We were rushing back to my car, but it was across campus, and it seemed like we would never make it. He said there was a place we could go, so he took my hand and pulled me off the path into a little shack hidden off in the trees. When I got inside, it looked like a gardener's tool house with a lot of lawn equipment. He seemed certain that it wasn't going to be frequented. I was more skeptical, because I was a virgin, but he started kissing me, and peeling off my wet clothes and his own. Next thing I know, we were on the ground making love to the sound of the rain pattering on the tin roof above us." As Jill recounted the memory, she remembered all the emotions that came with it. She remembered the smells and the sounds of the damp earth and the rain drops on the metal roof. She remembered how beautiful she felt the whole moment had been, and before she could stop it, a small tear ran down her cheek. A mark of betrayal for the abomination of a memory she held so dear. They had slept together many times since then, but she had often thought none of the other times had been as perfect as that moment. None of them had even come close. She had always felt happy to have such an amazing story of her first time. Now, that memory was tarnished. He didn't actually love her, and for all she knew he had sex with someone else earlier that day and possibly even later that night.

"Can anyone corroborate your story? Did anyone in your classes know what was going on? Did anyone ever see y'all walking to your car together?" The dean asked all of these questions knowing the answer she would give him.

"No, Jason is smart. He has done this before, and he is still doing it, so he knows how to cover his tracks." Jill said trying to keep her voice light without any hint of the emotional turbulence going on inside of her. "Does it matter if there are witnesses?" She asked wondering if coming here had been a mistake.

"No, but it helps. I'm sure his story will not align with yours. In fact, he has issued a statement that you were caught plagiarizing. He has asked that you be removed from his class." The dean said this all while holding up the manila folder in his hand.

"I have text messages from him." Jill said hopefully now knowing Jason's true intention in being in the dean's office waiting room that morning. Now, she realized she looked like she was trying to burn him before he burned her.

"That's definitely a start. Having another witness would be excellent though. There will be an investigation, so the more evidence we have, the better." The dean stated.

Julie spoke up then and offered her own information about the names in his phone and the messages that accompanied them. Jill's excitement rose slightly until Julie admitted she hadn't taken screen shots of anything, so she also had no proof. Now that Jason had seen them in there together, Jill was sure he would wipe his phone clean and not let Julie anywhere near it. Jill knew their best bet was to try and figure out who at least one of the other girls was, and she would have to convince her to come forward with her own statement. She had no idea how she would accomplish this, but she knew it had to be done. She finished giving her statement, and Julie put her own statement into record about nights he had worked late claiming work functions that didn't exist, and the evidence about the names and text messages in his phone supposedly being linked to colleagues he had at work that didn't exist.

When they were finished, and the dean thanked them for coming in, he rose to open the door and Jill felt her heart catch in her throat. She did not know if should face him right now. She was somewhat relieved to see that when the door opened, the chair he had been previously occupying was vacant. He had come to turn her in, and then he had left. He didn't want to see her, speak to her or have anything to do with her. He was finished with her. Jill let that sink in for a moment and harden her heart a little further against Jason. She needed to stay focused right now, and she didn't need to be charmed by fantasies of their time together.

Once they got outside, Jill and Julie agreed to go sit and grab a bite and work on strategy. Jill found herself in a "his word vs hers" scenario, and she wanted to prove beyond a shadow of a doubt that he did what she claimed, and he deserved to pay for it. She wasn't going to let anyone think she was just an upset student who had gotten caught plagiarizing a paper and made accusations in lieu of being expelled.

At the restaurant, Jill dove right in to making a game plan. She knew they would have to have one to make sure this came out the way she wanted. She really had no idea where to even begin finding one of the girls, but then she had a thought. She remembered that Julie had gone through Jason's phone, and she had read messages. Maybe there was something in the messages that was a clue. She decided it wouldn't hurt asking Julie about it. Worst case scenario, Jason was even better at covering his tracks than she had hoped.

"Julie, didn't you say you read the texts in Jason's phone from all of those random male colleagues he was always going to dinner with?"

"Yeah, I did read most of them until I thought I might get caught. Why?"

"Okay. This is a long shot, but I really need you to think about what specifically was in those messages. Did it say anything about specific locations maybe somewhere one of the mystery colleagues worked? Anything that would help us find one of them to have as an extra witness."

"Oh, awesome idea!" Julie said excitedly. "Okay, let me think about this for a second."

As they sat in silence for a few minutes while Julie thought through all the information, she had ingested in the past 24 hours, Jill teetered on the verge of hope and despair. She wanted to get her hopes up, but she was too afraid to let herself go there.

"Oh! I do remember seeing something about the Tasty Freeze. I know a lot of college students hang out there, but I was thinking based on the information in that specific message that it seemed almost like Robert worked there which was really odd. I knew Robert was supposed to be a colleague, so it didn't seem to match up for me. Now, I know exactly why that is."

"Then, the Tasty Freeze is where our search will begin!" Jill said unable to keep the hope and excitement from her voice this time. They paid for their drinks, and they left and headed onto the main walkway which would take them from campus right to the local college hotspot, the Tasty Freeze.

Ch.25

Later that day, Charlie was thinking back over the conversation he'd had with Annabelle at lunch. He decided to pray over everything they had talked about.

"God, I come before you now to ask for your provision and guidance to help Annabelle and Jill mend their relationship. Guilt is an ugly thing, and I don't want either of them left with guilt when all is said and done. I know you have a plan for both of them, and you have great things in store for them. Please allow me to help guide them in this journey. Annabelle is doing such a good job seeking you, Lord. She is thirsty for the truth and the living water only you can provide. I am so honored to have been chosen to go alongside her during this journey, Lord. Please wrap these sisters in your loving comfort and wisdom. It is in your holy name, I pray. Amen."

< < > >

Annabelle had returned to work with Charlie with the intention of finishing up a few things and then heading over to Rayne's house to make amends. In the midst of finishing things and getting everything sorted out for a visit to Rayne's house, she had felt an urgency inside of herself to pray which led to a search through the bible looking for the right words. She found later when she looked up from the bible, that she had immersed herself for a few hours in its pages. The time for making amends today had gone, but she felt a confidence that the right time would present itself another day. Somehow without knowing how, she just knew God was telling her today wasn't the right day, and she needed to be patient. She felt as though she was being lead on a journey of patience and trust in Him. She had read the story of the Israelites fleeing from Egypt, because of Moses. She felt a sort of kinship to Moses, and the fact that he felt unworthy of such a big task as he was given. She had often felt that way in her own life, and it reminded her of one of her favorite quotes, "For of those to whom much is given, much is required." She admired the patience needed by the Israelites to wander in the desert seeking the promised land. She was in awe of God taking care of them and providing for every need they had. She felt the strain of patience wearing on the Israelites as their journey seemed never ending. She had also been in that same place where she couldn't stay patient long enough, and she had given into the feeling of urgency and a need to make something happen instead of waiting on it to happen.

She was amazed by how much she thought the stories would be outdated, and she wouldn't have connection to them, but in reality, she had felt so many connections to their feelings. She had rejoiced with them, mourned with them, and most importantly, she had been in awe of God's timing and love. With a sense of peace surrounding her timing with Rayne, she decided to send her a card for now, and then follow up in person when God told her it was the right time. Before she left work that night, she wrote some of her feelings down in a card, and she left it in an addressed envelope on her desk. She would take it to the post office in the morning when she took the other items for her weekly mail run.

On her way out, she stopped by Charlie's office to let him know she was leaving. After saying goodbye, she headed outside to the waiting car. Since Jill had been gone, Annabelle had just been using her car. Today when she opened the door, she was hit with the familiar scent of her sister's perfume. It made her a little sad to think about her sister off dealing with big issues that had caused big emotions, but there was nothing she could do to help her right now. She understood how Charlie felt about wanting her to reach out to Jill and let her know she was here for her, but she felt like there were other things he didn't understand about the situation, so how could she be sure what she was supposed to do. She knew there was only one thing she could do, pray. In the past, she would've laughed at the thought that prayer actually did something, but now, she was sure there was something there. She cranked the car, closed the door and prayed for her sister and the entire situation surrounding her and everything she was going through.

When she finished her prayer, she felt certain she needed to send her sister a quick text to just let her know she could call or text her anytime, and she would be there for her. Charlie had been right. Annabelle wasn't so sure she would let him know that just yet, but it was nice to have a direction to go in. She took out her phone and sent a text to Jill's phone. She was pleasantly surprised to realize she didn't have any anxiety waiting for a response. She felt a peace and stillness and didn't need a reply at all. The fact that her sister would get the message was all she needed to know. Annabelle drove home in silence thinking about everything she had learned that day. She had vowed to take more in and think about how God would want her to respond to a situation before responding. She would wait to feel a nudge from God before proceeding in a situation.

She arrived home to an empty house. Her mom was out visiting her church friends, so she grabbed a piece of casserole left from the many they'd received after the funeral. She heated the casserole and got her bible out to continue on her quest for the truth. She was pretty sure Indiana Jones hadn't gotten so many movies from giving up halfway through his quests. She knew he had to be completing them, so she thought she owed it to herself to do the same. She read more bible stories she felt God was showing her as a way to speak to her own insecurities, but there was still one, she was keeping locked up tight inside. She wasn't ready to speak that insecurity aloud to God right now. She needed to pursue more truth first. Once she was filled with casserole and God's word, Annabelle cleaned up and went upstairs to bed.

< < > >

Jill and Julie had almost struck out at the Tasty Freeze. They had waited around all day asking the scoopers about the college and if they knew any of the scoopers who attended. They soon learned the early crowd of scoopers and the late crowd didn't seem to work together or communicate with each other. No one in the early crowd knew anyone who worked at the college except for a scooper named Matt. Once Julie and Jill met Matt and realized he was in fact a man, they knew that group was not going to be where they got answers. They found out what time the shift change would be, so they decided to leave and come back to talk to the next group of scoopers once their shift started.

Jill decided to take a nap once Julie dropped her off at the dorms. Julie would be back later to pick her up when shift change happened. The morning had been long and emotionally draining for Jill. She expected Julie felt the same way for similar reasons. They had both had their worlds shattered in the past 24 hours, and everything they thought they knew had turned out to be a huge lie. Jill realized that Julie had to be going through more than she was. Jill was mourning the loss of a lover, and Julie was mourning to loss of a husband. Jill wasn't naïve enough to think the two were similar. She knew Julie had more years of history with him, and she knew they both realized this had been going on a lot longer than any of them could have ever imagined. That couldn't have been an easy pill for Julie to have to swallow, but Jill realized selfishly she was glad she hadn't been the only one and the one to break up a marriage. She realized every part she had played in this was wrong, but she was truly hoping Julie would recognize that she never intended to break up a marriage since she'd had no idea he was even married. Jill knew things would get worse and there would be a longer grieving process before things were over for her, but she couldn't focus on all of that right now. Right now, her body was demanding sleep for a few moments where she could quiet her mind and tune it all out. She set the alarm on her phone and drifted off into a thankfully dreamless sleep where she could be at peace.

When the alarm woke her a few hours later, Jill felt tired by thankfully rested. Her body had needed those extra hours, but she still felt the weight of what they had to do weighing her down as she tried to prepare herself for what came next. She ran a brush through her hair, washed her face, and threw some shoes on just as there was a knock on her door. She ran to open the door, and she was surprised to see Jason standing where she was expecting Julie to be standing.

She stood in shock for a few minutes then remembered where she was and what was happening, and tried to close the door quickly, but he stuck out his foot and blocked the door from closing. No matter how hard she pushed, he wouldn't budge. She knew she was alone, and she started to get scared.

"Leave me alone!" She heard herself say in a small voice that she was ashamed to say belonged to her. This was the time for strength, but in this moment, she didn't feel strong. Truthfully, she didn't feel much more than fear.

"Jill, let me talk to you. I know how this looks, and I know what you're thinking, but please, just let me talk to you." Jason pleaded.

"There is nothing you can say that will change things now. I don't want anything to do with you." She said hearing the strength building in her voice.

"I know you think you know everything, but you're wrong. Julie hates me! She made up all of that stuff about other girls to turn you against me, because she knows I want to be with you. Julie and I have been having problems, so we are getting a divorce, and she doesn't want me to be happy. She knows that you make me happy, and you're the one I want to be with." He said.

"No, you turned me in for plagiarism today. You don't try to ruin the career of someone you love."

"You mean like you were there to do to me without even talking to me first?" He snapped.

"I was there to make sure this never happens to anyone else ever again. I was there to protect other girls from you like I wish someone had been there to protect me." Even as she said these words, she knew the harsh reality was that even if someone had been there to tell her she was being an idiot and making a mistake, she wouldn't have believed them. She felt what she felt, and that was all she had cared about at the time.

"I'm just coming here to tell you to stop this witch hunt and to think with your own brain about what you're doing."

"Jason, we both know you are just here to try and save yourself. This isn't about anyone else except for you." With those words, she took advantage of his shock, and she was able to push the door closed for good this time.

When another knock came about 10 minutes later, Jill made sure to check the peephole before opening the door this time. She was relieved to see Julie standing on the other side instead of Jason coming back for another round. She wondered if she should tell Julie about Jason coming there and what he had said, but she was afraid it would cause more pain than it would actually help the situation, so she decided not to tell her. She didn't want to make things awkward between them, and there was a small part of her, if she was being completely honest, that wanted to believe him.

With her resolve to keep quiet about everything that had transpired within the last half hour, Jill wasn't surprised to find that the entire ride back to The Tasty Freeze was in silence. The nervous energy radiating off of Julie was palpable, and Jill didn't know what to even say to her. She couldn't come up with anything comforting to say. She was just as nervous as Julie if not more. It was her career that was hanging by a thread here. If they didn't find someone else to come forward, she wasn't sure she would be able to win just purely on the fact that she was a female accusing her teacher of inappropriate behavior. With him bringing up the plagiarism accusation, she wasn't in a place to be looking very good.

When they arrived at The Tasty Freeze, Jill could see the atmosphere had completely changed. There were less families and older people and more teenagers, college students, and lots of people seeming to be on dates. She knew if you wanted to find a college girl, this would be the place to be. She had high hopes that their search would pay off tonight. Julie parked in a spot off to the side where they could easily get away if they needed to. Neither of them knew how this would go, and Jill felt reassured that they could leave quickly if they found the girl, but she got angry instead of wanting to cooperate.

As Jill followed Julie through the crowds of people gathering around to talk and eat ice cream, she was struck by the feeling that she really wanted some privacy for this. It had been a while since she had been around big groups of people, and she was finding she didn't really care for it anymore as much as she once had. She saw a lot of smiles and heard a lot of laughs in the crowd, and she was envious of the happy and carefree moods going on around her. She was hoping as she was passing all of the people maybe a little would rub off on her. They seemed to have plenty to spare. As they approached the counter, she sent up a silent prayer that God would lead them to the right person and towards answers. When they got to the front, they ordered scoops in cups, so they could have a reason for being there without just being nosey. Jill took a bite of her chocolate chip cookie dough and wished this was any other night, because she could tell if this was a regular night where she could come and feel free from all of this, she would really enjoy this ice cream. She could tell the ice cream here was really good, and she really wanted so much to be able to enjoy it, but she still had a sour feeling in the pit of her stomach that she knew no amount of sugar could take away.

As she took another small bite to blend in, she heard Julie inquire to the scoop girl about the girls who worked here, and if any of them went to the college. The girl pointed out a few. When she took out her phone and showed the girl a picture of Jason and asked if she had seen him here talking to any of the girls, this time the girl looked a little apprehensive, but she only pointed towards one girl off in the back. Jill didn't want to look at what she guessed would be her competition, but she couldn't help it. She looked in the direction of the girl's finger and followed it to the back of the room until she saw a girl who was breathtaking. She had beautiful smooth coffee colored skin, short cut hair, caramel-colored eyes, and a smile that Jill could tell could light up any room, and if her big, bold earrings were any indication, she had a huge personality.

Jill had no idea what Julie was feeling in this moment, but her own insides were a storm of emotions. She was disappointed there was a girl, because the part of her that wanted Jason's lies to be truths wanted there to actually be no other girls, but at the same time, she felt drawn to this girl, and she wanted desperately to get to know her. It was such a strange sensation, but she felt as though they were connected somehow, and Jill couldn't wait to introduce herself. With her feelings rolling inside of her, she took the first steps forward. She felt Julie start moving a few beats behind her. She didn't know if Julie was drawn to this girl the same way she was or not.

Before they got towards the back of the bar area to reach her, she came out with a broom and dustpan to start cleaning up. Jill didn't know what made her become so forward, but she walked right up to her, extended her hands and introduced herself.

"Hi. I'm Jill. I think maybe we have Econ together with professor Richmond." Jill decided it was best to play it this way instead of coming right out and admitting why they were there.

"Oh hey, I'm Keemera." She said extending her hand as well. "I'm sorry! I don't recognize you from my class, but I'm sure I've seen you before." She said sweetly.

Jill hated what she was about to do to this poor girl, because she seemed so genuinely nice, but she knew it had to be done, so she plunged ahead, but before she could get the words out, she heard Julie move beside her.

"I think you might know my husband." Julie said and she thrust the phone in Keemera's face.

Jill didn't need to look at the phone to know it was a picture of Jason, and with one glance at Keemera, she could tell that in fact, she did know him. Keemera's eyes got wide, and she looked at both of them and then back at the picture. She hesitated for the slightest second, and Jill noticed her resolve seemed to collapse before she picked it right back up and looked Julie square in the face.

"You must be Julie." She said smiling towards her.

"Yes, I am, but how did you know that? Oh my gosh! Have you known about me this whole time?" Julie said outrage and shock mixing in her voice.

"I only just found out about you recently. Look, Jason told me everything. I'm so sorry about your marriage, and I wish there was more I could do to help, but he told me he's tried."

"Jason? Wait, what has Jason told you?" Julie asked concerned.

Julie had no idea what Keemera was talking about, but Jill had a very good idea. She was certain now that Jason had visited Keemera that day too and probably several others to make sure he had covered all of his bases. Jill knew Jason wasn't stupid, she should've suspected this. He must have told Keemera everything he had told her about how she was the only one, and he and Julie were having problems, and Julie was trying to ruin him, because she was mad the marriage was ending. Jill had to hand it to him. He was good. He even had her believing him for a second, and she'd had solid proof he was a liar. Poor Keemera had no evidence to the contrary, so now, they booth looked like fools to her.

"Keemera, please." Jill interjected softly. "I know what he said to you, and I know what you must think, but what we are saying it true, and I can prove it. I have tons of text messages from him that I can show you. Please, just look at them." Jill said as she was taking out her phone and opening her texts.

"No, I won't look at them. I know you are mad, because he dumped you, and you want him back, and I'm sorry for that, but he is with me now, and we are so happy. I'm not going to ruin that by not trusting him. He hasn't given me any reason to trust him, so I'm going to stick by him. I'm so sorry for everything the two of you have been through. I really am, but this just isn't my fight. I'm sorry, but I have work to do, so I need to go do it. Y'all have a good night." With that, Keemera walked away and started sweeping trash from the concrete into her dustpan. She worked swiftly as she moved all over the concrete lot until she had disposed of all the trash. Before going back inside she looked back at Julie and Jill. Jill suddenly got the impression they were the next bit of trash she would like to remove from the sidewalk, so she gave Julie's arm a tug and pulled her back towards the car.

When they were inside the car. Julie slumped forward and her shoulders started shaking. Jill knew this was necessary, and Julie probably hadn't cried yet, so she let her have a moment. She put her hand on her back and patted it to let her know she was there. Finally, Julie looked up at her with red swollen eyes and streaked mascara. Jill saw the pain in Julie's eyes, and she felt for her instantly. She knew a small part of that pain, and she didn't want to give in without a fight if not for herself, she could do it for Julie.

"Listen. We aren't giving up. I'm not giving up. I'll continue trying, and we will get her to believe us." Jill said smiling at Julie.

"Are you sure?" Julie asked reluctantly "You heard her, she doesn't want to have anything to do with us, because he has her brainwashed."

"Yeah, I know." Jill admitted. "It seems like the end, but it isn't I promise. I know God has bigger plans for us than this."

"Really, God again?"

"Look, I know he isn't your favorite person right now, but I promise you later you will look back on this and understand why this was a necessary thing for you to endure. Do you trust me?" Jill asked hopeful.

"I guess." Julie said.

"Okay. I'm going to ask you to do something that won't be easy for you, but you have to trust me."

"What is it?" Julie asked hesitantly.

"We're going to pray together right now. We are going to make sure God is part of this, and we are going to ask him to point us in the right direction and help us know what we need to do next. Do you think you can do that with me?"

"I can try. Things can't really get much worse than this." Julie added.

"That's the spirit." Jill said smiling, and she closed her eyes and started to pray. She poured her soul into her prayer, and she felt Julie's hand find hers and squeeze it. That's when she knew that Julie was praying too. She prayed and prayed until she had no more words or emotions left within her to lay at God's feet. When she opened her eyes, and she saw Julie's eyes, she saw they were tear streaked again, but in a different way than before. They were happier tears on a face that had softened with the words of the prayer. The atmosphere in the car had also calmed and quieted, and everything seemed to settle around them with peace. Jill had no idea what they would do next. She didn't even know if they were going to be doing anything more with this, or if God would tell them to leave it, but she did know that God was now in charge of everything, and it was no longer her and Julie's battle.

Jill realized she had been thinking of this as a fight against herself and Jason, but now she realized it really had nothing to do with him. She was fighting the devil, and he had been winning. He had been making her warmer to Jason and wanting to believe the lies that she knew in her heart were untrue. She had been letting the devil win by not allowing God a place in this fight. The devil would always lose to God. Good would always triumph over evil, and she had been complacent with sheltering the devil and sin for too long. Now, it was time to kick them out! As she thought these things, she felt a buzz. She looked down, and saw she had an unread text on her phone from Annabelle. She thought for a moment about ignoring it, but then she felt a familiar nudge from somewhere deep in her soul, and she knew this was part of God's answer to her prayers somehow, so she opened it and smiled. After reading the message, she knew what she had to do.

"No worries, Julie. I have a plan." Jill said as she started typing a message back.

Ch. 26

Charlie had just received a frazzled call from Annabelle. She told him Jill had left and gone back to the college, and she had just called and needing her help. Annabelle apologized and promised Charlie she would be back before Sunday, and she would have everything finished in time for his sermon. She hadn't really gone into detail about what cause Jill to go back to school and what was going on now, but he knew one positive thing was it was going to bring the girls together. Jill calling and asking Annabelle for help made him happy, and he knew it was a step in the right direction for their relationship. He wanted nothing more in that moment than to thank God.

"God, thank you so much for your blessings each and every day. Thank you for sending your son to die for us, so we can all be made new through you. Thank you for your part in mending the relationship between Jill and Annabelle. Those two needed something to bring them together. I have no idea what the catalyst was, but God, thank you for following your plan and never listening to mine. You have so many blessings to bestow, and I cannot wait to see them, Lord. Please keep the girls safe with whatever they have going on, and let this situation bring this closer to you. It's in your holy name I pray. Amen."

< < > >

Annabelle was running around the house making sure she had everything packed and ready to go. She was going through a mental check list in her head. She had already contacted Charlie to let him know what was happening, and she would be out for a few days, and she had talked to her mom who had told her she was going to be staying with one of her friends who is also a widow. Annabelle knew her mother had been spending a lot of time with the friend, and she had seen her mother go through a great deal of healing while with her, so Annabelle was happy for her mother. She hadn't mentioned to her mom where she was going, because she didn't want her to change her plans or be worried about Jill. Annabelle knew they could handle whatever was going on together. Once Jill had responded to her text and asked her to come, Annabelle hadn't hesitated in preparing to go and help her. She had no idea what should be walking into, but she knew her sister needed her, and that was enough.

Annabelle had packed a bag unsure of the amount of time that she would need to stay. It was Tuesday morning, and she had made plans to be back at least by Sunday for Charlie's sermon, so she packed enough clothes to last until that moment. She put her bag in the car, and at the last minute, she ran upstairs and grabbed one nice outfit just in case this had to do with the school situation she had found out about with her sister. Once the car was packed and ready, and she made sure her mother had been picked up, she was on her way. She had a four hour car ride ahead of her, and she hadn't prepared a special playlist or anything for the drive, so she decided to play whatever her sister's XM radio wanted to play. She wasn't surprised at all when the first thing that came up was a Christian station. Her sister probably listened to this station often, and lately Annabelle hadn't been in the car long enough to turn anything on, so she'd never noticed it before. She listened to all kinds of songs about every aspect of God's love for her, and she could feel that for the first time in a long time her soul felt happy and complete.

When she arrived near the college, Annabelle called Jill to find out where her dorms were. It did not escape her that her sister was in college, and she had never been here to visit and had no idea where to even find her. She felt like a bad sister and started feeling bad about the person she had been to her. Maybe she could've prevented all of this if she had just been there for her from the beginning. Annabelle knew her feelings could create a bottomless spiral if she let them, and she wanted to get lost and wallow in them instinctively, but she also knew that wouldn't help Jill. She pushed the negativity away and focused only on helping her sister.

When Jill opened the door, Annabelle was so relieved to see her and to see that she looked okay. As she entered the dorm common room, she was surprised to see another girl sitting on the sofa drinking a coffee. Annabelle hadn't met any of Jill's roommates, so she assumed this must be one of them.

"Hey, I'm Annabelle. I'm Jill's sister." She said extending her hand with a smile.

"Hey, I'm Julie. I'm Jason's wife." Julie said extending her hand and shaking Annabelle's.

Annabelle stopped for a second. She knew the name Jason, but she couldn't quite place it. When it finally clicked where she had seen it, and the image of the text from Jill's phone flashed through her mind, she looked quickly wide eyed over at Jill. She had no idea what to actually say aloud about this odd situation, so she thought it might be better to try and communicate through her expression.

"Yes, we know it's weird that we're here together," said Jill, "but we are working together right now, so it just makes sense."

"Working together?" Annabelle asked confused. "What does that mean?"

Annabelle listened as Jill and Julie recounted the whole horrible tale. Annabelle was surprised at the part where Jill found out she had been turned in for plagiarism, and when they told her about Keemera and everything she had said to them. Annabelle felt like this was a lot for 1 day, and she didn't know how the girls were still standing and not a huge puddle of emotions. In fact, they seemed to be getting along and working together really well from what Annabelle could tell. When the story ended, she still felt like she had missed something.

"So, what do you need me for?" Annabelle asked suspiciously.

"Well," Jill said looking over at Julie with a mischievous grin. "We were hoping we could use you as bait."

"Bait? How and what?"

"Okay so here's my plan." Jill said taking a breath before pressing on. "I want you to put yourself in Jason's path and make yourself 'available' to him. If I know him like I think I do, he will take the bait without hesitation." Jill said confidently.

"Okay, but I don't see how that will help. I'm not a student here, and I'm an adult, so this is perfectly legal." Annabelle said confused.

"You're right." Jill said. "I don't need you to back up my story to the school. I need you to back up our story," She said while gesturing between herself and Julie, "to Keemera. She's the swing vote. We need her on our side to back up the "professor who has relationships with his students" angle, but right now, she won't say anything against him, because she thinks he loves her, and me and Julie are crazy exes."

"So basically, you need me to prove that he is the scum he is, so she can see it for herself."

"Exactly." Jill said excitedly. "So, will you do it?"

"I'd do anything to help you, Jilly Bean." Annabelle said smiling.

The words surprised Jill. Annabelle hadn't used her nickname for her in so long. It brought back so many memories of their time growing up and how close they had once been. Jill hadn't realized how much she had missed Annabelle and having a sister. It had been too long since she had left and so much had happened to get in the way of their friendship that Jill had even started thinking it could never be repaired. Then, here came God showing her with just one word how easily things could be repaired through him. Jill sent up a silent thank you as she jumped and hugged her sister tightly. She had a great feeling about this plan, and she knew with everyone working together, things would work out.

The three of them ordered take out, and as they sat and ate their noodles, meat, and vegetables out of white to go boxes with chop sticks, they worked out all the details of the plan. They would take tonight to enjoy some time together, and they would put their plan into action the following day. After Julie had left, Annabelle told Jill about everything going on back home with their mom, Charlie, and Rayne. She told her about the journey she was on to find truth and how God had led her to send the text Jill had received both texts were in response to a prayer. They talked about how much God had really been showing out in their lives, and how much closer they felt with him now. They read a little from the bible, talked about what it meant for their lives, and prayed before going to bed. They had a big day coming up, and they needed their energy to pull it off.

The next morning, Julie came over bringing breakfast for everyone. She made a joke that technically Jason had bought it, because she used his card, but whenever his name was brought up, the mood became heavy. Everyone could feel Julie's sadness surrounding the subject even Jill wanted to cheer her up, but she had no idea what to do or say to make it better. She knew Julie needed to grieve, so she was giving her the time and space to do it. They went over the plan again and again making sure each little detail would fall into place exactly as they were hoping. When they noticed it was nearing 11:30, they piled into the car and headed toward the south side of campus.

Annabelle had dressed in a white low-cut shirt with a colorful bra underneath that would easily catch someone's attention. She knew the old her would have loved the attention she'd receive from wearing something like this, but the new version of herself couldn't wait to cover up. As she started walking across campus with the girls to get into position. A light rain started to fall and Jill's confidence in this plan got boosted a whole notch higher. Jill and Julie hid inside the gardener's shack Jill has talked about in her recounting of her trysts with Jason. This place had once been so special and held so much meaning, but now it just seemed dirty and falling apart. Annabelle had to wait outside in the rain and make sure her shirt got wet to encourage the plan along as much as possible.

Soon enough Jason came down the path as predicted to head to his car to run and grab lunch. Annabelle readied herself with a notebook and a textbook over her head standing in the rain. At first, she thought he didn't notice her, but then she saw him look over and then do a double take. "Gotcha." She thought.

"Are you alright?" He said coming up to her and trying to hide his wandering eyes.

"No, not really." She admitted seeming upset. "I was leaving class, and it started raining, so I was going this way, because I thought it would be closer to my car, but my shoe got stuck in the dirt, and then my heel broke, and things just aren't going my way today. Well, that is until you came along." Annabelle said smiling at him.

"Then yes, today is your lucky day." He grinned. "I am all yours for whatever I can do to help."

"Well, I might have twisted my ankle, so I'm not sure I can walk to my car, but I need to get out of this rain before I'm completely soaked through. I definitely should've brought jacket or at least extra clothes. I hate wet clothes."

"Oh, I agree. Wet clothes are the worst. Let me help you inside here, and I can take a look at your ankle and maybe help you with your wet clothes." Jason said excitement creeping into his voice.

"Okay!" Annabelle said excitedly biting her bottom lip as she looked at him.

He lifted her and cradled her in his arms and started walking towards the shack.

"Oh my, you have such strong arms. You must work out right." Annabelle said as she felt his biceps through his shirt sleeve. On the outside, she was pretending hard to be very attracted to him, but on the inside, she wanted to vomit from having to touch him.

He brought her inside and sat her down on the floor. As he started to pull back to stand up, she asked, "How can I thank you for this?"

His eyes twinkled as he said, "Oh I can think of plenty of ways." Then he leaned back into her and put his mouth on hers kissing her as his hands roamed and groped all over her wet shirt and eventually found the buttons and began to unbutton them. Annabelle knew the girls only wanted a kiss and to hear him say enough to incriminate himself, so she pushed him back and stopped him.

"That was nice, but this is moving a bit fast for me right now. I mean I don't even know your name, and I'd like to at least go to dinner first, so I don't feel cheap."

"Oh, dinner can definitely be arranged." Jason said grinning. "How about tonight? Can you meet me at Ciao Bella's at 6:00?"

"I'll be there, and I'll bring the dessert if you know what I mean." Annabelle said winking at him. Then, she produced a key and asked him if he could possibly run grab her car and move it closer for her, and she would hobble down to get it. She told him if she didn't see him again, not to worry that she would be there tonight. The rain picked up as he left, and she and the girls gave him 5 minutes, before they hustled out of the shack and back the opposite direction toward their actual car. The key was an old key to one of their dad's old cars that no longer ran. Annabelle and Jill knew it would keep Jason busy for a while looking for the car.

Once they were back in Julie's car, they headed back towards the dorms to dry off and wait for shift change at The Tasty Freeze. The mood in the air was a little tense from everything that had just happened. Annabelle felt awkward having to kiss Jason in front of Julie and Jill. She knew why she was doing it, but it was still hard for her. She had grown to like Julie in the short time she'd known her, and she hated to do anything that would hurt Julie or Jill who she had finally started rebuilding her relationship with. Annabelle texted Charlie a quick update to let him know everything was good, and Jill was okay. He had been worried when she left, and he had offered to come with her. Now, she was happy she had told him to stay home. She would've hated him seeing her like she just was. She already felt gross after having Jason's hands on her, and she had an intense desire to take a shower. Now, she only had to play one more role tonight, and after that, she hoped she would never have to see him again.

When it was time, Annabelle started getting ready for her date with Jason while Julie and Jill left to head over to The Tasty Freeze. When they arrived, it didn't take them long to find Kemeera. Her personality and smile were electric, and her energy was palpable to everyone around her. She was actually at the front scooping ice cream, so Julie and Jill were hopeful they could easily make their move without scaring her away. They got in the back of the line and tried to blend in as much as possible. They had each worn hats for the occasion to try and conceal their identity enough to not be noticed right away.

When they got to the front of the line, Kemeera recognized them immediately, and she made a face to prove it. Jill spoke first.

"Listen, I know we're the last people you ever wanted to see again but hear us out. Just give me 2 minutes of your time, and I promise you won't have to hear from me ever again after that." Jill spoke quickly hoping not to lose Kemeera's attention, and when she was finished, she looked at Julie who quickly nodded her agreement. They both turned and looked hopefully at Kemeera trying to gauge any reaction they could get from her.

"Okay fine." She finally said. "But you only get 2 minutes, and not a minute more."

"Agreed! That's all the time we need." Jill said triumphantly.

Kemeera came out from the back, and the three of them went to one of the benches. They all sat down with Julie on the end and Jill and Kemeera in the middle. Jill took out her phone and cued the video. Then, when it was ready, she handed it to Kemeera, and Julie and Jill held their breath as they watched her push play. They stared at Kemeera's face while she watched the video, but her face stayed still and showed no emotion. Jill found it very unnerving after seeing how she usually was around people. When the video stopped, they were still staring at Kemeera while she took it all in. Finally, after what seemed like an eternity, she looked up and straight at both of them and said, "Take me to Ciao Bella's". Without hesitation, the girls grabbed their things and showed Kemeera the way to Julie's car.

The whole way to the restaurant, Jill hoped their plan would work. She prayed everything they'd done at this point hadn't been for nothing. They parked in a spot as close as they could get to the restaurant. Before getting out of the car, Julie flashed her lights 3 times which was the signal for Annabelle they had arrived. The three girls walked down the sidewalk in front of the restaurant, and they went in the front door.

Once inside, they were able to really assess everything, and it didn't take them long to spot Jason at a table with his hand on Annabelle's face guiding her in for a kiss. Jill looked away and back at Kemeera. She turned away from Kemeera's face quickly when she saw the fire ignite behind her eyes. Kemeera stepped away from them and headed straight to Jason and Annabelle's table.

"Hi, you must be Gary." Kemeera said extending her hand to Annabelle.

"No, my name isn't Gary. Are you okay? I'm not sure we've met." Annabelle said feigning surprise.

"To be honest, no, I'm not okay. My Boyfriend here," She pointed to Jason, "Told me he was having dinner with one of his colleagues named Gary tonight, and since the two of you seem to be having a lovely dinner together, I can only assume you're Gary." Kemeera said with a slight edge to her voice.

"Wait? You're boyfriend? You told me you were in the middle of a divorce from your wife, but you never mentioned having a girlfriend." Annabelle said looking straight at Jason.

"No, I..." Jason started to say before Kemeera cut him off.

"I don't want to hear anything you have to say. I've listened to you enough, and everything you've told me has all apparently been a huge bunch of lies. You even told me not to believe these girls," she pointed to Julie and Jill behind her, "but they have been able to present evidence of the kind of person you truly are. Honestly, I am *done* with you, and I am *done* with us. Don't call me." Kemeera said after she turned and headed back towards the door with Julie and Jill on her toes.

"Yeah, I'm finished with this too." Annabelle said as she got up from the table. "Have a nice life." And she left the restaurant behind the girls.

She was so happy to be far away from Jason and his hands and lips. It made her skin crawl to just think about him being close to her again. When she got outside, she could see Julie hugging Kemeera who seemed to be crying. Finally, someone was feeling their feelings from this mess and actually allowing them to happen. Annabelle knew at some point, Jill and Julie would break down too, and she wanted to be there for both of them when that time came. The girls asked Kemeera if she would be okay before taking her back to work. She said she would be fine, and she would just use this as her break time. She got in the car with them, and the three of them left. Annabelle went to Jill's car and drove back to Jill's dorm stopping only once to pick up a huge assortment of fried, spicy, and cheesy foods from the Mexican restaurant. Tonight, they would feast on some comfort foods.

When Julie and Jill got back, they told Annabelle that Kemeera had agreed to give a statement on Jill's behalf about the kind of professor Jason is. Jill was ecstatic, because it would help prove her story and prove she didn't plagiarize, so she wouldn't end up going down for a crime she didn't commit. She had made plans with Kemeera to meet outside the Dean's office in the morning to give her statement. Jill, who was glad to finally be getting somewhere with Jason being punished for his behavior, realized this would also help Julie in her divorce case. She told Julie to let her know whatever she needed from her to prove he had been unfaithful. With a chip halfway to her mouth, Julie started to cry. She hadn't even thought about getting a divorce attorney or filing paperwork, and she wasn't sure even where to start with something like that. Jill agreed to help her with whatever she could, and the three girls spent the rest of the night eating, consoling the tears that popped up here and there from Julie at the finality of the end of her marriage, and enjoying each other's company.

The next morning, Annabelle woke up to see that Jill was gone. She remembered Jill was going to the Dean's Office, and she hoped that wouldn't take too long. She started making breakfast which eventually roused Julie from sleep, and the two of them sat and ate while they waited on Jill to return. They were doing the dishes when Jill finally walked back through the door. She told them since the Dean had gotten her message in time yesterday, he was able to bring together some board members that morning to have an official hearing. Both girls gave their statements to the board, and Jason was summoned to give his own statement. With such overwhelming evidence, he had finally given in and admitted his guilt in the matter. Jill said she and Kemeera were able to leave after their statements, so she wasn't sure what would happen to him, but the plagiarism charges against her had officially been dropped which was really what she cared about the most.

Jill helped Julie look for a divorce attorney by calling around to some places they had found in an online search. Within an hour, she had an appointment with a respectable attorney to draw up divorce papers. The attorney was certain that it would be uncontested since the evidence against Jason was overwhelming. Jill agreed to stay another night before going home with Annabelle and go with Julie to the appointment for moral support. Jill was happy that even though things with Jason hadn't worked out, she would have a friend in Julie. They had grown close over all of this, and she couldn't imagine going back to not knowing her.

Ch. 27

Charlie hung up the phone and sighed a huge sigh of relief. Annabelle hadn't given him any details, but she did tell him she and Jill were on their way home. When she said it, Charlie could tell something in their relationship had changed. There was a kindness and excitement that hadn't been there before. He prayed this would last, and the girls would come to rely on each other in more situations. He knew they needed each other right now whether they wanted to admit it or not, and he was so happy they were finally starting to see it themselves. He was so happy, he immediately started thanking God for his answered prayer.

"God, thank you so much for blessing Annabelle and Jill with the gift of sisterhood and togetherness once again. I know they lost their way in their relationship before, but I can sense the bonds are stronger now, Lord. I don't know if they realize how much of a blessing, they are to each other right now, Lord, but I know they will one day realize it. I am so happy this was part of your plan, God. You know I have been praying they would find each other, and I want to thank you for such an amazing answer to my prayers. Tomorrow is going to be a big day for me and for Annabelle being in the sanctuary while I preach. Please Lord, let it impact her and leave an impression to help her come fully and wholly to you. I love you, God. Thank you so much for everything. In your most precious name, I pray. Amen."

When she arrived back home, it was Saturday, Annabelle ran up to the church to make sure there wasn't anything she needed to do to help Charlie get ready for the sermon the following day. When she went inside, she could see the light in his office was on, so she walked down the hallway towards it to see what he needed. When she neared his office, she could tell he was on the phone. He sounded excited, and she couldn't wait to hear all about it. She had really enjoyed growing their friendship, and she felt very blessed to have such a great friend in him. When she got to his office, she leaned against the open-door frame and smiled as he was saying his goodbyes and thanking someone on the other end of the phone before hanging up. Then, he looked up and saw her.

"Hey, I didn't hear you come in. How was your trip? Is Jill okay?"

"Oh, it was very eventful. I'll have to tell you about it sometime. Jill is good. I'm sure she will have to go through an emotional period when everything sinks in, but for right now she's doing good."

"That's good. I can't wait to hear about everything when we have time to sit and chat. I really want to be able to hear about the whole trip, but I have some news of my own that I really want to tell you about since its fresh and new."

Annabelle had never seen Charlie quite as excited as he was now. She was anxious to tell him about her trip maybe leaving out some parts instead of admitting to some things she wasn't proud of. She could always feel that old self of hers creeping in at the worst moments. It was always there to remind her that she wasn't good enough, and she would never be able to be better than the girl she'd been so long ago. Was it right? Was this most recent trip proof that she couldn't leave that girl behind, and she would be inside of her forever? She decided to think about that another day, and right now, she would be here with Charlie hearing about his good news.

"Okay shoot!"

"Okay, well, I just got a call from a friend who goes to a small church in an even more rural area than this one. It's a lot farther South, and they really need a new pastor. He remembers me from Seminary. We've been friends for a while, and I've preached there a few times whenever I've been between churches or whenever they needed someone to fill in for a Sunday. Anyways, he just called to ask me if I wanted the job to be their new pastor. So, what do you think?"

Annabelle was stunned. She didn't know what to say or what to do. She wanted to be happy and so excited for this incredible opportunity for him, but she didn't want to lose him. She had really connected with him while she'd been back, and she felt like they'd forged a good friendship. He understood her and accepted her in ways most people didn't. She wanted to be happy for him, but how could she be happy about this?

"That's great, Charlie. I'm so excited for such a great opportunity for you." Annabelle said honestly making sure to choose her words carefully.

"Wait, I haven't even told you the best part." He said excitement rising in his voice again. "The secretary for the youth department is leaving, and they have a spot to fill there. They asked me if I knew anyone I could recommend, and of course I thought of you. I want you to come with me."

"Oh wow!" Annabelle said completely shocked. "Are you sure you want me to come? I'm sure there are other more qualified godlier women than me who can really help the kids." Annabelle said ashamed and trying to find the perfect spot on the floor to avoid Charlie's bewildered expression.

"Annabelle, I don't think you understand what a gift you are. God chose you to be placed here with me, and you have done a phenomenal job. You reach the kids who feel unreachable like Rayne. You have a gift, and you don't even know it. Take this opportunity and see where it takes you."

"Charlie, I know that's how you see me, and maybe that's who I am now, but that's not who I've been. I don't think this church would want someone with a past like mine coming in to work with and potentially council their youth. Look, I just came to see if you needed any help getting things ready for tomorrow, but now it's time for me to go. I'll see you tomorrow."

Before Charlie could protest, Annabelle strolled hurriedly down the hallway and out the door into the parking lot. Fearing Charlie would follow her, she jumped into the car and sped away. What was wrong with him? Why would he think *she* would be the one to do that job? Maybe he didn't fully understand who she used to be. Maybe she needed to spend more time explaining it to him. She wanted to make sure he really knew, but she didn't want him to look down on her for her past. She decided she would tell him after church the next day. She would wait until after his sermon because she didn't want anything to mess that up. She knew he had worked hard to prepare it, and she wanted him to have his moment in the pulpit sharing God's word with the church, because it made him so happy. He would move on from this place without her, and she would remember him that way, at his happiest.

When she got back to the house, she called and told Jill everything that had happened. When she was finished, she was full of regret and sobbing. She cried for the girl she had once been who was gone, she cried for the life she could have had that she had thrown away with her bad choices, she cried and cried for so many things she feared she would never be able to get back or mend the damage from her past. As she cried, Jill cried also for the same reasons, and they both realized they seemed very different on the outside, on the inside they had the same fears and regrets. Neither of them knew how to move forward from this, but they decided to figure it out together.

The next morning, she got ready for church quickly. She arrived and was seated in the pew with at least fifteen minutes to spare. Charlie was walking around shaking hands, and he nodded in her direction when she came in. Annabelle had butterflies for him because she knew how hard he has worked on this sermon. She watched Charlie mingle and shake more hands until the first notes of music played to signify it was time for people to take their seats and a deacon appeared at the mic on the stage to welcome everyone and read that week's announcements aloud.

The singing went by quickly as Annabelle grew more and more anxious for Charlie as the time drew near. When she saw him stand up from his seat on the stage and approach the mic, she sent up a silent prayer for him. He got to the mic, and she prepared herself for the sermon he had talked to her about so many days ago, but the words she heard him utter surprised her for they were unlike any she thought she would hear here today.

"How much does our past define us? How much is God concerned with our past as he brings us to the place he has chosen and picked out for us?"

Everyone in the church sat silently listening, and Annabelle sat up a little straighter to listen to everything he had to say.

"Does God care about your past? I would say yes, but he wants you to acknowledge it, and repent and ask forgiveness and allow Him to work in you. Is he going to follow you around and remind you of it every chance he can? No, once you have repented those sins, you can move forward with Him a changed person. The issue of worrying about our past and being caught up in it is something we bring on ourselves. That is not God. That is the devil sneaking in to make us think we are not and will never be good enough which a complete and bold-faced lie. I bet some of you out there are wondering how I can speak to this with such clarity. Well, let's look at some important people from the bible. First, I want to highlight Esther. She was a Jew living in Exile in Persia. Her parents had died, and she was being raised by her older cousin. Her beauty attracted the favor of King Xerxes, so he took her captive along with several other women, and he essentially raped her when he was testing out the women to see which pleased him enough to be his wife. Now, maybe being in exile and being an orphan weren't so bad, but she had been defiled outside of marriage, so if Xerxes hadn't chosen her to be the queen, she could not have married anyone after that. She would've had to live among the concubines, and that would've been it for her, but God brought her through all of that, so she could risk her life to persuade the king not to kill the Jewish people, her people. God brought her through all of that, so she would be stronger on the other side. Her strength was on the inside, and God used what she had been through to create a better future for an entire group of people. Now, let's look at Jesus' own genealogy. Jesus could have chosen any blood line to be born into and any parents and any situation, but he chose women who were ordinary, tarnished by sin, and unlikely to make a mark on history. His great grandmothers: Tamar and Rahab who both possess sexually immoral backgrounds. Then his grandmothers: Ruth and Bathsheba. Ruth is known for her goodness, and she did not possess any sexual immorality, but Bathsheba did. Finally, we come to Mary who we know to be a virgin, but this should offer us some insight into Jesus' message to us about the past and how much our own past matters to his plan for us. Now, let's unpack the stories of these women quickly."

Annabelle was in awe. She knew this was not the sermon he had originally written. He must have rewritten the whole thing last night to speak to all the insecurities she had spoken aloud to him. It was his way of telling her he didn't care because he knew God didn't care. If she repented of her sins that's all it would take for her to be new and blameless in God's eyes, and what was good enough for God was good enough for him.

At the end of the service Annabelle had some big news to share with Charlie. She wanted to tell him right away about the prayer she had prayed today at the close of service and what it meant for the rest of her life, but she saw he had a line a mile long of people waiting to talk to him and share their goodbyes. At the very end of the service, he had announced his decision to leave and pastor a small, southern church. It seemed like everyone was very understanding and excited for him. They could all tell this was a step up for him, and this was the direction he wanted to go. As Annabelle watched him, she felt a tug on her arm. She turned around to see her mother standing there. She hadn't seen her mother in a while, and she hadn't seen her looking so good in years.

"Hey, mom. Wow, you look amazing!" Annabelle said smiling at her. Then she leaned in to hug her mom who hugged her and gave her a tight little squeeze.

"I have some exciting news to share. Claire and I have decided now that we are husbandless but still youthful women, it is time for us to travel and see the world."

"Wow, that sounds great, mom!" Annabelle said.

"Yes, we leave tomorrow for a Mediterranean Cruise. It is going to be heavenly. We booked spa treatments, and we are ready! I just wanted you to know not to be counting on me for plans anytime soon. I'm setting sail and exploring new horizons!"

"Okay well, thanks for the heads up." Annabelle offered enthusiastically. "Let me know if you need help packing or anything. Just remember I love you!"

"Thanks sweetheart, I'll call y'all when we're headed back. Love y'all too!" She said as she turned to go back and link arms with her friend Claire as they left to go talk to another group of ladies and share their exciting news.

Annabelle watched them go and felt another touch on her arm. She turned around this time to see a much older woman she didn't recognize. The woman had kind familiar eyes, but she wasn't sure where she had seen them before. She turned her body and gave this woman her full attention.

"Are you Annabelle?" The woman asked.

"Yes, I am. How can I help you?"

"I believe you sent this to my granddaughter, Rayne." She pulled out the card and handed it to Annabelle. "She asked me to give this back to you. I think maybe she wrote a little note inside for you. I just wanted to thank you for your kindness and friendship. She doesn't make friends easily, so she doesn't have very many, and I know your friendship really means a lot to her." The woman said smiling tenderly.

"Thank you, so you're her grandmother?" Annabelle said trying to fit all the pieces into place.

"Yes, I am actually her legal guardian as well. I live next door to try and give her mother a little space, but with that woman you give an inch, and she takes a mile. She's been gone a while this time, and I'm afraid that's why Rayne is leaving too."

"Leaving? To go where?" Then Annabelle remembered what she'd said about the tour and joining the band to go on tour with them. Annabelle pressed her palm to her forehead and couldn't believe she had been so stupid to forget about all of this. She had gotten distracted, and now another important person in her life was about to leave, and this one she wasn't sure she would see again after this.

"I don't know. Somewhere with that boyfriend of hers. You can't talk any sense into these young people now adays."

"Do you know when they're leaving?" Annabelle asked frantically.

"Yes, I think sometime this evening."

Annabelle thanked the lady, and she started to turn, but then had another idea. She had a very important question to ask her. After she finished her conversation, she headed to her car and called Jill. She could hear Jill's voice sounding happy and excited which was a sound she hadn't heard in a very long time. She was excited to be getting the old Jill back again completely. Jill filled Annabelle in on things with Julie. The papers were drawn up officially, and Jason signed them on his way out of town. Annabelle filled Jill in on her previous conversations with Charlie and Rayne's grandmother. After Annabelle finished explaining everything, Jill offered up the idea to Julie which she loved and agreed to instantly. Annabelle had a plan of her own, and when she explained it to Jill, she was pleased to see Jill agreed 100%. Now, she just needed to get Rayne on board.

When she got to the train station, she prayed a quick prayer for God's blessing over what she was about to do. Then she raced through the bus lots looking and searching for the girl. She started to worry she had missed her or would never find her in this maze of people and bus exhaust fumes, and Annabelle was about to double back and search from the front again when she heard a familiar voice. She followed the sound of the voice and found her standing on the outside of a group of guys. She didn't look excited to be there, and none of the guys seemed to be paying her any attention. Honestly, she looked like she'd rather be anywhere but there, and luckily that's what Annabelle had to offer. She ran over to her shouting her name until the girl turned to look at her.

"Rayne, oh my gosh! I'm so glad I caught you in time."

"What are you doing here Annabelle? I'm about to leave."

"I know, but I have an offer for you, and I really want you to hear me out on this one."

"What do you want?"

"Listen, I'm about to be moving to a new town for a new job, and I really want you to come with me. I've already talked to your grandmother, and she's on board with everything, but I need you to agree."

"Why would I want to do that? I have a good thing going here, and my life is finally about to start."

"I know it seems that way, but this isn't going to start your life. This is going to lead to years of pain, regret, and isolation. Trust me. I know. I've been there. I finally just crawled my way out of all of that. I don't want to see you making the same mistakes I've made. Please!"

"You're different, and you've become so much more like them. How do I even know I can trust you?"

"You're right, I am one of them. I prayed a prayer today to ask God to come into my heart, and I am changed for the better. I hope that same thing for you one day, but right now all I'm asking is that you come back with me, and you can come with me to a new place where we can all start over. You have one more year of school left, and then you are free to make your own decisions and your own choices. Please, let me be there for your last year, and let me show you what a real family is like. Remember what you said to me the first time we met?" Annabelle said anxiously.

"No" Rayne said turning to make sure the guys were still there and hadn't left her.

"You told me that you only wanted people in your life who *wanted* to be there, not people who felt obligated. This is me telling you I want you in my life, and I want to be in yours. I *want* you to come and live with us, not because I have to, but because I know my life would be better with you in it." Annabelle said sincerely.

Rayne paused for a minute before saying, "It would be nice to have a real family for a change." Then she took Annabelle's outstretched hand, and stepped away from the group. The doors of the bus opened, and the guys boarded. No one even seemed to notice she wasn't there. Annabelle felt sad for her about that, but at the same time grateful for this opportunity God was giving to all of them. She gave Rayne a tight squeeze and the two of them walked back towards the car. After they climbed in, Annabelle pulled out her cell phone to make one quick call. Charlie answered on the third ring, and she started talking immediately.

"Hey, boss, so when do we leave for this big adventure? Oh also, my family is coming with me."

Bethany Rodgers

Made in the USA
Columbia, SC
03 August 2021